A LOCKED-ROOM SUICIDE—OR MURDER

"If in fact the deceased was murdered," I asked Roulette, "how could the perp have gotten into the office?"

"He'd have to've had security clearance at the desk downstairs," she answered. "Plus an electronic card to activate the elevator, combinations to the corridor door locks, and keys to the suite."

I looked up at her from my scribbling. "Who at the agency has all those things? You?"

"Yes." Her large eyes widened further. "Does that make me a suspect?"

"'Fraid so."

"Ooh, how shivery." She looked at me with a half-smile. "May I say something in my own defense, before you drag me away in chains, or start beating me with hoses, or whatever it is you shamuses do?"

Shamus, I thought. Oh brother . . .

Also by Rob Kantner

The Red, White, and Blues
The Quick and The Dead
The Thousand Yard Stare
Made in Detroit
Dirty Work
Hell's Only Half Full
The Harder They Hit
The Back-Door Man

*Available from HarperPaperbacks

CONCRETE HERO

A Ben Perkins Mystery

ROB KANTNER

HarperPaperbacks
A Division of HarperCollinsPublishers

HarperPaperbacks   *A Division of* HarperCollins*Publishers*
                    10 East 53rd Street, New York, N.Y. 10022

Copyright © 1994 by Rob Kantner
All rights reserved. No part of this book may be used or
reproduced in any manner whatsoever without written
permission of the publisher, except in the case of brief
quotations embodied in critical articles and reviews. For
information address HarperCollins*Publishers,*
10 East 53rd Street, New York, N.Y. 10022.

Cover illustration by Larry McEntire

First printing: July 1994

Printed in the United States of America

HarperPaperbacks and colophon are trademarks of
HarperCollins*Publishers*

❖ 10 9 8 7 6 5 4 3 2 1

This one is for
CATHLEEN JORDAN,
with respect and gratitude.

And also, as always,
FOR VALERIE,
the one and only,
with all my love.

CHAPTER

ONE

The evening was supposed to be just another routine Friday night. Kick-back time at the Perkins apartment, starting with supper at the dinette table with my postnuclear nonfamily of the nineties: a boy who was not my son, his mother who was not my wife, and our daughter.

"Ma-*ma*," said Rachel, banging her high-chair tray with her fist.

I peered into the seven-month-old baby girl's dark blue eyes, the mirror image of mine. "More?" I translated.

"Ma-*ma!*" she agreed, and pounded the tray again.

"Sure, darlin'," I answered, and began cutting up a ham slice into bite-sized pieces.

"She's really putting it away tonight," Carole observed, as she scattered a few more chips onto the high-chair tray.

Rachel chanted nonsense. Will Somers, Carole's ten-year-old, grabbed the bag. "Can I finish these?" he asked, dragging a big mound of chips onto his plate.

"Help yourself," I answered as I sprinkled the ham

chunks on Rachel's tray. "Some potato salad?" I asked her.

"Oh, don't give her that," Carole said, sipping some iced tea while she had a chance. "She'll just smear it all over herself."

Rachel silently scooped up a couple of ham slices into her small strong hand, proclaimed "Ma-*ma*," reached past the edge of the tray, and, with a look of great concentration, proceeded to drop the food onto the floor.

"Oh, Rachel!" Carole said wearily.

"Sweetheart," I began.

"Ma-*ma*," she replied intently, as if explaining herself, as she swatted the chips off her tray.

Carole looked at me. "She doesn't really want more. That's just her word for the day."

"Ha?" Rachel asked, watching us quizzically.

"Seems to be making a study of gravity, too," I said.

"The other day, her word was 'bah,'" Will told us.

"Bah!" Rachel confirmed, beaming.

I bent, picked up the ham scraps off the floor. "Are we finished?"

"All set," Carole answered.

"I'm done," Will agreed.

"Ma-*ma!*" said Rachel.

And to think I once devoted Friday nights to babe-seeking, boozing, barhopping, brawling, and Battle of the Monster Trucks . . .

We stood. As Carole hoisted Rachel out of the high chair, Will and I gathered up the paper plates, deli sacks, and mostly empty containers of potato salad and bean salad and condiments. Will dumped the trash, I wiped off the table, and Carole took Rachel into the living room, where we reconvened a moment later.

It was a cool evening in early June. At the far end of the smallish living room, the doorwall screen gave out onto the wood deck, glowing warmly in the light of the fading sun way out in the west beyond Ford Lake. Inside, the living room was dim and shadowy and cleaner than usual. There was a dark leather sofa and love seat at right angles along the long wall, a matching recliner and oak coffee table, multishelved entertainment center on the opposite wall groaning under the weight of every audio/video gizmo known to mankind, and, presiding over it all from her place of honor on the wall above the sofa, the framed poster of a smiling, bikini-clad blond woman leaning on the fender of a Rolls-Royce above a caption that said POVERTY SUCKS. Welcome to Perkins's Place: cluttered, chaotic, and best of all rent-free, being part of my pay as manager of maintenance and security there at the Norwegian Wood apartment complex.

Which was not the only thing I did for a living, but at that moment my mind was not on detective work. In that department, things had been slow.

So far.

"Aggie called me," Carole said as she set the wriggling Rachel down on the floor by the coffee table. "She's very put out with you."

"Well," I said idly, going to the entertainment center, "I'm sorry to hear that." I fiddled through some tapes. "The last thing I want is for Aggie to be upset with me." Found it. "By the way, who the hell is Aggie?"

Rachel, in a pink top and bulging white Pampers, flopped over onto all fours and crawled briskly toward the doorwall, where lay the loose limp Raggedy Ann doll that was as bald as she was. As I flipped the new Buddy Guy tape and started it playing, I felt the usual mix of emotions at Rachel's moves: pride at her precociousness and a feeling of foreboding too. At this rate, any day now she'd be wanting the car keys.

"Aggie English," Carole answered, seating herself on the sofa. She was long and slender, brown-eyed and blond, her thick hair wavy to her shoulders. In her blue shorts and brown sandals and snug sleeveless tan tank, she looked idly lovely rather than aggressively lawyerly. She was as appealing as ever, but I knew her look was not for me. Those days were long gone. "Development director," she answered, "at WFOB radio. She tried to reach you last week, but you didn't call her back. So she called me."

Will had slouched into my recliner and was paging his way through one of his vast supply of comic books, his large easygoing face alight as he read. I stepped over Rachel, who was noisily mauling her doll, and went to the screen door, feeling the breeze coast in from outside, nature's evening air conditioning. A guilty feeling was gnawing at my conscience. "Oh, yeah," I said slowly, getting out a short cork-tipped cigar. "There was a message. I just thought it was one of those all-purpose beg calls, so I—"

"No-no-no," Carole said, shaking her head. "She wanted to tell you about the outcome of the auction."

"What auction?" I asked uneasily, flaring a kitchen match on my thumbnail.

"For the WFOB radio fund-raiser," Carole said patiently. "You donated an investigation for the station to auction off. Remember?"

Before I could light up, the breeze from outside blew the match out. From below, Rachel was watching me intently. I dug deep in my jeans pocket for another match. "Well, sure," I answered Carole. "Now I do. But hey, it was months ago when you talked me into that. I hardly remember what I ate for supper last night."

"Pizza?" Will ventured.

"Hell of a guess, old son."

"The auction was last week," Carole said. "Aggie was calling to give you the name of the person who bought your investigation."

"The things I do for work," I said.

She smiled. "I assured her you would come across. That you hadn't called her back because you were too busy hanging out at the saloon, and bowling, and flying your ultralight airplane, and pursuing your love life—"

"Not me," I said, flaming the match. "You're the one with the love life." The match blew out. Damn.

"Be that as it may," Carole said, ignoring my unasked question, "I've got the information for you. You need to get on this right away."

"'Kay. Who was it who won?"

Carole was sort of enjoying this. "Aggie doesn't know you, of course. But considering WFOB's normal auction items are things like microwaves and movie passes and life-size ceramic Dalmatians, they thought auctioning off a detective investigation was a real giggle."

"Glad they enjoyed it. Who was the lucky winner?"

"I thought it showed real growth and maturity on your part," Carole went on. "Contributing your time and skill to the cause of public radio."

"Mister Good Citizen, that's me," I said, twirling a finger, an index one. Rachel scooted on all fours toward the coffee table, chanting Na-na-na. "So," I asked Carole, "who was the lucky top bidder, and what am I to do for him in return for the pretty penny my services no doubt fetched?"

"Top bidder?" Carole asked blankly. "Actually, there was only one bidder. A woman from Ann Arbor. I wrote the name down; I'll give it to you before we go. As to what she wants, I have no idea."

Digging deep in my pocket, I retrieved my last match. "I just hope it's something slam-dunk simple," I said, "like a license-plate check or something."

Will looked up. "Maybe it's a murder," he said dramatically. "Maybe somebody died, see—and the police can't figure it out—but you track down the bad guy, and there's a shootout, and—"

"Oh, Will," Carole cut in, annoyance angling her face, "that kind of thing hardly ever happens."

I flared the match. The phone started ringing. The match went out. I stuck the unlighted cigar in my teeth and hoofed over to the phone, on the end table beside Will. "Except when you least expect it," I added.

"Whatever the winner wants," Carole said to me, "you will take care of it, won't you?"

"Sure." I picked up the phone. "Public-Spirited Perkins here. Talk to me."

It was a short conversation. As I listened and talked—mostly listened—I watched Rachel use the coffee table to pull herself up onto her feet. She looked at me and I smiled at her and then she walked herself around the table with short self-conscious steps of her bare feet. At the corner she got crossed up, wobbled, then thumped hard on her diapered butt, but after a quick shake of her fuzz-blond head she resolutely pulled herself back to her feet and continued walking herself along the table. My little gal, a Perkins through and through. Knock us down, we get back up, with a flick of the middle finger. That part she hadn't mastered yet, but hell, she was only seven months and change.

I hung up the phone. Carole had turned on the big fifty-inch Sony and was half watching Rachel as Leeza Gibbons flirted with sensitive, scholarly, bespectacled

Sly Stallone. I said, "Rookie's gonna be walking pretty soon, isn't she."

"Looks like it," Carole replied. "Any day now. Do you believe it, she's not even eight months old yet. Will didn't walk till his eleventh. Who called?"

I shrugged. "Deputy sheriff at the airport. I gotta run over there for a minute, help somebody out. Do you mind? Won't be long."

For an instant that wary professional focused look came over her. "Can I help somehow?"

"No need, thanks. Routine deal." Looking at Rachel, who was at the coffee table corner nearest me, I hunkered down in a crouch and held out my hand. "Whaddya say, rookie? Let's go help somebody."

"I'd rather she stayed here," Carole said calmly.

Rachel, half smiling, was looking at me with her large dark blue eyes. She let go of the table with one hand, took a very short step, let go with the other, wobbled, and fell hard on her butt again. Her round face creased, but she didn't cry—just scowled and gave me a resentful look and, as she tumbled over to crawl back to the coffee table, muttered a string of syllables, of which the only intelligible one might have been "mongo."

"See that?" Carole marveled. "She almost walked that time."

"Pretty cool," Will agreed.

I rose, went to the stereo deck, booted Buddy Guy, and tucked him in my shirt pocket. "You work on it while I'm gone, rookie," I said, and with a jaunty wave to the others left the apartment.

Luckily, I had spare matches in the Mustang, and the first order of business before heading for Metro was to get my cigar going. The second was to start rolling the Buddy Guy tape in the cassette deck. Only then did I fire up the big 302 motor and wheel away. Priorities.

The sun, at my back as I roared east on Huron River Drive, was almost down. Its red death rattle bathed the wooded, green, glacier-flattened landscape in an eerie glow as the town limits of Belleville advanced on me in ever-denser clusters of stores and houses and subdivision streets. The town was growing and changing—strip malls, strip malls everywhere, a stop for every DINK. Plus, in a burst of urban renewal zeal, the city parents had funded a refurbishment project that gentrified Main Street with brand-new antique brick sidewalks and Gay Nineties street-lamps. But I didn't see much of that, because I swung north at Belleville Road, snaked across the chain of lakes, and just up from there grabbed Interstate 94 eastbound for the airport.

As I drove and smoked and listened, I did not think about the errand ahead. It was odd but not especially arduous. What I thought about was the group I'd left back there, waiting at my apartment—Carole and Will and most of all Rachel, the most obvious evidence of the changes that had overtaken me since December when, as the outcome of an incautious interlude with Carole during what now appeared to have been the last great passionate fling of our lengthy and checkered and never-formalized relationship, my daughter had come yelling into my life.

Oh, I'd figured that fatherhood would change my life some. Especially this kind of nontraditional father-hood, being one half of unmarried parents who lived several suburbs apart. But Christ, I'd had no idea.

There were many "little" changes. At Carole's urging I'd cut back on the cigars when Rachel was around, smoking only in well-ventilated places. I was lighter by three C's a week, having finally convinced Carole to take my money; this cut a hunk out of the funds I'd normally invest in other things, like poker. My Friday nights were committed to get-togethers with Carole and the kids, alternating between their place in Berkley and mine in Belleville. I kept my .45 automatic safe and out of sight, either under the Mustang seat or up high on a closet shelf in my bedroom, instead of just lying around the place. A child safety seat now floated in the Mustang trunk alongside the tire iron, road stars, smoke bombs, and my bag of burglary tools.

Little changes, no big deal, hardly worth mentioning. Especially when compared to the big ones.

For one thing, being Rachel's father meant that I was, for the first time in my life, really dug in. While I'd never lacked for companionship—female and otherwise—I'd always lived pretty much alone. For better or worse, quite often the latter, I'd called my own shots. But now, with Rachel, for the first time I no longer had the option simply to throw my duffel in the back of the Mustang and take off and never come back. For a bang-around go-with-the-flow guy like me, this was a mighty big switch—bigger even than marriage would have been, had Carole said yes rather than no.

Rachel also had the eerie power to speed up the passage of time. No joke, folks. A minute or two ago, she was just a warm, noisy, but mostly inert thing that merely inhaled, exhaled, ingested, and excreted. Now, a blink of an eye later, she was a big, vivid, active baby woman who seemed to have inherited her mother's build and blond hair and brains, as well as my dark blue eyes and jaunty grin and—well—independent spirit, to put it kindly.

Now, suddenly, signs of time passing seemed to

be everywhere. The election season was upon us again already, unleashing the politicians and their handlers upon a helpless public. The interesting thing that year was the uphill and somewhat oddball reelection campaign of U.S. Senator Paul Proposto. Since last go-around he'd shed his longtime wife, let his hair grow out, and started keeping open company with Zanna Canady, a faded blues singer who'd emerged from oblivion and had been stumping the state at the senator's side. I'd never voted for a Republican, but I'd been a major fan of Canady's way back when, and I must admit I was tempted.

Other changes. A week ago an obituary had appeared for Emilio Mascara, the union boss with whom I'd spent the darkest chapter of my life—and, as one of his enforcers, had nearly shared his penitentiary cell. Under New Management, my longtime favorite down-'n'-dirty saloon, was still down and plenty dirty but was increasingly patronized by sleek suits and yups from the tiny, tony, high-tech businesses sprouting along the Interstate 275 corridor. The Ford plant where I'd hung car doors many years before had closed, a Japanese assembly plant had opened, and my older brother, Bill, had turned over another decade and was suddenly looking stooped and beaten and old.

Last, but not least, was the deal—or, more properly, the Deal—that Carole and I had made. In short, I'd agreed, after a lot of pestering, to lay off the rough stuff for one year. No strong-arm, no bodyguard, no gun duels or fistfights or murder investigations. "You owe it to Rachel to give it a try," Carole pointed out. "And who knows? Maybe you'll come to enjoy not getting beaten up or shot."

So, for the time being, I was in full Ozzie mode. Ozzified, as it were. And so far it was okay. In fact, most everything seemed okay just then. The work was okay, the friends were okay, the money was okay. The detective work—background checks, skip traces, process service, insurance work—had been the very best kind, easy and lucrative. Surprisingly, for four months now no one had even shot at me. What the hell, I thought as I exited Interstate 94 at Middlebelt Road, if I'm changing from a strong-arm detective to a paperwork one, so what? Take the money. Avoid trouble. Heroism is for kids, and once you have a kid of your own, it's time to stop acting like one.

Of course, just this evening the detective work had taken a definite turn toward weird. Tomorrow, I planned to touch base with the woman who'd "bought" my services in the public radio auction. That, no doubt, would be slam-dunk simple: an easy locate job or something, I hoped.

And now I was about to ride rescue to an old acquaintance who'd strangely and almost literally fallen out of the sky. As I neared the sheriff substation, I had that figured for easy, too. I'd spring him loose, bunk him down, clean him up, dry him out, and by sundown Saturday have him on a plane back for the West Coast.

I mean, how tough could it be?

The Wayne County Sheriff's Metropolitan Airport facility was a two-story brick building on Middlebelt Road on the east side of the sprawling airport. The gravel lot in front was less than half full, and I parked in a visitor's space next to a white Ford Explorer bearing the sheriff's emblem and blue and red overhead lights. As I got out, a Northwest Airlines 727, looking almost close enough to touch, shrieked by from the northeast on its final landing approach. Another one was visible a couple of miles back, making its approach to the parallel runway. Seemed to be a busy night out there.

I pushed my way through big glass doors into a paneled lobby that stretched wide and deep. To the right hung glass cases displaying police arm patches and other insignia. On the left-hand wall were a couple of plaques, along with pictures of the sheriff and the Wayne County executive smiling knives at each other, as well as a lineup of visitor chairs, all empty. In the painted cinder-block wall dead ahead was a large open reception window and desk, unattended at that point. I walked over to it and waited for a minute, listening to the almost incomprehensible squawking of a police radio booming from somewhere back of there. The air hung with a pukey, unpleasant scent of sweat and disinfectant. Police stations, hospital waiting rooms, bus station lobbies—for some reason, places where people don't want to be always smell like that.

Presently, a deputy wearing a brown uniform, black leather belt, and suspicious stare appeared behind the window. "You been helped?" he asked abruptly.

"Ben Perkins," I said. "Somebody called about a guest you've got out here."

The deputy was thin-bodied and thin-headed, with thin brown hair for which he'd compensated by shaving most of the rest of it off. Leather popped as he moved, and his uniform creases were crisp enough to crackle and set at precise right angles. He stared down at me, either because he was much taller than my six feet or was standing on a platform I couldn't see. "You're for Squire," he said.

"That's the guy. Can I see him?"

He nodded toward a door to my left. "Push when I buzz."

I did so and went through. The deputy, who was now magically my height, led me through a coatroom and into an area that stretched along the back of the building. It was divided into three barred holding cells about eight feet square each. In the center cell, on one of the two cots, sprawled a shoeless male form in gray pants and a pale blue shirt. His unconscious face was only in profile to me, but I recognized him, even though he looked different from the man I remembered. "Yup," I said. "That's Dennis, all right."

"You want him, then?" the deputy asked.

"You kicking him?"

"If you'll take him."

"What happens if I don't? Just curious."

Unlike you and me, the deputy didn't talk; he recited. "We'll render him over to Romulus police and book him for UBAL."

"Unlawful blood alcohol level," I translated. "Just drunk, huh? So he wasn't disorderly or violent or anything?"

"No. When his plane got here, he turned up passed out unconscious in first class. Airline people deplaned him and called us. He came to long enough to mention your name as the deputy was driving him over here. Been like that," he added, gesturing with a thumb at Squire's inert form, "ever since."

"He say why he came here?" I asked.

"No. But take a look at this." Behind us, a legless table hung on the wall. Above it was gray metal rack with parallel slots. From one of them the deputy took a large manila envelope, opened its flap, and dumped the contents onto the tabletop. The mess included keys, glasses, lint, a lot of change, a quantity of flimsy papers, a silver flask, a black wallet, and a gold money clip packed with tightly folded U.S. legal tender, of which the top denomination appeared to be 100.

"Over a thousand dollars in cash there," the deputy said, answering my unasked question as he sifted through the papers. I whistled. The deputy showed me one of the papers. "Here's the memo copy of his airline ticket. This individual started out in San Jose, California, ten days ago, and went to Las Vegas."

From inside the cell, Squire made an unpleasant sound but otherwise did not move. We ignored him. I was looking at the other papers. They were memo copies of more airline tickets. I sorted them by date. "San Jose to Vegas," I said. "Vegas to Houston. Then, uh—a week later, New Orleans to here." I looked at the deputy. "This boy's been through it."

"You want him?" the deputy asked.

"Has he had his shots?" I asked. The deputy stared stonily at me. "All right, you talked me into it."

The deputy began putting Dennis's belongings back into the envelope. "What is he, kinfolk?" he asked.

"No."

"Ben?" came Dennis's deep voice, quavering and husky.

"Friend of yours?" the deputy asked, handing the envelope to me.

"No," I answered. "Actually, I only met him one time. But I owe him."

The rumpled Dennis had eased himself into a half sitting position on the cot. Definitely thinner, definitely wasted. I felt a little sick, remembering how he had been. "Thanks for coming, man," he said faintly, through dry lips.

"Besides," I told the deputy, "anybody who gets out of both Vegas and New Orleans with over a grand in his pocket deserves to be saved."

Dennis made it out to the Mustang more or less under his own power. I buckled him into the bucket seat, handed him his envelope of belongings, and got in on the driver's side. The first thing he did was put on his glasses. But instead of checking his money next, as I expected, he opened the flask and took a long pull of it. Bourbon, from the smell.

"Welcome to Detroit," I said, as I rolled the Mustang onto black, street-lighted Middlebelt.

"Thanks, I guess," he said dully, and drank some more. "Wow, what wheels." He blinked behind his glasses. "Elegant. What is this, your middle-aged fantasy car?"

"Nope," I said, glancing at him. Elegant? "I bought her brand new, back in 'seventy-one. Put some work into it since then."

Dennis Squire was somewhere in his late thirties. When I last saw him, nearly two years before, he was tall and lanky with reddish blond hair, pale white skin, a flamboyant mustache, and a slight paunch. He still had the height, as well as the blue eyes and wide mouth, but his skin was, if anything, more pale now. The paunch was gone. He badly needed a haircut and a shave and a shower. The passing of time accounted for some of the change, but time had not been the only force at work on him. The focused, razor-sharp, adrenalized achiever I remembered so well had dissolved into a soft-looking, slightly trembling wreck sitting beside me in the other bucket seat.

"Where's my jacket?" he asked, as I cruised the Mustang to a stop at Ecorse Road.

"What you've got," I answered, "is what you're wearing, plus what's in that-there envelope."

"Shit," he whispered, slumping in the seat. What he was wearing had evidently started out as a business suit, but all that was left was gray trousers, an opened-necked pale blue shirt, and dull black wingtips. "Where are we going?"

"Motel, I guess," I said, swinging west on Ecorse. "That all right with you?"

"I guess." He drank some more. In the light of a passing streetlamp, his gold wedding ring glinted briefly. Obviously, he hadn't been rolled or robbed, wherever he'd been, whatever he'd done. "You know," he said presently, "I don't remember booking the flight here. Isn't that something."

"How'd you get from Houston to New Orleans?" I asked.

"Don't know that either." He giggled, a high-pitched, scared, and scary sound, and took another swig. "Detroit," he said breathily. "Is this frigging bizarre or what."

"Wanna tell me what happened?" I suggested, sticking a cigar in my teeth.

For a long time he didn't say anything. I'd reached Merriman Road by then, fixing to turn south toward motel row down at the highway. Presently he said, "I just . . . couldn't deal with it anymore."

"With what, Dennis?" I prompted, lighting my cigar.

"Any of it." With numb movements he adjusted himself in the seat. "You know, I really put out for the bastards. For twelve years. Fifteen-hour days, Ben. Endless meetings. Putting up with morons. I was the fair-haired boy, did you know that? When-ever some other division started circling the drain, they'd send in old Dennis to straighten it out. And I always took care of it. Put up great numbers. Growth, share, profits—up, up, up. What more could they want?"

"Beats me," I said patiently, waiting for him to get to the real story.

He took another slug from his flask and held it toward me. I shook my head. He drank again, sighed heavily, and said, "Now I find out my division is on the block. They're shopping us, but they never told me. Which means I'm out. After everything I've done, they're sticking it to me, Ben."

We neared the Interstate 94 viaduct. Ahead gleamed the lights of motel row. I hurled the car west onto Wick Road. "Come on, Dennis," I said gently. "This isn't about business, is it?" He did not answer. "You're married," I said quietly, "aren't you?"

He shot me a look, with the instant belligerence of the offended drunk. "You just leave her out of this."

"Fine, suits me."

"Don' wanna talk about it." He pressed on, slurring. "Jes' drop it. Right now."

"Okay, Dennis," I said patiently.

He was crying, but since it was mostly dark we both pretended not to notice. Just then we reached the ramp to Interstate 94, and on impulse I swerved onto the expressway headed west toward Belleville and home. Dennis did not ask any questions and he didn't say anything more, just slumped in his seat, staring out the passenger window at passing scenery, lost in the darkness.

Fifteen minutes later I led Dennis into the apartment and closed the door behind us. Carole and Will, who'd been watching TV, gaped silently at us; Rachel, who was playing with her rubber ring pyramid, clapped her hands and said, "Da!"

"Hey, rook," I answered. "Gang, this is Dennis. Dennis, this is the gang. Carole, Will, rookie."

"Honored," Dennis said blearily.

"Hello, Dennis," Carole said, eyes narrow.

I gave her a quick headshake. "Dennis is pretty tired from his trip," I said. "Come on, man."

I led him back to the spare room, opened the door, and gave a quick inspection. "Yep, good, there's still a bed in there," I told him, flicking on the light. "Move those boxes against the wall and help yourself. Shower's off the master bedroom over yonder, if you need it. Okay?"

"Elegant," he mumbled, staring around blearily. "Don't know what to say. Thanks." Suddenly he fell against me in a clumsy aromatic embrace.

I patted his shoulder awkwardly and then stepped back. "This is important, Dennis. Are you in trouble?"

He was unable to look me in the eye, but that could have been because of the situation. Here he was, a proud man used to controlling events, beholden to a stranger a long way from home. "No," he answered softly.

"Anybody after you?"

"No."

"Anyone looking for you?"

"No."

"Does your family know where you are?"

He smiled bitterly. "She doesn't give a shit where I am."

In the living room, Carole and Will had been watching a video of *Tender Mercies,* one of my favorites. I picked up Rachel and sat with her on the love seat and looked at Carole. "It was worse than I thought."

"So I gathered," she replied, and paused the tape. "I could smell him from here."

"Is he a friend of yours, Ben?" Will asked.

I shrugged. "He helped me with a case out in California, a couple years ago. I called him last winter and he helped me again, found a computer hacker for me."

"I remember," Carole said. "But my God, he looks dreadful. What happened to him?"

Rachel had taken a half-smoked cigar out of my shirt pocket. I relieved her of it and stuck it behind my ear. She did not complain or struggle to get away, sure signs she was getting tired.

"Life happened to him," I answered.

Carole stared heavenward. "Oh, puh-leeze."

"He flamed out," I explained. "I think he's taking a vacation from his life. I think he needs to rest and eat and sober up and think."

"What are you going to do?"

I shrugged again. "Give him a day or two to get

wheel side down again and then send him back home where he belongs."

"That's good of you," she noted. "Is it fair to say he'd be in a cell someplace, if you hadn't stepped in?"

"I owe the guy."

We watched the rest of the movie as Rachel, who had started skipping her naps lately, fell asleep in my arms. I did not see Dennis again that night. I heard the sounds of the shower running and the toilet flushing and doors closing, and then all was silence from back there.

By eleven, Carole and the kids were ready to head home. I walked them to the building door and only then handed the sleeping Rachel to Carole, who bundled her in a blanket against the chilly evening. Will hugged me and I gave Carole a wave. "'Bye, darlin'."

"See you, Ben. Don't forget to take care of that auction winner ASAP."

"You didn't give me the info."

She smiled. "I taped her name and number to the six-pack in the refrigerator."

"Ah," I said, grinning, "you know me all too well. I just hope what she wants is something real simple, like an employment verification or something."

"Oh, don't worry," Carole answered. "I'm sure that's all it is."

CHAPTER

THREE

"My husband died," said Wendy Dilworth. "The police called it an accident. I have my doubts. Your assignment is to find out if he was murdered. If so, you are to determine who did it and why."

"Uh," I answered. "Hm. Ah," I added.

It was Saturday, the morning after I "rescued" Dennis Squire. Late morning, to be precise, the type of bright, clear, cool morning with which Michigan sometimes rewarded us in June for the misery it put us through in February.

Wendy Dilworth and I were walking up her street in the Geddes Hills section of Ann Arbor, sort of halfway between the Huron River and the University of Michigan campus. Actually, the pace she set was far from a walk. Quick-time was more like it. She was, evidently, a prodigious walker. "Five to eight miles a day," she'd told me on the phone earlier that morning. "Come to the house at ten and we'll discuss the assignment while I do my second leg of the day."

I'd arrived right on time. The neighborhood oozed

old money: rolling hills, tall trees, hedges, large rambling 1920s and 1930s homes of fieldstone and brick, sporting multiple chimneys and skylights and banks of windows and three-car garages tastefully hidden around corners. Dilworth's house was a tad more modest, a 3,000-square-foot white frame ranch on a dead end north of Geddes Road. An array of recycling bins waited by the sidewalk for curbside pickup, and Dilworth herself was in the front yard, doing stretching exercises under the majestic trees as I pulled up.

She was past fifty, I figured. Tanned, weathered, sinewy, and unshaved everywhere. Her hair was gray and streaked with white, dumping straight from a middle part just to her shoulders and held in place by a blue headband embroidered all around with yellow—excuse me: gold, maize, whatever—University of Michigan logos. She wore a baggy gray Michigan sweatshirt and loose blue Michigan shorts and white low-topped Reeboks that surprised me only in that they did not sport the U of M logo as well. This was, I could tell, a serious fan. I could picture her in the stands at Crisler and Yost and Michigan Stadium—no doubt possessing most excellent seats everywhere—watching the action through those hard skeptical gray eyes, tanned fists clenched in her lap.

Her greeting to me was brisk and detached and accompanied by a firm, formal, almost Teutonic shake of her small, strong, leathery hand. Then, with a gesture, she started us walking up the sidewalk, setting a brisk pace, stomach in, shoulders back, muscled arms swinging smartly. I kind of loped along beside her, focusing mainly on keeping up—until, that is, she told me what the assignment was.

Dead husband. Accident—or murder, maybe.

Now *there's* a slam-dunk easy one for you, old son.

I looked at her as we rounded the corner onto the Geddes Road sidewalk. She was smiling. Then she laughed, a quick haw-haw, through large teeth. "What do you think, Mr. Perkins?"

"What I think is, if your husband was murdered, it's work for the police. Not for me."

"Of course," she answered crisply. "But the police have concluded that his death was accidental."

"You don't think so?"

She paused. "I think, in the end, they'll be proven to be correct."

"Then why me, and this, and—"

"The WFOB fund-raising auction," she said patiently. "I won you, Mr. Perkins. I paid good money. You volunteered your service. I must give you *something* to do."

"Oh."

"Unfortunately, I was badly outbid for the trip to Málaga," she told me. "I have no use for a life-size ceramic Dalmatian, of course. Hence, you."

We were heading down a long slope, which was a good thing, because it gave me a chance to coast a little. Dilworth obviously didn't feel the pace one bit. She was all thrusting elbows and knees, chin up, shoulders back as she marched.

"So," I said presently, "you want me to double-check the cops' work, and if I sign off on their explanation I'm done?"

"Yes." March, march. "I must confess," she said after a minute, "this is very embarrassing for me. If any of my acquaintances found out—"

"Embarrassing? How?"

"The very idea of a private detective," she answered. "It conjures up such distasteful images. Sexist, chauvinist, anachronistic ones—"

"Lost you after sexist," I cut in with a grin.

A flock of joggers streamed by. "The idea of employing someone to snoop," Dilworth went on. "Invading the privacy of others. Employing devious techniques. And, sometimes, violent ones." She glanced at me. "Judging from your nose, you're no stranger to rough-and-tumble."

"Run into a door or two in my time," I agreed. This wiry little woman was getting on my nerves. People like her, in neighborhoods like hers, always made me feel cloddish and clumsy and slow and stupid. But I kept quiet. You promised, I told myself. You owe. Just get it, do it, and forget it.

We came to a corner. The light was red our way, but the joggers waded into the street anyway, and we tagged along with them as the cross traffic waited on their own green. Civilized town, Ann Arbor. Over in Detroit, where I was much more comfortable, some crack-blasted yo would've bulldozed his clunker right through that crowd—*thumpa, thumpa, thumpa*—leaving a red flopping, screaming swath strewn with Reeboks.

"I would think," Dilworth observed as we reached the other sidewalk, "that your breed is dying out pretty fast. No wonder you're forced to advertise by participating in the public radio auction."

Now that was too much. "Actually, business couldn't be better," I said. "You'd be amazed how many people need help."

She shook her head. "But to turn to you? I find that hard to believe, in this day and age, with all the resources available. There are government agencies and self-help groups, counselors, books, tapes—I myself am a strong believer in discussing matters and finding consensus."

"Sometimes, ma'am, discussing just don't cut it," I said. I realized I was laying on the hillbilly tone, a relic of my raising by emigrants from north Georgia, no doubt to offset her clipped, bookish, fake-British sound. "Sometimes, things get to a point where violence is the only way to resolve them."

"Perhaps in your shrinking world," she said stoutly. "Certainly not in mine."

"As for the auction deal, I was talked into it by a friend of mine who's some poobah on the WFOB board. I doubt," I added pointedly, "that I'll do it again."

Abruptly, she spun around and started us marching the other way. Uphill, this time. Lord, Lord. My legs could take it just fine, but I wasn't sure about the lungs. "Be that as it may," she said, "we now have this task before us, so let us get on with it. How shall we proceed?"

We recrossed the street, on green this time. I'd considered lighting up a cigar, as long as we were outside, but the long uphill slope ahead of us changed my mind. "How about you tell me what happened?" I suggested. While, I did not add, I shut up and focus on breathing.

There wasn't much to the story. Her husband, Chris Cloyd, was a copywriter for an advertising agency in Detroit. A month ago, bright and early one morning, he was found in his office with a rope around his neck, stone cold dead. The police had investigated but had found no signs of foul play.

"Rope around his neck?" I echoed. "How do you get accidental out of that?"

"Oh, it is complicated, to be sure," she said in a hard, fussing tone. "Suicide is another theory that was mentioned."

"You don't buy that either?"

"My husband," she noted as we turned up her street, "was not the sort to take matters into his own hands."

Aw, who knew? In my experience, spouses didn't know any more about each other than about anyone else. I asked the obvious question. "Was your husband—uh, intoxicated?"

Her street was level, thank God. Breathing had become work. Dilworth shot me a look. "Certainly not. Chris and I were extremely health conscious. Strict vegetarians, of course."

"No drugs of any kind?"

"Of course not."

"Was he—um, a depressed person? Moody or whatever?"

"No." She sounded annoyed. "He was a thinker, an idealist, a citizen of the planet. When he had problems, he worked them out rationally, by reaching out and sharing and arriving at a consensus. He did not run."

Still, murder by rope seemed a tad excessive. I wondered what kind of physical evidence there was. "They found him in the morning?" I asked. "He stay late, or—"

"Chris often worked all night," she answered, stooping to scoop up an errant pop top tab.

We were drawing up on her house now. I felt fairly sure that Dilworth was leaving major parts of the story out, for purposes of her own. Instead of bearing down, I decided to back off for a bit. "Tell me about him."

She glanced at me. So far, she had shown no emotion at the passing of her husband. Very controlled and resolute, with walls way, way out from where she really was. "Chris was an artist," she said. "He was only working for that horrid little agency until he could finish his play and get it produced."

"How long had he worked there?"

"Eleven years."

"Long play, huh?"

She led me across the lush lawn toward the side of the house. "He was struggling with the arc of the protagonist."

I nodded, as if that made any frigging sense. "Married long?"

"Six years."

Around back there was a patio, surrounded on three sides by a tall white trellis crawling thick with vines. Dilworth led me through an archway, up some steps, and through a sliding glass door into what appeared to be a den. "Second marriage?"

"First for Chris. I had a brief involvement while an undergraduate." Dilworth slid the door shut behind us, slipped off her headband, and shook loose her gray hair, which seemed to be damp at the roots. "Please have a seat, Mr. Perkins," she said. "I must pay a visit."

She left. I looked around. The den was long and sun-splashed, with beams along the ceiling and scatter rugs on the hardwood floor, and armored on three sides with solidly packed bookcases. No TV, no stereo, no video games, no guns, no dead heads on the walls—just books. On the fourth side was a fieldstone fireplace that had obviously seen a lot of use. So had the heavy, elderly stuffed furniture, and the exercise bicycle in the corner, and the bushy gray-and-black tabby cat sprawled in a sun splash by the door.

Above the fireplace was a pair of framed portraits of two half-smiling people: the left chest up and head on, the right chest up and profile. His-and-hers mug shots. Each showed Dilworth, looking very much as she did that day, except in the pictures she wore a dark business suit. Next to her was a thin man with seriously receding dark hair, wearing small wire-rimmed glasses and a suit. He looked remote and anonymous and unapproachable—and a good ten to fifteen years younger than his widow—

Who chose that moment to come back in. She carried a gray metal briefcase by its handle and a thick brown cardboard expanding wallet under her arm. As she set them on the coffee table she said, "I presumed you would want some clues to work with."

"Clues are good."

"This is the best I can do. I will need these back, of course."

"Sure." The bulging cardboard wallet was tied shut with string, but I could see it probably had forty or fifty well-packed slots in it. I prodded it with my finger. "What's in this?"

"Chris's business papers," she said. "Bills and receipts and so forth. We kept our business affairs separate, of course."

"Of course, of course."

She had her sinewy arms folded and was watching me with narrow gray eyes. "I do not know what is in the briefcase. It is locked and I do not have the combination."

I glanced at it. Each of the two clasps was accompanied by a triple-tumbler combination lock. I shrugged. "I can bust it open if you want."

"I would rather you did not," she answered. "I may have use for it someday." Her smile flickered large teeth. "You claim to be a detective. Surely you have skills of some sort. Can you open it without breaking it?"

"Probably."

"Show me."

The big bushy tabby had bestirred itself and was circling my ankles, staring up at me with yellow eyes. "And give away a trade secret?" I asked, grinning. "Get out of town."

"Take it with you, then," she said, stooping to scoop up the cat. "But please don't damage it."

"Sure." At that point, Dilworth had just about given up trying to hide her lack of enthusiasm, and all

I wanted was out of there. But there was work to be done, and to do it I needed a few more basic answers. I got out my tattered little spiral pad—down to its last three or four raggedy blank pages now—and a stub of pencil. "Six years married," I murmured as I jotted, "eleven years on the job. Okay," I said brightly, looking at her. "Who were his enemies?"

The cat struggled in her arms, and with an exasperated sound she let it drop to the floor. "He had none. I will not say he was a big bruising hail-fellow-well-met, like you. He was intelligent—quite brilliant, actually. Quite shy and withdrawn, of course, and sensitive and intuitive. But he had no enemies."

"How about friends?"

"No one special."

"Family?"

She shook her head.

I jotted something else and then looked at her and let the silence grow large in that sunny room. That technique can make your questionee uncomfortable, causing him or her to rush in with helpful information. Right on cue, Dilworth spoke up. "Will there be anything else?"

"Not now," I said cheerfully.

"I had the card of the police detective who investigated the case, but I must have misplaced it. African American fellow."

"Don't worry, I'll muddle through."

"I will see you out then."

I picked up the briefcase, which was lighter than it looked, and the wallet, which was heavier. Dilworth led me through a square, bright, white-tiled kitchen, down one level, and into a two-car garage that looked out the big open door to the street. In the driveway sat a blue utilitarian Honda Accord. Inside the garage, covered with just the faintest sheen of dust, was a Pontiac Trans Am, candy-apple red, a big muscular car, now unwanted and ignored.

"Wow," I said, looking it over. "Bet you love driving this, huh, ma'am?"

"Certainly not," she retorted. "When I must drive, I drive the Honda."

"I see. Must have been your husband's, then."

She looked withering. "If this is an example of your detective expertise, it is no wonder your business is dying out."

"Beautiful wheels," I said, staring at the car as I wandered toward the driveway.

She was looking steadily at me, one foot tapping. "Mr. Perkins, I cannot tell if you are really this dense or just putting me on for some reason."

"Well, ma'am, that makes us sorta even."

"In what sense?" she asked warily.

"I can't tell if you're really detached about your husband's death or covering up a completely broken heart."

She gave me one last look, shook her head, and went back into the house.

Before starting the Mustang, I studied the briefcase latches. Turned the tumblers experimentally, squinting at them. Then, without hesitation, I dialed up the combinations and pressed the levers and the latches sprang open.

Like most people, Cloyd had kept the tumblers in the unlocked position most of the time. Exposed to the air, the combination numbers were much more tarnished than the others. Almost like a signpost. Sometimes the answers you need are right in front of you. You just have to learn to look.

Unfortunately, the briefcase was empty.

CHAPTER

FOUR

As I headed south on U.S. 23, I dialed up Detroit police headquarters on the cellular. Luckily, Elvin Dance was on duty and in the building. Even more luckily, he was willing to talk to me, if I got down there in time for his lunch break. "Can't use city time to talk to no honkies from the hostile suburbs," he told me. Kidding around. I thought.

I swung the Mustang east on Interstate 94 and set a trajectory toward the city of Detroit. The big Mustang motor purred a rumbling, comforting bass counterpoint to the crooning of Buddy Guy from the half dozen speakers, and I smoked a cigar as I easily and swiftly negotiated the heavy traffic on the four-lane freeway.

I thought about Chris Cloyd's death, but at that point there wasn't much to consider. I had two more stops to make on that one: the Detroit police and then Martin Ketchum & Martin, the ad agency where he worked. By the close of business Monday I expected to have it wrapped up, no muss, no fuss—and, I had a feeling, no foul play. Death came to everyone, in all shapes and sizes, and I was unaware of any law that said it always had to make sense.

Which brought to mind Dennis Squire, my unexpected houseguest. I hadn't talked to him that morning. When I left for Dilworth's, he was still comatose, sprawled across the guest-room bed dressed only a pair of worse-for-wear skivvies. Now, in the bright light of a Saturday morning, my decision to take him in felt ill-advised. I was hoping to dust him off, rest him up, and propel him onto the next westbound plane. But what if he didn't want to go?

Worried, I called the apartment but got only my own recorded voice for my trouble. Hm. Maybe, I thought, he'd woken up, hungover and embarrassed, called a cab, and even now was airborne, headed into the sun and out of my life. . . .

Elvin Dance, as it turned out, wasn't waiting for me at police headquarters. I was told he was busy, and to wait. I cooled my heels in the hallway on the fifth floor, stomach growling from too many cigars, too much coffee, and not enough lunch. It was past two when the police captain came charging up the hall. "You still here?" he boomed at the sight of me.

"I know you're on city time," I said, "but this is business."

Elvin strode toward me, a solid, threatening presence. "City bidness?" he pressed, glowering, "or Perkins monkey bidness?"

"It's about a death you investigated. We doing lunch or what?"

"No time for that, man," he said, glancing at his watch. "Go ahead, ask me quick. I got to run."

Elvin Dance ran the Detroit Police homicide unit, and had for a dozen years or more. The captain was blocky and bull-like, with black-on-black skin and short black hair and a heavy, hard face to which expression hardly ever rose. He wore a tailored baby blue dress shirt, a silk tie of mottled red and blue, gray trousers, and black alligator shoes. He also wore a Smith & Wesson .38 Police Positive holstered high on his right flank, as well as a tiny .25 caliber Beretta automatic tucked in an ankle holster under the custom-tailored right trouser cuff. Elvin Dance was a complete cop, a tough customer, a survivor. I liked him, and I suspected he liked me, to the extent that a man like him could like a man like me. But that didn't mean he'd hesitate to throw me in jail, if the opportunity arose.

"Chris Cloyd," I said, stepping aside to make way for a pair of strolling uniforms. "He was found dead in his office at—"

"*Uh*-huh," Elvin rumbled, and for an instant I thought he looked disappointed. "Profile case. Puzzle. What about it?"

"His wife asked me to check it out."

"His wife."

"Yup."

Elvin stared, then tipped his head. "Over here, boy." He led me to a dark wood pew along the wall, away from the doors. As we sat, he slipped a Kool cigarette out of his shirt pocket and lighted it with a gold Zippo. "Case is still open," he said, exhaling smoke.

"I know. What about it, Elvin?"

The police captain sat hunched forward, thick arms resting on his knees, cigarette angling whitely in his fingers. Again, his face betrayed nothing, but I sensed he was struggling with something. "I'm s'posed to close it," he said. "The ME ruled it accidental. We ain't got nothin'."

"So why haven't you closed it?"

He glanced at me. "Just haven't gotten around to it. What'd the wife tell you?"

Something smelled here. "Said he worked at an ad agency in the David Whitney. Found dead in his office one morning, rope around his neck, like he hung himself or something."

"That what she told you?" He grunted.

"She seemed a little confused," I answered, sticking a cigar in my teeth. "First she said it was accidental, then she said possible suicide."

Elvin was shaking his head. "Not confused at all," he said. "Fact is, looks to us like his death was a little of both."

I flared a big kitchen match on my thumbnail and stared at Elvin. "Run that by me one more time?"

He scowled. "Lemme fill you in on the whole thing. See what your take is. 'Kay?"

I puffed my cigar to life, shook out the match, and got my tattered little pad out, hardly believing my good luck. It was not like Elvin to be so forthcoming. "Shoot."

"'Kay. This Cloyd dude, the victim. Worked all night a lot of the time."

"Artist type, the wife told me," I said.

"Weird little geek," Elvin agreed. "'Course, she's a weird little geekette." He grinned. "Ann Arbor."

"You got it."

We shared a mutual made-in-Detroit smile. Abruptly his grin vanished. "This agency he worked for, Ketchup somebody—they had a open house the night before," he said. "Hundred people or more. Big event, limos around Grand Circus Park, the whole deal. That all shut down about midnight. Story is, Cloyd stayed after to work all night. They locked up the offices with him inside. There was the usual building security, no one could get in or out without being seen. But the next morning, receptionist showed up and unlocked the place and found him dead."

"Oh, goody," I said. "A locked-door mystery."

"Well, not 'zackly," Elvin commented, smoking. He was looking 'at me oddly. "She really didn't fill you in, did she?"

"Fill me in on what?"

He looked both ways. The hallway was congested, but we might as well have been alone for all the attention we attracted. "Ever heard of sex-associated asphyxia?" Elvin asked.

"Oh, sure. Rough stuff that goes too far." I thought. "You mean somebody was with him?"

"*Uh*-uh," the detective answered. "He was alone, all right. He done it to himself."

"Wait a minute." I looked at him, looked away, looked at him again. "You think Cloyd tied *himself* up as some kinda . . . solitary sex ritual, and—"

"It went wrong somehow," Elvin answered. "We seen it before, a few times. Accidental autoerotic asphyxiation. See, it gets complicated what they do with those ropes. Loop around ankles and wrists and neck, tied to a chair or desk or overhead . . . They get off on the near-asphyxia, see."

I worried my cigar. "Gawd-amighty," I murmured. "You'd have to be funny-turned to do yourself that way."

"He tripped, or moved the wrong way, or something," Elvin continued. "Strangled hisself."

"Mm. His wife knows all this?" Dumb question, I realized. Of course she did. She just didn't want to tell me. "Sounds like an open-and-shut to me then, Elvin."

"Yeah," he said, troubled. "Couple things don't fit the profile, though."

"Such as?"

"Well, it's always men does this, supposably. Even married men, men with children, so all that fits, sorta. But usually they do it at home; bedroom or basement. Not a office."

"'Course, Cloyd almost lived at work, sounds like," I observed.

"And usually we find 'em with pornographic materials in view," Elvin added. "Need I say more?"

"Found nothing like that, huh?"

"Nope. So, I'm . . . not sure we should close it."

I fiddled with my pen, considering. "Was this, uh— was the open house by invitation?"

"*Uh*-huh."

"Well, I mean—suppose somebody slipped in during the open house. Hid away till everyone was gone but Cloyd. Came out and did for him, and then, um— anybody seen leaving first thing in the morning? Anybody they couldn't account for?"

Elvin Dance leaned back on the pew and stretched his thick arms till the cuffs nearly popped, squinting at me through cigarette smoke. Maybe he was impressed a little. "This here's the reason we ain't closed the case all the way," he told me. "Detective Hoosie had the same thought as you. Security man on duty at the Whitney, there, swore he saw nobody leave the building first thing that morning. Then he says, well, maybe there was a man. Left out of there eight-ten, eight-fifteen or so, while the security man was chatting with a magazine delivery person."

I meandered a note. "Description?"

"None. Not till we hypnotized the desk dude."

"You did what?"

Elvin's grin opened again, briefly. "Hoosie's idea. Had the desk man hypnotized. Got a description—not much of one."

"Can you get me a copy?"

"I'll fax it to you. You do have a fax, don't you?"

"'Course." I scribbled the number and gave him the slip. Elvin made it vanish into his big black hand. "'Preciate it, Elvin."

"It won't help," Elvin said. "Guy could be anybody. Assuming he was there at all."

We sat there for a long moment, thinking, as uniforms and perpetrators and informants and attorneys trooped to and fro, clumped and unclumped, their urgent and mostly male voices arcing around the old walls. The detective bureau never slept. I said, "Well, obviously, we could be dealing with a real professional here. Someone who did the research, learned about Cloyd's work habits, found out about the open house. Planted himself inside. Did the job, made it look accidental—hell, even knew the security man liked to flirt with the magazine delivery woman every morning—"

"Delivery *man*," Elvin put in.

"Whatever."

Elvin snorted.

"So, was that your thought? A very elaborate hit?"

"That was our thought," Elvin agreed. "Just one problem. We got no motive, no perpetrator, and no physical evidence."

"That's three problems, Elvin."

"Three *big* problems."

"Which is why no collar yet?"

"Which is why." He ground his cigarette out under the sole of his highly polished shoe.

"Hoo. How about snitches?"

"Dead silent, man."

"No stray prints, huh? No incriminating matchbook covers? Not even a stray chain of DNA layin' around?"

"I said we got *nothin'*, boy." Elvin ticked thick

fingers. "Cloyd didn't do drugs. He didn't gamble. He didn't run around. He didn't frequent no grade school playgrounds. He didn't write crank letters. Had no police record an' no past worth mentioning, had nothin' anybody else wanted, far as we can tell."

"Straight-arrow type," I observed.

"Only interesting thing ever happened to this little dude," Elvin said, "was this. Somebody whacked him."

"I thought the ME said accidental." Elvin did not answer. "You really think otherwise, huh?"

"Not really. Oh, sorta." He glowered. "I go back and forth," he added, looking away, voice low.

"I see that."

"Don't quote me."

I couldn't think of much else to ask him. It sounded like the cops had worked the thing pretty hard. Which made sense, considering it involved a white professional victim employed by a prominent company headquartered in one of Detroit's landmark buildings—what Elvin called a profile case. I could tell he badly wanted to prove the ME wrong, to validate his own gut feel, to close the case with a collar. He wanted it so badly, he was willing to let me elbow in edgewise and bang around a bit.

At least briefly.

Too bad I had to disappoint him.

I stood. Elvin did likewise, looking at me expectantly. "Well," I said, "I'm gonna hit the ad agency first thing Monday. Then report back to the client. Then I'm out."

Elvin's stare did not flicker. "Ain't gonna work it, huh?"

"There's nothing here, man," I said mildly. "You guys put the blocks to it and came up empty. What makes you think I can do better?"

"'Cause you're a private dee-tective," Elvin answered,

tiny eyes boring into me. "You specialize at making us grunts look bad. You get all passionate an' involved an'—"

"Not this time," I answered. "I'm outa all that." Damned if I'd tell him about my deal with Carole, though. "My bits these days, they're about paperwork. Employee background checks, workman's comp claims."

"Nice nine-to-five shit." Elvin grunted.

I nodded. "This is a flukey deal anyways. Not a real case."

"*Uh*-huh. No money, in other words?" the big cop rumbled.

"Well, that. It's what Carole would call a pro bono."

"Hey, I'm impressed," Elvin said. "Pro bono. Imagine that," he said as I started up the hallway. "Let me know, if anything—"

"Thanks, Elvin."

"Hey."

I looked back.

"How's your friend Barb?"

"Barb Paley?" I remembered learning a while back that Barb, a recovering alcoholic, had met Elvin at some Alcoholics Anonymous meetings. "She's doing okay."

"Haven't seen her in a while," Elvin said.

Come to think of it, neither had I.

On impulse, I went from police headquarters to the main branch of the Detroit Public Library to check the newspapers for the period just following Cloyd's death. Apparently, Detroit's paper pundits hadn't thought it the story of the century. The *Free Press* ran a paragraph about it in their "Other News" column, between items about a stickup at a saloon on Cadieux and a smash-and-grab on Washington Boulevard. The *News* didn't print anything about it at all—it was too busy printing tantrums about Senator Proposto, campaigning for reelection in the company of what the paper indignantly described as "a frumpy, frowsy, failed saloon singer"—and neither paper followed up on the story, as far as I could tell. I was surprised. With five or six hundred homicides a year to write up, editors were picky as hell. To make the paper, you had to die grotesque or grisly. A sex-associated asphyxia like Cloyd's? I'd have expected them to front-page the sucker, above the fold.

For the hell of it, I checked the library's *Crain's Detroit Business* file also. There I found a puff piece about the Martin Ketchum & Martin open house that Elvin had mentioned, held the night Cloyd died. It sounded like quite a gala event. There had been hors d'oeuvres and an open bar. A string quartet performed in the atrium of the building. A singer, a comic, and a juggler had entertained. And there had been a special appearance by Brucie, the little chimp the agency featured in its motor oil ads. Tastefully, *Crain's* said nothing about Cloyd's death, not even in the "Comings and Goings" column.

Big help.

It was past four when I got home. I was in a hurry; I had plans for the evening and, besides, I had to find out what was going on with Squire. Maybe he'd come to his senses, bought a plane ticket, and headed for home.

Could I be that lucky?

CHAPTER

FIVE

The apartment door was suspiciously ajar. Inside, the living room was even a worse cluttered mess than usual. Before I could assess that, I heard noises from the back—muffled thumping and a female voice. I hurried back to find Barb Paley in the hallway, gripping the limp, half-naked Dennis Squire with a from-behind bear hug, dragging the pale, insensible, barefoot Californian out of the guest bathroom.

"Oh, thank God," she gasped when she saw me, and lowered the limp Dennis to the carpet.

Christ. "Is he all right?" I asked as I went to them. "What're you doing here, Barb?"

She stood back, seriously out of breath. "Something wrong with my car. Wanted you to look at it." *Puff, puff.* "Let myself in. Found him like that on the bathroom floor. He's all right, I think. Out cold, though. Who is he, Ben?"

I dollied Dennis up and hoisted him under the armpits, not especially gently, but he was in no condition to care. Barb opened the door to my bedroom as I dragged. "Sort of a drop-in guest from out of town,"

I told her. "Not in there, he'll puke all over my bed."

"Well, he already puked all over the guest-room bed."

"Aw, shit." I hauled him into the master bedroom and tumbled him over onto my bed. He made a few sounds but was otherwise inert. Barb, arms folded, stared down at him. "Poor guy."

"Don't worry, I'll be all right."

"I meant him, hon."

"I know," I said, grinning.

We went out to the kitchen. Barb Paley looked more freckled than usual that day, probably from working on her flowers around her little house over in Taylor. She was a vivid woman in her late thirties, with creamy skin, chin dimple, and bright blue eyes that understood and accepted. Her red curly hair was a solid mass about her round cheery face, and she carried herself with the assurance of a self-taught survivor. That day she wore jeans and sneakers and an open-necked sleeveless plaid shirt in blues and greens. Since it was late afternoon, she obviously had the day off from her Heritage Hospital typing job.

We were lovers once, briefly, a long time before. But that was a different Barb in a different era. These days she was sober and working hard to stay that way via AA. We went to concerts together, hung out together, occasionally worked cases together. She was the best woman friend I had, in the sense that our relationship was mutually enjoyable and uncomplicated by sexual tension. Though I would never have dreamed of telling her this, I was plagued by low-grade worry about her. She was good-hearted and self-sufficient, but also highly emotional and impulsive—"a typical drunk," as she herself frequently said in her no-holds-barred way.

So I watched out for her.

"Has your friend Dennis been alone here all day?" she asked as we surveyed the evidence in the kitchen.

"Yup." I picked up the empty Rebel Yell bottle that had been rolling around on the floor. "Wonder where he found this."

"Drunks are ingenious," she said. She was glancing at the open yellow pages book on the dinette table. "First he drank up your inventory. Then he found a party store that delivered. What'd he do for money, Ben?"

"You wouldn't believe the roll he had on him when I rescued him from the airport last night. Thousand bucks easy."

Her eyes glinted. "You rescued him from the airport?"

"Sheriffs had him in the jug."

"You should have left him there," she told me. "He has to hit bottom sometime. Rescuing him won't help."

"Reflex."

"I know, hon."

"What's this about your car?"

"Oh, yeah, let me show you."

We left the apartment, went down the stairs, out into the parking lot. On the way, at Barb's prompting, I told her all I knew about Dennis Squire. She didn't say much, but I knew what she was thinking, knew what she would suggest, and it was all right with me. Anything to get him up and running and back into his life again—and out of mine.

"So where you parked?" I asked, looking around the parking lot.

"Right there," she said, smiling.

The car at the nearest end was a brand-new shiny gold Ford Taurus four-door, glistening in the late-afternoon sun from a very recent wash. It bore a cardboard temporary tag, and the dealer sticker was still pasted to the driver's side rear window. "Well, I'll be damned," I said. "You dumped the Escort."

"Finally," she said happily. "Rotten old alcoholic car, even you couldn't keep it running. And now that I'm sober, I suddenly have money for nice things."

"Smart choice."

"Hey," she said, nudging me playfully. "My best friend is an old Ford Motor man. What would you have said if I'd bought a Honda?"

"I'd of said, 'Good for you, darlin',' " I answered innocently. Laughing, she fake-slapped at me. I hugged her. "Good for you, darlin'. So," I added, letting her go, "this bit about something wrong with it, that was just a con to get me out here, right?"

"No, it *is* kind of running rough," she said. "Maybe you could adjust it a little for me."

"Sorry. Wish I could."

"Why not?"

I gestured at the Taurus. "These new cars are all way beyond me. It's all computer stuff. They got no carburetors, distributors—engines are put in crossways—can't find nothing in there, and can't fix what I *can* find."

"Oh," she said, crestfallen.

"Sorry I can't help."

"Oh, that's all right," she said, touching me briefly. "I can always take it to the dealer. I just feel bad for you, hon."

"Why?"

"I know how important car work is to you."

"Hey. Time hurries on, that's all. And speaking of which, I have a date in exactly one hour, so I'd better haul ass."

"A date?" she asked, peering at me, half smiling. "With an actual woman?"

"Ha. Nothing special, kind of a duty thing, actually."

"What about your friend up there?" she asked casually.

I hesitated. "What about him?"

She looked at me with level calm, the parking lot breeze ruffling her red hair. "He really shouldn't be alone. How about if I stay here while you're gone? I'll clean up, and make him something to eat, and try to keep him from drinking. And I'll talk to him."

"This is what you call twelfth-stepping, right?"

"It helps me," she answered. "You know that. I need to help other drunks. It helps me more than it'll help him. So how about it?"

I squelched my reservations. "I knew you'd offer," I told her.

"And I knew you'd accept," she replied, smiling.

Arm in arm, we went back in.

"Can I ask you a question, Ben?" Raeanne asked as we slid into the booth at the Pancake House in Dearborn.

"Fire away," I answered, signaling the waitperson for coffee.

"Does this mean we're dating?"

I looked at her. Raeanne's oval pretty face, framed by smooth short black hair, had its usual sardonic cast. High cheekbones, even teeth, long neck, smile just slightly wider on one side than the other. I figured her for around thirty, within a click or two either way. She wore blue stirrups and a soft white linen blouse. Whip-thin, trim, vivid.

"Does *what* mean we're dating?" I echoed.

The waitperson dealt cups, poured, left. Raeanne cradled hers with long slender fingers. "This," she answered. "Going out tonight. There seems to be a pattern developing. But it's been so long since I 'dated' anyone, I'm not sure."

"Me too," I confessed. "But don't forget, you started it, with that dinner at Too Chez."

"Yes, but that wasn't a *date*-date."

"Oh?"

"It was to thank you for saving my life that time, remember?"

I remembered. It had been a bad, ugly, messy business, into which Raeanne had wandered quite innocently. "All in a day's work," I said jauntily.

"You saved me," she repeated softly, "so I took you to dinner."

"You really didn't have to do that."

"Did so. It's right there in Miss Manners," she told me. "Look it up. When a man rescues you from a certain and excruciating death, the appropriate response is buy him a good meal."

"I see."

"But now you've changed the dynamic by taking me to Moby Dick's with you tonight," she said.

"This isn't a date-date either."

"Oh?"

"It's to thank you for taking me to Too Chez."

"You really didn't have to do that."

"Did so. It's right there in Miss Manners," I told her. "Look it up. When a woman buys you a hundred-buck dinner, the appropriate response is to take her to a rhythm-and-blues club."

"I see."

"Besides, I couldn't let you miss George Gritzbach. One of the great blues artists."

"Like Zanna Canady?" she asked.

"Yeah. You know about Zanna, huh?"

"Hey, she's all over the papers, with the senator and all. Isn't doing any singing, though."

"Which is too bad," I added. "I loved her stuff. This political bit she's into now, campaigning with that lard-ass—"

"Proposto," she affirmed, smiling. "I can't figure it either. Talk about contrasts!" She sipped her coffee. "Why'd she quit singing, do you know?"

"Nope. Lotta years since then," I said, feeling old. "I loved her stuff, though, way back when. I had a couple of her records."

"Records," she repeated, smiling. "No one has records anymore."

"I did. Still do. Hers vanished on me, somewhere up the line."

Raeanne studied me. Then she reached into my shirt pocket for one of my short-tipped cigars, stuck it in her teeth, came out of her little purse with a Bic lighter, fired the cigar up, and then put it in my mouth. She drank some coffee, evidently amused at my reaction. "You surprise me," she said.

Her? I was the speechless one. Well, nearly. "How come?"

"Bringing me here. Most men," she went on, "would have suggested we go to my place after the concert. Or taken me to a bar, gotten me giggly, and *then* suggested we go to my place."

"Reckon I'm not most men."

"Clearly."

"I'm a rehabilitated, sensitive, nineties kinda guy."

"I could see that, yes indeed." She sipped some more. "Are you involved?"

The abrupt question made me hesitate. A smart-aleck answer rose to my lips—*Not this week*—but I squelched it. A truthful answer would have been, *No,* not since

Ardyce, but I squelched that too. I liked Raeanne, but I couldn't be that open with her. I never told anyone everything. "Not involved," I replied, puffing smoke. "You?"

"I was married once. Not anymore."

"Oh. Sorry."

She tried to be offhand. "It went wrong from the start," she told me. "We both wanted to make each other over into someone else. Didn't work. And neither of us could stay married to the person the other one really was." She squinted at me. "Am I confusing you?"

"No, why?"

"You look puzzled."

"I look like that a lot. Occupational hazard."

She peered at me. "If something's puzzling you, ask away."

"Okay. What happened to the accent?"

"What accent?"

"The one you had, back when I met you," I told her. "Kind of Texas twangy. Gone now, though."

She thought. "Oh. That was when I was in *Hell's Belles* up in Pontiac. I understudied Maggie."

"So the accent stuck to you?"

"The character stuck to me. They usually do, for a while."

"You mean you act like the character, even when you're not performing?"

"It's not that explicit," she said. "And it's not by design. Some of the character traits bleed through, that's all."

"So back when I met you, you were Maggie?"

"Partly, I suppose."

"Who are you right now, then?"

"Who do you think I am?" she responded, amused.

"Well, I know who you want me to think you are. The question is, who is that?"

"Right now?" She thought. "Me. Just me."

"Just you, huh?"

"Yes. I sit before you, exposed for what I am: nobody." I eyed her. "Nah. You're definitely somebody."

"When you find out who," she said, "would you please let me know?"

"Sure," I said, smiling back. In the pleasant pause I drank some coffee, which had cooled already. "Question for you," I said. "At any given time, how do I know it's you I'm dealing with and not some character?"

"Oh, you can tell," she said. "Look into my eyes. "I leaned forward. Pretty eyes, a perfect gray surrounded by clear whites. The nearness to her felt tingly. I eased back. "Okay."

"Now watch." She turned her head, touched her short hair aimlessly. Hiked one foot up under her rear end, kind of rolled her shoulders, and then looked at me again. Now she looked different. Her face seemed heavier, slantier. Her eyes were dull and a little buggy. She blinked a couple of times and said, in a piping, breathy voice, "Free padding? And free labor, too? Why, that's just unbe*leeeeee*vable!"

Our waitperson, who had cruised up to administer refills, just stood there staring at her. Then something seemed to switch, to let go, behind Raeanne's eyes. She shrugged and blinked, and disengaged her foot, and smiled at me. "See?"

"Jesus," I breathed.

"You're the dumb blonde!" the waitperson bleated, slopping coffee as she poured. "From the Century Carpet ad!"

"You know," I told Raeanne, "I've seen that ad a million times, but I never made the connection."

Self-mockingly, she said, "It's my claim to fame. It's also my curse. It's typecast me in this town. They're after me to do another one, but I told them I've retired the wig. I'd rather go back to doing Miss Plywood radio spots, even."

"That was you too?"

She nodded somberly. "At least I've got a shot at something better. I'm auditioning for *Jubilee* in a couple of weeks."

"That's the one coming to the Fisher, right?" She nodded. "Sounds like big-time stuff."

"About as big as it gets," she answered. "I've been killing myself rehearsing my audition number."

"I'll bet it's pretty."

She cocked her head. "Would you like me to sing it for you sometime?"

"Very much."

She smiled but said nothing.

"I hope the *Jubilee* thing works out for you," I said presently.

"Me too." She shrugged. "If not, that's all right. There's always the radio spots, and training videos, and spieling at Cobo and the Palace and the Silverdome, and good old Kelly Services. If it weren't for them, I'd have starved long ago."

A few minutes later we were in my Mustang, returning to Moby Dick's, where Raeanne had left her car. "So tell me," she said. "Are we going to start dating, or just keep reciprocating, or what?"

"Can't answer that," I said. "I don't know what dating is anymore."

"Me either," she admitted.

"It's like everything else," I observed. "Changing. You let go for a bit, it gets hard to catch a hold again. So I've been hanging back, for the past year or so. Watching."

Suddenly I was acutely uncomfortable, conscious that I'd said more than I meant to. Raeanne answered easily. "Can't do that, Ben. You've got to hang in there. Keep doing what you do and being what you are, no matter what."

"You're right," I said doubtfully.

We swept into the deserted club parking lot and over to where her white Pontiac Sunbird sat parked by the fence. "One thing you can be sure of," she said.

"What's that?" I asked, rolling the car to a stop.

Her oval pretty face was half visible in the light of the distant streetlamps. "I had fun tonight."

"So did I."

A long silent stillness. Then she asked, very softly, "You're afraid we'll mess this up, aren't you."

Being read felt funny. "Uh-huh," I answered presently.

"Me too."

After an instant, we smiled, said cheery goodbyes, and she left the Mustang. I watched and waited as her Sunbird lights disappeared up Michigan Avenue, and then I set out for home.

The bathroom door was closed, water running inside. I tapped. "Dennis? I'm back. We got to talk, man."

No answer.

I tapped again. "Hey! You all right?"

"Ben," came Barb Paley's voice, "would you mind going out to the living room? I'll be right there."

It was late, I was tired, I didn't get it. "What's wrong?"

Pause. "I'm naked, hon. All right?"

CHAPTER

SIX

A few minutes later, Barb appeared in the living room. Clothed. I was on my feet, lighted cigar in hand and not all that calm, but articulate as ever. "What the hell, Barb. I mean—Christ, you know?"

"Just take it easy, hon," she said resolutely. "Please."

Her reddish hair was limp and had been hastily brushed. Other evidence of recent action was her pale complexion, which could have been due to lack of makeup—and exhaustion—and a reddish welt at the base of her neck.

I flopped down on the arm of the sofa. "I'm really surprised, kid. You've told me about the twelfth step. What does the Big Book call this, the thirteenth?"

She did not smile. "Don't be mad."

"I'm not mad. Just surprised."

She sighed. I expected her to sit, but she just stood there, not defiant, not reticent either. "He woke up. I fixed supper and we ate. We talked. And from the get-go, Ben, it was—it was special for me. He's very special, did you know that?"

Oh no, oh no. "I barely know the guy. Hell, I've

hardly talked to him since he crash-landed here."

"He's had an awful time of it," she said. "That marriage of his . . . just a poisonous thing. Job-wise he's totally burned out. And then the boozing on top of it . . . he just lost it, completely flipped out."

"Yeah, but—"

"I like him," she said. "He's smart. He's successful. He's special. He can be saved. There's nothing wrong with him that sobriety and love can't cure."

Christ! "Love? Already?"

"I know what you're thinking."

"Sex is what you're talking about. That's all there's been time for here."

"What difference does it make?" she shot back. "I'm an adult, I've been alone a long time, I'm entitled."

"I just don't want you hurt, darlin'. That's all I'm saying. You don't know this guy, I don't know this guy. God knows what the story is—"

"I know what his story is," she said deliberately. "It's the same as mine."

My cigar had gone out. I struck a match on my thumbnail and flamed the cigar again, dragging on it so hard it popped sparks. "I wouldn't build no elaborate plans around him, if I were you," I said grimly, shaking out the match. "I suspect come Monday he'll be on a plane back to somewhere."

"Oh," she answered evenly, "I doubt that."

"Just back off him now, darlin'. Please."

She stiffened and moved toward the door. "Don't tell me what to do."

"I can ask you not to do it in my bed, thank you kindly!"

"Go piss up a rope," she said crossly, and left.

I stared at the slammed door with mute anger, expecting it to reopen any instant. It did not. Gradually, I calmed down. Briefly I entertained myself with the notion of going back to the bedroom and continuing the discussion, but with Dennis this time. But right away I determined it wasn't such a hot idea, considering my frame of mind. Plenty of time for that tomorrow.

It was—oh shit, 2:30 A.M. , something like that. Way past bedtime, but I wasn't ready for sleep, especially not on the living room sofa. I went into the kitchen and rescued myself a Stroh's beer. Cracked and sipped and looked around, noticing that Barb, good as her word, had cleaned the place up. What a kid.

The big brown expanding wallet, the one Wendy Dilworth had given me, was on the end of the counter by the phone. The sight of it reminded me that I had a case, of sorts, to work on. Not much I could do until Monday, when I'd go nose around the ad agency where Cloyd had died. But I hadn't looked through the paperwork yet, and now seemed like a good time. Paperwork: the perfect tranquilizer.

I untied the flap and sorted the masses of papers out of the wallet's slots and onto odd piles on the dinette table. There was all kinds of trash in there. Utility bill stubs, carefully notated with check number and date paid. Credit card receipts. ATM slips. Copies of handwritten time sheets with MARTIN-KETCHUM-MARTIN printed on them. Even wads of receipts from grocery stores and others, some for purchases as small as three bucks. Nothing there of any consequence. Yawnville, man. I was just about to call it a night when I came upon a yellow sheet mixed in among several car repair invoices. That made me crank both eyes open again.

It was a towing company invoice that had been stapled to a car repair bill. It was dated the previous January, for a thirty-six-mile tow of Cloyd's Trans Am to a garage on Industrial Highway in Ann Arbor. What jumped out at me was the origin of the tow. Walnut Street in Wyandotte.

Cloyd lived in Ann Arbor. His office was at Grand Circus Park in Detroit. Wyandotte, a downriver Detroit suburb, was nowhere near either and way off the straight line between the two. I had to wonder what the hell he was doing down there.

But that was the old nosy detective instinct, working overtime and to no purpose. I reminded myself that the Cloyd matter, though twisted and grim, was not really a case but a throwaway. On Monday, I'd go through the motions and interview his co-workers at the ad agency. But to press on I'd need a lot more than a vague theory and Elvin Dance's gut feel. I'd need, say, a clue or two. A lead. Some evidence. A motive. Anything.

I put away the paperwork and made a bed for myself on the sofa in the living room. Before turning off the light, I called Barb's number. She answered sleepily.

"Sorry," I said.

"Me too," she answered.

I hung up, cut off the light, and kicked out.

"Let us review," I began, leaning back in the booth and lighting a cigar. "Since I rescued you from the sheriff's on Friday night, you puked on my spare bed. You drank up all the booze in the house, including even a fifth of Rebel Yell I clean forgot I had. You trashed the living room, you left a tray of ice to melt all over the counter, and, last but not least, you boinked my best friend." I blew smoke. "Does that sum it up pretty well, pal?"

Dennis was calm, amiable, deliberate. "If I've offended you, or taken undue advantage of you, I'm sorry," he said quietly.

I waved that away. "All I want to know is what the hell gives here. I think I'm entitled to that much."

It was Sunday afternoon at Under New Management. Patrons were sprinkled about the dim wood-walled joint, in booths and at tables and along the bar at the far end, groovin' on the booze and the tunes from the juke, mainly Garth Brooks as usual. The Foosball machine was unattended, though, and the volume of noise and tobacco smoke had not risen to anything like its usual level. On this spectacularly sunny nearly summer afternoon, most folks had better things to do than to sit around a saloon.

I was there because it seemed like a good place to talk. I'd actually bunked in until late morning and got up to find Dennis out on the deck, reading the morning *Free Press* and drinking coffee. He was withdrawn and a bit jittery and seemed disinclined to talk. But when I suggested coming over here for a healthful brunch of burgers and beers, he readily agreed.

For the occasion, I'd outfitted him with an old pair of my blue cutoff jeans and a white Detroit Pistons T-shirt. He'd shaved and mashed his blond hair flat. But he looked goofy as hell, sitting there in the booth across from me, the bespectacled West Coast business-suit type, dressed raggedy-assed and plopped down there in that backwoods saloon. I remembered how he'd been out at his Sunnyvale office, surrounded by bright shiny twinkling computers and bright eager employees aching to do his bidding, sitting and fidgeting, bouncing from place to place, talking in that booming voice of his, the very image of Silicon Valley brilliance, oozing power from every pore. And now look at him.

For a long moment he stared into his untouched mug of beer. Then he said, "This is really about Barb, isn't it. She told me the two of you were close once."

"That was years ago," I answered. "We're friends, that's it. But yeah, this is about her, mostly."

"I really like her," he said.

"Married man," I said mildly, "on the lam, and you bounce the first babe you—"

"I suspect you're no angel yourself," he pointed out.

"This is about you," I countered. "And a woman for whom I happen to care quite a bit."

"My marriage is over," he said tonelessly.

"Well, I'm sorry." He did not answer. "Kids?"

He shifted. "One. He started college last fall."

I stared at him. "Hoo boy, you started early."

"Married at eighteen."

Bill Scozzafava, the massive aproned bartender, arrived at the booth with our burgers on paper plates. "Eddie wants to talk to you," he told me, sliding the food in front of us.

Oh, Christ. Must have been about my tab again. "Sure, Bill, send him on over."

"At the bar," he said, and wheeled away.

All in good time, I decided. I looked at Dennis, who was shaking ketchup onto his burger. "What about your job?"

"I've had it with them. *Had* it."

He handed me the ketchup. I splurted some under the lid, took a mouthful, swallowed. "So," I asked, "does that mean you're not going home?"

"I don't know what I'm going to do." He washed down a large mouthful with some beer. "Best I can tell you right now. If staying at your place is a problem, I understand. I can move out."

I let that go. "This thing with Barb. One-night stand or—"

"I don't know that either." He looked at me, and

for the first time his blue eyes had that shrewdness I remembered. "I really like her, Ben."

"Yeah, you said that." I ate another couple of bites. "You should know, Barb's had it rough. She went into recovery last year. She's sober, but it's been tough. She walks close to the edge, way too close."

"I'd never hurt her," he said, chewing.

"Hope not."

He paused in his eating and smiled thinly. "Do I sense a threat in there somewhere?"

I set my burger down, no longer hungry. "No," I said lazily. "I always liked you, Dennis. You seem like a nice guy, just messed up as hell. You helped me out a couple of times, and I don't forget. I want to help you—I been helping you—but I got priorities, and on that list Barb is way higher than you. Sorry."

"I understand," he replied, and tore off another bite. "And I'm grateful to you, Ben. Just give me a few days. I got to think, and rest up, and figure things out."

I picked up my mug, swirled the last mouthful, and downed it. Dennis polished off his burger with dispatch. For a guy coming off an extended binge, he had one hell of an appetite. Iron constitution, I decided.

"You want that, Ben?" he asked, gesturing at my sandwich.

"Nah, help yourself. Be right back." His mug was still full, so I carried mine over to the bar and slid it in front of Bill for a refill. "What's Eddie want?" I asked as Bill drew me a fresh Stroh's dark.

"Dunno," Bill murmured, "but he's agitated as hell." Bill Scozzafava was a massive man, an ex-member of the Chicago Bears' "Gorilla Gang," but even he stepped lightly around Eddie Cabla. He slid the mug to me. "I'll get him."

Bill went through the doorway into the employees-only area. I leaned on the bar, waiting. The bar noise had picked up a bit. At regular intervals the front door thumped open and shut, open and shut, shooting a beam of piercing sunlight into the dark bar each time. I waved and nodded as the regulars started to check in: Norris, Jimmy Joe, Harry, Darryl, and the rest. Presently, Barb Paley came in. I waved and called. She waved back, then saw Dennis and headed straight for him without hesitation. He stood and they hugged and I felt that old uneasy feeling, oh shit, oh shit—

"Perkins!" came Eddie's high flat voice as he barreled out from the employees-only area. "Where ya been? Been wanting to talk to you."

I looked down at the bald-headed little bar owner. "It's okay, Eddie, I'll put a C against the tab today, and then—"

"Forget the tab," he said impatiently. "Who cares about the tab? You been coming here a dozen years, I know you're good for it."

"Hey, Ed, that's a mighty obliging attitude."

"That's me," he said, grin toothy. "A real obliging guy. You know that."

"Sure."

His forehead wrinkled, his imitation of sincerity. "You know mucky-mucks in state government, right?"

"Uh—"

"That judge guy you play poker with!" he rapped.

"Well, sure, him I know. Why?"

"I got a hell of a problem." He leaned on the bar, looked both ways, and said quietly, "It's the goddamn tree huggers."

"Who?"

"The DNR! Department of Natural Resources," he translated unnecessarily. "They're crawling up my ass crack. I need some pull, some serious pull."

"What's the problem? The bar in violation of the state eyesore ordinance or something?"

"Very funny. Nah, it's worse than that. They're gonna dig up my driveway if I don't find a way to stop 'em."

"The driveway? Why for?"

Eddie's lined face was sour. "This building was a grocery store once, back in the fifties, right? Sold gas too. Well, the state says there's gas tanks still under the driveway, leaking into the ground water or some pain-in-the-ass thing."

I glanced back at the table. Barb and Dennis were sitting side by side and together, I mean very together, heads practically touching as they talked. God knows what their hands were doing under the tabletop. If those tables could talk . . .

"Well," I asked Eddie, "are there tanks under there?"

"No!" he said, with a swatting gesture. "I had 'em dug up way back in sixty-eight. Sold 'em to a guy over in Taylor. But I can't prove it no more, and the state says they're still down there, and they're gonna send backhoes and shit and tear up my driveway and shit. And I don't need that shit."

"My buddy's a judge," I said. "I don't know what pull he has. I can ask."

"Wouldja? Thanks, pal."

"Don't mention it."

He started away but darted back. "Your tab *is* gettin' a little high," he told me. "Better knock it down, or I'll have to cut you off. Nothing personal."

"Okay, Ed," I answered, reaching for my wallet.

Barb and Dennis got to their feet as I returned to the table. "I'm taking Dennis for a ride," Barb told me, face alight. "Show him the sights."

I could just imagine what kind. "You kids be careful," I said. "And Dennis, you know what your curfew is."

"Yes, Dad," he answered, and they snickered.

"Gotta roust you early tomorrow," I told Dennis. "I'm interviewing some people downtown on a case, people in suits. I could use somebody who speaks the language."

"Sounds elegant," Dennis answered. "Glad to help."

Barb tugged at him. "'Bye, Ben!" she called, and they left noisily.

I watched the door close behind them, then looked toward the bar. Bill, pulling a shell, and Jimmy Joe, drinking at his, were looking at me owlishly. Like me, they had never seen Barb Paley like that before, and I'm not talking about the fact that she was wearing shorts.

On impulse, I carried my beer into the little hallway that ran back toward the bathrooms, fed the pay phone, and mashed out a quick chrome number. Raeanne's cool voice gave some sort of short taped spiel, and then her answering machine beeped. I pictured her typing at a computer terminal somewhere, or posing under hot lights being ogled by cameras, or maybe even standing in the living room I'd never seen, belting out her audition number as her stereo played accompaniment. . . .

"Thinking about you," I said, and hung up.

CHAPTER

SEVEN

To any native Detroiter, the name David Whitney Building conjured up images of dentists and doctors. The twenty-story tower was, in fact, built for the medical profession back in 1915 or so—the year, as it happened, that my daddy emigrated to Detroit from north Georgia—and as kids we all spent many hours soaking up the splendor of the Whitney's marble and glass Italian Renaissance decor, waiting to have temperatures taken, orifices probed, or cavities filled. That was, of course, before postwar flight, which never really stopped, drained Detroit's communities, confidence, and cash.

These days, landmarks like the David Whitney struggled to survive on "aggressive" rents paid by the likes of dim little flacks, flimflammers, fortune-tellers, and financial planners. The odd exceptions were outfits like Martin Ketchum & Martin, companies that, influenced by civic consciousness or psychosis, stayed bravely in Detroit, outposts of optimism.

The ad agency occupied the entire tenth floor, surrounding an interior courtyard that rose up twenty floors to the translucent ceiling. Double glass doors, emblazoned with the agency's name, led into an oval-shaped foyer decorated in chrome office modern with blue and gray predominating. The receptionist took our names, inquired as to our business, and invited us to sit.

We stood. Dennis, with the help of Barb Paley, had bought himself some clothes during their "sightseeing" trip the afternoon before. He wore gray slacks and a blue Ban-Lon shirt and bright white Nike Airs and looked like an executive on an off day. I was a little more formal, wearing blue dress slacks and a white open-necked dress shirt and my blue blazer, into which I'd hastily changed after putting in several hours at the Norwegian Wood maintenance office.

Finally, beckoned by a beep at her console, the receptionist led us out of the foyer. We wound through narrow cluttered halls, past noisy offices and bustling cubicles, and into a squarish conference room that looked out over Grand Circus Park. A big slab of mahogany table, attended by high-backed chairs, dominated the room; at the far side, beneath the windows overlooking the park, a low-slung conversational grouping of heavily stuffed furniture clustered together around a mirrored coffee table. The receptionist asked us to wait—"Mr. Martin will be with you shortly"—and retreated with a quiet click of the double doors.

Dennis was drawn to the windows overlooking the park. "Elegant," he breathed, staring down.

"Whole town was supposed to be built around circles like that," I commented. "Just like D.C. But Grand Circus Park is about all that's left of that bright idea."

"What happened?" he asked.

"What always happens around here. People got greedy."

"It's not just here," Dennis said grimly. "You want

to see government at its greedy rip-off best, go out to California."

"Thanks, anyhow."

The double doors sprang open and in marched a short black-haired man in a dark double-breasted pinstripe, beaming and gesturing like a prizefighter entering the ring. He acted like there was a crowd of cheering people in there, instead of two guys standing around waiting. "Gentlemen, gentlemen!" he sang warmly. "Welcome to Martin Ketchum & Martin." Before I knew it, he had my hand in both of his and was shaking it with a moist and curiously limp grip. "Such a fine day to be out. I envy you fellows." He motored on. "We're all stuck inside here, producing some brilliant creative, asking the questions and questioning the answers, ha-ha."

"Ben Perkins," I said, noticing that Martin, if that was who he was, had been accompanied by a tall and extremely attractive young woman, who stood at the wall by the door, watching us expressionlessly with hands linked behind her. "This here's Dennis Squire," I added. "Appreciate your seeing us. We won't take up much of your time."

"You can have all the time you need," the man said expansively. "I'll stay with you all day if you need me."

The woman spoke for the first time, in an even, calm voice. "But, Larry? You told Debbie to wait exactly six minutes and then announce that you have an overseas phone call, didn't you?"

The short man tossed his head and laughed. "All the time you need," he repeated. "This, by the way, is Roulette Burke, one of my people."

"Brooks, Larry," she corrected. "Roulette *Brooks*. Maybe after six *more* years you'll learn my name, huh?" Larry just laughed. Brooks stepped forward and offered me her hand, which I shook. "It's a pleasure, Mr. Perkins."

She was probably twenty-four or twenty-five, and on the tall side, even without the aid of her pumps. Her shoulder-length blond hair was fashionably tangled and moussed—today, looking good means looking like you just got up—around a pale, full face and vivid dark eyes. She wore a long sleeveless ivory-linen vest, with big buttons up the front, over a snug ivory skirt that went down to her ankles. She had striking looks— various washed-out shades of white and off-white, set off by bright red at her lips and fingernails.

"Same here," I answered. "I appreciate y'all—"

"I think it's great that you're doing this," Larry Whoever said with narrow-eyed sincerity. Like most little guys who worked in the public eye, Larry made up for his slightness of stature with continuous motion, and he paced and gestured as he talked. I could see right away that he was used to being the center of attention wherever he was. I could also tell, right from the start, that he'd be of no help to us whatsoever. "You have to understand something about advertising agencies here in America," he churned on. "We're very much public-service oriented. We're people oriented. We believe in serving the community. That's why we—"

"People oriented?" Brooks asked lazily. "Tell us, Larry. What color is the sky on the planet you live on?"

"—dible situation with Chris Cloyd," Larry continued, wheeling on Dennis, who had eased himself onto the sofa by the window. I remained standing and so did Brooks, who half leaned against the wall by the door, aimlessly examining her red fingernails. "Just one of our best people," Larry chattered, "one of our top people, an absolutely phenomenal and eclectic person. Oh," he intoned, "the impact of his loss is just incalculable. I just can't say enough good about him."

"What you *have* said," Brooks remarked coolly without looking up, "is that Chris was a sociopathic grotesque. Untrue, of course, but that's what you've said."

Larry was bearing down on me now, gesturing at me with both hands as he paced. "—you to do, Ben, is find out everything you can. Absolutely everything. And then report directly to me. You'll have total access; you'll have all the power I have. Of course I'm close friends with the mayor and several people on the Common Council. I can pull some strings for you. It's important that we ask the questions and question the answers, to put his wife's mind at ease. So that she can put this behind her. I feel such incredible empathy for Wendy. Such a dreadful time for her—"

"How about some empathy for your own wife?" Brooks asked, again in a quiet voice, again without looking up. "Or are you too busy flying your mistress around the country with you to—"

"And," Larry charged on, "I've given all our staff strict orders to be truthful—"

"Which everyone takes really seriously," Brooks commented, smile icy. "Coming from such a barefaced, reflexive, utterly brazen liar."

The doors opened and a young woman with spiky hair leaned in. "Larry, your call from Amsterdam is on seven four."

"Take a message," Larry commanded dramatically.

"He said it's urgent," the woman said meekly.

"Oh, my God," Larry said, looking at each of us, hands in the air in a patient how-can-I-help-it gesture. "International business. It's a twenty-four-hour world, gentlemen. Ms. Brock will take care of you two," he added, loping toward the door. "Have a great day!"And with that he was gone.

Roulette Brooks left her lean and folded her arms and looked from me to Dennis and back. Her smile was wicked and knowing, white teeth and bright red full lips. "That, gentlemen, was Mr. Larry Martin. He never bothers to introduce himself, being utterly convinced that everyone he meets knows who he is."

"The boss, huh?" I asked.

"Boss," she affirmed, "owner, founder, curse."

"What about Ketchum and the other Martin?" Dennis questioned.

"If there ever was a Ketchum, he was gone long before my time," Brooks answered. "And there is no other Martin. A merciful God wouldn't do that to us. May I send for coffee or soda or something?"

"We're fine, thanks," I answered. "Why don't we set a spell."

"Surely," Brooks said coolly. We took seats on opposite sides of the mirror topped coffee table, Dennis to my left on the sofa. I was, I must admit, intrigued with Roulette Brooks. So was Dennis, I could tell. And I was all crossways about the situation there. I had expected to conduct a rather boring and predictable question-and-answer, and instead I seemed to have stumbled into a rather bent and curiously hostile corporate soap opera.

"I'm asking around at the request of Wendy Dilworth, Chris Cloyd's wife, as you know," I told Brooks. "I'm not here to interfere with the police. Just to double-check, sort of."

"I understand," Brooks replied. "How can I help?"

"Well," I said, getting out my spiral pad, "what's your job here?"

"I'm an administrator," she replied. "A glorified gofer, in other words. I worked for Chris."

"Okay."

"Actually," she said, "I was Chris's—how can I explain this?—liaison with the world."

Dennis and I exchanged looks. "Mind explaining that?"

"I'll try." Brooks crossed one leg over the other under her ivory skirt. "Chris Cloyd was a copywriter. By far the best here. Probably the best in Detroit. Certainly one of the top people in the country. He was brilliant," she said earnestly. "Really brilliant."

"Okay," I said, writing nothing.

"He was also rather—unconventional," she said slowly. "Do you guys know anything about ad agencies?"

"Nope," I said.

"I've always done my stuff in-house," Dennis put in.

"Okay," she said. "It's sort of a cliché that agency creatives are supposed to be eccentric. It's gotten to the point where most creatives act eccentric because they think that's what clients expect of them. But Chris didn't have to fake it. He really was different. Very much so."

"In what way?" I asked.

"Well, he loved his work," she replied. "He loved doing it. He worked fiendishly hard at it. He'd work three, four, five days straight, all night long, locked up by himself, sometimes not even eating." Her large dark eyes were looking off somewhere, reflecting in the light from the windows overlooking Grand Circus Park. "He didn't care about deadlines. He didn't care what anyone else around here thought. He'd just work on his own until he had it exactly the way he wanted it. And once he did, it was always perfect."

"Real wordsmith," Dennis observed.

"Chris's failing, or weakness, or liability—I don't know the right word," she confessed. "I'm sorry.

Anyway, Chris's big problem was that he couldn't stand other people. Being around or dealing with them. Especially people here at the agency. He didn't socialize. He didn't go to meetings. He didn't have any friends. He refused to go see clients or to meet with them here."

"God," Dennis said slowly. "A copy guy, a guy in the communications business, and he refused to communicate."

"Just couldn't handle it," Brooks said. "He'd get input in writing from the account executives and then work on his own. He'd talk to people on the phone; he spent a lot of time on the phone. Then it was just him and his computer. Just him and it. Staring into the screen, *rat-a-tat-tat* at the keyboard all day long. All by himself."

"Except for you," I said.

"Oh, sure," she agreed. "I talked to him. I even went in there sometimes. But only briefly. And I was the only one. He wouldn't meet with account executives, account supervisors, media people, anybody. And they stayed clear of him too. They were all scared to death of him."

"You were his buffer," I said.

She nodded. "For some reason he liked me," she said. "So I became his interface with the world."

Interface. Interesting term. "I see," I said, doodling. I had a notion but decided to hold it for later. "Is it fair to say he had a lot of enemies around here?"

"The police kept asking me that," she said, irritated. "But it's not true. Chris was antisocial and odd, but nobody disliked him. I think they really respected him. Except of course for Larry. To Larry, 'respect' isn't a feeling, it's just a word to use on people. To Larry, the world exists only on the sidelines of his own life. To

Larry, other people aren't human beings, only insects."

I kept my voice deceptively mild. "Think Larry killed him?"

She laughed, truly amused. "If someone killed Chris—"

"Do you think someone did?" I cut in.

"No. I don't."

"You buy the accidental asphyxia theory?"

A pause, and then she said impassively, "I told you he was odd."

"But *that* odd? To get off by tying himself up and—"

"It's not unheard of."

"Did you know he did that kind of thing?"

"Of course not." She snorted. "What a stupid question."

"There are no stupid questions," Dennis put in calmly.

"Well, that one sure was," she said sourly. She swung on me. "Do you think someone killed him, Mr. Perkins?"

"What a stupid question," I answered.

"There are no stupid questions," she put back, half smiling.

"Well, that one sure was," I retorted. "I don't 'think.' I check things out with an open mind. I draw conclusions from the available evidence."

"What if there isn't any evidence?" she asked.

"Then I wing it." That grew her smile, brilliant red and white. I pressed, "Let's get back to the idea of Larry Martin as a killer, shall we?"

Brooks crossed her legs the other way and took a deep breath. "If we must. Now. Let's say someone did kill Chris. If that's true, it required careful planning. Larry doesn't have the attention span for that. It also required ruthlessness. Larry doesn't care enough about people even to be ruthless."

"Could have jobbed it out," I noted.

"And how would he do that?" she came back. "There's no entry for 'assassins' in the yellow pages. And Larry just doesn't move in the kind of circles that would give him access to people like that."

"I see."

"Besides," she went on, "Larry above all protects his own interests. Chris's death is not good for him, it's very bad for him. Chris's brilliance made up for this agency's shabby performance in other areas. Larry couldn't afford to lose Chris, and somewhere deep inside he knew that. So why kill him?"

"You're sticking up for Martin pretty good," I pointed out. "Guys like him, at that level, they can be pretty dangerous."

"Please don't misunderstand," she said evenly. "Larry is a truly contemptible human being, and a corrupt menace, and I suppose he could be dangerous in some sense—but not in the way you mean. Hey," she added with a laugh, "if I could realistically pin Larry with this, don't you think I'd do it?"

"Faster than Hogan's goat," I agreed, taking a moment to jot some things. I was getting hungry for a cigar, but I'd seen all the little THANKS FOR NOT signs around there, so I forbore. This was yet another of a growing list of places where I could no longer be me. Dennis, seated relaxed and watchful on the sofa, seemed to be doing okay. Looked pretty good for a guy coming off a binge. Must have been the good Detroit air.

Or—I could hardly bring myself to think it—the love of a good woman.

I scanned several pad pages, from my talks with Wendy Dilworth and Elvin Dance. Elvin's people had combed through Cloyd's coworkers and pronounced them beyond suspicion. That was a judgment call, of course. I'd have to make my own, if this went that far, which I doubted. "About the open house," I began.

"Surely," Brooks replied expectantly.

"Took place in the suite here, right?"

"Yes."

"Lot of people show up?"

"Mm. We had clients and suppliers and media people and so forth coming and going all evening. There could have been fifty or sixty here at any given time."

"And Cloyd was here too."

"Chris was working down in his office," she corrected. "The open house was centered here in the conference room and the rooms at this end."

"He ever join the party?"

She sighed. "Haven't you heard a word I said? Does Chris sound like the party type?"

"Well, he was here, right?"

"He was working," she said patiently. "He wasn't about to let something like an open house affect his schedule."

"'Kay. Did you see him at all, that night?"

"I took some dinner in to him."

"What time was that?"

"I have no idea. I want to say, eight-thirty or nine."

"What'd you bring him?"

"Some stuff from the deli spread here. He just picked at it. Ate the meat, if that helps."

Strict vegetarian, Dilworth had called him. Hm. "It does help, thank you, ma'am," I answered, matching her sincerity. "He was here after the party then?"

"He was still here when we locked up."

"And that's pretty usual, I gather."

"Mm. He had keys, he had an elevator card, he had the combinations to the corridor door locks, he had security clearance downstairs."

"Takes all that to get in, huh?"

"For someone to get in and get at Chris that night," she said, "he'd have to have security clearance at the desk downstairs. He'd have to have an electronic card to activate the elevator. He'd have to have the combinations to the locks on the corridor door outside, and then he'd have to have keys to the suite."

I was scribbling. "Gotcha." I looked at her. "Who else at the agency has those things? You?"

"Yes." Her large eyes widened further. "Does that make me a suspect?"

"'Fraid so."

"Ooh, how shivery," she said.

CHAPTER

EIGHT

Roulette Brooks glanced over at Dennis and then looked at me, half smiling. "May I say something in my own defense, before you drag me away in chains or start beating me with hoses or whatever it is you shamuses do?"

Shamus. Oh, brother. "Go ahead," I told her.

She held up a long soft white hand and ticked each sharp red fingernail as she talked. "If I came back here to kill him, the security guard would have recorded my visit. He didn't. If I'd stayed behind and killed him and then left, the security guard would have recorded my departure. He didn't. And," she went on, overriding me, "if I killed Chris and then hid in the office until morning so as not to be seen leaving, my sitter would not be able to testify that I showed up at her house to pick up my children at a little after midnight." She smiled earnestly. "Feel free to check."

She was enjoying this, I could tell. Some people were like that, innocent as well as guilty. "All right. Who else has after-hours access?"

She clouded. "Well, Larry does, of course. At least in theory. Not that he ever comes in after business hours. And even if he wanted to, I'm sure he lost his elevator card years ago and could never remember the lock combinations either."

I looked at her. "Now, don't get the idea I'm doubting you, Ms. Brooks—"

"Call me Roulette."

"Okay, thanks. But look here, Roulette. If Larry Martin is as dumb as you say, how'd he get to be president of all this here?"

"Born salesman," Dennis put in.

"Surely," Roulette Brooks said, with a smile for him.

"All right." I made a note. "Who else had elevator passes and clearances and combinations and so forth?"

"The senior secretary, Linda Poniatowski. But she flipped her car and hasn't been to work in two months. Joe Morgan, vp–creative director. But he was on a shoot in Arizona. That's it."

"That's it? Nobody else has the keys?"

She shrugged. "Chris usually unlocked the place in the morning, around eight-thirty. I usually lock up at night. The building is very strict about controlling who has keys and so forth."

I leaned back and shifted my legs a little. The sofa was nowhere near as comfortable as it looked, and this dragged-out back-and-forth was stiffening me up. I hated just sitting. Give me action. "What about former employees? Any of them have keys or cards or whatever?"

Her eyes mirrored. "Now, that's a really good question. Even the police didn't ask that question, Mr. Perkins. Congratulations."

"Ah, it's nothing."

"And so's the answer," she said agreeably. "The combinations are changed every two months. And the elevator cards are remagnetized then too. They have new code doodads fed into them."

Of course I'd have to confirm all that. If I cared to. Frankly, my judgment was that Roulette Brooks was being just as honest and helpful as she could be. The inconsistencies with Dilworth's statements did not trouble me. Dilworth, it was obvious, had more than her share of Ann Arbor illusions about her husband, herself, and the world. Brooks was out of a tougher school. I liked her. She seemed smart and stubborn and streetwise and skeptical, a survivor, a striver who hadn't soured on the world yet. Of course, at twenty-five or whatever, it was still easy to believe that everything was going to work out all right. I also had the feeling, just an instinct, that she had cared very deeply for Chris Cloyd. I'd been wondering how far she had taken that.

"Did you ever see Cloyd outside business hours?" I asked.

She chuckled. "Listen, Mr. Perkins. I helped Chris. I liked Chris. I was fascinated by Chris. I'd have done anything for Chris. And I *did* do a lot for Chris, including some things that weren't in my job description. But I never screwed Chris."

"Were you attracted to him?"

She considered that. "It could have been interesting. But my taste runs more toward big and dumb in all the right places. And young. I like them younger than me." Her dark eyes glittered. "You, Mr. Perkins, for example. Once—"

"Yes," I cut in easily, "once, a passel of presidents ago, maybe." And not just maybe, I reflected.

"It could have been interesting," she repeated. "Sex with a man as deep and brainy and complicated and imaginative as Chris . . . interesting. On the other hand, it might have gotten complicated. Perhaps even messy."

"Never took him around the block for a spin though, huh?"

"No, Mr. Perkins," she said easily. "Never even came close. Frankly, I don't think Chris was interested in sex."

"Really? You don't think so?"

"Just a suspicion."

"But he was married," I noted.

"Your point?" she asked.

Dennis laughed and nodded. I let it go. "Well, then," I asked, "who would want to kill him?"

"I have no idea," she answered. "Nobody here. That I'm sure of. You wouldn't believe how upset everyone has been. I mean, this agency went into a state of shock and it hasn't come out yet." She leaned forward. "Here's how bad it is. Chris has been gone all these weeks, but no one took over his office. That's amazing. He had one of the best ones, third down from the corner, great view, and, best of all, about as far away from Larry as you can get. Normally, somebody would've grabbed it, there'd have been war over it, it would have been like Lebanon around here. But so far, nothing. I think people are afraid even to go in there."

"Can we have a look?" I asked.

"Surely."

We left the conference room. Brooks led us through several narrow, winding halls, past brightly decorated offices and brilliantly lit carrels, from which issued sounds of arguments and rock-and-roll, and computer printers spewing type with ripping metallic sounds, and faxes humming and beeping. As we walked I said casually, "So, you found a new job yet?"

She laughed. "Whatever for?"

"Well," I said, "the way you were talking to Martin, I figured you want him to fire you."

"Oh, not at all," she retorted. "I need this job."

"I don't get it," Dennis observed.

We turned a corner into a quieter hallway. Roulette had produced a key from somewhere. "You just don't understand the agency business," she told us as we walked.

"Well, clue us in," I suggested.

"This business has no product, as such. It's all intangible," she explained. "Everything here is illusion, and impression, and perception. Fine so far?"

"Gotcha."

"I have no skills," she said. "I can barely type. I hardly know anything about computers. I'm too moody to manage people, and my voice sounds awful on the phone. I got hired because of a friend of a friend, and I survived here because I was important to Chris and Chris was vital to the agency. Now that he's gone, there's really no reason for Larry to keep me on."

She unlocked the wood windowless door and pushed it open. We followed her inside. "But as I said, I need this job desperately. I'm too lazy to go find a new one. How can I keep Larry from firing me? Remember," she said, eyeing each of us, "everything here is impression and perception. The best way to keep him from firing me is to give him the impression that I'm utterly confident he wouldn't dare. So, as you saw, I stay in his face."

The oblong office had a high ceiling, three large windows along the far wall, and blue carpet. The desk was bare except for a phone and a computer; the shelves hanging on the wall behind the desk were empty also. The place looked like someone was half moved out or half moved in. "So you bought yourself a stay of execution, huh?" I said.

"Mm." She put a finger under her chin. "Right now

Larry's wondering: Why does she talk to me that way? Does she know something I don't? Does she have an account in her pocket?" She chuckled. "He's so supremely arrogant in his ability to handle us, it doesn't occur to him how easily we all handle him."

"Risky strategy," Dennis commented.

She shrugged. "This is the ad business. Everything is risky."

Considering Cloyd had been a writer person who played with papers all the time, his office was surprisingly uncluttered. And, considering how successful Cloyd was, the furnishings—gray steel desk, older secretarial chair covered in threadbare brown fabric, credenza, mismatched file cabinets, single brown leather visitor chair—were quite plain and very worn, obviously old hand-me-downs. Roulette was reading my mind.

"Chris could have had brand-new furniture any time he wanted," she commented. "But this was the stuff he inherited when he came here, and he insisted on keeping it. Superstitious. Like most people in this business."

"Even the computer's ancient," Dennis observed, wandering over to it.

I mean, *I* couldn't tell. The computer, which sat on an ell off the desk, consisted of three pieces in two shades of ivory, connected with cables: a screen, a steel box underneath it with slots, and a keyboard. All three pieces said IBM. As Roulette watched, I walked around behind the desk, peered under the chair, examining the carpet and so forth. Mr. Detective, sniffing for clues.

Nothing, nothing—nothing on the floor but dust kittens, a paper clip, a scattering of three-hole punch dits, and an unattached phone cord. Cloyd had been found lying dead there, but I saw no sign of it: no blood, no nothing. Frankly, I didn't know why I'd even bothered to check out the office. It was highly unlikely I'd find anything the cops had missed; this was not, after all, *Murder, She Wrote.*

"Seems awful empty in here," I observed. "Didn't he have books and files and things?"

"Wendy Dilworth asked us to ship all that to her house," Roulette said. "Anything else I can do for you?"

I kept coming back to the computer, like a mosquito drawn to fire. "What about that?"

"What about it?"

"Cops check it out?"

"Well," she answered, "one of them turned it on and did something. I don't know. Those things are totally lost on me."

Dennis was across the room, staring out the window, oblivious to us. "Hey," I said. He looked at me. "Wanna make yourself useful as well as decorative? Fire up that idiot box, see what he's got on there for me."

His brow wrinkled. "Ben. Come on. You can't just—"

"You know computers, don'tcha?"

"Well, a little," he allowed, "but it would take real time to check everything out."

My beeper went off then, a silent insistent vibrating in my trouser pocket. "I think we better," I said, "especially since the cops don't seem to've." The read-out said Carole's number, at her law office in Berkley. "Can I use the phone?" I asked.

"Sure," Brooks said. "Help yourself. Oh"—she caught herself—"dial nine to get out, then one-zero-zero-six-zero, then your number." She smiled. "We have equipment that tracks who makes what calls to where," she said. "Larry doesn't have money for decent wages but plenty to spy on his own employees."

I dialed her numbers, then Carole's, and sat on the edge of the desk as the line rang. Roulette guided Dennis to the far window, and they spoke quietly as they waited for me.

"So what's up?" Carole asked briskly when she came on.

"In what sense?" I asked. "Dilworth?"

"Yes. Have you seen her?"

"Yep, Saturday. Cops, too. As we speak, I'm at the ad agency where her husband died."

"And?"

"Nothing."

"Oh, really."

"No."

Which wasn't exactly, precisely true. There was that oddball tow bill in Cloyd's papers. But that, I thought, could have been any of a million things.

"Are you sure?" she asked. "You're not just . . . rushing through, because of how—"

"Carole, please."

"Beg pardon?"

I kept it light. "I've been reasonable about this, right? So ease up a little, darlin'."

"Yes, of course," she conceded. "You'll square-end it with the client?"

Dennis came over to the computer and seemed to be inspecting it. Roulette watched him, arms folded. "Yeah, I'll run out there later," I told Carole. "How's the rookie?"

"Oh," she said, warming up, "last night she got into the pantry and dragged out every single bottle and can and—um, arranged them all over the kitchen floor."

"Hoo boy. Some mess, huh?"

"Buck helped put it all away," she told me.

"Nice of him to stop by," I said. "Things a little slow in the unexploded ordnance business these days?"

"He's headed back to Sarajevo in August," she answered. "Anyway, he couldn't get over Rachel walking herself around furniture the way she's doing."

Dennis led Roulette to the open door, and they talked some more. "When rookie walks for real the first time," I said to Carole, "it'd better be with me there and not your friend Buck."

"Well, I hope so too." She paused. "So does Buck. He really likes you, you know."

"Seems to like you too."

"He does," she agreed, with satisfaction. "A lot."

"Buck," I repeated. "I just can't get over your getting involved with a guy who sounds like a comic book character."

"Why not?" she asked warmly. "I was involved with you for all those years, wasn't I?"

Roulette had left. As I hung up, Dennis clapped his hands together and bounced a little on the balls of his feet, a big smile on his face—the first real smile I'd seen him make. No, the second. The first was when he saw Barb come into Under New Management the day before. "Guess what."

"I'm afraid to. But what?"

"She's giving it to you."

"Whuh?"

"The computer. She's giving it to you. Or rather"— he tumbled on—"selling it to you for a buck. She went to cut a bill of sale."

"Jesus," I said, standing. "I don't *want* the damn thing, I just want to know what's on it."

"So, we take it to your place, and I take the time to check it out for you. Once that's done, then maybe . . ."

"What, Dennis?"

His eyes glinted behind the glasses. "Maybe you could let me have it."

"I guess. But what do you want it for?"

His voice was more like I remembered, too: the deep-toned, rapid-fire syllables. "Hey, if I open an office here, I'm going to need equipment."

"Here? You're setting up shop in Detroit?"

"I'm thinking about it. I—"

He cut short as Roulette strode back in. "Here you go," she said, handing me a paper. Sure enough, it was a bill of sale for an IBM something or the other, serial numbers blah blah blah, one dollar cash in hand. She was smiling. "Enjoy, Mr. Perkins."

I shuffled over to the desk, glanced over the machine. "I don't get it," I confessed. "You don't have to *give* it to me."

"You're doing me a favor by taking it," she said. "No one in this office will touch it. They're superstitious, like I said. Same thing with the furniture. I'm going to have to sell it all or give it away. It's yours. Take it."

"Well," I said doubtfully, "thanks, I guess."

"Thank you, Roulette," Dennis chimed in.

"You're both welcome," she answered. "Nice doing business with you." A T-shirted teenager in a backward baseball cap slouched through the open door, dragging a red dolly. "Mark will carry it down to your car," she said, turning to me. "Washington Street side."

"Okay. Listen, Roulette, appreciate your help here."

"My pleasure," she said, with a quick smile. "Killed some Monday time for me."

"One other thing?"

"Yes?"

"Can I have an employee list? I may need to talk to a few more people."

"I'll get you one on the way out."

* * *

It was way past lunchtime by now, and I had a lot of work to do that day yet, and I was hungry enough to eat a bug. So I took us through a Burger Barn drive-through on Michigan Avenue in east Dearborn, and since it was a gorgeous day we ate in the parking lot behind the place, sitting in the open-doored, top-down Mustang, awash in the soft sounds of the new Buddy Guy tape. Dennis was, if anything, hungrier than me; he gobbled his half-pound bacon and cheese and large curly fry and even finished my fries for me as I lighted a cigar.

"So," I said, after a slurp of my Coke, "what's this about setting up shop?"

"Oh, I don't know," he said, wadding up his trash. "I've been thinking, you know, this is a pretty nice area here."

Somehow, I suspected it was not the physical charms of metropolitan Detroit that had him bedazzled. "We like it," I said.

"You look at California, man," he said. "Goddamn disaster. No jobs, no money, no water, no future. Plenty of taxes, though."

"And," I pointed out, "you've got the climate."

"Can't drink climate."

"That's true," I noted. "You've got the weather, but we've got the water."

He glanced at me. "There's talk of someday diverting Great Lakes water out there, to help us reclaim more desert land."

"Can't have any," I told him. "Not so much as a tin cup full. Sorry."

"Okay. I'll pass the word, if I ever go back."

I tapped ash into the loaded ashtray. The Buddy Guy tape flipped over. "You're really thinking of staying here, huh?"

He pulled a gulp of Coke through his straw. "Yes."

"What kinda work?"

"Marketing consulting, I guess. It's what I know. I've got a reputation. And I've got contacts. All over the country. I can really do it from anywhere."

"Big move."

"Tell me about it." He leaned back in the Mustang seat, the sunlight glinting off his glasses. "What I need," he told me, "is a brand-new start."

"No such thing."

"Sure there is. People do it all the time."

"No way. Not really. You're still stuck with being you. We all are."

"I can change me, though," he said quietly. "With help."

"I reckon."

A City of Dearborn DPW truck chugged past us in low gear, diesel roaring. I could feel Dennis looking at me. "I won't hurt her, you know."

"For chrissake," I said mildly, "you just met her two days ago. Let up on the pedal a little."

"You don't understand," he said rapidly. "It's like I've been hit by a thunderbolt."

"You're on one huge-ass, transcontinental, midlife-crisis rebound, is what you're on."

"It's more than that," he said.

I leaned toward him, bearing down. "And I don't know how long it's been since you had sex with your wife. Or with someone *other* than your wife. But it could just be that doin' the big bounce with someone new has got you—"

"That's a shit thing to say," he remarked, glaring at me. He didn't back down an inch. With abrupt angry gestures he took the trash, got out of the Mustang, walked over to the trash barrel by the building, and came back. I fired up the Mustang as he got back in, jammed her into gear, and wheeled us over to Michigan Avenue.

Now, with the top down and the warm June air rushing past us over the rumble-roar of the Mustang engine, it was a little harder to talk. Just as well. I felt caught between the devil and the deep blue sea. My good-faith effort to lend Dennis a hand was turning into something bigger, and I could not predict the outcome. Wouldn't have mattered, much, except now Barb was being pulled into the whirlpool.

Dennis didn't say anything until we drew up to the light at Evergreen, kitty-corner from old Henry Ford's estate. "Listen, Ben," he said, staring through the windshield, "I respect the fact that you two are friends. I'd like to think that you and I are friends, too. I've helped you a couple of times, haven't I? And you've helped me out here, big-time. And I appreciate it, man."

"Well," I answered, "maybe I shouldn't be so edgy."

He straightened and stared up the street. "Would you mind stopping at the Egghead store there for a minute?"

"Sure," I said. I wheeled north on Military and found a parking spot. "I'll just wait here."

"Thanks." He got out, shut the door, looked at me. "I was impressed with you, back there at the agency," he said. "Nice mix of smart and dumb. You handled her well."

"Thanks," I answered, "but to be fair, this one's a no-brainer."

He hesitated. "If you want me to move out," he said, "just tell me."

"Okay."

"Do you want me to?"

Yes. "No."

NINE

I really needed to get over to the Norwegian Wood maintenance office to check on my boys. First, though, I helped Dennis carry the computer into the apartment, where we set it up on the card table in the guest bedroom. Once upon a time, this was the room Will slept in when Carole used to stay over. Since those days, it had gradually collected junk and clutter, the way unused rooms tended to. Dennis had stacked the half dozen boxes along the wall next to the door and put my spare tools in the closet. Someone—could have been Barb—had given the place a thorough vacuuming. It was looking good, in the light that notched through the half closed blinds over the bed. It also looked foreign, a piece of my house being taken over by a virtual stranger—and now the computer.

Dennis was like a kid on Christmas Eve, connecting the cables from the screen to the box to the keyboard, plugging the machine into the wall, ripping shrink-wrap off some software disk boxes he'd bought at the Egghead store. "Can't wait to see what's on this thing," he said.

"Me neither," I said, giving the machine a suspicious look. "I'm gonna head over to work for a couple of hours."

"Fine," he said, distracted, as he dragged a stool up to the dark brown card table. "See you in a while."

I went to the door and looked back. "You didn't by any chance pick up *Battlestar: Galactica* at that store, did you?"

"Not this time," he said, grinning. "I'll get it later for you, if you want. Gotta clean off the hard drive, reformat it and everything."

"Oh," I said. "Just breeze through the data thingies first, willya? Give it the old smell test. Anything jumps out at you suspicious-like, give me a shout, *capiche?*"

"No problem, chief," he said briskly, the rapid-fire intent businessman I remembered.

I went out to the living room. The red message light was blinking on the answering machine. I hit the button. It rewound, played a couple of hang-ups, and then a woman's voice said, "Hi there." I could hear the smile in Raeanne's voice, and I felt myself smiling back. "Been thinking about you, too." Then she hung up.

Next to it, a lip of white stuck out of the fax machine. I ripped off the paper and found it was from Elvin Dance at Detroit police headquarters. It was the description of the man the David Whitney guard had seen leaving the building the morning Chris Cloyd was found dead. The description was—what's the word?—pithy. A medium-built male, it said. Caucasian. Short black hair. Narrow face. Casual clothes.

Real helpful.

But that reminded me of the employee list Roulette Brooks had given me. I went to the dinette table with the wallet of Chris Cloyd paperwork, retrieved the tow bill, and compared the address in Wyandotte from which Cloyd's car had been towed with the addresses on the ad agency employee list.

No, no, no, no . . . yes. A match. Close, anyhow. Maybe.

It was in Wyandotte, an address on 19th Street. Cloyd's car, according to the tow bill, had been towed from Walnut. Downriver was not one of my stronger areas, geography-wise. I dug through the junk drawer under the counter and found my old dog-eared Detroit area street guide. Did some crisscrossing with streets and numbers and—

Just then I heard knocking at the door. I went and opened it, and a smiling Barb Paley swarmed me with a big hug and a kiss on the cheek. "How are you?" she asked, and rushed on. "Is Dennis still here?"

"I'm good," I said, smiling back, "and he is. Hey, come on in, I got an interesting bit here."

She followed me into the kitchen. She wore new duds today, an orange tank top and gray, loose-fitting shorts. Obviously, she had the day off work. Her red hair was pushed back under an orange headband, and she wore just the slightest bit of makeup on her round cheery face. "Where is he?"

"Back in the bedroom. Fully clothed," I added.

"Well," she said playfully, "I'll just have to do something about that."

"He's got him a new play toy," I added.

"I know," she said, with a private smile.

"You've been replaced," I informed her, "by a computer."

"Ha," she said, with a rich laugh. "We'll just see about that. So what are you up to, hon? Dennis told me you've got a case?"

"Ah, not really." I sketched out the facts for her, told her a little about Chris Cloyd, then showed her the tow bill, as well as the ad agency employee list with one name prominently circled. "You've got good instincts," I said. "What's your take on this here?"

She straightened. "He was screwing her," she said, offhand. "Next question."

"That's what I think too."

"I mean," she added, "it's just too big a coincidence. Of all the jillions of side streets in metro Detroit, he picks that one to break down on? A block from her house? Come on."

"Yep." I closed the directory. "Question is, what do I do with it?"

"Maybe," Barb said slyly, "you should go ask her some very pointed questions."

"Holy shit," came Dennis's deep voice from the back.

Barb and I exchanged looks. "Let's go see," I said, in my mind's eye picturing the computer ablaze. We headed back there. "Yeah, I could press on and bang around a little," I said as we walked, "but I think I'll just let it go."

"Really?"

"Yeah. So he was screwing her. Big deal. By itself it doesn't mean anything." Except, I reflected, that Chris Cloyd apparently had not been as uninterested in sex as Roulette Brooks had suggested. "The man's dead, all evidence says accident; why dirty him up?"

In the spare bedroom, Dennis stood over the computer, which looked all right to me. Not on fire, anyhow. It was running—I could see white words on the black screen—and Dennis had removed the cover from the big box that held the guts of the machine. The inside looked surprisingly empty. All kinds of room in there, just some circuit boards and components, all merrily humming, and—most disconcerting to an old Ford Motor man—none of it moving.

"Hi, lover," Barb said, and went to him, and they kissed hard.

"Hi," he said, smiling. He had his hand on her shorts and gave her rump a hard squeeze. I had to admit they looked good together, the blond and the redhead. They had that edgy urgency of newly minted lovers that made me think the polite thing to do would be to excuse myself for a couple of hours, or weeks. But Dennis seemed able to operate on more than one level. "You won't believe this machine here," he told us, letting Barb go.

"What about it?" I asked, keeping my distance.

"It's a monster," he said, eyes gleaming behind his glasses. His tone reminded me of the way we used to talk about our cars. "I thought it was an old moldy XT, ten-year-old box. Well, the case is XT, but the insides . . . I think it's got a Pentium processor. Latest thing. Makes Madonna look slow." He was pointing excitedly at things inside the box. "About a four-hundred-meg hard drive. Sixteen K of memory on the motherboard."

"The mother what?" I asked.

"Board," he repeated, not getting it. "He's got an Intel modem here, the fourteen four job. Plus this is a super VGA monitor, and—"

"Greek, gibberish, garbage," Barb said, smiling. "I can type on them; that's about it. Good to see you excited, lover."

"You ain't seen nothin' yet," he said, and winked, and they kissed, just a light one, but full of anticipation and promise.

I had to get to the office, *had* to. "What about—uh, information?" I asked. "In the memory or whatever? Is there anything I should know about?"

"I don't know yet," he answered. "I haven't even

looked to see what's on there, datawise. He does have an old WordPerfect and Lotus and some kind of moldy DOS, three point three, I think."

"Is that supposed to mean something?" I asked.

"No," Barb assured me, and gave Dennis's neck a caress. "Come on, lover, we've got to get going."

"Oh, yeah," he answered, and shut off the machine.

"Where?" I asked.

"Going out for a while," she answered, avoiding my eyes. Dennis looked subdued now. I knew then where they were headed, and I guess I was surprised. By God, I thought, she's got her hooks in him, but good.

Two hours later I came back from the Norwegian Wood office. The chore list had been heavy that day, as it usually was on Mondays, but the guys had taken care of everything. I initialed the paperwork, made the rounds, chatted with a few of the tenants, and got back to my apartment just as the home-from-work traffic was pouring into the parking lot, weary cash-strapped Norwegian Wood tenants relieved to have whipped another tough Monday.

Barb was alone in the silent living room, stretched out on the recliner, when I went in. "Oh, Ben," she murmured, and stood up. "It was such an experience."

"You took him to AA," I said. She nodded and came to me and hugged me, just a brief light touching all over. "Where is he?" I asked.

She let go. "Back in his room." She went to the sofa and sat and, leaning forward, shook a cigarette out of the pack on the coffee table. "He took his first step," she said, lighting her cigarette with a little butane lighter, and exhaled a quick expert funnel of smoke. "He admitted he's an alcoholic. And he listened, and he shared, and he opened up." Her eyes were glassy as she looked right through me. "Afterward out in the car he started crying. I just held him. I felt so—"

"That's good, sweetheart," I said uncomfortably.

"Nothing like this has ever happened to me before," she said, smiling uncertainly.

I couldn't think of anything to say. I was, after all, just plain old uncomplicated Ben. A straight-from-the-shoulder, nuts-and-bolts, ways-and-means man. This world they were in, living inside their heads, it was all foreign to me. I resisted the impulse to caution her, to rain on her parade. She can take care of herself, I thought resolutely. And if she can't, she has to learn how, sometime.

"That you, Ben?" boomed Dennis's voice from the kitchen. He bounded into the living room. "Glad you're back. We have to talk."

He wore blue shorts now, and a white Belleville Yacht Club T-shirt, obviously swiped from my drawer. For a man who, just a while earlier, had been crying in Barb's arms, he seemed upbeat and cheery. For a man who had just ended a long drunken binge—or maybe just interrupted it, a bitchy little part of me pointed out—he looked pretty damn sharp and energetic. With each hour that passed, he seemed more and more like the old Dennis. It was as if some coilspring inside him were slowly rewinding, giving him strength. Was it the power of love? I thought. Or the tables at AA? Or just native resilience?

There was more going on with him than I'd thought. A lot more. I sensed it, but I wasn't sure Barb did.

She was smiling at him. "What have you been up to, honey?"

"Booted the machine up," he answered. "Been

checking out the hard drive. You know what?" he told me. "I think somebody did some serious tampering with that machine just recently. Come on back, I'll show you."

He scooted out. Barb rose and we walked back. Dennis had closed the computer up again. He sat on the stool, hunched over the keyboard. The screen was all multicolored now, white background, blue and red and green boxes filled with white lettering. Lists, it looked like.

"What kind of tampering?" I asked him, imagining a masked man with a screwdriver, tinkering inside the computer case.

"Somebody wiped out a bunch of stuff," he answered, tapping keys. "Or at least tried to."

"What kind of stuff?"

"Data," he said patiently. "Information."

Hm. "Tell me," I said.

"The last time the computer was used," he told me, "was May eighth. At least that's the last time anybody wrote a file to the disk."

I had my tattered spiral pad out and consulted it to make sure. "That's the day Cloyd died."

Barb, sitting on the bed, smoked her cigarette and watched us. Dennis was pointing at the screen. "And on that date, a whole raft of files and directories were wiped out."

"Destroyed?" I asked.

"Not exactly." He looked at me. "You can delete files off the computer, Ben. But they're not really gone. They're still on the disk and they stay there until something is recorded on the disk over them."

"But if they were deleted"—I fumbled—"how do you know?"

"I've got a program that recovers them."

"I didn't realize you were such an ace at this."

He shrugged. "It's pretty routine stuff."

Not in my building. "Okay, so what about these deleted files?"

Dennis pointed at the screen again. "Here they are. They were all deleted on May eighth. Of course, it doesn't have to mean anything. Cloyd might have deleted them because he didn't need them anymore."

"What's in them?" Barb asked.

"That's the problem," Dennis confessed. "I can't open them. They were saved in compressed form and protected with passwords."

"Oh, God," I said. "These things use passwords?"

"All the time." He turned on the stool and faced us. "Any ideas what Cloyd's password might be, Ben? I've tried some obvious things, like his name and initials."

"How about his phone number?"

"Eight digits max. Give it to me."

He turned to the keyboard. I found the phone number in my pad. Dennis typed the first eight digits. ACCESS DENIED, the computer screen printed. Tried the last eight. Ditto.

"Try his work phone," Barb suggested. I read that to Dennis, who entered pieces of it. ACCESS DENIED, over and over.

Brainstorm. "I know!" I said. "His briefcase combination."

Wrong.

You get the idea. We wasted probably twenty minutes on that little exercise. We tried Cloyd's address, and his birth date, plus the name and birth date of his wife. We tried all kinds of harebrained things. ACCESS DENIED, the computer kept saying. Nothing. The computer stubbornly refused to cough up. Well, to call it "stubborn" was to credit it with emotion it did not have. That computer was about as emotional as a clerk in the Secretary of State's office.

I was getting hungry. The afternoon was about out, and I still had to shoot over to Ann Arbor to, as Carole put it, "square-end" Wendy Dilworth—if, as planned, I meant to shut down this so-called case. But now I was wondering. Those deleted files were bugging me. If they were important enough to protect with a password, why did Cloyd wipe them out? And did it mean anything that he happened to do that on the day he died?

"Is there any other information on the computer we can look at?" I asked.

"Oh, yeah," Dennis said. "He's got data files up the kazoo. Text files, spreadsheets, the works." He flickered some keys. The screen went white, then black, and then up popped a screenful of words. The headline said TOWELETTES . . . FOR THOSE ON-THE-GO MOMENTS. Some kind of advertising bizz-bazz, which figured. Dennis showed me a few other screenfuls. Same trash.

"Okay," I said, and rubbed my eyes.

"Nothing suspicious," Barb concluded.

"Cops must've at least looked at the data, anyways," I added. "So forget it. Gotta roll, kids, see you in a while."

"What about the password-protected stuff?" Dennis asked. "Should I blow 'em away?"

"Any chance of breaking the password?"

"No chance in hell," he answered.

"Blow 'em away then." I left the room and hoofed up the hallway toward the front of the apartment, thinking about seeing Wendy Dilworth once more. The thought of the woman, and the house, and the garage . . . "Hold it!" I shouted, and bolted back to the bedroom.

Dennis was poised over the keyboard, Barb crouched beside him watching the screen. "What is it?" Dennis asked.

"Don't touch those files yet. Hang tight." I went out to the kitchen and dug Cloyd's tow bill out of the cardboard wallet. Scanned it once, then again. *Shit*, not there. I grabbed the phone, consulted my pad for Dilworth's number, and dialed. She answered on the first ring, sounding a little out of breath; probably just completed a fifty-mile walk or something. "That car of your husband's," I said to her after exchanging greetings.

"Yes? What about it?" she asked.

"What's the tag number?"

"I have no idea. Is it important?"

Barb was watching me from the kitchen door. "Can you give it to me, please?" I asked Dilworth.

"Just a moment." Pause. Barb gave me raised eyebrows. I shrugged back. Dilworth returned. "Nine-five seven-D-W-X," she said.

"Thanks, I'll get back to you." I hung up. "Got another password candidate," I told Barb, and we returned to the bedroom.

"Does the password have to be eight digits?" I asked Dennis. He shook his head. "Try this," I suggested, and recited the license number.

Dennis typed it in his rapid hunt-and-hit, then pressed enter. ACCESS DENIED. "Doesn't work," he said.

"Shit," I answered.

Dennis was typing some more. "But backward it does," he added calmly.

TEN

"Wow," Barb said, as the screen filled with rapid-fire commands. A *clittery-click*ing sound was coming from the computer, like a thousand mice dancing. Uncrunching, the screen told us. Decompressing, it advised. Along with pithy little character strings spurting onto the screen in rapid sequence, each ending with the letters CHF.

"What are those?" I asked.

"File names," Dennis answered. "Like I told you, this stuff was all saved in compressed form. He took a shitload of files and compressed them under one file name. That's to save room on his disk. Then he protected it with his password. To keep people from prying."

"But you said it was deleted, though."

"It was," he said patiently. "I brought it back with an undelete program. Now that we have the password, we're breaking the big compressed file into individual files." He leaned closer to the screen. "Looks to me like most of those are graphics images."

"Whazzat?" I asked.

"Pictures. That's what those CHF suffixes mean."

"Pictures of what?" Barb asked.

"I don't know," Dennis said. "He was in advertising. Could be clip art or something like that."

"Well, let's have a look," I suggested.

He sighed. The screen went still. "Can't," he said. "You need a graphics viewer. A program," he added hastily. "There's not one on here. Have to pick one up tomorrow."

Barb had already lost her enthusiasm and now seemed bored and fidgety. "Do you think it's important, Ben?" she asked.

"I don't know what's important or not." I lighted a cigar, a smart thing to do on an empty stomach. "Believe me, people, I want to be done with this, just dump it off and forget it. But something's bugging me."

"What's that, Ben?" Dennis asked, turning on the stool toward me.

"Check me out on this," I said, sitting on the edge of what had been Dennis's bed until he and Barb took over mine. "We've got this computer here, right? It's got a bunch of files on the disk, all innocent-looking stuff. But then you found that someone wiped out some other files, on the day Cloyd died. Question: Who wiped them out? Is there a way to tell, Dennis?"

"No," he said readily. "Cloyd himself, I imagine."

"Or," I countered, "maybe his killer."

"But why?" Barb asked.

"I don't know," I said. "But hey, as much as I'd like to just shrug this off, before I can do that I have to see what's in those files. That's something the cops never got into, right, Dennis?"

"Couldn't have," he agreed. "If they had, the files would have been decompressed already."

"Okay. So, tomorrow we can look at those picture files?" I said, standing.

"Tomorrow," echoed Dennis.

They left right after that. Barb told me she wanted to show Dennis her house over in Taylor, and I got the definite impression they would not be coming back that night. Fine with me. I changed the sheets on my bed, showered, threw on slacks and a T-shirt, then left to grab some grub over at Under New Management. I planned to have a good old-fashioned Ben Perkins night out: shoot the shit with my friends, guzzle a couple of cold ones, smoke cigars, kick back a bit. Before I left, I peeked into the spare room at the computer. It sat there, boxy, dark, and silent, quite dead. And yet, when you applied electricity and skill, it became a living thing that possessed secrets, not all of them good.

I was not sure I wanted the thing in my house.

Under New Management was raucous that night, better than half full and jumping with juke sounds and hard heavy laughing from a table full of UAW Local 735 softball players. I took a stool at the bar and, while waiting to be served, caught a snatch of *Entertainment Tonight* from the TV set mounted up high. Leeza Gibbons, giving "the lowdown," read a small item about "one-time blues great Zanna Canady," who had, Gibbons stated, "scandalized Michigan voters" with her relationship with longtime Republican senator Paul Proposto. But now, Gibbons said, Canady had vanished from the campaign. Proposto's campaign, comfortably ahead in the polls, had had no comment as to why she left or where she went.

Just then Eddie Cabla, who was working the stick that night, descended on me. "Didja call your judge friend for me?" he asked urgently, leaning close.

"Christ, Ed, that was just yesterday you asked me."

"I gotta know, Ben."

"Wednesday night's poker night," I told him. "I'll ask the judge then. Pull me a cold one, okay?"

"Oh, Christ," he moaned, running a hand over his bald bullet head. "They're gonna bring steam shovels and dig up my goddamn driveway if I can't find a way to stop them."

"So let 'em, Ed. What's the big deal?" I asked.

"I like my driveway."

"Your driveway's all gravel and axle-breakin' chuck-holes. They can't help but leave it better than they find it."

"It's just the goddamn principle," he growled, leaning on the bar half facing away.

"You could use this to publicize the bar," I suggested. "When the DNR comes out, call the papers, get 'em to come out and write it up. We'll have a tailgate party, brewskis and beer nuts, and have a good laugh while the DNR people make asses of themselves, when they dig up the driveway and find no fuel tanks down there."

"Goddamn," he muttered.

"Can you bring me my beer now?"

"Whole goddamn country's going communistic," he grumbled.

"My beer, Ed?"

"Why dint you ask? I'm not a frigging mind reader."

Tuesday was wall-to-wall work. Not that I actually lifted a tool or anything; my luck wasn't that good. Instead, Tuesday started with a meeting with Mr. Horner, the bespectacled balding bean-counter type who passed as my boss whenever he was in town, which was, thank God, not often. He was some sort of honcho with Fantastico, the faceless holding company that owned, or so I was told, a ton of properties around the Great Lakes.

As usual, he met with me and Marge, who handled rentals and tenant relations. After delivering his litany of numbers—all "disappointing," of course—he rendered rulings on the latest raft of requests. On raises for my boys: no. A new answering machine for Marge: no. Flue dampers for the building furnaces: no. And, of course, on my request for a switch to an apartment facing the goddamn lake: just take a guess.

Mr. Horner did have other business. The Company (as he put it) approved funding to repave the east parking area—not a burst of generosity, since the city of Belleville had threatened to lift our C of O if we didn't. And, he informed us, plans were under way for the long-awaited—like, since about the Carter administration—Phase Two of Norwegian Wood, consisting of a half dozen more units on the parcel south of us beside the golf course. If that went through, I'd have to hire more people; I'd have a lot more to do, and I'd lose my shed on the back forty where I'd always kept my ultralight airplane.

Swell.

Mixed in with the chores that ate up the rest of the day, I did some other things. Called Carole to tell her I was still on the Dilworth deal, at least for the moment. Called Raeanne's house again, too, and got her answering machine. At the infamous beep I said, "We've got to stop meeting like this." Then I tracked down Dick Dennehy, my inspector buddy on the state police, and had him run Chris Cloyd through "Fat Bob," the state's all-knowing computer system. Fat Bob came back with the advice that Cloyd paid his taxes satisfactorily, had run a stop sign on Cadieux back in '82, held library cards in Ann Arbor and Detroit, was a major ATM user, subscribed to a little sailing magazine out of Wisconsin, adopted a cat a few years back, and had declared himself a Democrat in the '88 primary.

A lot to go on, huh?

As expected, Dennis had spent the night at Barb's, but after breakfast they came to the apartment so he could work on the computer. They were gone by the time I knocked off, a little after four, gone God knew where to do God knew what. Well, I could guess.

I scrambled up some eggs for supper and had just finished eating when Barb and Dennis breezed in, hand in hand. As it turned out, they'd been to an AA meeting, and Dennis had bought himself a copy of the Big Book. They had that glow about them: companionship and sobriety and self-discovery, not to mention continuous sex. I'd never seen Barb so radiant. It made me leery, and it made me a little jealous, and it made me want to corner Dennis in private somewhere and hold him against the wall with a forearm across his throat and make him swear a number of very specific vows.

I took myself to task for that. What's the guy ever done that's so bad? Just trust him, okay?

After listening to their chatter about the AA meeting, I brought them to the subject. "Did you open up those files on Cloyd's computer?" I asked Dennis.

His face clouded. "Oh, yeah. Better have a look, Ben."

Barb's cheerfulness had vanished too. "Yup," she murmured. "You better."

We went to the spare room. Dennis had brought one of the dinette chairs back there, so now there was room for three to sit: Dennis on the stool facing the keyboard and screen, me on the chair to his right, Barb on the edge of the bed behind us. Dennis cut on the computer. As the hum rose to a medium-pitched drone, I noticed he'd added an additional unit. "What's that?" I asked. "Printer?"

"Yup. H-P Laserjet," he said, and committed a burst of typing in his rapid hunt-and-hit. The screen, which had shown only a few words, went blank. Then it popped to blue. Dennis said, "Okay, here we go. Remember those files I uncompressed? The ones with the CHF on the end of the name?"

"Yeah."

"Those are graphics files. Like computerized pictures."

"Yeah, you told me. What're they of?"

"Look."

He hit a key. A funny little hourglass graphic showed in the center of the screen. Then the screen changed and colors poured into it, from the bottom rising to the top, as if it had rapidly filled with multicolored liquid. Only this was a picture, a full-color picture, brilliantly sharp and clear, of a naked woman on all fours. She was silently gasping and clutching the sheets as a man standing behind her, invisible from the chest up, gripped her hips, penetrating her anus almost all the way up.

"Christ!" I said, jolted, as Barb made a soft wounded sound.

"Just wait," Dennis said quietly.

The image vanished and another one poured in. This was a tight blurry shot of the face of a dark-haired woman wearing heavy glasses, committing fellatio on the man who was very obviously taking the picture. I felt the tension of the people with me, especially Barb, who seemed frozen in place. The picture wiped to yet another, a grainy black-and-white of two naked and extremely well-endowed women, standing on either side of a single bed on which lay a tanned, muscled, naked man, looking up at one of them, showing every symptom of intense appreciation. That in turn gave way

to another color shot of an extremely young woman—
a girl, really—wearing a cheerleader uniform top and
low white sneakers and nothing else. She was squatting,
knees flung apart, and penetrating herself with two
fingers as she squinted at the camera, smiling dreamily
and with profound pleasure.

"All right, that's enough," I said. My voice sounded
tinny in my head. Dennis hit a button and the screen
went black. I looked at him and Barb. Dennis was
impassive, but Barb was pale, obviously upset. I myself
felt glum and grim. In theory, smut didn't bother me.
In theory, I thought of it as part of the cost of living in
a free country. But the fact was, I felt just a tad sour and
sickish, sitting there with the memory of those pictures
smeared across my thoughts like bug guts on a windshield. And I felt intensely curious. My impression of
Chris Cloyd had taken a good hard hit. Computer smut,
huh? Question was, Did this have any bearing on what
had happened to him?

"There's probably a hundred more in that directory," Dennis volunteered. "We only looked at the first
ten or so."

"I couldn't stand any more," Barb said. "I made him
turn it off."

"High-tech smut," I said. "I'll be damned. Here I
thought computer geeks were straight-arrow types."

Barb had a cigarette out and flamed it and exhaled
heavy and thick. "It's disgusting," she said shortly.

"It's also big business," Dennis told us. "People buy
'em, sell 'em, trade 'em with their friends. They're called
'chiff' files because the file name always has CHF at
the end."

"How come you know so much about it, Dennis?"
Barb asked coolly.

"I told you why," he answered patiently. "I go on

line all the time. You hear about things. Hey," he added, reaching back for her leg, "I don't need that stuff to get off, honey."

"On line?" I echoed.

"Computer services," he explained. "On-line services. Computer bulletin boards. You tie your computer into them over the telephone. That's obviously what Cloyd was doing. I told you this machine has an internal modem."

That still meant nothing to me. But I did remember the unplugged phone line I'd seen on the floor of his office. "I get it," I said, as some old TV ads oozed up through the murk of my memory. "He was dialing up those places from work, huh? Places like Prodigy?"

"Ah, not quite," Dennis said, smiling. "These are private outfits. Most of them are small and specialized. Obviously, our friend Mr. Cloyd knew all about them."

Barb stood up and stepped away and smoked. "Sickening," she said.

Dennis ignored her. He looked at me. "So what do you think?"

"What I think," Barb cut in, facing us, "is that Cloyd was a sick son of a bitch who deserved what happened to him. As for you two, for you to sit there and drool at those things—"

"Who's drooling?" I cut in.

"This is business, honey," Dennis said.

She was flushed and staccato-voiced, gesturing with hard jabs of her red hot cigarette. "What that shit is," she said, "is women being victimized. Plain and simple. It's violence against women. It's men controlling women and using women and abusing women. And the fact," she said, charging over something Dennis started to say, "that it's in the computers now—well, that shows you that nothing has changed. It's all high tech now, but nothing has changed. All we are to you sons of bitches is prey."

"Just for the sake of argument," Dennis began.

"Year of the woman my *ass*."

"I suspect," Dennis went on patiently, "that those women posed for those pictures voluntarily."

"You sick little *shit!*" she shouted.

"Kids, kids," I said.

"I'm just telling you the facts, dear."

"Don't play Mister goddamn Know-It-All with me."

"Your first big fight. How sweet," I said.

"This is about you too," she flared at me. "I was watching you. You couldn't take your eyes off those pictures."

"I'm working, darlin'," I said.

"Wipe them off," she said.

"Wipe them off?" I echoed. "Well sure, once we—"

"Right . . . now!"

"Not till I look at everything," I said.

"Then color me gone," she snapped, and stomped out.

With a heavy sigh, Dennis rose and went out after her. I stayed put, left alone with the drone of the computer. I was thinking about what Roulette Brooks had said: "I don't think Chris was interested in sex." Well, maybe not in *doing* it. Maybe. Did this make Cloyd a sick little shit, as Barb charged? Not for me to say, or her either.

Dennis trudged back in. "She's gone," he said, sitting heavily back down on the stool.

"She'll be back."

"Yeah, I know," he said unhappily. "We've got another AA meeting before she goes to work. Assuming she still wants me to go with her."

"So you've taken the oath, huh?" I ventured.

Dennis looked tired now. He slouched in his chair, fingers drumming the edge of the computer keyboard. "I don't know," he answered. "What I do know is, sobriety is a sensible strategy for me right now. And," he added quickly, "there's Barb, and it's all so important to her."

"That's right," I echoed. "Important."

"So," he said briskly, gesturing at the patiently humming computer, "are you going to look at the rest of the pictures?"

"Reckon so. Guess I'd better."

"You think they're tied in with Cloyd's death?"

I considered for a moment. "What I think," I said, "goes like this. Cloyd got killed, supposedly through an accident. But on that very same day somebody wiped out all these files. Maybe it was Cloyd who did it, for some unknown reason. But if someone killed him, that person might have wiped off those files. Could be Cloyd knew something, had something on his computer, that someone else didn't want him to have."

"Like a dirty picture?" Dennis said.

"Yep."

While he thought about that, I stood up and lighted a cigar. The room was stuffy and getting smokier by the minute. I notched the window under the blinds and said, "I noticed something about those pictures on there."

"What's that?"

"They look kind of clumsy to me. Blurry in spots. Light's not so good. And one of them's black-and-white."

"They're amateur shots," Dennis explained. "Ordinary people take them. What you've seen before in porn, that's pro stuff. Notice with these, how some of the people are not all that gorgeous? Amateurs."

"And Cloyd was part of it," I said.

"That's right. Pretty active too, I think," Dennis said. "Let me show you something else."

I sat back down on the chair. Dennis flickered some keys and the screen went through a couple of changes, then spit up big dense paragraphs of black words on white background. Each wad was separated by strings of equal signs. "E-mail," Dennis told me.

"Whassat?"

"Computer letters. You do these on line too. Write letters back and forth to your friends. Delivered instantaneously. Go ahead, take a look."

I read.

FROM: SinThigha
TO: ChrisCo
ATT: ME_BED. CHF

Hi Chris, I hope you like this one! :) My boyfriend took it last year before I got shaved. I've got some new shots now you might like better, soon as my scanner is fixed I'll upload those for you. Enjoy! :)

SinThigha

P.S. Do you have any girl/girl with toys? I already have all of LindaLix's but any others you might have I appreciate it. Thanks!

"See," Dennis said, "this SinThigha person was sending our buddy Chris a picture called 'me space bed dot chiff.' He saved the pictures, and he also saved his E-mail. There's several files of these."

"All about his trading," I said. "God. So they use aliases on these services, huh? This SinThigha. Any way we can find out who she is?"

"Doubt it," Dennis answered. "Hell, man, we don't even know what service he was on. Could be any one of hundreds."

"Hm."

"And SinThigha could be anywhere in the country," Dennis added. "The world, even. But probably California," he added maliciously. "Land of fruits and nuts."

I glanced through the note again. It was so breezy and casual, they could have been talking about bubble gum cards. Something else jumped out at me. "What's that thing there, after the first sentence?" I asked. "A typo or something?"

He squinted through his glasses. "Nope. That's an expression mark."

"What the hell."

"See, with E-mail you've only got words. No expressions. No emotions. So people on line use symbols to express moods, their facial expressions."

I looked again. Colon and right parenthesis. "Still don't get it."

"Turn your head ninety degrees to the left," Dennis said. "Now it's a little happy face, see?"

"Wow," I said, trying it out. "Boy howdy, is that high tech or what?"

"That particular one means smile," he told me.

"Nice friendly folks on line, huh?"

"You betcha."

There and then, Dennis gave me my first computer lesson. He showed me how to turn the thing on and bring up Cloyd's E-mail files. He also showed me how to activate what he called his slide show program, so I could review the rest of the pictures. I was nervous, plunking away at the computer keys. Felt clumsy and stupid. Dennis was kind enough not to laugh. He only cautioned me not to hit the keys so damned hard. News to me. I thought I was just tapping at them.

Barb came back to take Dennis to their AA meeting. She'd gotten over her anger, as I knew she would. Once again I had the impression I wouldn't see them anymore that night. Another evening alone in the apartment for good old yours truly, but that was okay. I had work to do.

After cleaning up the kitchen, I lined up beers on one side of the computer and cigars on the other and started the thing up. It whined and flickered and silently said all sorts of things, then the screen went clean and it sat there staring at me, patiently waiting, with only the letter C showing in the upper left-hand corner.

Me and it, sitting there.

Laboriously I typed the commands Dennis had given me. After several false starts, I whooped as the E-mail files came up. Then, hitting the page-down key to move from screen to screen, I read Chris Cloyd's mail.

There wasn't anything terribly thrilling. In fact, it was bland and cryptic and downright boring. The aliases of his correspondents were interesting at first. In addition to SinThigha, with whom he exchanged a lot of files, he wrote back and forth to people calling themselves things like PassionIt1, Mystrie, FaithannN, and Debby 33. Some seemed to be women. Many aliases could have been either gender. From the tone of their writing, and their liberal use of those little sideways smiley faces, I got the feeling they liked old Chris.

After reading thirty or forty notes I got burned out

on that, so I switched the computer over to the slide
show program. Uncracked a beer and drank as the
images flowed over the screen, a new one every twenty
seconds or so. They were a real motley collection of
porn, in all different sizes and shapes. Most pictures
filled the screen; some only took up part of it. There
were color shots and black-and-white and psychedelic
tints and swirly dot patterns. As to the subject matter,
it varied all over the place too. Mainly Cloyd liked
women: solo, in pairs, or in trios; posing or in action;
unequipped or using various kinds of devices and
apparatus. And all the shots seemed to be what
Dennis called amateurs, taken by computer-equipped
exhibitionists for their fellow voyeurs.

After a few dozen of those, my eyes started to glaze
over there too. I no longer felt sickish and sour. I felt
bored and utterly burned out. I was getting ready to
shut the thing off when something on the screen roused
me. The face—the face of the woman in the picture—

I managed to stop the slide show. I didn't know how
to skip to particular shots or whatever, so I started it
all over. Sat there numbly for twenty minutes, waiting and watching as the shots marched by a second
time, and then there it was again. That face—the face
of a woman on her back on a bed, knees drawn up,
impaling herself with a long black dildo, eyes alight,
toes curled with excitement.

Abruptly I shut the thing off.

Damn.

"How may I help you today, Mr. Perkins?" asked Roulette Brooks.

"Well," I said, "I'd like a complete listing of all calls made from Chris Cloyd's phone for the past ninety days. *Both* phones," I added.

Roulette Brooks wore the same expression as on Monday: cheery, open, candid. Had the same basic look, too, from the heavily moussed, deliberately tangly white-blond hair to the glint of Ferrari red on her full lips and long nails. Same type of attire, pale jacket and skirt over an open-necked white blouse. And we were, once again, in the conference room of Martin Ketchum & Martin, in the David Whitney Building in Detroit.

But this was Wednesday. This time, I was working alone; Dennis had business. This time I had a specific objective. And this time I knew things. Things about Cloyd, things about her, things I was sure she wanted kept secret. But I wouldn't use any of it unless I had to. I didn't want to embarrass her. She'd been cooperative before. Perhaps she'd give me what I needed without my having to become, shall we say, insistent.

"Sorry, Mr. Perkins," she replied. "Can't do it."

On the other hand, perhaps not.

I tried the silent bit. Didn't work. Brooks seemed content to sit there as long as I liked, with that half smile on her red lips. Presently I said, "Of course you can do it, Ms. Brooks, and you know it."

"Call me Roulette, please," she answered. "And frankly I'm baffled by your reference to 'both' phones."

"He had a modem in his computer," I told her, as if she didn't know. "Hooked up to a separate phone line. I saw the cable lying on the office floor in there the other day."

"Surely I'm not familiar with—"

"Besides"—I overrode—"you yourself told me this joint has equipment that tracks the numbers of all calls placed. So the records are here somewhere. I want them. Now."

That open, candid pose of hers was slipping badly. Now she looked tense, remote, almost glacial. "I fail to see the importance of this."

"Frankly, I'm not all that sure where I'm going with it either," I confessed. I grinned, trying to win her over with the old aw-shucks. "But that's detective work. You have to paw through a lot of garbage to get at the good stuff."

She drew herself up on the sofa, crossed her legs the other way. "Even the police didn't ask for any such records," she told me. "So I'm not inclined to hand them over to you."

Oh, well. Try to be nice, try to go easy, and what did it buy you? I reached under my blazer for a folded paper, flicked it to a skidding landing on the mirrored coffee table between us. She did not move, barely glanced in its direction. "What's that?"

"Take a look."

She bent, picked it up, unfolded it, looked at it incuriously. "Ace Towing," she said. "So what?"

"Cloyd's car," I said. "Towed from Walnut Street in Wyandotte. And guess who lives right around the corner?"

She snorted, and let the paper fall to the table, and leaned back. "This is such bullshit."

"That so?"

"So he broke down near my house! Big deal!"

"Come on, Roulette."

"He was dropping off some materials for me to work on. That's all."

"Oh, please. I didn't fall off the turnip truck yesterday."

"If I was screwing him," she insisted, "I would tell you. I've got nothing to hide."

"Oh?"

"Oh," she said defiantly.

I sighed, reached into my blazer for the other paper, and held it up unfolded. "You really want to look at this?"

"If you insist."

I sailed it over. She picked it up on the skid, snapped it open, stared. Her only reaction was a sharp intake of breath and a single toss of an ivory pump. Nothing more.

"Anyone you know, Roulette?" I asked quietly.

She folded it up. Her full oval face seemed compressed now, dark eyes remote. "How," she said without inflection.

"What do you mean, how?"

She did not answer.

"I guess what you're saying," I went on, "is that you thought you had wiped all this stuff off Chris's computer."

Still silent.

"Dennis had some kind of program that brought it back. Don't ask me how it worked, it's way over my head."

She crumpled the paper in both red-tipped hands, staring toward the bright window. "He was dead," she said quietly. "No one had to know. It didn't matter."

I felt a wave of—I don't know, elation, maybe. It was one of the mental rewards of detective work, busting through the crust of someone's pretense and getting a little closer to the truth. You never got all the way to the truth; I mean, come on. But if you were persistent and, most of all, lucky, you sometimes got close.

"Tell me about it," I said.

Her dark eyes found me, and something about her expression made me alert. She did not seem ashamed at all, or guilty, or even self-conscious. "I only lied to you a little," she said.

"That so?"

"And I don't have to tell you anything now." She gestured with the crumped wad. "You can't blackmail me with this."

Since I had no intention of blackmailing her, I let it go. "Just tell me," I suggested. "It'll go easier for everyone."

"All I wanted was to protect Chris," she said. "His memory, his reputation. I know it sounds corny."

"So you did have a relationship with him."

"I loved him." Her voice was uncharacteristically small. "I was crazy in love with him. That's something I did not tell you before. But I didn't screw him."

Still resisting. I tried to ease her. "Come on."

"No," she said, shaking his head. "I wanted to. Oh, God." She recrossed her legs and inhaled deeply, thoughts making her face an open book. "But *he* didn't want to. He didn't want sex, Mr. Perkins, I told you that. I told you he was different."

"That's different, all right," I said doubtfully.

"He lived inside his head," she said. "That's how I look at it. Nothing outside his head was really important to him. Either that, or he was scared. All I know is, he didn't want any real-world stuff. Too risky for him, I guess. But he had his outlet, like everyone else. He liked to look."

"I'll say," I observed, remembering the computer pictures.

Having crossed the big divide, Brooks now seemed more relaxed, more like her normal open self. "He told me all about it. The on-line pictures, the trading, everything."

"Why'd he tell you, do you think?"

"He liked me," she answered, sounding proud as well as wistful. "Everyone needs one person to tell things to. I was his. Besides, he wanted my help. He needed something to trade, something no one else had."

"Pictures, you mean."

She just nodded.

"Which," I said, gesturing at the wad in her hand, "you were only too willing to give."

"I loved him," she said.

Yeah. For everyone there is a limit, except when love is involved. Then all bets are off.

Having unburdened herself, she now seemed to loosen up a little. "Can I be totally honest with you?"

"Hey, don't let me stop you."

"It was a hoot, actually," she said. "I enjoyed it. Knowing that . . . you know," she said, and she seemed to blush a little, "knowing that my pictures were being flashed from computer to computer, all over the world.

That people I'd never meet were looking at me. I liked that."

Time to start nudging her back toward the objective. "Why didn't you just tell me all this to begin with?"

"I didn't take you seriously," she answered. "Whoever heard of a private detective investigating something like this? And like I said, I wanted to protect Chris. These things about him, people don't need to know them. Do they?"

"Which is why you wiped the files off his computer?"

She straightened. "Oh, no," she said. "I didn't do that. They were already gone before I ever went on."

I stared at her steadily, hiding my surprise. "Really?"

"Surely. I went on the night after Chris died, after the police had been here," she said. "I was going to wipe the pix and the E-mail files. But they were already gone."

"You're sure?" I prodded.

Her glance was scornful. "What I should have done," she told me, "was reinitialized the hard drive, or deleted the FAT or the partition, or run the defragment routine or something. If I'd done that, your cute little undelete utility wouldn't have found those files in a million years."

I smiled. "But I thought you didn't hardly know anything about computers. Another one of your little lies?"

"Yes," she replied. "But I never touched those files, honest to God."

"Who did, then? Chris?"

"I don't know why he would want to destroy them. But yeah, I guess."

I let her puzzle with it.

"Chris," she added, "or whoever killed him."

* * *

The hole saw whined shrilly, filling the air around my face with drywall dust. I steadied the tool in both hands until it worked its way through, then shut it off and laid it down and squinted into the hole. Sure enough, there it was, the phone line: right where I'd fished it. Nothing like guessing right the first time. Luck had its uses, as I had proven umpteen times over the years, but it was also helpful to know what you were doing once in a while.

By now it was late afternoon. After seeing Brooks, I'd put in a few hours at the Norwegian Wood office, then returned to my apartment to run an extension from the fax machine line back to the spare bedroom. Dennis had told me we could go on line using the regular phone line, but I didn't want it tied up. Now I was done, and just in time too, because I heard the front door open, followed by Dennis Squire's booming greeting.

He came into the room just as I finished installing the jack. "All set," I told him. "It even works."

"Excellent," he answered. He wore new navy blue trousers, a striped dress shirt, and a mottled blue-and-white tie knotted a third of the way down his chest. His blond hair was neatly combed, and he was certainly all business, down to the new hand-tooled leather briefcase that he casually tossed onto the bed. "Busy day," he told me, catching the loose end of phone line that I tossed him.

"Making progress?" I asked, gathering up my tools.

He ran the phone line along the wall and then over to the card table. "Making contacts. That's about it," he said, bending and peering at the back of the computer. "There's work out there for me. That's for sure."

I put the hole saw up on the closet shelf, set the toolbox in the corner in there, and pulled the folding doors closed. "How's Barb?"

"Went to work. Pulled a double shift today." With a *click* he inserted the phone line into the jack in the back of the computer. Then he sat down on the stool, clapped his hands once, and cut on the machine. "We hit a meeting this morning and another one between shifts. And I'm meeting her after work, and we'll do the midnight at the Alano Club."

"Sounds good," I said.

"This is all good," he said expansively. "Being here, and with Barb, and in the program, and helping you." He looked up at me through his glasses. "I really owe you, man."

"Forget it."

"Okay," he said with a quick grin, and turned to the computer. "I'll fire up the communications program. You got some phone numbers for us to try, I hope?"

I dug my tattered spiral pad out of my pocket. "Yeah," I said, flipping it open. "His computer line at the agency was almost constantly in use. Bunch of different places he contacted. But there was only one he used every day. "I read him the number, which was in our 313 area code. "What now?"

Dennis tapped in the number in his rapid hunt-and-hit. "We'll dial her up," he said easily, "and see what emerges."

Suddenly I heard a dial tone from somewhere. It came from inside the computer, followed by a rapid electronic beeping and the purring of a phone at the other end. Dennis just stared at the screen. Then came a high-pitched whine, like the sound from a fax machine, followed by another, higher one. "Negotiating," Dennis said softly. The whines became unison. "Handshake,"

Dennis added. The whines cut off and the computer beeped rapidly, the screen flashing the words CONNECT 2400 over and over again. "We're on line," Dennis said casually.

As I sat down on the chair beside him, the screen wiped clean and then filled with giant block letters:

ContaXX bbs

It hesitated, then printed a line asking for my password, followed by a flashing question mark sign. Dennis looked at me. "Try Chris's," I suggested. He typed it in. The system hesitated again, then the screen wiped clean and displayed a big box with a whole bunch of listings in it.

"How about that," Dennis said. "His ID is still active."

"Nobody knew about it," I said, "except Roulette, so nobody was likely to cancel it. Are these things free, or what?"

"You kidding?" he retorted. "More like nine plus bucks an hour. They take your credit card and milk it dry."

I was scanning the screen. "What's this now?"

"Main menu," Dennis replied, pointing. "These are rooms. Wow, look at this. Pretty hot stuff."

There were almost a dozen of these "room" names: Bound for Glory, Foreplay Lobby, Hot Tub, Women4Women, Lez for Me, Let's Go Private, Leather Heaven, Bi Highway, Pictures of Wives & Girlfriends.

You get the idea.

"What the hell is a room?" I asked.

"It's just an area of the system where people come in and chat," he explained.

"You mean on the computer," I said clumsily.

"Well, yeah. Obviously, Ben."

"'Scuse me," I said shortly, a little ticked at his tone. "This is all new to me, so you'll have to go slow."

"The room names indicate areas of common interest," he said blithely. "What's your pleasure? Leather? Bondage? Bisexuals?"

"What I want to do," I answered, "is track down some of these people he was trading with. And writing to." I had my pad open. "How do we do that?"

"I don't know. We're just going to have to fool around with this thing, see what the capabilities are—"

Just then the computer beeped rapidly and a box popped in the middle of the screen.

HOT FLASH!
from: SweetPea
Hey, baby,
How hard are you today?

CHAPTER

TWELVE

"Good God, willya look at that," I said. "What the hell?"

Dennis was smirking. "So they have this! How elegant."

"What is it?"

"An instant messaging function. Anyone on line can contact anyone else on line, privately, like this. It's like sending a telegram. Is this SweetPea some friend of Cloyd's, do you know?"

I checked my list of Cloyd's on-line contacts. "Not on here," I answered. "Can we just ignore it?"

"I don't know." He hit the ESCAPE key and the hot-flash box vanished. "Yes," he amended, grinning.

"Christ," I muttered. "People hitting on people over the computer."

"Remember, Ben, this is all live, all interactive," Dennis said, clittering some buttons. "There's God knows how many people on line right now, all over the place. They're chatting with each other, and writing E-mail, and doing God knows what."

"But I mean, you can't see 'em!" I retorted. "You can't

touch 'em! You don't even know who they really are!"

"That's the idea," Dennis said. "And the whole attraction."

"All right," I said. "Whaddya say, let's see if we can track down these people and then get the hell off this thing."

"Not so fast," he murmured, dickering with the keys. "This is fun. . . . Ah, here we go. A help screen."

"Hey, that's handy."

"In computers," he told me, "we have a saying. 'When in doubt, RTFM.' Means 'Read the Manual.'"

"Read the what?"

"Manual."

"Oh."

I sat back in the chair, barely paying attention as Dennis jotted down a bunch of information off the screen. I was getting tired and my eyes were squinchy already from staring at the screen. Plus I was dry as a powder house, but with Dennis there it seemed, on balance, not a good idea to open up a cold one.

So I felt a tad resentful, and the feeling was made worse by this whole computer situation. I mean, I'd never been to a foreign country, unless you counted Canada, eh? But now I was getting a taste of what foreign travel might be like. The whole "on line" thing was utterly alien, entirely unreal. Strange language, a hobble-gobble mix of tech talk and funny little symbols like that smiley Dennis had shown me. An invisible landscape with no map and no signposts. Strange rituals. An almost total lack of physical action; everything was on the screen or in your head. And the oddball population of on-line people, floating around somewhere behind the screen like electronic ghosts, hot-flashing you at will, saying things they'd never have the courage to say anywhere else, like in a bar, for instance.

```
HOT FLASH!
from: SweetPea
I'm so hot and wet
:(
```

I turned my head sideways. "Big frown," I said. "See there, Dennis? I figured it out."

"You're learning." Dennis hit ESCAPE and the box vanished. "Here's the deal," he said. "We can see a list of people who are on line right now. We can also lurk the rooms if we want. We can also bring up little profiles of the people you're after."

"I want to get at them somehow, Dennis. I want to track them down and talk to them face to face."

"Problem is," he pointed out, "everyone on here uses aliases. That's part of the scene, the anonymity. You can't break through that. There's no way to find out who these people really are."

"One impossible challenge at a time," I answered, flipping a pad page. "All right, bring up the list, let's see if any of them are on line right now."

He took us to a screen with a single column of aliases. There was a Juggz, JailBait, 1forU, KareBare, PamL69. But there weren't any names from the list I'd made of Cloyd's contacts.

"Can we get profiles then?" I asked.

"Sure. Give me the first one."

I consulted my pad. "Puss4U."

I felt silly even saying it, but Dennis made no comment, just rapid-tapped the name into the computer. After a moment a box popped up.

```
HANDLE: Puss4U
NAME: Beth D.
LOCATION: Holt, MI
LIKES: Participant sports :)
QUOTE: Take me out to the ball game
```

"Oh, that's real helpful," I said. "We can't get an address or phone number or anything, huh?"

"No. I told you, Ben, they're going to guard their anonymity, most of them. Want to try the rest?"

"Might as well." I gave him the other names. The profiles Dennis brought up were, if anything, even more cryptic. Three of the handles generated no profiles at all, just the response ID TERMINATED.

"Terminated?" I said. "What does that mean?"

"My guess is, their IDs have been discontinued for some reason. Credit card tapped out, or they quit, or something."

"Huh. In my work, terminated sometimes means dead."

"This isn't your work."

"I am completely and totally aware of that thank you."

"Don't get bent out of shape," Dennis said patiently. "What I meant was, this is the computer world. The language is different. Jargon tends to be very direct and blunt."

"Like these aliases," I murmured. On my pad, I circled the aliases who'd come up terminated: Shadwbabe, SherryDoes, and HardRodd10. "Any other bright ideas?"

"Let's go into a room," Dennis suggested, and hit a few more keys. The screen switched over to a blue background with white letters. At the top it said YOU

ARE NOW IN FOREPLAY LOBBY. Below that were lines of type. The lines were moving too. Slowly scrolling up, one at a time.

"This is the chat thing?" I asked.

Dennis nodded. "These people are all on line now, chatting in this room."

The lines of words crawling slowly up the screen looked like a script, with the name of each "speaker"—JailBait, KareBare, and LauraMore—at the left and their clumsily typed and sexually explicit observations to the right. Besides the words, they used goofy little symbols and cryptic abbreviations, like ROFL and LOL. The symbols weren't tough to figure out, but some of the jargon was lost on me. "What's LOL?" I asked.

"Stands for 'laughing out loud,'" Dennis answered, squinting at the scrolling screen. "ROFL stands for 'rolling on the floor laughing.' These ladies are having a pretty good time."

"Well, it's not helping me any. Let's shut it off, huh?"

Without comment, Dennis hunt-and-hit his way out of the program. He did not turn the computer off, though. I stood and stretched and stuck a cigar in my teeth and flamed it with a blazing kitchen match, exhaling a smoke cone out of the corner of my mouth as I hoofed to the hall door and back, hands stuck in my back pockets. Dennis was watching me expectantly, one arm draped across the computer keyboard in a pose that almost seemed protective. I took the cigar out of my mouth. "Gotta find a way to track these people down," I told him.

"What do you expect to find out?" he asked.

"I don't know. Nothin', prob'ly."

"Then why bother, Ben?"

"Look," I said, sounding reluctant even to myself. "I took this job. It's a nothing job, but I took it. Basic deal is to check around Chris Cloyd's life, look for something that smells, something that might have led to his death by foul play. Now, his life's already been gone over pretty good by the cops. I know the Detroit people; they're good. If they found something to go with, I think they'd still be working on it."

"Okay," Dennis said tentatively.

I jerked a thumb in the direction of the computer. "That-there they sorta slid by, looks like. From what you say, they never found those picture files. I know they never got the phone records. So they never went on line, never found out about this ContaXX place. So what we have here is a whole area of Cloyd's life, a great big area, that needs to be checked out. I can't just walk away from it."

"Got it," he said. "What are you going to do?"

"Gonna track down this ContaXX place and talk to them. Get them to tell me the real identities of Cloyd's on-line pals so I can check them out."

"Two challenges," Dennis noted. "First, to find out where ContaXX is. Second, to get them to spill the beans."

"It's what I get paid these big, big bucks for," I answered.

"Judge?"

"Ten," Lonnie murmured, tossing.

"Yes, Ben?"

"See that," Max said, and clinked a chip to the center.

"Know anybody at DNR?" I asked.

"Gonna bet or fold, Ben?" Loel prompted.

"I'll call," I answered, flicking a chip in.

"Not really, why?" the judge said, squinting at his cards first through his reading glasses, then over them at arm's length. Neither view seemed to please him, but then, with the judge you could never be sure.

"Got a buddy, small business owner—"

"Heart of American business enterprise," Lonnie said.

"The engine that drives our economic machine," Loel chimed in.

"—who's in a jam with them," I finished.

"Cards?" the judge asked.

"One," Lonnie said.

"Damn near impossible to hold DNR off," the judge said, passing out cards. "Ben?"

"Two. How come?"

"I'm good," Loel said.

"I've heard," Max said, smiling.

"Practically limitless power," the Judge replied, picking up his hand and reordering it. "A little like U.S. Customs."

"And the IRS," said Lonnie. "Ten," he added, tossing.

"And the media," Max said. "I fold."

"And state supreme court justices," Loel added, smiling.

"If only that were so, dear," the judge observed. "You going to bet, Ben, or admire that hand the rest of the night?"

"Ain't nothing to admire here, sir," I answered. "Ah, call, I guess," sliding in the chip.

"I'm out," Loel said, giving me a suspicious glance.

"Triple sixes," Lonnie announced, spreading them.

"Full boat, heavy tens," I said.

"I knew it," Loel said.

"Shit," the judge snapped, slamming his cards down.

"So, judge," I said, "my buddy's got no recourse, huh?"

The old man was glowering. "Tell him to lie back and try to enjoy it. Now can we get down to more important business?"

"Deal the cards," I answered, raking it in.

The message light was blinking when I got in.

"I agree we must stop meeting like this," came Raeanne's amused voice. "Suggestions?"

Temperance was a village way down in the flatlands of Monroe County, within a hearty hike of the Ohio line and hovering on the frontier of what some called "greater" Toledo. The closest I had ever been to it was its exit sign off Interstate 75, which ran along the Lake Erie shore about four miles east of the village. I had heard once—God alone knew where; probably one of those trivia columns in the paper—that the place was named Temperance because its founders incorporated an alcohol ban as a covenant on every lot within its borders.

Evidently, I noticed as I rolled through the village limits on Lewis Road, the covenants hadn't stuck. There was a beer store just inside the village line, and another one coming up on the right, and yet another way down yonder. If there was such a thing as truth in advertising, I thought, they'd have renamed the place Boozeville.

It was Thursday, just past noontime now, a sullen hazy still day, hotter than a three-dollar pistol, the kind of day that bottled up the heat in your pores—

more like August than June. I'd gotten an early start
that morning, wrapping up my end of the Norwegian
Wood work, and grabbed an early lunch before heading out. I didn't know exactly where Dennis was, or
Barb either. He'd gone to Barb's the evening before
and never come back or checked in. When I prowled
the bathroom and the spare room of the apartment, I
found his personal stuff was gone. Looked like he was
moving in with her.

Good news / bad news.

Okay, at least he was out of my apartment. That
was part of the good news. Not that I disliked Dennis.
You can like a person and still not want to live with
him. Or her. The other part of the good news was that
he was able and willing to help me with this computer
mess. I'd have been up shit creek without him.

And the bad news? The bad news was, he'd been
here almost a week now and showed no signs of, or
even interest in, going home. Quite the contrary, in fact.

Much as I hesitated to do it, if this kept up I'd have
to have a long talk with Barb, before she got herself in
any deeper.

I didn't have an atlas or anything, but the address
wasn't too hard to find. Hench Road intersected Lewis
in the southern end of Temperance. On a guess I
turned right and chased the numbers west to 6250, and
there it was.

I pulled in and parked as close to the road as I
could get. The building was a flat-topped brick struc-
ture, obviously intended to be a strip mall once. But its
big windows had been bricked over a shade lighter,
and there were no store signs, no ads, no come-ons of
any kind. The place wasn't abandoned—there were a
dozen or more cars parked in the lot, and a big white
unmarked panel truck was just pulling around to the

back—but there were no business names posted, at least where I could see them.

A handful of small little companies, I decided, who didn't need to advertise and who wanted the lowest possible rent out there in the middle of nowhere. Their odds of succeeding did not seem great, considering the fact that the building was neighbored by a huge old quarry to the west and a weedy, fenced-off drive-in theater across the road, both long abandoned.

Well. Nothing to do but go do it. I got out of the Mustang and hoofed across the blacktop toward the building. I hadn't dolled up that day. I didn't think Temperance rated the blazer routine. I wore a white sport shirt and gray slacks and my low leather loafers with the cute steel toes concealed inside. The look was half business and half blue collar. Perfect.

There was one public door, a heavy gray steel job, at the north end of the building. It had nothing on it but the street number. I pulled the handle and stepped inside. Nothing but a hallway that ran all the way down to the end, it looked like. Quiet, anonymous, dim, soundless, with several doors showing on each side.

I walked. The first door, on the left, said A CO. INC. The next said WELCOME PRODUCTIONS. Further down was DIVERSIFIED PRODUCTS, and then, at last, was the whole point of this exercise: CONTAXX. NO SOLICITING.

I knocked brusquely on the door and then turned the handle. It opened, admitting me into a small cubelike reception room, brightly lighted with overhead fluorescents. Everything was clean and seemed relatively new, but it was also cheap stuff: thin carpet over concrete under my feet, thin plyboard with seams showing under the watery layer of off-white paint, plastic molding and trim inexpertly nailed around the doors and along the floor, two-by-two drop-ceiling squares. A mismatched pair of cushioned chairs flanked a corner table that had no lamp, no magazines, no ashtray, nothing at all but one of those THANKS FOR NOT signs. The detectable odor of tobacco smoke in the air suggested that the warning wasn't taken very seriously.

"Yes?" asked the woman at the small desk opposite the door. She had an enormous phone console in front of her but had no nameplate or name tag or any sort of welcoming look in her dark expectant eyes. Her mouth was made for the word no. My sense was that they didn't get many visitors here.

"You the person in charge?" I asked mildly.

She was forty or more, heavyset and olive skinned, with a telephone headset clamping down her tightly curly black hair. She wore some kind of dark blue twill uniform like what the rappers were wearing. "No, that's Mr. Cockrum," she said tonelessly. "May I say what it's about?"

Hm. "Just business," I said, offhand.

The door opened behind me, and I saw a young slender blond woman slip in. She stood against the wall, watching expressionlessly. The receptionist paid her no mind. She got my name, pressed a console button, murmured into the mouthpiece, listened, then murmured again and looked at me. "He'll be out. You'll have to wait."

I didn't sit. Cockrum would be on his feet when he came in, and I wanted to meet him on equal terms. The other visitor stayed standing also. She and the receptionist did not exchange so much as a word. I figured she was expected, but there was something not quite right. The woman's limp lifeless blond hair hadn't been washed lately, and her jeans and blue checked shirt had a lot of miles on them, and she stood kind of hunched and hesitant, as if waiting her turn at the principal's office and getting her story straight: Sure I was there, sir, but I dint do it, it was them other girls—

The door beside the receptionist pulled open and a man stood in the frame. He was middle-aged, of average build, a little soft all over, and sported a soccer-ball belly that pushed against the buttons of his open-necked white dress shirt. His shiny, combed-flat hair was the dark color of his glasses, and he had a pale jailhouse complexion with that mottled scarred look that suggested he'd enriched the dermatology profession over the years. At first blush he struck me as a meek weenie geek type. Even his voice, when he spoke, supported that notion; it was nasal and high pitched and lisping.

But.

"I thought I told you to stay the fuck away from here," he said mildly to the young blond woman.

She straightened. "Please, Mr. Cockrum."

He was smiling and bobbing his head just slightly, looking altogether agreeable. "You fucked me, Jenny."

"Please," she insisted, lower lip trembling. "I'm sorry. I'm *sorry*. I promise I won't do it again."

The receptionist seemed wholly engaged in some paperwork. Cockrum too was casual, almost bemused. "Of course you will, Jenny. You just won't do it to me."

"I got nowhere to go!" she cried.

"Of course you do," Cockrum said in the patient manner of a kindly tutor. "Go up to Front Street and get on the bus either north to Detroit or south to Toledo. I'm sure a girl of your qualities can find all sorts of work."

"But my baby—"

"I'd suggest"—he overrode simply by raising his voice a notch—"that you try harder to obey the rules, wherever you end up. Otherwise you may face consequences less pleasant than these. Not everyone is as kindly and understanding as I am."

"Kindly?" she retorted, thin face a mask of tearful, scornful anger. "You're a miserable cock-sucking, ass-fucking son of a bitch."

"Goodbye, Jenny," he said placidly as she slammed out.

The receptionist turned a page and did not look up.

THIRTEEN

Cockrum was facing me, half smiling but utterly indifferent. "What do you want?"

What I wanted was the story. But one thing at a time. Maybe someday Cockrum would tell me all about his beef with the blond woman, once he and I became best friends.

Ha-ha.

"I'm Ben Perkins," I said, stepping toward him. "You run this ContaXX bulletin-board computer network thing, right?"

He stayed in the door frame, unassuming, non-threatening, but not welcoming either. "That's right," he lisped.

"I'm a private detective," I told him. "I'm working on a bit, involves somebody on your computer network or whatever. *Was* on it, anyway. Can we talk?"

He did that little aw-shucks bobbing thing with his head again, half smile showing bad teeth. "I don't think so," he answered.

"The guy died," I pressed. "Odd circumstances. Could involve other people on your network. I have to—"

"Listen," he said in his reedy voice, "it doesn't matter

what your 'bit' is. We have nothing to discuss."

"Maybe," I said, with cold, deliberate precision, "you could invite me into your office and we could talk this over."

"Maybe," he returned, sounding about as threatening as Woody Allen, "you can just turn around and walk out that door, and get in your car, and go back to Tennessee or wherever you're from."

"Detroit."

"Good day," he said calmly, and stepped back and closed the door between us.

The receptionist looked at me, a glint in her dark eyes. "Thanks for stopping by, Mr. Perkins. Do have a nice day."

I took back roads home, instead of the freeway. It was a longer drive, but much more scenic: woods and fields, Otter Creek and the River Raisin, villages with names like Samaria, Ida, Grape, Maybee, and Whynott. I motored with the top down, played Buddy Guy loud, and smoked cigars and thought about what I'd seen back there.

It was a mixed bag, all right.

I mean, take the surface picture. Crummy building with a handful of tiny businesses in it, smack dab on a deserted highway by an abandoned quarry and drive-in. The low-rent ContaXX office with its prototypical fat receptionist. The boss himself, Somebody Cockrum, spectacled and a little seedy, soft and lisping, from all appearances a bumbler and borderline loser.

But look at how he treated that blond woman.

And then there was the way he pushed me away without a second thought. That was the thing that really interested me.

See, in my experience, most people—except politicians, media people, and other diseased egos—tended to at least talk to me. Many had no intention of cooperating; most told lies, at least to some degree; but they would always at least talk to me, if only to find out what the hell I was up to.

This Cockrum guy was different. It didn't matter to him what I was after. He just instantly swatted me away. I puzzled at that a little, because I sensed it meant something, and then it came to me. Cockrum acted like a man who was in almost constant trouble with someone. Maybe lots of somebodies. Therefore, he operated always in bunker mode, living by the jailhouse code: Never say nothing to nobody.

That theory didn't seem to square with his weak grin and bobbing head and the tinny, tiny, lisping voice. I could see him in his house somewhere, living under the thumb of his mommy, padding around in carpet slippers, beginning each day by picking at his pimples and smearing salve on himself. But, I reminded myself, even wimps commit crimes. I had to forget how he looked and focus on how he acted. He was, in fact, a hard case.

Research time. As I made the final dash north on Rawsonville Road, I mashed buttons on the cellular and raised Dick Dennehy's office up in Lansing. He was out on a case, so I left word. Surprisingly, he called back just as I walked into my apartment. "What's up?" the state cop barked, sounding like he was on the moon.

"Need a little research from ya," I said. Stretching the phone cord, I went to the apartment door and picked up the mail scattered around on the carpet. "Fat Bob up and running?"

"I can log on when I get back to the office," Dick said. "Whaddya need?"

Normally, police officers, state cops included, weren't terribly anxious to help backdoor bang-around guys like me. But Dick Dennehy and I went back years and years. We'd mostly been on the same side, pretty much. He'd always rather gruff-cheerfully helped me out when he could. But earlier that year I'd helped extract him from some severe career trouble, and since then I'd found him to be, while not exactly slavish, at least willing to take my calls more of the time.

I braced the phone receiver against my ear with my shoulder and sat on the recliner to sort my mail into the usual categories: good stuff, work stuff, and trash. "Fella down in Temperance, of all places," I said. "Last name Cockrum. First name unknown."

"Cockrum, U. ," Dick said. "What's his game?"

"That's what I want to know." Trash, work stuff, trash, trash.

"Well, what's your interest?"

I filled Dick in on the case, such as it was. Trash, trash, work stuff, trash. "I know it seems like a big huge zero," I said. "But—"

"Zero, hell," Dick said. "Computer crime's getting to be a biggie. I've heard of this on-line porno stuff. Cockrum doesn't ring any bells with me, but I'll nose around. Question, though."

"Shoot."

"How'd you find out ContaXX was in Temperance?"

"For shame, Dick. I ran the number past my mole at Michigan Bell."

"You just got everybody you know falling all over themselves to help you, don'tcha, boy?"

"They scratch my back, I scratch theirs." Trash, work stuff—then the last item, a small dark-brown padded envelope.

"I hear that." He paused, probably to light one of

his endless Lucky Strikes. "You think maybe one of your victim's pen pals tracked him down and whacked him?"

"I don't know," I said, looking the padded envelope over. Handwritten name and address, return address in Dearborn. Something small and hard inside. "Seems far-fetched."

"How so?" He puffed.

"Well—"

"If you leave the computers out of it," Dick said, "you've still got people at both ends. And you know as well as I do that people are capable of anything."

"Yeah," I reflected, tearing the envelope open. "And you know, this is a case that just doesn't want to go away. I push a little, and I find out a little, so I push some more, and I find out some more. Maybe all you'll get for me is the brick wall, but—"

"But you doubt it?"

"Yeah. Somehow, I doubt it."

"Later, Ben."

"Thanks, Dick."

I hung up, then shook the open end of the padded envelope over the coffee table. Out dropped a plastic audiocassette box with a slip of paper taped to it. The paper said, in the same fine hand, *I thought you might like this. Raeanne.*

The cassette box had obviously been around for a while. The colors of the printed cardboard insert were faded, but the pictures and the text were instantly familiar to me:

BLUES ANGEL. *Zanna Canady.*

I stared at it for the longest time. Turned it over, read the list of songs, even the copyright information and details of the Zanna fan club and everything. Then I picked up the phone and pressed Raeanne's number.

Got her machine, of course. Story of my life. Everyone's life, now.

Beep. "What this is," I said, "is her very first solo LP. I know. Nobody has LPs anymore, but I do. Anyway, this goes back to—God, sixty-seven, I think, after she busted up with Zanna and her Blues Dudes. She covered 'Sally Sue Brown' on here, and I remember she took some heat because of the lesbian implication. But God, this record! My first copy I wore out from playing so much, you know. Had the eight-track, too, till it got et up by the deck one time." I didn't know if her machine was still recording, but I rushed on. "Anyway, thanks. What an incredible thing."

I wanted to play it right then. But I was good. I went over to the office and finished off the day, then came back and did the tape two, maybe three times, with pizza and beer and cigars. Just me and old Zanna, getting reacquainted. She'd held up well. Better than me.

Before going to bed I tried Barb's house. No answer. Was no news good news? I hoped so. I was just turning in when my phone rang. I hoped it was Barb, or maybe even Raeanne. Wrong again. Dick Dennehy.

"You're gonna love this," he said.

This time I didn't knock first. I just opened the door and went inside, with Dick Dennehy right behind me. The heavyset woman was right where I'd left her the day before, wearing, I swear, the same dark twill uniform. She looked at us with the same incurious dark eyes. If she remembered me she gave no sign. "Yes?"

"Mr. Cockrum, please," I said.

She didn't ask for details, just pressed a button and murmured something into her headset mike. I glanced at Dick. He was a tad taller than me, six one or two maybe, with blondish gray hair and aviator glasses on a face that had seen many hard miles. He wore a cheap gray suit, a white shirt, and a nothing tie, but otherwise he looked rather unmemorable. Unless, of course, you counted the pervasive menace of the professional cop—menace that, though as much a part of him as his fingernails, he seemed capable of adjusting at will, as if with a rheostat. Dick worked at a lot of levels, and even I could never tell where he was really coming from much of the time. It was what helped keep him alive on the street. That, and his Colt Cobra.

The door behind the reception desk opened and Cockrum appeared there, looking much as he did the day before, except today his open-necked shirt was pale blue. The eyes behind the glasses flickered over us and he lisped, "Yes, what is it?"

"Morning, Mr. Cockrum," I said. "We'd like a word with you, if it's not too much trouble."

He smiled. "No trouble at all. Please, gentlemen, come in."

He stood back, grinning and bobbing, and I walked past him, followed by Dick. The office was small, and bright from banks of ceiling fluorescents, and just as cheaply done as the rest of the place. He had a black steel-and-Formica desk, laden with papers; a high-backed executive chair and two low thinly upholstered guest chairs facing the desk; and a single bank of adjustable shelves on the wall behind the desk, sloppily stacked with magazines. Instead of drywall he had dark paneling, and the gray carpet was, perhaps, a slightly higher grade of fuzz. To our right were two closed doors, leading God knew where.

He also had a computer. It sat on a small wheeled table at right angles to his desk, its screen glowing in what I recognized was the ContaXX bulletin board main menu. I couldn't help noticing that his machine looked a lot newer and glossier than mine. Christ, I thought, don't you go getting the bug too.

Cockrum went behind his desk and faced us to see Dick displaying his state police ID, casually cupped in the palm of his hand. "Dick Dennehy," the cop said. "Inspector, Office of—"

"Yes," Cockrum said readily. "How can I help you gentlemen? Please," he said, gesturing with both pale hands, "sit."

We did so. "Well," I began, "I was here yesterday, and I—"

"I'm really sorry about putting you off," Cockrum said. "I'm so short-handed right now. I'm glad you could come back today, Mr. Perkins. What is it you need?"

I felt Dick's presence in the chair beside me, pent up, ready to strike. Though unsure as to where Cockrum was headed with this, I decided to play it straight, for now. "I need the names and addresses of some people who are members of the ContaXX network. Yesterday you told me—"

"That information is highly confidential," Cockrum said, folding his hands, expression and tone quite reasonable.

"Listen," Dick began.

"But," Cockrum said, raising his fingers briefly, "as long as you promise to respect the privacy of our members, of course I have no problem giving it to you."

"You don't, huh?" Dick asked suspiciously.

"Certainly not." Cockrum rolled himself to his computer keyboard and smiled at me expectantly. "May I have the screen names, please?"

"The what?"

"Their aliases," Cockrum explained, gesturing. "The names they go by on the network."

"Oh. Sure." I got out my little pad and flipped through the pages. "First one's Puss4U," I said. "That's Puss, then the number four, then—"

"If you'd just give me the list," Cockrum said, "it'll be much easier for me. I know you gentlemen are probably in a hurry, and I don't want to detain you unduly."

"Okay," I said, tossing the pad across. "Thanks."

Cockrum arranged the pad next to the keyboard, poised, and began tapping. In the occasional pauses, the screen changed colors; boxes came and went, commands streaked across and faded away. Cockrum didn't look like he was working very hard, but his weak-looking white fingers danced on the keyboard with great precision. Unlike Dennis, Cockrum was a ten-finger touch typist.

Dick Dennehy had slouched in his seat. We exchanged looks once or twice but said nothing. Presently, the printer next to Cockrum's computer began making a nasty grinding sound. Cockrum handed my pad back wordlessly, and when the printer was done he tore off the first two sheets and handed those to me too. "There you are, gentlemen," he said. "Anything else?"

"Anything, Ben?" Dick echoed.

"You know, I'd kind of like to tour your place," I said. "I've never been through one of these computer network joints before."

Cockrum chuckled. "There's not much to see," he lisped modestly, "but if you have a minute or two, I'd love to show it off. Right this way."

Thanks loads, Dick mouthed silently as Cockrum led us through one of the doors in the far wall.

The tour was indeed a quickie. There were just two other rooms in the ContaXX suite. One was a large open area with several long rows of tables, lined with what Cockrum called "servers" but what looked to me like more computers, maybe a dozen of them. All running, all humming, the unison drone an almost touchable thing in there. They were connected by snakes of cables to posts that ran up into the drop ceiling. At the far end were two desks with one computer each. One of these was manned by a bearded, stooped individual who stared dully at the screen and, according to Cockrum, was something called a "siss-op." The other room was the size of a walk-in closet, practically filled by one big metal cabinet from which emerged snakes of wires and conduit. Cockrum said it was the computer-controlled telephone system.

The tour ended in Cockrum's office. "Anything else today?" the boss asked.

Dick looked to me. "Nope," I said. "Reckon not."

"I'll let you go, then," Cockrum said, stepping to the door. "Be sure to get in touch if I can help in any other way."

"Yeah," I said. "Thanks. See ya."

"Good day," he said, opening the door for us.

We were barely out of the ContaXX driveway when Dick, slouched in the Mustang passenger seat, made an ugly sound. "Do you believe that son of a bitch."

"Yeah. I mean, no, I don't believe it."

"Just ain't fair," Dick muttered. "I had all the poopy lined up like ducks in a row, ready to drop on his head, one by one, like a buncha bricks. I had my lines, I was all ready to go, I been looking forward to it, it's the whole reason I agreed to come down here to this asswipe town. So we get here and what happens? One look at us, and he just folds like a friggin' tent."

I was doing about eighty on the twin lane blacktop, and just then I bore right at Whiteford Center, headed northwest toward U.S. 23. "Your reputation preceded you," I said.

"Wasn't me," he admitted.

"Sorry you didn't get to have your frolic," I said. "And I appreciate your help. I got what I needed."

"He's a smart one," Dick said. "He knew he couldn't win, so he tried to win brownie points by playing ass-kisser."

"Exactly."

"Assholes like him take all the fun out of police work," Dick grumbled.

CHAPTER

FOURTEEN

We reached U.S. 23 and I shot down the northbound entrance ramp. Dick leaned back in the bucket seat, spun a Lucky to his lips, and lighted it from the dashboard lighter. "Promise you one thing, pal," he said grimly, "I'm gonna make it my personal business to get the lowdown on that asshole. Starting with, How come he ain't in jail?"

"Maybe there's never been enough to go on."

"That," he said, "is an assessment I plan to make for myself."

"Dick Dennehy, on the warpath."

"I'm gonna take him down," Dick said. "He's dirty. I can feel it, I can smell it. Know what I mean?"

He had that gonzo glint in his eye, signaling imminent violence. "Oh, yeah," I said. "I know. But there's this small matter of, like, probable cause, preponderance of evidence, and due process. Not to mention innocent unless proven guilty."

"You mean *until* proven."

"No. Unless."

"With me it's until," he said quietly.

We drove for a bit, neared and passed the smokestacks of Dundee.

"So," Dick said, puffing smoke with the words, "you becoming some kinda computer guru now or what?"

"Hell, no. It's just where this thing seems to be taking me," I said, playing lane slalom with a bunch of trucks. "Beyond that, computers? Hell, no. I'm a car guy, first, last, and always."

"Never too late to learn," Dick jibed.

"Well, I got no intention of learning," I said obstinately. "I got me some expert help." I told him about Dennis, and I also told him about the complications with Barb. "So on the one hand I don't want him to leave," I said, "because I need him on the computer till I get this case squared away. On the other hand, I want him out of here bad. Because he's gonna mess Barb up. I just know it."

"The Ben Perkins Soap Opera."

"Tell me about it."

"Wouldn't be just the slightest bit jealous now, would you, my son?"

I glanced at him. "Shit no. Her and me was a long time ago."

"And so was Carole," he prompted.

"So was just about everybody," I admitted.

"Yeah," he drawled. "You've been between sweeties, more or less, a long time now."

Which he knew full well, because he and I had lain drunk in the gutter together a few times, under which circumstances you tend to blab. "Hey, I'm seeing somebody," I said.

"Oh yeah? Who?"

"Woman I met on the Boccarossa thing," I said. "Brunette in the van, remember?"

"Oh, sure," he said. "Cute."

"It's not heavy or anything."

"No. One-twenty, one-thirty tops."

"Not what I meant, old buddy."

He just smiled. "Is it gonna get heavy, you think?"

"Not at this rate," I answered. "It's sort of a . . . I don't know. Voice-mail relationship. We play telephone tag."

"C'mon," Dick said. "You can do better than that."

We were nearing Milan now. Big signs advised us that it was a prison area and warned us not to pick up hitchhikers. I had plenty on my mind, what with Barb and Carole and the case and all. But my thoughts zapped back to a whole different deal I'd been puzzling over since the night before. "Lemme ask you something," I said.

"Ask away," Dick intoned, as the massive Federal Correctional Institution drew near to our right.

"Is it still okay to send flowers?"

"What?"

"To women, I mean."

"Well, I didn't think you meant to me."

"Not you, no. Grateful for your help, but—"

"Though I am partial to lavender roses."

"Oh yeah, right."

"Truly. But don't tattle," he whispered, winking. "Our little secret."

"You'll have to buy 'em for yourself, sorry."

"What fun is that?" Dick asked, annoyed. "At any rate, terms of sending flowers to women, sure it's okay. Haven't you seen Merlin Olsen on TV?"

"But despite that," I persisted, "it's still all right?"

"Why not?"

I gripped the wheel with both hands and stared straight ahead as I drove. "You just never know," I said. "Everything's changing. People don't always take things the way you mean 'em. You kind of have to feel your way through, if you don't know the ropes." Dick smoked and stared and said nothing. "You know how long it's been since I've done real honest-to-God dating?" I asked. "There's been Carole, off and on all these years. Few others in between."

"A few," Dick agreed, grinning.

"I know, I know. A slut, is what I've been."

Dick laughed. I didn't. "You been around," he said. "But what you're talking about now, that isn't dating."

"It's not?"

"Sounds more to me like courting."

Now it was my turn to laugh. "Courting went out with button shoes. Didn't it?"

"You like this woman?"

"Yeah, I like her. But hey, cool your jets here, pal. At this rate you'll have me picking out an engagement ring for her by suppertime. All I asked about was flowers, the advisability thereof, et cetera."

"All I know," Dick said, "is that when Ben Perkins talks about sending flowers to a woman, he's getting a bad case for her. Whether you realize it or not."

It had been a hot day, and it carried on into a warm muggy evening, a leading indicator of July nights to come. The stands at Diamond No. 3 at the Detroit Artillery Armory—which was in Oak Park, not in Detroit—were sprinkled with spectators watching the Ferndale Flyers take on the Berkley Buccaneers in a Mustang Division 7 showdown. Bottom of the eighth, no outs, runner on first, Berkley clinging to a one-run lead.

Carole Somers and I sat at the end of the bottom bleacher on the first base side, about three feet apart, the space between us occupied by the canvas baby bag. Rachel stood in front of Carole, supporting herself by holding her mother's knees. She wore a bright yellow sundress over tightly taped Pampers; Carole was in light blue denim shorts and a white T-shirt and, perched atop her thick wavy blond hair, a dark blue Berkley ball cap that matched the one worn by her son, roaming his turf out around third base.

"The catcher," intoned the announcer over the loudspeaker. "Number eight. Bokos. Bokos."

Our usual Friday night get-together had begun with spaghetti at Carole's house in Berkley, followed by a quick drive down for Will's softball game. I filled Carole in on the Wendy Dilworth / Chris Cloyd case, such as it was, as best I could. She took it all with virtual silence, eyes narrow, face set in her trial-lawyer concentration mode.

"So the state police had already been investigating Cockrum and this—um, ContaXX organization?" she asked.

Strike two. "Yup. That's what Dick found out."

She looked down at Rachel. "Go see Daddy. Go see Daddy."

Rachel, who didn't necessarily do anything we said even if she understood it, seemed agreeable tonight. She stepped down to me, a little clumsily, holding the bleacher seat to keep from falling, and then hung onto my pants leg and grinned up at me.

"Any day now," I told Carole.

"Any day," she agreed. "What did the state cops have on Cockrum?"

Ball two. "Oh. Well, there were reports of child pornography being shopped around on the network," I told her. "Cops thought maybe Cockrum himself was involved."

"Oh, God. Sick."

"Yeah, it is."

"So the plan was for Dick to stick the state police investigation into Cockrum's face, to make him cooperate with you," Carole said.

"Exactly." I looked down at Rachel. "Go see Mommy."

The batter swung and connected and pulled the ball hard down the third base side. Will Somers, sturdy and solid, was perfectly positioned. He caught the ball before the hop and made the easy out to second. One down.

We finished clapping and sat down. "Well?" Carole asked, trying to pull Rachel into her lap. "Is he?"

"Is who what?"

"Is Cockrum pushing child pornography?" she said, letting Rachel go after loud complaints. "Go see Daddy," Carole told her darkly.

"Dunno. What Dick found out was, the investigation got put on hold. No idea why. Hey, rookie," I said as Rachel reached me.

"Not enough evidence, maybe," Carole speculated.

"Yeah. What do you want?" I asked Rachel, who was prying at my pocket with insistent noises.

"The center fielder," intoned the announcer. "McKnight. McKnight."

"Another problem," Carole said, "is that the existing laws are virtually silent on the subject of computer networks. Hardly any regulation at all."

"Oh, yeah? Ooh, wicked swing." I dug into my pocket, came out with a teething biscuit, unwrapped it, and stuck it in Rachel's mouth like a cigar. "Enjoy, sweetie."

"I read somewhere there's a bill before the Senate," Carole said, glancing at the batter. "But it's been bottled up forever."

Rachel propped herself against me, gumming her biscuit happily. "Uh-huh," I said. Ball one.

"I take it you've said nothing of this to Wendy Dilworth," Carole said.

"And I won't, either," I answered. "Not unless it turns out he was popped and I can prove it."

"Probably wise."

"Merciful, too." Strike two. "I mean, this whole thing, she's getting a lot more than she bargained for."

"And so are you," Carole said without looking at me.

"Meaning?"

Carole fixed me with her dark eyes. "It doesn't enthrall me that your friend Dick is mixed up in this. People always seem to get shot when he's around."

"He's a state cop. A good guy, even. I—"

"We have a deal, Ben, you and me."

"I know." I changed the subject. "Here's a radical thought. What if Wendy knew all about her husband's picture fixation? Hell, maybe she was into it with him."

She scoffed. "What a ridiculous notion. Women don't—"

"Look at Brooks. She posed for him."

Full count now. Real duel brewing. "Thanks," Carole said dryly, "I'll pass on the look. And one errant exception does not disprove my position. Ninety-nine point nine percent of women are not even remotely interested in pornography."

I thought about the aliases of some of the people I'd seen on ContaXX. They were female, or claimed to be, and from what I'd seen they'd been actively trading smut with Cloyd. "I really do doubt that Dilworth knew, though," I conceded. "She doesn't seem to be the type. Whatever that is. It doesn't seem to've been a close relationship."

Foul ball. Carole looked right at me and said, "Oh, Ben, it doesn't matter how close you are. You never really know what's going on with the other person. Not really."

I could tell that the batter was going to jump all over the next pitch, and she did, smashing a screamer down the third base line. Will, playing the hole, looked hopelessly out of it, but he'd been watching the signs, just like I'd taught him, and he lunged to his right as the ball left the bat and made a loud, smacking, bare-handed catch as he crashed sliding longways to the turf. The base runner, who'd thought he was headed for home and had already rounded second, turned to trot back to first to tag up and started to run when he saw what Will was up to, but too late. Will, stretched out flat on the ground, pulled up on one elbow and flung the ball toward first. I thought it would sail on him, but the first baseman snagged it and swept down at the sliding base runner and tagged him in a cloud of thundering dust. The umpire hesitated, then did a kind of hip-hop and ripped a huge yanking gesture in the air with both fists and bawled, *"Out!"*

We were on our feet cheering. I had an arm around Rachel, holding her against me as she clung fiercely to her teething biscuit and made excited noises, drumming her bare heels against my hip. As Will strode toward the dugout below us, I gave him a thumbs up. For a ten-year-old to acknowledge even the existence of a sort-of parent was definitely not cool, but Will tipped his hat in response and grinned.

The applause subsiding, Carole turned to me and asked, "Did I tell you Buck was joining us?"

And quite suddenly Longstreth was there, all right, standing beside her. "No," I said, adjusting Rachel against me. "Must have slipped your mind. Hey, Buck."

The tall tan man smiled his handsome adventurer smile. "Evening, Ben. Hope I'm not intruding."

"Well," I said mildly, "it's just my usual Friday evening with my daughter, is all."

"Ben doesn't mind," Carole said, tiptoeing up to give Longstreth a kiss. "That's because he and I are the best of exes."

"Outstanding," Longstreth said. His long brown hair was ponytailed tight against his head. He wore a white loose open-necked shirt and khaki shorts, which showed off his lean limber body and its numerous scars. Looked to me like he had forty under control, but it must have cost him plenty. "Sorry I'm late," he told Carole, returning her kiss.

We sat. Rachel squirmed on my lap, but I didn't let her go. "So I hear you're headed to Sarajevo, Buck," I said, about the cheeriest thought I could think of at that moment.

"August," he answered. "Any news?" he murmured to Carole.

"No," she answered, and nudged him. "Will's batting cleanup tonight, he'll be up after this girl here."

"Something big going on?" I asked casually.

"Nothing important," she replied.

They sat close. I held Rachel, who'd lost her biscuit but didn't seem to mind. I was watching the game but was only marginally aware of it. I'd picked up things the past few weeks, and I turned them over in my mind. Some kind of changes in her law office. Her book was coming out and the publisher wanted another one. She'd been named chair of some kind of national advocacy committee.

I looked at them, and saw them holding hands and smiling. "You never know what's going on with the other person," Carole had said. But right then I knew, all right. I knew.

FIFTEEN

"Perkins's Night Owl Café, Ben speaking."

"Hi, hon. I know it's late."

"Barb!"

"How's Rachel?"

"Rookie's good. Will's team didn't do all that well, though. Lost in extra innings, squibber dropped in between two outfielders. Real shame."

"Too bad."

"How's Dennis?"

"Good."

"You got that glow in your voice."

"Ah . . . we have to talk, you and me."

"I've been wanting to, darlin'."

"I've been avoiding you."

"I know. Been since Tuesday. I know you've been busy."

"I know you have things to say, Ben."

"You want to talk, I'm ready."

"Not on the phone. Are you busy this weekend?"

"I'm on the road solid, all day tomorrow. Want to come along?"

"Is it the case?"

"Yup. Interviews, you know the deal. What do you say? You working?"

"I'm off. Dennis wants to hit the library; he doesn't need me for that. What time?"

"Nine sharp? In your driveway?"

"I'll be the one with the doughnuts and the smile."

"Perfect. 'Bye, darlin'."

"See you, hon."

I hung up and went into the living room to lock everything up for the night. Barb had sounded cheerful but a little jumpy, as if afraid I'd scold her or something. I sure didn't plan to land on her. I'd probably tell her some things she would rather not hear, but that was what best friends were for. All I hoped was that maybe I could get her to slow down a little. Slim chance. She was certainly in lust, if not more than a little in love, and had been alone a long time, and when you were that hot and bothered, you didn't pay much of a nevermind to possible consequences. I could sure relate to that.

The phone rang as I was turning off the kitchen lights. I grabbed it. "Yeah!"

"Well," came Raeanne's marveling voice, "how about this!"

"Hey," I said. "Hey. Ain't this something. We meet up."

"You were out all evening."

"Oh, was that you who committed the about ten thousand hang-ups on my box?"

"I'd have left a message," she said, "but I couldn't think of anything clever. Voice mail gets tiresome by and by."

"Yeah," I said. I wheeled myself down into the dinette. It was late and I was beat but didn't notice. "Personal contact does have its attractions."

"Mm. Were you out having fun?"

"How could I have fun? I wasn't with you."

"You outrageous flirt. You must be drunk."

"Actually, it was Rachel night, up at her mom's this time. Went to a softball game. Pretty cool. How 'bout you?"

"Oh, I've just been sitting here admiring this absolutely exquisite white rose that came."

"For all evening you did that? G'wan."

"All evening. You must understand, I don't receive things like this all that often."

"Don't give me that. You're an actress, you've been in plays, I happen to know the leading lady usually gets an armful of roses at the end of a performance."

"You may be thinking of the opera," she observed, "which is one of the few venues I've avoided being mediocre in, thanks. But Ben . . . this rose, it's just beautiful. Thank you."

"Well, thanks for the tape. It's sensational. I don't know how you could have found it. Don't tell me you just had it laying around the place."

"Sam's Jams in fabulous Ferndale," she replied. "In the nostalgia rack."

"Well. It's really thoughtful, kid. I'm, uh . . . well, are you—"

"Yes?" she inquired softly.

"I was just thinking out loud."

A pause, and for that instant I thought she'd back off. "How about dinner at my place?" she asked.

"That'd be great," I said. "Just great. Don't want to rush you—"

"We won't rush anything," she said. "We have lots of time, Ben."

"Think so?"

"Yes."

I took a deep breath. "Tomorrow night?"

"Fine," she said readily. "If you like barbecue, I whip up a pretty mean steak."

"But isn't red meat supposed to be bad for you?"

"Let's chance it," she said confidently.

Overnight the muggy spell snapped, pushed east by a cool dry front that eased down from Canada. As I rolled the Mustang into the gravel driveway of Barb's tiny unshaded ranch house in Taylor, the last wispy morning cloud withdrew from the sun, leaving it hanging in blinding brilliance in a perfect unblemished sky to the east of us, over the city of Detroit. The rumbling of the idling Mustang motor reverberated off the houses around me, and right on cue the front door of Barb's house opened and she came out and skipped down the stoop steps toward the car, Donut Hole box in hand, as Dennis Squire trailed after.

"Morning," I said, pushing open the passenger door. Barb handed me the box and got in as Dennis came around to my window. She wore blue stirrups, a white sleeveless top, and a white headband in her brilliant red hair. Dennis was Saturday slob in shorts and a T-shirt with a cartoon of a man urinating on a computer system, over a caption that said COMPUTER WHIZ. "Looks like you're all dressed for the library, pal," I noted.

"If I have to be cooped up inside all day," he replied, "I might as well be comfortable."

"I left the car keys by the front door, hon," Barb told Dennis.

"Thanks, babe."

"Day like this," I said, gesturing, "better to be outside."

"Where I come from, every day is like this," Dennis answered. "Have a good one," he added with a quick businesslike smile as I stuck the Mustang into gear and backed out.

"Coffees are on the floor in back," I told Barb as we headed for Telegraph Road. "Route's under your visor."

She retrieved the folded sheet and snapped it open and studied it. "Wow," she said. "What are there, fifteen here?"

"Yep," I answered. "All Cloyd's buddies, chatted with him on the ContaXX network."

"How'd you get their real names and addresses?" she asked. "Dennis said you wouldn't get those names in a million years."

Well, I thought, Dennis had his ways, I had mine. "Met with the owner," I answered. "Reasoned with him."

"I see. Coffee?" she asked.

"Please."

She reached for the two big travel mugs from the back seat, checked to determine which was double-double, and gave me the other. Her red hair gleamed in the morning sunlight, and her blue eyes sparkled and always seemed to be smiling. She looked less tired around the eyes too. It would have been nice to think her pleasure was due to my company, but I knew better.

I swung south on Telegraph Road and booted the Mustang into high and drank some coffee. I felt good, better than I had in days, weeks. Though I was sure the day's work would be a bust, at least I was spending it on the road and with my best friend. No apartment work. No paperwork. No computer work. And then that night I was seeing Raeanne. Life was good. Better, anyhow, now.

Barb lighted a cigarette as I negotiated the crossover to northbound Telegraph and pointed us in the general direction of Lincoln Park. "Know what I like about hanging out with you?" I asked.

"What's that, hon?"

"I can smoke without feeling guilty."

"Yeah, us walking chimneys are becoming a threatened species, aren't we," she said, exhaling a plume.

"In more ways than one."

"Ha-ha. No, I mean, we can't hardly smoke anywhere anymore."

"Getting tougher," I agreed, lighting a cigar. Complicated job, negotiating the Mustang shifter and coffee and lighted cigar, but I managed. Multi-dextrous.

"Used to be," Barb said, "I had to keep an eye out for signs saying where I couldn't smoke. Now I have to look for signs saying where I can."

"My barbershop banned smoking," I told her. "Do you believe that? No smoking in a barbershop?"

"My home AA meeting too," she said.

We were headed east on Wick Road now, coming up on Interstate 75, more or less the boundary line of Lincoln Park. The street we wanted was a piece past that on the right. "AA don't want you addicted to anything, I reckon," I observed.

"Nothing but doughnuts," she agreed. "Of course the hospital went totally nonsmoking. Now I have to stand outside the entrance to grab a quick weed. There's a handful of us from different departments; we've kind of become friends."

"Doorway people," I told her. "The new lost tribe. Marooned on a stinky smoky desert island."

"It's like we're criminals or something," she muttered. "I can't see where we're doing anything so terrible."

"No law against slow suicide," I agreed.

She glanced at me. "This the place?" she asked as I turned us right down a strip-of-tar elderly residential street.

"This is it. Your side."

"Three up," she said. "There we go." She crushed out her cigarette as I parked the Mustang in front of the gaunt clapboard two-story house. "What's the act?" she asked.

"No act," I answered, checking the sheet. "Go in straight and play it by ear."

"Gotcha," she said, and was smiling as we got out.

The house towered over a narrow treeless lot and stood within arm's reach of its almost identical neighbors. Now, with the Mustang motor turned off, I could hear the sound of a lawn mower nearby. As we went up the walk toward the steep porch steps, a big beefy man in T-shirt and baggy shorts came marching around the corner of the house, practically being dragged by a bright orange Snapper mulcher mower with all the fixings. When he saw us, he let go of both safety handles and the mower stopped abruptly.

"What is it?" he asked, looking warily at us from beneath the bill of his ball cap. More at Barb than at me, which was good, because she looked generally friendlier.

"Morning, sir," I said, half friendly, half not. "My name's Perkins, this is Barb Paley. I'm a private detective doing some asking around. Talk to you for a minute?"

He mulled that over. "What's it about?" he asked.

"Your name's Jesse Dolan?"

He thought about it. "Yeah, that's me." Vacant voice, empty eyes, Hoffa haircut.

"There's a computer network you belong to, Mr. Dolan," I said. "Called ContaXX. Know what I'm talking about?"

He said nothing. Seemed frozen in place.

"You go by the handle of 'Hott1' on there," I went on. "And we were just—"

Without changing expression, without looking at us, and without a single word, he left his mower and went quickly and purposefully up the steep flight of wood steps to the porch.

"This is all strictly confidential," Barb said to his back.

"Just want to talk," I added. But without a pause or even indicating that he'd heard, he opened the door, went in, and closed it behind him. For an instant I thought maybe he was going after a weapon, but then I heard a couple of deadbolts clonk home in the big wood door.

In the silence, Barb eased over to me, bemused. "So what now?" she murmured.

"Well, I could kick the door down and tie him to a chair and sweat the information out of him."

"What's the other option?"

"Go see the next person on the list."

"I vote for that one."

"Sold." We started for the car. "This is going to be trickier than I thought."

The Saturday morning traffic was building as we headed north on Fort Street. "Where's the next one?" Barb asked.

"Allen Park. Almost Melvindale."

"'Kay." She lighted a fresh weed. "You don't smoke around Rachel, right?"

"Not indoors." Well, I thought, here goes. "How 'bout Dennis? What's his odor on it?"

"Oh, he doesn't like me smoking," she said with a small smile, "but he puts up with it."

"Hey. An open-minded guy."

"*My* open-minded guy," she agreed.

In the silence I found myself looking for somewhere to send the conversation, but it was a one-way chute, and we were in it. "So," I said. "Dennis."

She was smiling tightly. "We're to that now, eh?"

The traffic cleared and I pulled a fast tight left into a subdivision street. Dark brick homes, well-groomed lawns. "Reckon so," I said. "After we do this one, huh?"

"Are we here?"

"It's that last one yonder, at the corner."

"'Kay, hon."

There was no driveway, so I parked at the curb and we got out. The small snug ranch looked like all the others along that cookie-cutter street, except that it had a big weathered wood wheelchair ramp on the front, with thick guard rails and a switchback. The sidewalk running up to the house was newer than the house, judging from the condition of the concrete, and wide enough to accommodate a wheelchair. "Who's this one?" Barb asked, walking beside me.

"Ann Lee," I said. "Known to her ContaXX friends as Shadwbabe."

"Let me lead," she suggested, preceding me up the gently sloping ramp.

"Be my guest."

CHAPTER

SIXTEEN

The main door stood open behind the glass storm door. From inside I could hear a TV set and the droning sound of a window air conditioner. Barb pressed the doorbell button and we waited, and then waited some more. Then a wheelchair rolled into view from the right, occupied by an enormous dark-haired woman wearing black-framed glasses and a blue housedress. The bare calves and ankles of her useless legs were chalky white, but her thick arms were taut with muscle as she edged her chair at an angle to the door. "Yes?" she asked, voice muffled by the glass.

"Hi," Barb said, all sparkly. "I'm Barb Paley, and this is Ben Perkins. Are you Ann Lee?"

"I'm Annie," she said shyly, voice faint behind the glass.

"Hi," Barb repeated. "We're talking to people who use the ContaXX computer network. Can we come in?"

"No, I don't let strangers in," Lee said, sounding matter of fact, easy, and slow. "What network?"

"ContaXX," Barb answered.

Lee's eyes were large and dark and kind and looked

younger than the rest of her. It was sometimes hard to tell with very heavy people, but I put her at thirty or so. Her voice was muffled by the glass door, but we could hear her all right. "What do you want to know?"

"There was a man on the network," Barb said, "who had an accident and died. We're talking to his friends about it. You wrote back and forth to him." She glanced at me. "What was his handle again?"

"ChrisCo," I supplied.

The name didn't startle Lee any. "ChrisCo," she echoed. "I don't know. I chat with lots of people," she said laconically. "This is the ContaXX network you're talking about?"

"Yes," Barb said.

"I'm not on that anymore," she said.

"We know," I said. "Your ID was terminated."

"I spend most of my time on the Internet," she explained.

"What about ChrisCo, Annie?" Barb asked gently.

"I don't know," she said.

"You wrote to him," I put in. "A lot."

"I write to a lot of people," she said. "That's all I do. That and my stories."

"There were pictures, too," I said.

Barb shot me a narrow-eyed glare. "No, Ben," she whispered fiercely.

"Pictures?" came Lee's muffled voice.

"You know what I mean," I said evenly, ignoring Barb.

She looked uninterested. "No, I don't," she answered.

Barb turned her back and I heard her mutter, "So what now, big guy? Gonna tie her up and sweat it out of her?"

I looked at Ann Lee, who had me and knew it. "Sure there's nothing you can tell me about ChrisCo?"

"I'm sorry," she said.

Barb was already on her way back to the car. When I caught up with her, she said, "You could have just talked to her, you know. You don't have to be mean."

"Barb, I have to ask about the damn pictures. They're part of this."

"Well, don't expect me to like it," she said. She got into the car and slammed the door before I could close it for her.

As I went around to get in my side, I glanced back at the front door. Vaguely I could see Annie Lee through the glass, watching us, an enormous woman with useless legs, trapped in a chair for what would probably be decades—but then in a rush it came to me, how she sat at her computer keyboard for hours on end, living her life on line, making conversation, making friends, perhaps even making some sort of love, all with people who could not see her, who did not know what she was really like. She could be precisely who she wanted to be. Not overweight, not paralyzed, not Annie Lee, but Shadwbabe.

The next destination was Dearborn Heights. I picked up Outer Drive and worked my way up the winding, wooded boulevard across Dearborn. Barb, smoking again, was silent at first. I didn't know if that was because of the spat over the pictures or because of the conversation we'd been having when we arrived at Annie Lee's.

Testing, I finally prompted. "Dennis."

"Yes," she said, sighing. "You wanna go first?"

"Nah, you better start."

"Okay." She looked composed, almost somber, but somewhere back of her round freckled face I could sense the pure pleasure she felt, bubbling hard against the back of her mask. "It does seem awful fast. I've only known him a week. But it's . . . the way I look at it is . . ."

"Go on, darlin'."

She shifted in the bucket seat. "This is gonna sound real corny," she told me. "But through all the years and all the—everything I went through," she amended, "I never stopped believing there was just one special man for me out there somewhere."

"Uh-huh."

"Little girl stuff."

We were in the heart of Dearborn now. I paused for the light at Michigan Avenue. "Not little, and not girl," I said. "Everybody wants somebody. Even big goony guy types."

She snorted. "But my dream guy, I did sort of assume he was around Detroit somewhere. In Michigan, anyways, or maybe Ohio, or northern Indiana. I had no idea he was way the hell out in frigging California."

"So Dennis sort of fit in with a fantasy of yours, huh?"

"It wasn't a fantasy. It was just something I believed. And no," she confessed, "I'd have to say, when I pictured this guy in my mind's eye, he looked pretty much like—well, Clint Eastwood."

"Turned out to be Dennis, though, huh?"

"Yes," she said quietly. "Turned out to be him."

"Hoo, boy."

"What, hon?"

I wanted to say, This is worse than I thought. Instead I said, "This is tough."

"I know what you're going to say. That it's too quick, that it's just sex, that it'll never last."

Getting sticky, I thought. We were crossing the thin

shank of Dynamite Park, bearing down on Ann Arbor Trail. I didn't answer until I'd made the turn northwest, cutting across a slim corner of the city of Detroit. "Nope. That wasn't what I was going to say."

"Okay." She retreated. "Your turn."

"I'm not trying to tell you what to do," I said. "I just want you to think about some things."

"Such as what, hon?"

"People," I answered. "They tend to stay like they are."

She thought about that. "Meaning what?"

"Well, let's start with you, 'cause that's easier. You're from Detroit, you're a plain hard-workin' stiff, you're a straight shooter who tries to help people. Just like me, in other words, except a whole hell of a lot sexier."

"I'm also a drunk," she pointed out.

"Recovered," I said, checking numbers. We wanted one of the apartment towers right along there.

"Recovering."

"Okay," I said. "That's you. Now to Dennis. A whole 'nother story."

"He's a drunk too."

"He's from California, he's a management type, had to've had a big fancy education—"

"I almost got my associate's, you know."

"I know, darlin'," I said patiently, pulling into the parking lot. "And last but not least, Dennis is married."

"He's separated," she corrected.

"Not officially he ain't. Or is he?"

"No. But that's just paperwork."

"Paperwork?" I asked, and shut off the engine. The silence seemed deafening. "There's more to ending almost twenty years of marriage than paperwork."

"His marriage is over," she said stubbornly.

"Okay," I said. "Shall we get back to work?"

"Yeah, sure."

The apartment tower overlooked the Warren Valley Golf Club. You couldn't just go to the guy's apartment; you had to be announced from the front desk. The ID plaque there said PUBLIC RELATIONS ADVISER, but the guy sure looked like a security goon to me. "No answer," he told me, hanging up his phone.

I scribbled some numbers on a pad slip and gave it to him. "Ask him to call me, okay?"

"Damn," Barb muttered as we headed back out for the car.

"Gonna be a lot of that today," I told her. "Not to worry. With any luck Mr. Joseph Stuart, aka HumpD, will give me a call."

"On the other hand," Barb said, "maybe he won't."

Now we were up against a long drive, all the way across town to the east side and an address in Harper Woods. That meant Interstate 94 most of the way. For a while we were quiet, alone with our own thoughts. Barb smoked a cigarette and sipped at her coffee. Mine had gone cold. Sort of like this damn case.

If it *was* a case. It occurred to me for about the thousandth time that I was going on next to nothing. Well, that wasn't exactly true. I had that bad old tingly edgy feeling about things. But that could have been due to the novelty of the whole computer network thing.

There was, obviously, more going on in that car than simply the case and the coffee and the smokes and the sounds of Buddy Guy singing about how it felt like rain. As we entered the freeway interchange area, with its requisite trucks and potholes and disableds and gawker slowdowns, Barb said, "I guess you're having trouble believing in Dennis's sincerity, huh?"

"I don't know. I mean, people don't move from California to here. Usually it's the other way around."

"Believe it," she said. "Dennis really is cutting his ties with everything out there."

"So now," I said deliberately, "he's going to settle down here, start a new career, and be with you. He's going from California and his gig out there and his wife, to this here. Right?"

"Right."

"Hate to say this, Barb, but I'm scared to death of it."

"I'm not," she said evenly.

I hated to do this, just hated it. "Can't buy in," I told her. "In the end, I just don't think it'll happen."

"It will too," she said stubbornly. "He promised. He wouldn't lie to me."

"I don't think he would, either," I said. "But I don't think you're dealing with the real Dennis. I think you're dealing with a temporary Dennis, a burned-out, drunked-up, beaten-down Dennis. Sooner or later he'll become himself again, and then odds are he'll go back to what he has and what he knows and what he is."

"He's changing his life. He told me so." Resolute.

"People's lives are like ruts. They just get wider and deeper as the years go by, and pretty soon there's no getting out."

"That's not always true. Plenty of people start all over." Matter-of-fact.

"Would you leave Detroit, Barb? Would you move way the hell out to—uh, Arizona or somewhere, and—"

"For Dennis I would." Utter certitude.

"It's just all theory, darlin'. And wishing. And hoping."

"We'll make it happen."

"He'll go back to his life, Barb. He'll go back to his *wife*."

That seemed to rattle her a little. "He hates her," she shot back. "She was so mean to him. You wouldn't believe the things the bitch—"

"You can't fight history."

As she thought about that, tears suddenly glittered in her blue eyes. Brow furrowed and jaw set, she lashed out. "You're just jealous of him. That's what it is."

"Oh, bullshit."

"You just can't stand it that he's so smart—"

"Married, Barb."

"—rich—"

"*And* a parent."

"—funny—"

"Married."

"—handsome—"

"A suit, besides."

"—and educated."

"Married, darlin', he's a married married *married* man."

Suddenly we were silent, aware that we'd been shouting at each other in the small Mustang. Barb was flushed, her mouth set and pinched as she crossed her legs and lighted herself a cigarette and stared out the side window.

And so we stayed, silent and separate, all the way to Harper Woods and the house of Carlo King, known to his ContaXX pals as Luger. The house was a well-kept bungalow on the north side, a short hike from Eastland Mall. The houses on either side sported FOR SALE signs, like a half dozen others on the street. This was, I figured, yet another inner-belt suburb slowly bleeding people to the more pristine climes of Harrison Township and White Lake.

As I shut off the engine, Barb said sullenly, "You do this one. I want to think."

"'Kay, darlin'." I got out and headed up the walk. It was a lively neighborhood, well kept up, air dense with bird chirps and mower roars and clipper snips. And here I am, working, I thought grumpily as I pressed the doorbell button, doing my level best to help a friend, but alienating her instead.

The door opened to reveal a tall, thin, very tanned man in his fifties somewhere, wearing a green short-sleeve shirt and even greener shorts. His wire-rimmed glasses gave him a scholarly look, and he peered down at me over them with the thin-lipped disapproving look of a study hall proctor. "What is it?" he asked, with exaggerated politeness.

"Ben Perkins," I said. "I'm a private detective doing some asking around. Talk to you for a minute?"

He was bald on top but had grown the side hair long and bundled it to the back of his head. "What do you require?"

"You belong to the ContaXX computer network," I said. "You go by the handle Luger—"

"But this is outrageous." He drew himself up and scowled down at me. "An absolutely *outrageous* invasion of my privacy."

"I'm not invadin'," I said, "I just—"

"You horrible, wretched scum," he hissed furiously. "Are you aware that federal law *prohibits* the type of—"

"Can I assume"—I overrode—"that you're not particularly willing to—"

"—before I call the authorities," he shouted, wrathfully righteous and practically spitting. "You filthy *plumber* person, you *spook,* you sniveling little *snooper!*" And he slammed the door on me.

I got in the car. "No luck," I told Barb.

"I'm sorry," she said.

"We got a lot more yet."

She reached to my shoulder and squeezed it. "No," she said softly. "I'm sorry I yelled."

"Me too, kid." We were both uncomfortable. I started the motor. "Grosse Pointe Shores, next."

"Roll it," she answered.

I headed us north to Vernier and then east, bound for Lake St. Clair. Barb got a cigarette going. I sensed we weren't through yet after all, and I was right.

"So," she said quietly, and with bitterness I could almost touch, "you think Dennis'll just turn tail and go back home. You think he'll remember me once in a while as good old what's-her-name. That fat old drunken redhead he banged back in Michigan. Right?"

The way she said it made me heartsick, because I knew she was really expressing her own worst fears. "C'mon. You're not fat, and you're not old, and you're not drunk."

"Then what am I, huh?"

"To me," I answered, "you're precious. So precious, I'm gonna keep telling you what I really think, even if it makes you hate my guts for five or ten minutes."

She made a scornful sound. "I don't think that's it. I think deep down you think of me as that fat drunken redhead you used to stick it to—"

"No, Barb, no."

"—years ago. And you want her *back,* is what it is," she went on, tone deadly. "You can't stand it that I've changed."

"No. Your kind of change is the good kind."

As I made the right on Lake Shore Drive, Barb's eyes searched me. "Do you really and truly believe that?"

"Course I do," I said gruffly. Looked like the place I wanted was just two doors down. No, three. Coming right up.

She studied her smoldering cigarette, took a big hit. "I think about it a lot, you know," she said. "You get sober, a lot of things look different to you. I've had to face up to what happened and what I was like, and it wasn't a pretty sight."

"Yeah," I answered, and shut off the motor.

"I used to be—" She stopped short as the sight around us registered. "Holy shit," she breathed. "Is this it?"

"This is it. Wanna go in?"

"It's a mansion!" she said.

"Home of an individual known as Nice Ts," I answered. "Shall we go?"

"By all means," she answered, opening her door.

Mansion was probably overstating the case a little bit, but the place was definitely better than shabby. It was a single-story Spanish villa, quirky and asymmetrical, with a red-tiled hip roof and large arched openings on the front porch. I'd parked on the curved driveway, but there were no other cars around, and as we walked toward the house under the shade of the tall oak trees I wondered if this was another dead end, and what kind of taxes a joint like this cost, and whether we'd come all this way for nothing.

"Pool," Barb noted as we entered the porch. "Hear that?"

Splashing sounds and indistinct voices reached us from somewhere near, next door or around back. "Try this first," I said, and rapped the brass knocker. No answer. Rapped again. Still nothing.

Barb was making for a brick walk that cut around the front. "Let's go see," she said, beckoning. I followed her around the side of the house, where a tall brick wall protected the back, guarded by a black wrought-iron gate. I pushed it, and it *whonng*ed open on heavy iron hinges. The splashing sounds were louder now, punctuated by male voices, and we emerged from the shady area onto a pool deck behind the house, a pool deck scattered with men.

Young men, well-muscled men—who lay supine to the sun, spread-eagled, creased, greased, and totally naked.

CHAPTER

SEVENTEEN

Well, not totally. A second look informed me that the two men nearest us wore just the skimpiest of skimpy suits—not even bikinis, more like anorexic G-strings that left nothing, and I mean nothing, to the imagination. The young men were almost identical in appearance: chiseled, tanned good looks, muscular, tanned, greased bodies, short hair, Robocop sunglasses, earrings, ID chains on wrist or ankle.

Barb shot me a quick look but said nothing.

The pool was a large blue kidney with a little bump in the near end for the spa. It was surrounded by a dense bank of low greenery and fruit trees, all enclosed by the high brick wall. Two men were sunning on the deck, two sat in the humming, burbling spa, and two others were in the shallow end of the pool. I had the sense that they were the ones who'd been doing the cavorting we had heard. One of them said curtly, "Hey. Private residence."

Chiseled handsome heads stirred and raised and turned to look at us with invisible eyes. I said, "We rang the knocker or whatever. Greg Allbright here?"

The speaker, still annoyed, said, "I'm Greg. What do you want?"

"Need to talk to you about your computer networking hobby."

"What about it?"

"You are Mr.—uh, Nice Ts, aren't you?"

He considered that, laughed, and sloshed toward us, rising out of the shallow end by climbing several short underwater steps. He was the only blond of the bunch, a stocky, practically hairless five feet ten, wearing a bikini that wouldn't have covered my finger. "Come on down here," he said.

"Problem, Greg?" asked the man in the water, with a hostile look at us.

"No problem, Gary. Hang tight, boys." We followed Greg down to the end of the pool, where several sets of heavily upholstered patio furniture sat grouped under brightly colored umbrellas. Barb seemed edgy to me, and on the one hand I understood that, but on the other hand I didn't. If anyone had reason to be edgy, it was me. I was the one being picked apart by all those invisible eyes.

Allbright dropped into one of the chairs and bent forward to put his face within range of the large concave makeup mirror that sat on the circular glass table. The mirror was surrounded by little jars and tubes and strange looking implements. He pushed his Day-Glo green sunglasses to the top of his head and peered into the mirror, inspecting himself with gray eyes, feeling his face with brown water-wrinkled fingers. "What do you want to know?" he asked.

"Curious about the handle, for one thing," I said. "Makes you sound like a woman."

"And?" he prompted, squinting, changing the angle of his reflection as he studied.

I let it go. "My name's Perkins, by the way. This is Barb Paley. We're investigating the death of a man who was also on the ContaXX network. Went by the handle of ChrisCo. Remember him?"

"Sure, I remember," Allbright answered. "If you'd care to sit, be my guest."

I really didn't feel like sitting, but this was the first reasonably live one we'd found today, and I didn't want to blow it, so to speak. I caught Barb giving me a small private smile as she sat down, and I took the chair beside her, across the table from Allbright. "Thanks. Mind if I smoke?"

"Yes, I do," he answered, still inspecting.

Ah, well. "Okay. So. What do you know about Chris?"

"He's dead?" Allbright asked, looking straight at me for the first time. He had piercing gray eyes and the most handsome, regular features I had ever seen outside of a magazine.

"Yes."

"Accident?"

"Well," I answered, "let's just say he got a little too tight with some ropes and strangled. I'm looking into the theory that he might have had some help, if you catch my drift."

Allbright didn't confess, or turn pale, or even react all that much. "It's a shame," he said. "Chris was a nice guy."

"Did you ever meet him?" Barb asked.

Allbright was inspecting his inventory of tubes and jars and little tubs. "He had some great pictures," he told us.

"What kind?" I asked.

Quick smile. "You know what kind." He selected a tube and uncapped it.

"I've seen some of them," I said. "But I'd like to know what went on with you and Chris."

He squeezed some brown stuff out on a finger. "All right," he said reasonably. "There's a board on there—a club, sort of—called Pictures of Wives and Girlfriends. That's where he hung out, mostly. I'm not into straight hetero, but a lot of bi's upload their group shots, and that can get pretty hot. Chris liked those and I had a few, so we traded from time to time."

"How long did this go on?" Barb asked.

"We chatted too," Allbright went on, smearing goo on his face with small precise motions. "He was always looking for new suppliers of amateur pictures. He told me he had over two gig of pictures in chiff and BMP formats. That's over double what I've got."

I could tell that Barb was getting annoyed. I threw her a cautioning look. "What's a gig?" I asked Allbright.

His eyes found me for an instant and then went back to the mirror. "Gigabyte," he answered. "A thousand megabytes."

Hoo. Sizable. "Did you ever meet Chris in person?" I asked, repeating Barb's question.

"No," he answered. "I know some people use the network to meet new people. Not me. Lot of losers on there."

"I see." One of his pals belly-splatted into the deep end and began to backstroke down toward us. Barb watched idly, bored now. "So what about Chris? Any reason you know of why someone would do him in?"

He snorted and began capping his goo tube. "Now, that's a really stupid question, Perkins."

"Why?"

"Because why ask me? I didn't know the guy."

"You chatted with him, traded with him."

He swatted that with a brown hand. "You don't really get to know anyone on the network. Not in the sense you mean. We all use aliases, we all lie like politicians. Everyone on there is beautiful and desirable. The women have enormous teats and the men have huge cocks. When in fact most of the people, I suspect, are shut-ins and social misfits and pizza-faced teenagers."

"Well, not everyone," Barb said. "Look at you."

He stood. "All I know about Chris is this," he told us. "He was one hell of a fast typist. Accurate, too. On the chats, he'd be right back at you with his answers. And he knew how to write. A lot more articulate than most of the people on there. And he loved pictures. Boy-girl and girl-girl, toys and come-shots, and strictly amateurs. That's what I know about him."

"Okay," I said, standing also.

"Don't know what he did," Allbright said. "Don't know who he knew. Don't know where he lived or what he was like. I barely know who he was. And I sure as hell don't know why he died. Okay?"

"Thanks for the help, Greg."

He popped the sunglasses off the top of his head and Frisbeed them onto the table. Looked at me again and smiled. "Thanks for stopping by," he said. "I'll bet you were quite tasty when you were younger."

"Still is," Barb said.

I shrugged, resisting the urge to laugh. "If I don't appeal to you, pal, it don't break my heart."

"If you weren't such a bigot," he answered, "it would."

He turned and flung himself out into the pool as Barb and I walked out.

"What an asshole," Barb said as I fired up the Mustang.

"At least he talked to us," I answered, wheeling us around the horseshoe driveway.

"He talked to you. He never talked to me. He was a rude son of a bitch, and he wasn't much help."

"Well, a little bit. Perspective-wise."

"What do you mean?"

I rolled us north on Lake Shore Drive. "What he said about relationships on the network. I didn't realize it before, but it sounds like nobody really gets to know anybody else on there. If that's so, why would someone on the network want to knock Cloyd off?"

"You're saying," she said slowly, "that we're wasting our time?"

"Maybe." We drove in silence. "If you want to go home, just say so."

"No. If you're keeping on, I am too."

"Thanks, darlin'."

"That son of a bitch," she muttered. "Never once looked at me. Never even answered my questions." More silence, and then we both laughed. She said, "For once, you were the one getting the guy-eye instead of me."

"Yeah," I said. "Pretty funny. St. Clair Shores next. Then we'll have lunch."

"Okay."

"Gonna hit an AA meeting today?"

"Later on," she said vaguely, "with Dennis." She lighted a cigarette. "You know, I don't get the guy-eye all that much anymore. Not like the old days especially."

"People's taste has gotten worse," I said.

"Ha-ha. No, that's not it. I'm no spring chicken anymore. And I changed, besides. Remember what I used to be like, Ben? T-shirts and jeans, and my hooker 'do, and all those rings and junk jewelry and makeup?"

I remembered. As my daddy would have said, she was anybody's dog who'd run with her.

She slid down a bit, rested her head on the seatback. "Guys wanted me and I knew it," she said, "and I just went with the flow, let them have me, have their way. Everyone got to have their way with good old Barb. While other girls were getting educations and jobs, and husbands and houses and babies, I was on the street and in the bars and working crap jobs, and screwing and partying and drinking and drugging. And the whole time, in the background, there was this gigantic sucking sound, and you know what that was, Ben? The sound of my life going down the drain."

We had reached 11 Mile Road, and I made the left. "Well," I said, "you turned it around."

"I'm working on it," she answered. "It's my program. And Dennis is part of it, whether you like it or not."

Back to Dennis, I thought. "It's not a question of liking it. It's whether to trust it or not."

"But you see," she said earnestly, "you don't really know him. When he's with you—"

"Like, after one week *you* know him? G'wan."

"When he's with you," she repeated, "he's completely different. He does the guy thing. Frankly, when he's with you he comes across like a jerk."

"That's me," I said. "Bringing out the best in everyone I meet."

"That's not true either," she retorted. "It's just that he doesn't really know you. He doesn't know how to act around you. You're good at keeping people off balance, you know."

"Detective reflex."

"It's more than that. It's part of your act."

We passed Little Mack, and I slowed the car on the

divided boulevard—Wampler, Wexler, Whistler: bingo, hang a right.

"But when we're alone he's different," Barb went on. "He shares—are we here?" she interrupted herself.

It was a narrow high-curbed street with small clapboard Cape Cods on large, treed lots. "Next block," I said, scanning house numbers. People should make them bigger, easier to read, to help detectives out.

"Okay," she said absently, thoughts still on Dennis. "He tells me things. He wants to know everything about me. He holds hands with me. He says sweet goofy things. It's a romance, Ben. I don't think I've ever had a real romance before."

"Me neither," I said, and thought of Raeanne. We passed an intersection. Passed a yapping dog, a vacant lot, a kid on a trike.

"Plus, we're a lot alike," she said. "More than you would think. In his own way, Dennis has been as badly used as me. We're both damaged goods. We're both swimming away from a shipwreck. We're in our own little world already. We're soulmates. It just took us almost forty years to find each other."

"Wait a minute," I said, hitting the brake abruptly. "Must have overshot it." Stopped the car, jammed into reverse, propelled us backward a ways, and then a ways more.

"Which is it?" she asked.

I checked the house numbers on both sides and then I knew. Damn. "Right there," I told her.

The vacant lot had a single tall tree in front. In its center, the low rim of a concrete foundation formed a rough square and was circled by an irregular bright-orange snow fence, for safety, I assumed. Scraggly weeds covered the ground, and among them I could see scraps of wood and other debris littering the ground. The gravel driveway was blocked by two leaning sawhorses, guarding what from whom I could not tell.

"What happened to it?" Barb asked.

"Shit if I know," I said over the rumbling idle of the Mustang engine.

"Sure this is the right address?"

"Yep. No wonder her ID was terminated." I wheeled over to the curb and turned off the motor. "Let's prowl," I suggested. "You take the east side, work north. I'll take the west side and work south."

"Straight or fake?" Barb asked, opening her door.

I got out. "Wing it," I told her. "Maybe you're an old high school friend or something."

"Maybe I should know who I'm looking for, then."

I grinned. "Good point. Betty Brody, alias SherryDoes, but I'd suggest keeping that part to yourself. Meet me back here?"

"See you, hon."

I was halfway through a cigar when Barb got back. A little breathless, she flopped into the bucket seat and gratefully accepted the lighted cigarette I offered her. "Sorry it took so long," she said, taking a deep hit. "Lady down there didn't want to let me go. We're invited to lunch, by the way. Tuna-fish sandwiches."

"Thanks anyhow," I answered. "I know a good Burger Barn right around the corner. What'd you find out?"

She had left her door open and propped a sneak-ered foot on the curbstone. "Probably the same as you," she answered. "Place burned down—what, five weeks ago. Betty's dead."

"Presumed dead," I corrected. "They found human remains, but they couldn't positively ID her."

"They couldn't? How'd you know?"

I pointed over my shoulder with a thumb. "Found an ex-Marine back there, was in Naval Intelligence for a while and never got over it. Thrilled to have an actual 'suspicious circumstance' on his street. That's what he called this, a 'suspicious circumstance.'"

"I see."

"He pestered the police and the medical examiner and the arson investigators and got all kinds of lowdown."

"And," Barb noted, "was eager to share it with—who were you, by the way?"

"Oh, I was Harv O'Gannon, the friendly appraiser from Homer Mortgage," I answered. "Seems Ms. Brody had applied for a second, and—"

"I gotcha." We sat silent for a moment or two, smoking. "Got to admit," she said, "this is pretty suspicious."

"Maybe. Seems to be arson. And whoever did it knew what he was doing," I told her. "Fire burned so hot, it incinerated the house down to nothing. Only took two Dumpsters to haul away what was left, the man told me. Like whoever did it wanted to absolutely destroy Betty and everything she had."

"Meant business, huh?"

"Yep."

She tapped ash out the window. "Okay, Mr. Detective. What do you think this means?"

"Not sure. Probably nothing. What does poor old Betty have to do with anything? Aside from her being on ContaXX and writing to Cloyd, there's no connection between them."

"They both died violently," she pointed out.

"But this," I said, nodding at the barren lot, "ain't how Cloyd bought it."

"True."

We thought for a moment.

"On the other hand," I said, "it would be a little hard to do this to the David Whitney Building, wouldn't it?"

EIGHTEEN

The Burger Barn was a block or so west, where 11 Mile met the interchange of the Ford and Reuther freeways. We did the drive-through bit but then pulled into a small city park and ate in the Mustang with the top down, in the bright June sunshine, to the quiet sounds of an old Stevie Ray Vaughan tape.

Barb was always a silent, focused eater, so there was little talk as we put away our double bacon cheeseburgers. I should have been thinking about the case, but instead I was thinking about Barb, about how good it was to hang out with her, even on a mission as long and boring as this. I could see why Dennis wanted her. She brightened her corner of the world, and accepted people as she found them, and had such hope and optimism for herself that you felt there had to be hope for you too.

I knew my doubts came partly out of selfishness. I did not want to lose her, and I'd learned, over the years, that there was no faster way to end a friendship than for one of you to fall in love with someone else.

Even so, this thing with Dennis was bad news. She did not have her head on straight. What we were dealing with, I felt, was impulsive, emotional Barb, betting her fragile recovering self, the whole shooting match, on a man I did not entirely trust.

But enough was enough.

As I jammed our trash into the can in front of the Mustang, Barb pulled hard on her Coke straw and said, "Okay, boss! What's next?"

I got back into the car. "Hazel Park, Clawson, and points west." But I did not start the car. Instead I took her wrist and squeezed it. "Hey. I'm sorry."

"What for?"

"Dennis. It's not right to question you or doubt you."

She reached and hugged me quickly, cheek warm against mine. "Just don't resent him," she said, releasing me. "I know he's a suit, but he's all right. Really."

"I'll be watching out," I told her. "Just in case."

"Of course you will," she noted. "It's the guy thing."

"Best friend thing, more like," I countered. "And something else I'm gonna do for you."

"What's that, hon?"

"I'm gonna shut up about it," I answered. "I've said my piece. Whatever happens, whatever you decide, whatever you do, I'm with you, kid, all the way. I'm in your corner. Look over this way, any time, and you'll see me right here."

She touched my hand. "Thanks, hon."

"If it goes blooey, I'll pick up the pieces," I said. "If it goes the other way, I'll pin on a flower, and throw rice, and put gravel in your hubcaps, and snuffle and dig for my hankie."

She looked away. For a long and longer moment she said nothing. Then she let out a long breath and said, "Dennis asked me to marry him. And I said yes."

"Well," I said after a moment. "Congratulations."

And that was where we left it. For the rest of the day, Dennis's name hardly came up at all. As we drove our slow, traffic-clogged route, we talked about a million other things. The election, Senator Proposto's wisdom-defying relationship with Zanna Canady, and the tape that Raeanne had sent me; the bar, the people we'd known there for so many years, and Eddie Cabla's upcoming confrontation with the backhoes of the DNR; our jobs, our friends, even our relatives, what was left of them. It was as nice a time as you could have, on an errand like that, which proved what good friends we really were. There was no better test of a relationship than spending hours and hours stuck in a car together.

And the car was where we spent practically the next couple of hours as we worked our way west. In Hazel Park, Yvonne Mack, known as JessiBi2, wasn't home. Ditto Rich Pickton, the legendary HunkOMatic, in Clawson. The situation got little better as we penetrated deeper into Oakland County. Hannah Lingle in Birmingham angrily denied any knowledge of the ContaXX network, or computer networks, or computers, or even her handle, though the latter, Juggz40DD, seemed a pretty close fit. In Beverly Hills, Adam Zentz peered at us through the peephole in his apartment door and, upon hearing mention of his alias, ToesLover, turned on a tape of an angry dog barking and shouted that he was calling the police.

Next destination was an address in Lathrup Village, a town of subdivisions built around gentle green wooded slopes and crisscrossed by five-lane highways. The street we wanted was called Hickory Landing, in a subdivision called Walnut Knolls at Sandy Creek, and the individual we sought was named Alex Capitani, known to his on-line friends as HardRodd10.

"Gosh," Barb said dryly, "wonder what the 'ten' is supposed to signify?"

"Signifies the man's a midget," I answered.

"You wish!"

"You just don't remember," I told her. "You were having booze blackouts in those days, you told me so. Besides, you were in such ecstasy, such sexual rapture from the way I was playin' you like a violin—"

She couldn't help laughing. "A ten I'd remember," she said, "no matter how drunk I was. What else do we know about this guy?"

"Terminated ID," I noted, checking my list as we rolled along the gently curving street.

"Hm," Barb said. "Could be interesting."

"Could also mean nothing. Remember Shadwbabe, down in Allen Park? Her ID was terminated too."

"Here it is, here it is."

I swerved left and into an asphalt drive and parked behind a champagne-colored Ford Escort SHO. The house was a brick flat-roofed fifties relic, well maintained, with slotlike windows peering over high hedges at the painted-on, putting-green lawn. It was the height of the afternoon now and the sun blazed down at us—July intensity in June—as we strolled along the intermittent patio-stone walk to the front door. I knocked and we waited, entertained only by the throaty drone of a central air unit, part of a chorus of hundreds of others in the neighborhood.

The door opened to reveal a very young woman, sixteen or seventeen tops, blond and detached and wearing red shorts and tank top. "Yes?" she asked, ready to close the door again, and quickly.

"Alex Capitani, please," I said.

She rolled her eyes, turned, and yelled, "Mom!" And disappeared into the house, leaving the open door to pour cold air out at us.

"Mom?" Barb echoed softly.

Presently another woman bustled to the door. She was short and blond also, an older rendition of the original, except rounder and softer and wearing a large chin dimple. "Yes?" she asked, looking harassed.

I smiled my best. "Alex Capitani," I requested.

"He's deceased," she said, businesslike. "How can I help you?"

"He's dead?" Barb blurted.

"Deceased, dead." The woman huffed. "Expired, *morte*, out of the picture, pushing up daisies, bit the big one, whatever. Okay?"

"Sorry," Barb said, though the woman obviously wasn't.

"What did you want Alex for?" she asked me.

"Are you his wife?"

"No," she said, exasperated. "His widow."

"Well, right. I'm, uh—"

"If he owed you money," she said, "you'll just have to get in line."

"It's not about money. I—"

"Whatever scam he was into with you," she charged on, "I had nothing to do with it. I never knew what the little sneak was up to." She was gradually closing the door. "You got a problem with that, call my lawyer. Harvey Laitch in Southfield."

"This is about the computer network he was on," I jumped in.

"The what?" she said, blinking, as the door eased open again.

"ContaXX," Barb said.

"Computer network," I added quickly.

The widow was giving me a fixed stare. Behind her, I saw the younger one hovering at an archway, watching us. "Well," the widow said, "this is a new one."

"Can we talk?" I asked.

"I think we'd better," she answered.

She let us in, slammed the door, and led us past a living room into the back of the house. It was brighter back there, a country kitchen merging onto an eating area merging further onto a carpeted, beamed family room a half step down. The color scheme was glistening blues and greens, from appliances to wallpaper to flooring, and she favored porcelain engravings of farm animals, having mounted a herd of them on practically every available vertical surface. The place smelled like grilled cheese sandwiches and cigarettes. A loaded ashtray sat on the counter. Barb smiled.

I thought we'd talk in the family room, but the woman led us to the big blond wood table in the eating area and took a seat with her back to the bay window. "Sit," she invited curtly. "I'm Stephanie Crocker, by the way. You're—?"

"Ben Perkins," I said. "Barb Paley. So you dropped your husband's last name, huh?"

Crocker wore a light sleeveless blouse over faded jeans and had a red bandanna on her hair. I had the sense that we'd interrupted her in the midst of scrubbing a bathtub or something. As we sat, she slipped a cigarette out of her shirt pocket and lighted it with a brisk snap of a tiny butane lighter. Barb, beaming, lighted up one for herself. I held off and took a chair at the head of the table, placing Barb between me and Crocker.

"I never took Alex's name." The widow answered me. "Everyone can spell Crocker. No one can spell Capitani. Life is so much better when it's simple."

"That's right," Barb said exuberantly. "Kiss."

Crocker stared. "Beg pardon?" she asked uneasily.

"'Keep It Serenely Simple,'" Barb explained, exhaling smoke. "KISS."

I caught something in the corner of my eye: the daughter, if that's who she was, at the archway to the dining room. When I turned to see, she was gone.

"Tell me about this computer network," Crocker said.

"Well," I said easily, "first I'd like to hear what happened to Alex. Fair trade?"

Outwardly, Crocker looked like the soft, vulnerable, quiet mouse type. But something about the way she sat—tense and wary—told me this was a hardened person, not to be trifled with. Maybe she'd been soft and vulnerable once and ended up paying dearly for it. There was real emotion just barely hidden behind her placid blue eyes: bitterness, maybe; anger, probably. Sure as hell wasn't grief.

"Alex," she said matter-of-factly, "died in an accident. A very—bizarre—accident."

"Oh," Barb said softly. "I'm sorry, hon."

The women locked looks. "Don't be," Crocker said.

Already I knew, was certain: bing-*go*. Though I suddenly felt like I didn't have enough air in my lungs, I stayed calm and bland till the spell of inner elation passed. I did have the fleeting thought that detective work wasn't all brains and persistence and muscle. You needed a special instinct too. Something had made me press on with this.

"—you and your daughter," Barb was saying.

"Not at all," Crocker said stiffly. "The only regret I had was that I didn't kick him out months ago. Years ago. This was just the final episode in a long miserable story for us." She looked at me. "Now, what's this about a computer network?"

Cigar time. I flamed and puffed. "Your husband had a computer, right?"

She turned and unlatched a window and notched it. "Yes, of course. He was a salesman, he worked out of his office downstairs."

"Could we see it, please?"

"Nothing to see," she answered. "I got rid of it all."

Well, well, I thought. Not keeping the office as a shrine for old Alex, huh? "He belonged to an on-line computer network called ContaXX," I told her. "Double X," I added.

She nodded slowly. "Computer porn?"

"Yup."

"Figures," she said sourly. "When it came to filth, the man was positively ingenious."

"One of the clubs on there was called Pictures of Wives and Girlfriends," I said. "These people came on and traded and—"

She laughed humorlessly. "I guaran-damn-tee you, he never traded any pictures of me! Even if I was that kind of degenerate, who'd want to look at a fat falling fortyish frump like me?" She straightened suddenly and shot a look past Barb into the kitchen. "Faith!" she called sharply. "This is private business. Go to your room."

Barb looked at me. I shook my head slightly. "One of the people your husband traded with," I told Crocker, "was found dead a few weeks ago. His death was a—uh, very bizarre accident too."

"Oh," she said quickly, "Alex's definitely *was* accidental."

"I didn't suggest it wasn't," I said.

She tapped her cigarette ash against the rim of the ashtray, about twelve times too many. "You think . . . this other person . . . that perhaps it wasn't an accident?"

"I don't think," I answered. "I check and see. That's why we're here. It looked like an accident. Or was made to look like one. Could have not been, though. We're checking out the people my victim traded with on the ContaXX network."

"What a nice way to spend the day," Crocker said dryly.

"Up till now," Barb told her, "they've all been alive, mostly."

"And now," I added smoothly, "we'd appreciate it if you'd tell us about your husband's death, Ms. Crocker."

"You can tell us," Barb said gently. "It's just information we want."

Crocker shook her head just slightly. "It's so hard," she said, voice constricted.

"You were the one who found him?" I asked.

She nodded and looked down.

Barb reached over and patted Crocker's forearm. Crocker did not react. Remembering how she'd talked about her husband, I had a hard time buying the act. But maybe it wasn't an act. Love/hate is often a package deal. I asked quietly, "How did it happen?"

She looked at me, eyes narrow and fierce, and hissed through her locked jaw, "He strangled himself, all right? He strangled himself. That's all there was to it. The police called it open-and-shut accidental, and that's good enough for me. Now I'd like you to leave."

Neither Barb nor I stirred. "This is important," I said gently. "Exactly how did he—uh, 'strangle' himself?"

"I don't want to talk about it."

"Ben," Barb said.

I held up a hand. "Then let me tell you, all right? I'll tell you just how it was, and you tell me if I'm right."

The woman did not react. Barb gave me a pleading look, but she knew it was hopeless. I said, "He was on his back. Mostly naked. There was a rope or strap secured to his ankles and around his neck." Crocker's face had eased into her hands. "And," I went on, feeling reckless, "the only thing that puzzled the police was that there was no pornography in view. Right, Ms. Crocker?"

She dropped her hands. "Wrong," she said hoarsely.

Silence.

"There were dirty pictures," she added, and burst into tears.

NINETEEN

"Sick stuff," Barb said as I started the Mustang.

"Yep." I wheeled us away from the Capitani house.

Barb shifted on her seat and faced me, red hair fluttering in the warm slipstream around the open convertible. "I saw the look on your face, hon," she said.

"You saw nothin'," I answered. "I was the great stone face."

"Not to me," she countered. "To me you're an open book. You think we're on to something, don't you."

"Don't you?"

"Mm-hm. When I give it the Ben Perkins smell test," Barb said, "I get a strong whiff of something not right."

"Tell me," I invited, and with a punch on the accelerator flung the car out onto Southfield Road.

Barb hung on silently until we'd steadied into the traffic. "Well, hey. Two members of this ContaXX network, chatted, swapped dirty pictures, right? Both end up dead in almost identical strangulation accidents."

"Accidental autoerotic asphyxiation, is what Elvin Dance called it," I said. "He'd seen it before."

"Elvin's seen everything before," she observed.

"Got that right."

We motored along the endless car-packed avenue of office buildings and strip malls.

"But doesn't it strike you as a mighty big coincidence that it happened to Cloyd *and* to Capitani?" Barb asked. "Within days of each other. Almost exactly the same."

"Sure it does. Too big a coincidence."

"So somebody killed them?"

"Could have."

"Ha-ha," Barb said grimly. "I knew it."

"There's some vague similarities beyond the sex angle," I said. "Alex was alone in the house. Chris was alone in his office. No sign of forced entry in either place. Biggest difference is the porn. Alex had it, Chris didn't."

"What do you make of that?"

I shrugged. "Alex had some laying around, so the perp used it," I said. "Chris didn't. Could be as simple an explanation as that."

We were quiet for a bit, headed west by now on 11 Mile Road, almost to Northwestern Highway. As I propelled us onto the expressway, Barb said, "Sounds like this perp, if that's what we have here, went to a lot of trouble."

"Sounds also like he—"

"Or she."

"—is a solid professional at this kind of thing. Getting in and out of the Capitani house wasn't that big a deal, but penetrating the David Whitney Building and getting out unseen took some doing."

"There's one thing I don't understand," Barb commented.

"Only one? For me there's a bunch. But there's one great big one," I said.

"Uh-huh." Barb nodded. "Why."

"Why," I agreed.

"Why kill them?"

The afternoon pushed on, and so did we. Barb seemed to be tiring, but the Capitani business had charged me up. We were on to something, I was sure of it, and I was sure, also, that there was more to be learned from the rest of the people on Cloyd's pen pal list.

Which meant, almost predictably, that we bombed out with the next few. In West Bloomfield, DoriL had moved away and left no forwarding address. The man who answered the door at RamJam's apartment in Novi seemed unduly suspicious and told us the man we wanted to see was away and would not be back any time soon. We actually laid eyes on Moana, whom we found playing Frisbee with a man on a country road in Canton Township, but she gave us the same denial routine we'd heard from several of the others.

Well, at least they were alive, as far as we could tell, which set them apart from Capitani and Brody.

Fourteen down, one to go: Linda Steckroth, alias BiJudy, at an address on Plymouth Road in Livonia. We got there about four to find that the address was a trailer park along a commercial/industrial strip in the eastern end of town. The park, called Imagine Acres, looked depressing. Faded tin trailers of 1960s vintage and indeterminate colors were jammed together on cinderblock footers along gravel lanes in a grim treeless sprawl that seemed to go on forever. Jammed in among the trailers were tiny tin utility sheds, parked cars, barbecue grills, storage items under tied-down tarpaulins, and motorcycles. The whole thing was surrounded by various types of fence, including basket-weave, shadowbox, board-on-board, as well as section after section of that good old standby, rusted-out saggy-looking chain link. There was no residence directory, and the long row of mailboxes at the front had numbers on them instead of names. A sign on one of the trailers just inside the entrance said OFFICE. Helpful.

I found a place for the Mustang between the office trailer and the fence, and we went inside. The trailer, a bulbous silver job at least thirty years old, had no interior partitions, and the windows were shuttered tight except for the one in which hung a big air conditioner, dripping water and emitting chilly air with a loud rattling bellow. Despite its efforts, the trailer was stuffy and uncomfortable, probably from having sat in direct sunlight all day, and the two young men near the back wore nothing but dirty jeans and backward ball caps and tattoos.

They sat—maybe lounged is a better word—at either end of a small desk. Between them on the desk stood quite a few opened beer cans. Along the wall behind them was a rack of tools and several industrial steel shelving units holding what looked to my experienced professional eye like odds and ends and junk. A boom box above them blared atonal grunge rock. Closer to us was another desk, unattended, strewn and stacked with papers and a big console telephone and flanked by a typewriter stand and two low file cabinets. The desk also held a little circular bell and a note that said RING FOR SERVICE.

I looked at the two young men, who stared back at us silently. Then I hit the bell a few times and said, "Ringy-dingy."

Barb snickered. The taller of the men, a buzz-cut number with a tattoo that said LIQUOR IN THE FRONT / POKER IN THE REAR, bestirred himself. "Girl's gone for the day. Come back Monday."

They were giving Barb the old narrow-eyed once-over. I said, "How do you know I'm not one of your tenants, with something busted that needs fixing?"

"We know everybody that lives here," the other one said.

"Good," I said brightly. "We're looking for Linda Steckroth."

They looked at each other. "She ain't here," Poker said.

I waited, then made a beckoning gesture. "And?"

"And what?" asked the other.

I stepped around the desk and stopped. "And," I prompted, "where is she?"

"Moved away," Poker said.

I waited. Made the beckoning gesture. Waited again. "And?" I prompted, tone darker.

"Oh, no," Barb breathed behind me.

"And," Poker said, "she ain't here, mister. What are ya, hard of hearing?"

"Sometimes," I admitted. "I didn't catch the part where you told me where I could find her. Would you mind repeating that?"

"Please, guys," Barb said.

"Shut up, fat ass," said one.

"Would you mind getting the fuck out of here?" said the other.

I looked at them. Behind me Barb sighed. "Oh, no," she said. "Now you've done it."

As I moved toward Poker, the two men stood, bare chests tensed, arms poised. Looked to me like they wanted some sort of choreographed dance, but that was never my style. Without hesitating, I grabbed Poker under the jaw with one hand, the heel of it hard against his throat, wheeled him around, and jammed him back against the wall and held him there as his ball cap slipped off. He was so surprised he did not resist much, just stared at me, giving off the stink of sweat and beer breath.

"Now," I said, quietly, "I know it's Saturday, and it's time to knock off and kick back, and you boys've been drinking beers and are feeling a little cocky, a little belligerent. But it seems to me you need brushing up on your public relations skills. Buddy," I interrupted myself sharply with a glance over my shoulder, "if you're thinking about coming at me with a pipe wrench or something, better think again."

"I ain't doin' nothin'," came the other man's voice. "You're some kinda fuckin' maniac, you know that?"

"He gets this way sometimes," Barb said lazily. "Especially after a long frustrating day like we've had."

"Had a bad day, huh?" Poker asked me, face pale under his tan, voice constricted by the pressure of my hand against his throat.

I nodded. "Just tell us where Steckroth is and we'll be on our way."

"She had an accident," the man behind me said rapidly. "They took her back home, her dad did. I helped him load her stuff."

I let Poker go. He didn't lunge or swing, just stood there. "What kind of accident?" I asked.

"Can't talk about it," Poker answered.

"Lawyers said not to," the other said.

"We could get fired," Poker said quickly.

I turned to the other. "Where's her dad live?"

"Fox Hills," he answered. "I don't know where," he added quickly. "The girl knows."

"Girl ain't here, though," Poker said, massaging his throat.

"Girl took off early," the other said, "left us stuck here to do the work."

"Girl," Barb drawled, "probably didn't want to be alone in a trailer with a couple of half-naked guys getting shit-faced."

Poker and his partner exchanged looks. "We didn't do nothin' to her," he said.

"Nothing serious," added the other.

"Just joking around," claimed Poker, a little sheepish. "Look in the file drawer there, ma'am, there's gotta be a address where they sent the deposit money back."

Barb knelt by one of the file cabinets, opened a drawer, picked along folder tabs while we watched, extracted one. "Here we go," she told me. "And don't call me ma'am," she told Poker.

"Write it down," I answered. "Thanks, guys," I told the men. "You've been a big help."

"Any time," Poker said.

"Have a nice day," the other chimed in.

"Nice playacting, Ben," Barb told me outside as we walked toward the Mustang.

"Oh," I said. "Was that what that was?"

As I understood it, the purpose of the interstate highway system was to improve transportation and trade among cities and states. In Detroit, its effect was somewhat different. The freeways destroyed many neighborhoods, served as walls between others, and ghettoized still more; wrecked existing transportation systems; provided fast exit routes for the racist exodus that cut Detroit's population in half in just thirty years; and served as a handy site-planning guide for the creation of a seemingly endless series of new suburbs like Fox Hills. Now, don't get me wrong, I loved freeways—where else could you wind out your Mustang to 140 or 150 mph when the mood struck—but they should only have run freeways *to* big cities, not smack dab *into* them.

Fox Hills was the fruit of all this. I thought of it as a "second generation" suburb, being filled up by people from original suburbs such as Dearborn, Southfield, and Warren, which, having become too diverse for many folks, were gushing people outward as the decaying urban core expanded. Fox Hills was about thirty miles northwest of town, tapping, like an IV needle, into Interstate 96 just below the U.S. 23 interchange. It was a region of rolling wooded hills and winding country roads and even a farm or two, interrupted at odd and jarring intervals by half-occupied strip malls, gleaming office developments, new subdivisions pocked with excavations that looked like rectangular bomb craters, and large fields filled with huge red dirty dump trucks and yellow Caterpillar earthmovers—our finest technology at work, flattening forests, rerouting rivers, driving off wildlife, wiring and piping and paving, and every inch of it FOR SALE, all part of the great economic shakedown that we pretended was growth.

"So don't move out here already, Ben," Barb said crossly as I threaded the Mustang carefully through a series of orange road-construction warning barrels. "Jeez, the things you rant about sometimes."

"If the regional population was growing," I insisted, "I wouldn't piss and moan about it. But it's been stagnant for years. We just use up one area and bulldoze down some more."

"I happen to think it's pretty out here," Barb said. "But then, what do I know? I'm just a drunken slut from Taylor. Is this it, coming up?"

"I think so. Wait. Yeah." I swung the Mustang right and motored up a wide subdivision street, thick with dirt from construction traffic. Around us were new houses in various stages of construction, big high-gabled jobs with portholes and fanlights and faced with vinyl siding and weird speckled brick. The house we wanted was on the right. It looked just like the others, but, judging from its look of immaculate completion, was probably the original one in the sub. It even had a lawn, and a birdbath, and a pink porcelain pelican.

I pulled into the driveway and shut off the motor. "One more time, darlin'."

"Let's get it over with," she answered. "I'm tired, I want to go home."

The air was odoriferous with mixed scents of newly poured mortar, fertilizer, and freshly sawn lumber. I heard the distant machine-gun hammering of construction in progress, even this late on a Saturday afternoon. There was nobody to be seen, anywhere on the street or around the house. Probably nobody home, I thought grumpily, as I pressed the doorbell. That's how we'll end this, with one more—

The door opened, and a pudgy stubby man in nondescript dress beamed up at me, blinking. "Yes?"

"We're here to see Linda Steckroth," I said. "Is she in?"

His face clouded, but he said, "Where else would she be? Ha. Who're you?"

"Barb Paley," I answered, indicating her, "and Ben Perkins."

His blinking quit as his eyes widened. "Perkins?" he repeated.

"Yes," I said, puzzled at his reaction. "Can we see Linda?"

He stepped back, pulling the door farther open. "Well, I think you'd better. Ha."

"Why do you say that, sir?"

"She's been asking for you."

CHAPTER

TWENTY

"She's whuh?" I bumbled.

"Come in, come in," he urged. "Ha." We did so. He closed the door. "I'm Herb Steckroth," he piped, blinking. "I'm Linda's father. Right this way, right this way. Ha."

He led us up a big winding staircase, his carpet slippers flipping against his heels with each step. The house still smelled new, of drywall and paint and carpet, and was neutral in color if not in scent. I could hear a TV playing somewhere, and country music playing somewhere else. The stair curved left along an oaken banister and ended at a hallway that ran athwart the house. "Where did you know Linda?" he asked, leading us past a bathroom to a bedroom door.

"Well, we don't," I said. "We got her name from the computer network she was on. ContaXX."

He opened the door and blinked up at me, a confused expression on his kindly pudgy face. "What's this about, then?"

"What happened to Linda, Mr. Steckroth?" Barb asked.

He did not answer, just pushed the door open. The

bedroom was all pinks and yellows, redolent of pot-pourri and Lysol and bathed with afternoon light from the broad westerly windows. On the ornate canopy bed, under a single sheet, lay a form, a human form, a woman, youngish and dark-haired, facing away from us, motionless. Something was odd about her posture, and then I realized, as did Barb, who gasped softly, that the woman's limbs were twisted under the sheet, her whole body bent into a fetal position.

Steckroth bounced over to her. "Your friends are here, sweetheart," he said, placing a gentle hand on her forehead. He looked at us and beckoned. "Come on, come on. Ha."

"Perkins," came a voice from the bed, low, raspy, toneless.

We went to the foot of the bed. Linda Steckroth was skin and bones under that sheet, her black hair choppy and short as if amateurishly cut, probably by the kindly beaming man who was caressing her shoulder and smiling down at her. Her dark eyes were huge in her thin tight waxen face, fixed on nothing and hardly blinking. Her lips looked swollen and dry, and as I watched her I realized she wasn't entirely motionless; every now and then just the slightest shudder went over her entire body, as if there were a short circuit sizzling somewhere inside her.

"Perkins," she droned again, and shuddered.

Her father looked at me expectantly. I glanced at Barb, who was pale and grim. "Yes," I said down at Linda, then looked at her father. "Man. This I don't get. Not at all."

"Why is she saying your name over and over?" Barb asked.

"Did you work with Linda or something?" her father asked.

I faced him. "Sir, I never met her before in my life."

He blinked and grimaced. "But she's saying your name, you see," he pointed out in his high breathless voice. "Your name, over and over. Ha."

"Doesn't make sense," I answered.

"Perkins," the woman droned, and shuddered.

"Of course," Barb pointed out, "Perkins is a reasonably common name."

"That's right. Her sayin' it has nothing to do with me, Mr. Steckroth," I told him.

"I see," he murmured, crestfallen.

"What happened to her, sir?" I asked. "We were told she had an accident."

"Oh, no accident," he answered, jowls jiggling as he shook his head. "No accident at all. Ha. Let's go downstairs, why don't we. You tell me and I'll tell you."

We left the room. On the way down, Steckroth explained that nurses came to care for his daughter for one shift each day, and he looked after her the rest of the time. The doctors had told him her condition was deteriorating, and that sooner or later she would probably contract pneumonia and die, but he did not believe it, not for a second. "I'm gonna make her better," he vowed. "She'll turn around, and recover, and walk out of here. Ha. I even kept that mobile home of hers, still paying rent on it, kept it just the way she left it, so it'll be all ready for her."

We were walking through a stunning kitchen, all white and stainless steel. The whole house was absolutely immaculate, but I had the sense that this gentle, easygoing man had little to do with that. "Lovely place," Barb said as we went through a window wall and out onto the deck.

"We love it out here," he answered, beaming, blinking, nodding. "So quiet and peaceful. I took early retirement out of Chrysler's, when Linda got sick, so I could take care of her." He dropped into a wicker chair, his carpet slippers barely reaching the deck. "Don't say anything to Alice about Linda's trailer," he said, showing us his palms. "Ha. She don't know about that. She's upset enough about all the expense."

"Alice?" I asked politely.

"Your wife?" Barb inquired, seating herself on another wicker chair facing Steckroth.

He glanced toward the house. "She's at Bordine's right now," he said, voice low. "When she comes back, don't let on this is about Linda, okay?"

"Sure." I leaned against the deck rail. The back yard was deep green, each blade of grass perfect, running down a gentle slope to virgin woods that rose like a green-on-black curtain, blotting out a great deal of the late afternoon sky. The construction noise was almost imperceptible back there. Steckroth's jovial, good-living face had gone a bit cloudy, I figured at the thought of his wife. "Tell us about Linda," I suggested.

"I'll tell," he said, blinking. "But first you, okay? Ha. Please?"

"Okay. First off, I'm a private detective."

"And I help him out," Barb added.

"Okay, okay," Steckroth wheezed. "What about Linda?"

Oh, boy. How could I do this? "This ContaXX network I told you about, it's a—"

"I know about networks," he cut in, nodding vigorously. "Linda told me. She had pen pals and chats."

"One of her pen pals died accidentally a few weeks ago," I told him. "We're tracking down the people he knew on line, just asking around."

"Accidentally," he echoed. He gnawed on his thumb.

"Wouldn't have had anything to do with ropes and being tied up and that, would it? Ha."

Barb threw me a look. I said, "Yessir."

He was blinking again, but this time I thought there were tears. "That was Linda too," he said. "Accidental autoerotic asphyxiation. That's what they called it."

Same as Capitani. Same as Cloyd. My heart was hammering and I could hardly breathe, so quite naturally I took out a cigar. "Okay?" I asked Steckroth, holding it up.

"Sure," he mumbled, and wiped his eyes. Barb lighted up. I stood pat, using the interval to organize my thoughts, but Barb got there before I did.

"Didn't Elvin say it's usually only men who do that?"

"He did," I answered.

"Who said that?" Steckroth asked.

"Detroit police detective, investigated the one we're on," I said. "Said he's only seen men engage in this . . . autoerotic deal with the ropes."

"I knew it," Steckroth said shakily. "I knew someone did it to her. Ha. This proves it, don't it?" he pleaded. "This proves somebody did it, did all of them."

"It's possible," I said. "Tell us about Linda. How was it she survived?"

"Pure luck," he answered. "Her cat Puffie had gotten out. Her neighbor was leaving for the early shift at Detroit Diesel; he collared Puffie and brought her to the trailer. Found Linda inside on the floor, all tied up. Ha. She'd stopped breathing." Steckroth paused and looked away, composing himself. "He did CPR. Called nine-one-one. They brought her back."

To what? I thought, unwillingly.

"The cops told us Linda tied herself up, some kind of sex thing. Did it to herself." He went on, having trouble with the words. "And it went wrong and she almost strangled. But I never believed it. Ha. I knew someone did it to her."

I believed it now, too. One accident maybe, two possibly, but three, within days? Come on.

"Alice said it was God," the father told us.

"God?" Barb asked, startled.

"God's punishment," Steckroth said. "Linda is a lesbian, you knew that."

"We gathered something to that effect," I answered. BiJudy, her handle was.

Steckroth was calm, matter-of-fact. "She's always been a rough one," he said, blinking. "Hung out with the tough girls in high school. Got into fistfights. Started living with girls when she was seventeen. Likes leather and chains. I know she's done a lot of different sex things. It's just the way she is. Alice couldn't accept it. She threw Linda out. I had to meet her on the sly. Buy her dinner and take her to parks so we could spend time together and talk. After the accident, Alice wanted to put her in a home. Said she never wanted to see Linda again. But no, I said. Ha. I'm bringing my little girl home, and I did."

Barb nodded at him and smiled. "Good for you."

Steckroth was blinking and shaking his head. "Linda can't help the way she is," he said. "I wish it was different, but I can't change her. I don't care what she does, or who she does it with. She's my little girl. I love her. Alice can say whatever she wants, but I'm going to keep Linda here, no matter what it costs. Ha. I'm going to make her better. And there's one other—"

He stopped abruptly, held up a hand. I couldn't hear anything, but then the deck door slid open and a tall gray woman in slacks and shirt appeared. I straightened from my lean as she eyed Barb and me and Steckroth, who smiled. "Hi, honey!"

"Who are these people, Herbert?" she asked, voice neutral.

He was on his feet, nodding and blinking. "They're thinking about building on that last empty lot to the north, dear," he said. "Nice young couple, see? I was telling them about the neighborhood."

"It sounds so grand," Barb said, beaming.

"Just what I always wanted," I added.

"A house of our very own," Barb said dreamily.

The woman's mouth smiled, if ever so briefly, and she threw her husband an impatient look. "Once they're gone, start the grill," she said. "We're having the Howards over."

I gathered we weren't invited.

"Sure, dear," her husband answered, nodding, "whatever you say."

She eyed us once more, cold and appraising. "Welcome to the subdivision," she said flatly. "Bring lots of money." She slid the door shut.

Barb stood. Steckroth ambled over to me. "Hooee," he whispered, blinking. "Close one."

"Pretty smooth, sir," I told him.

"I'll walk you around the side," he said in a low voice, and went down a flight of wood steps to the grass. We tagged along. Out of the corner of his mouth he said, "What I want, more than anything, is for the son of a bitch who did this to my little girl to pay. Ha. What would it take to get that done?"

"I don't know, sir," I answered. "First we have to find him."

"I'll help," he vowed. "Whatever it takes."

We were crossing the front lawn headed toward the Mustang. "'Preciate it. Listen, she had a computer, right? What happened to it?"

"I brought it back here," he replied. "Left her other

stuff in the trailer, but I was afraid the computer would get stole, so—"

"Can I borrow it for a few days?"

"Will it help?"

"I don't know," I confessed. "I'm just winging it right now."

"I understand."

We reached the Mustang. Barb went around to the passenger side. "To find out who's behind this," I told Steckroth, "I have to find the common link between your daughter and my victim. The answer might be in the computers."

"You can have it," he said.

"Thanks. I'll bring it back."

"Yes," he said, glancing back at the house. "Linda will need it when she gets better."

"Of course," Barb said.

"I'd like to take it with us, sir," I told him.

His kindly face turned furtive. "Ooh. How'm I going to work this? Ha." Alice, I thought, as Steckroth considered. "You know that little Mobil Mart at the corner, by Leander Road, where you turned off to come up here?" he asked. "Meet me there in fifteen minutes."

"You got it."

He bustled across the lawn to the house. I got in the car, cranked her, and motored us up to the Mobil Mart. I parked most visibly by the pay phones, went inside for a pair of iced teas, and gave one to Barb to drink while we waited. "Thanks, hon," she said, cracking it open. "I was just thinking about old Herb back there."

I hoisted myself up onto the passenger-side fender of the Mustang and, finally, lighted my cigar. "Yeah, he's something else, isn't he."

The warmish air had the faint odor of diesel exhaust,

and the breeze wafted through the topless Mustang, ruffling Barb's brilliant red hair. "Imagine what it would have been like," she mused, "if our fathers had accepted us the way he accepts Linda."

I snorted. "My daddy? Not in a million . . . not in a *billion* years."

"What about Rachel?" Barb asked slyly. "How do you think you'd handle it, if—"

"If she turned out to be a cigar-smokin', chain-totin', bulldyke type?" I asked.

"I know she won't," Barb said hastily. "I shouldn't have said that, I'm sorry."

"Hey, how do we know?" I countered. "I've been wondering that myself, here. Don't know how I'd handle it, frankly."

"Sure you do." At my expression she pulled an impatient face. "You'd do like Herb. You'd love her no matter what."

We drank and smoked and waited, as the cars and trucks processed endlessly in and out of the Mobil Mart gas bays. I thought about Rachel at the softball game the previous night, busy, active, vivid, involved. And I thought about Linda Steckroth, imprisoned forever in an inert body. This was the terror of parenthood, that such things could happen no matter what you did, how hard you tried, or how good and decent you were. How Steckroth handled the pain of it I could not for the life of me figure.

"Hey," I said presently. "While I'm thinking of it? I'm gonna need Dennis tomorrow, help me out with these computers."

"Sure, hon. Why not tonight? We're not busy."

"I am. Got a date," I told her, sliding off the fender.

"Oh." She sounded surprised and warmly curious. "Anyone I know?"

"Not yet."

"Mm. Secret lover, eh?"

"Not a lover."

"But soon, huh, Ben?" she asked, bemused.

I didn't answer.

"I thought maybe it was Angelina at the bar," Barb said. "Bill told me you've been flirting with her."

"My charms," I answered, "are lost on her, evidently."

"The woman's an idiot."

"Gorgeous idiot," I grumped.

"Poor Ben," she cooed. "Ten plus inches with nowhere to go."

I looked at her. "Nothing more insufferable than someone who's getting laid regular."

She laughed. "And by just one person, too!"

"Yeah," I said, laughing along. "Good old safe sex. I'm even safer, more's the pity." I looked up the road toward the mouth of the subdivision. "Where the hell is old Herb, anyway?"

We waited and watched for a bit. Barb looked tired but was smiling and content. "We did good today, you know?"

"Yeah, we're somewhere," I agreed.

"You sound doubtful."

I shrugged. "In a way, things are tougher now."

"What do you mean?"

"Before, we weren't sure Cloyd was killed. Now that it looks like he was, our job just got worse."

"Because now we've got to find the perp," she concluded.

"Not just find him. Fix him."

TWENTY-ONE

"And how, O Detective Hero, are you going to manage that?" Raeanne asked.

"Can't wait to find out myself," I admitted.

We were strolling along the sidewalk of Nona Street in Dearborn. The old-fashioned streetlights of the historic homes district had already turned on, though it was not quite dark. Despite the relentless sun, it had never gotten really hot that day, and the evening air was still and cool and fragrant from the flowers that blossomed around nearly every home in sight. After a long day in the bucket seat, followed by an exquisite char-broiled steak off Raeanne's grill, it felt good to walk, and talk, and just mosey around—"watching the lightnin' bugs," as my mother would have said.

Raeanne wore a simple white cotton tank top over gold twill walking shorts and sandals. She'd put a twinkly little earring through each pierced lobe, and had picked up some tan somewhere, and had had her smooth black hair trimmed just a tad shorter around her slender pretty face. Her walk was limby and lithe and easy, arms folded, head tipped slightly, half smiling as we talked.

"Wellll," she said presently, "if one person really killed those people for some reason, he's committed a series of virtually perfect crimes."

"True."

She looked at me. "Means he's pretty good."

"Yep."

"Better than you?"

"Lots better, probably."

"Then how will you catch him?"

"Pull some sort of fast one."

"And assuming you catch him, how will you keep from getting killed?"

"We'll see when I get there." I glanced at her. "Does it matter?" I asked playfully.

"Of course it matters," she said seriously.

"Well, I'm touched."

"You're as close to a boyfriend as I've had in a long time," she explained. "I'd hate to have to start all over."

"Don't get all mushy on me now, darlin'."

"A woman has to be practical, sooner or later," she said. "I'm thirty-one now. The young hard studs with nice firm butts don't flock around my door as they once did. So if it isn't inconvenient or anything, I'd rather you didn't get killed just yet."

"I'll keep it in mind."

She laughed. I laughed too. To our right, an elderly woman, stooped over a flower bed, straightened and looked at us. "Hello, Raeanne," she said in a quavering voice. "Who's your young friend?"

"This is Ben," Raeanne answered warmly. "How are you this evening, Mrs. Scott?"

"Fine, dear," the woman answered, bending back to her work with a hand rake.

"Know everybody on this street?" I asked.

"Practically," Raeanne said happily. "I grew up here."

The easy answer surprised me a little. Earlier, at dinner, she'd kept the conversation resolutely on me: my raising, my family, my so-called career. "In the house you're in now?"

She nodded. "I was raised by my grandparents."

We passed a colossal oak. "Oh? What happened to your folks?"

"Well," she said lightly, "they split up when I was a baby. My father was crushed in a stamping machine accident shortly after. My mother went to California to get herself reestablished. Never quite got around to coming back for me."

"Oh, jeez. I'm sorry."

"It all worked out," she said easily. "My grandparents were lovely people."

"Uh-huh."

We walked in silence for a half dozen steps. "Now I've got the house," she said finally.

"Well, it's a great neighborhood," I said stoutly. "I was here before, you know."

"Oh, really? When?"

"When I was little," I told her. "My Uncle Dan brought me here for some reason. Had friends in the neighborhood, I guess."

"Was he with Ford's?"

"Yeah, but just a foreman. These houses were all built for Ford executives, right?"

We were approaching her place now. Like the others on the street, it was a small, tidy, two-story gem, brown brick down and white siding up, with a steeply pitched roof and wide windows. Beside the front door was mounted a small black oval plaque that said FORD HISTORIC HOMES DISTRICT / 1919. "Mid-level supervisors," she answered, leading me up the steps. "I don't think any of the bigger shots lived here. Buy you a beer?"

"Sure."

We went in. The living room was to the left, and I loitered there while Raeanne went into the kitchen. The room was arranged densely with dark early American furniture—sofa, love seat, chairs—as well as floor lamps and end tables and a semicircular brick fireplace in the far wall. The mantel and tables were clustered with knickknacks and framed photos, most of them black and white, and the furniture had an elegant, preserved antiquity about it, as if Raeanne had consciously kept the place just the way her grandparents had. Her only concession to the late twentieth century was the tall oak shelving unit next to the fireplace, on which perched the requisite VCR, stereo with CD rack, Infinity speakers, and massive Sony Trinitron.

It was a nice room, quiet and comfortable. But I wasn't comfortable at all. Anything but. The woman, let's face it, intimidated me. She was such a composite of opposites: realistic and idealistic, intimate and remote, witty and serious, alluring and standoffish. I felt there was something really important going on between us, but without a reliable reading of her, I didn't know what to do. I wanted her, and I knew lots of moves, moves that had served me well, once upon a time. But things were different now. I was feeling my way along ever so slowly, almost frozen in my tracks. I felt that any move, including no move at all, could be the wrong one. That was the danger of wanting something—someone—too badly.

Gun-shy, I thought sourly. You got it broke off in you. That business with Ardyce was too recent yet—

"Here's your beer," Raeanne said, strolling in. I

took the glass of Stroh's dark—pleased anew that she'd remembered my brand—and thanked her. She went to the stereo system. "Would you like to hear my audition number?" she asked briskly.

"Love to," I said.

She cut on the stereo, and just then the phone rang in the kitchen. She ignored it. We heard her box give her spiel, and then a man's muffled, echoing voice said, "Raeanne, this is Derek at the agency. Listen, honey, I was just with the client, and they really want you for the next one. The focus group, the Q numbers—it all says you, love. They won't take no for an answer. Let's do lunch, okay? Can we talk about it? Call me, okay? Please?" *Click.*

Raeanne, clicking home the tape transport, rolled her eyes and smiled at me. "Don't you just love the sound of an ad man begging?"

"What was that about?"

"Century Carpet."

"Oh, the dumb blonde ad?"

She twiddled buttons. "Yes. Part two. I told Derek already, and I was very nice to him, but I told him I'm moving on. And I meant it. Ready?" she asked, facing me.

"Ready," I answered.

I'd thought she was going to play a tape of her song. But as the orchestral intro emerged from the big speakers, and Raeanne moved ever so slightly in time to the music, looking away, taking deep breaths, preparing herself, I realized she was going to sing it for me.

It was the love theme from the musical *Jubilee,* a slow, plaintive, romantic ballad. Like most people, I'd heard it a million times, on the radio, in the movie version, in clubs, and in elevators, even. Liza Minnelli's version was probably the most famous, but Raeanne's take was different. She put more sweetness and vulnerability into it without being at all submissive. To me, it was hypnotic, sitting there on the sofa as Raeanne sang—her voice, so much richer than you'd expect from hearing her speak; her body, long, lithe, limber, rhythmic, flowing in time to the music; her pale gray eyes casting about, beseeching her unseen audience. As the final chorus wound down with the repeated words, "Only you, you and me, eternity," I realized there was a cigar in my hand, unlighted. I did not recall taking it out. I let it drop to my lap, as the music faded away, and clapped and smiled as Raeanne gave a little bow.

When after a pause she straightened again, I could see her eyes glistening and a tear trail down her left cheek. I got to my feet. "What's the matter?"

She shook her head, still smiling, and fussed nervously with her hair. "Nothing, I just get into it, that's all. Such a beautiful number."

"No. What's beautiful, darlin', is the way you sing it."

She looked swiftly at me. "You liked it?"

I moved toward her. "I loved it," I answered. "You know something? Nobody ever sang for me before."

She smiled. "I got your virginity?"

"You blew me away," I said, very close to her now.

"Mm." Eyes on me.

"You're gonna knock 'em dead at the audition."

"Remains to be seen," she whispered.

Gently I took both of her hands, which were down at her sides, and leaned close and kissed her. There was just the barest answering pressure of her lips, cool and sweet. When I let go, her eyes were still open, and she smiled. "You're a nice man."

"And you're a nice woman," I answered, and kissed her again, just lightly. "And talented." Kiss. "And sensuous."

She laughed softly and eased herself against me and wrapped her arms around me, her hands snaking up my back, her head tucked under my chin as she gave me a long hard squeeze with the whole length of her long firm self. And then, quite definitively, she let go and stepped back. She didn't have to spell it out; she didn't have to say anything at all. I got the message. Funny thing was, I wasn't disheartened.

Well, maybe a little.

"You've had a long day," she said, "and I've got an early appointment at Producer's Color. Looping a training video—the client hated the original actor's voice. Do you mind?"

"I'm devastated," I said, smiling, and then fibbed, "but yeah, I am a bit tuckered." The clock said past ten. Later than I thought. We headed for the door, hand in hand. "Call you tomorrow?"

"I'd like that," she answered.

"Thanks for dinner."

I opened the door, turned back, and kissed her lightly. Her eyes had gone serious, and she caught my head as I started away and kissed me back, hard. Then she gave my butt a solid hand smack. "Better scoot," she whispered.

"Hey," I said impulsively, "I got an idea. Whyn't you come out tomorrow afternoon? You showed me your place, now come out and see mine."

"Okay," she said readily. "Three?"

"Three's good. 'Bye, Raeanne."

"No," she said, holding up a finger. "Not goodbye. Good night."

"Good night, Raeanne."

"Good night, Ben."

*   *   *

It was early yet, and a Saturday night, and though I was a little beat I wasn't really in the mood to go home. So I swung over to Under New Management and pushed my way inside the raucous saloon, which overflowed with chatter and laughter and the booming bass of the big juke. I waved at some people, winked at others, as I made my way to the bar and took up position at the curved end between two solitaries who sat staring unsmiling into their half-empty glasses.

Eddie Cabla, working the other end, caught sight of me and wheeled down, scowling. At the sight of him I had an attack of the guilts. "Chrissake," he screeched as he reached me, "where ya been, Perkins? You talk to your judge buddy or not?"

"Yeah, I did, Ed. I'm sorry, I've been busy."

"Well? Whuddy say?" he demanded, pulling me a mug of dark.

"He can't do nothin'," I told him. "Says DNR is a law unto itself. Said to let 'em have their way with you."

He clonked the beer down on the bar and gave it a push that slid it perfectly to me. Twenty years of practice. He leaned close to me, beady eyes crafty. "That's what he says, huh?" he groused. "Well, we'll just see about that."

I grinned down at him, getting out a cigar. "Whaddya got in mind, Ed?"

"*My* business," he answered.

"What'd you do?" I asked playfully. "Dump a dead body down there?"

He snorted and waved his hand in dismissal. "Just butt out, Perkins. I'll fix those DNR people. They ain't never digging up my driveway. Not ever."

*   *   *

I had just fetched the Sunday paper from the front door when the phone rang. Sliding into the dinette, I grabbed the phone as I snapped the front section flat on the table. "Just woke up," I said, "so take it slow."

"Ben?"

"Well, good morning, Dennis. Bright 'n' early, huh?"

"Yes," he said crisply. "I have a lot to do today. Barb said you needed help with the computer?"

"Yeah, if you could swing by."

"I'll try. I'm meeting some people in Troy for brunch." He was very businesslike, almost formal.

"Getting your business going, huh?"

"Can't tell yet," he answered.

"Well, can't expect a ton of progress overnight," I said.

"Especially in Michigan. What did you people do, sit down and plan out a system to ensure that no one in his right mind would want to start a business here?"

"Don't ask me, man. Way over my head."

He made a sound. "So what do you need on the computer?"

"Grunt work," I told him. "Need to print out all the pictures on there and all the E-mails."

"You don't need me for that. Got a pencil?"

"No," I said, turning to the counter. "Wait. . . . Okay." I flipped my little spiral pad open. "Shoot."

Slowly, laboriously, he recited several strings of Greek-like computer commands. I read them back to him to make sure they were right. "It's a batch program," he explained. "You just run that, and—"

"Just keep it simple, okay?"

"Okay. Make sure there's paper in the printer."

"Okay, all right."

"And make sure it's turned on."

"That much I understand."

"And plugged in."

"Dennis—"

"You said to keep it simple."

"Much obliged."

"Anything else?" he asked briskly.

"Yeah. Barb told you we brought that woman victim's computer here?"

"And?"

"Place is getting to be a goddamn computer lab."

"Hey, back home I've got three."

Back home? "I need that computer checked out like you did with Cloyd's. Top to bottom. Soonest."

He sighed. "Does it have to be today?"

"Yes, it has to be today. For chrissake, Dennis, I'm on to something here, and I will not lollygag around. You gonna come across for me or not?"

"Yes, of course," he said reluctantly. "Let's, uh— well, later on today, okay? Can we leave it open like that?"

I smothered my impatience as best I could. "Can you make it before three, anyhow? I've got company then."

"I'll try. Okay? I'll try."

"Okay."

"Good luck, Ben."

"You too," I answered, but he'd already hung up.

I poured myself some coffee and turned to the paper. But I found myself uninterested in the stories. The campaign of Senator Proposto had gone dullsville since Zanna Canady had quit touring with him, though the political columnists were still speculating as to how much damage their relationship might have done him. The Tigers had lost again. The Bulls had won yet another NBA championship, causing a "delirious all-night celebration" in Chicago, the type of thing the national media called a "riot" when it happened in Detroit. I turned pages and skimmed leads, fixing to quit and give up and get to work. But a picture on the inside back page caught my eye. It was a blurry shot of a young light-haired woman with a thin face and fearful eyes. She looked familiar—very familiar.

POLICE SEEK INFORMATION
ON MURDER VICTIM

MONROE—The Monroe County Sheriff's Department is appealing to the public for information on the bludgeoning death of a young Temperance woman.

Maintenance workers discovered the body of Jenny Phelan, 22, late Friday in a trash Dumpster in the Interstate 75 rest stop south of here.

The victim's last known employment was with a Temperance-based escort service. Its manager, Gary Cockrum, told police she had terminated her employment earlier in the week.

Anyone with information is urged to contact the Monroe County Sheriff's Department at once.

Jesus Christ, I thought. It was Thursday when I saw Jenny in Cockrum's office. Just a day later she was dead. Beaten to death.

I remembered her palpable fear as she talked to Cockrum. But it appeared from the notice that Cockrum was not under suspicion. Interesting.

Well, it was grim, all right. Could be Cockrum was up to his hips in it. But I had more pressing things to think about. Those hieroglyphic computer commands on the spiral pad were calling to me. So I built myself a fresh coffee and headed back to the spare room to get to work.

I was troubled. Not due to Raeanne, or the case, or

the Tigers, or the death of Jenny Phelan, or even all this computer bizz-bazz. It was Dennis. Not what he said, but the way he sounded. Couldn't pin down why, but there it was.

TWENTY-TWO

More knocking came from the door. I trotted through the kitchen. "Coming, coming," I boomed, and opened it, expecting Dennis. Instead, Carole stood there, with Rachel in arms, under the hovering shadow of Buck Longstreth. They were all in brightly colored shorts and sleeveless tops and sneakers—except for Rachel, whose feet were bare. They were also smiling. "Well hoddy," I said, surprised. "What brings y'all out here? C'mon in."

They did so, and I collected the squirming, noisy Rachel from Carole. "We were in the neighborhood," she said, "and wanted to stop by to give you something. Glad we caught you here."

"I'm working," I said, peering grinning into Rachel's dark blue eyes. "How're you, rookie?"

"Hum!" Rachel said.

"Well, hum yourself," I answered.

"Ha!" she said dismissively, and looked away.

"Working on what?" asked Longstreth, glancing with his imperious air around the living room. His brown hair was loosely ponytailed, and I noticed he had a little ring in one lobe today. Trendy.

"Just a little paperwork," I answered. Rachel's struggles were too much, so I set her on her feet by the coffee table. She let go and wobbled and sat down hard. "Hum," she said, displeased. *"Hum."*

"The word you're probably gropin' for there, little darlin', is 'shit,'" I said.

"Ben, please," Carole cautioned.

I grinned at her. "So she's not quite walking yet, huh?"

"She'll get there," Longstreth observed.

"I know," I told him. "Where's Will, by the way?"

"At a friend's. Here," Carole said, and handed me an oblong red envelope.

"What's this?" I asked.

"Open it."

I did so. It was a greeting card. The outside had a caricature of a man and baby hugging, and the inside said HAPPY FATHER'S DAY above a suspiciously adult-looking execution of Rachel's name. "Well," I said, floored. "I'll be damned. It's today, ain't it. Clean slipped my mind."

"Your first one," Carole said, smiling. "Happy Father's Day."

I gave her a quick hug as Longstreth inspected the POVERTY SUCKS poster. "Y'all want to hang around, have some lunch later?"

"Can't," Carole said. "We've got errands in Plymouth. Ready, Buck?"

"Of course, love."

Rachel was walking herself around the coffee table, humming to herself and looking up at us for our reaction. She was getting better at it, more coordinated, less prone to falling. I asked, "How 'bout leaving the rook with me, stop by for her on your way back?"

"All right," Carole said readily, then her eyes narrowed. "You have diapers, and lunch, and—"

"Oh, yeah, I got all that stuff. What do you say, rookie?"

"Hum!" Rachel announced, and whapped the table with her hands.

"See you in a while, Ben," Carole said, as I walked them to the door.

"Bye-bye," Rachel added.

When they were gone, I collared my daughter and carried her back to the spare room. Some of her toys were in a box in the closet, and I got out her cone and multicolored rubber rings and bald-headed Raggedy Ann. She sat half under the card table that held the computer system and busied herself stacking the rings on the cone as I checked the computer's progress.

This was taking forever.

I'd managed to turn the thing on okay. Hunched over the keyboard, squinting at the screen, I'd even negotiated my way to what Dennis called the "command line," really just a letter and a little sideways V mark. But then I ran into all kinds of problems entering the first command Dennis had dictated to me. The miserable machine kept saying BAD COMMAND OR FILE NAME. Reminded me of an accountant or something, same words exactly over and over, BAD COMMAND OR FILE NAME. I swore, I fumed, I threatened vivid vengeance. Then each time I realized, upon inspection, that I'd erred in some small sense: mis-typed letter, missing punctuation, some dinky who-cares shit—I mean, why should that kind of thing matter? Never seen anything so bookkeeperish and niggly and anal in my life.

Finally, on about the fourth try, instead of saying BAD COMMAND OR FILE NAME or TRY AGAIN, DUMB

SHIT or something like that, the computer seemed to hesitate, and the printer increased in volume, and the screen streaked with a series of incomprehensible sentences, and the printer began to disgorge freshly printed pages.

The first batch consisted of E-mails. Most of these were short notes from or to Chris Cloyd, discussing picture trades and describing their interests in what sounded to me like relatively businesslike and clinical terms. Most of the E-mails were sent along with picture files, which were identified by file name, so once I had everything printed out I could match pictures to E-mails and figure out who sent what to who. Never could tell, maybe an interesting pattern would emerge. Some of the correspondents were the usual suspects: Shadwbabe, Luger, Juggz40DD, Nice Ts. But there was also stuff to and from BiJudy, HardRodd10, and SherryDoes, the ones who had met with "accidents." Those I put in a separate pile.

Then I entered the command to print the picture files. That only took me three tries before I got it right. Progress. As before, the computer started to print, but each one took an eternity, with long pauses in between, as if the sick son of a bitch was ogling the pictures before printing them out for me. And I couldn't just leave the room. I had to hand-write the file name on each picture so I could match them up with the E-mails later.

Still, I had all kinds of time to horse around with Rachel. I scattered the rubber rings for her and let her hunt them down. I hid one on her, and she actually found it, after crawling inquisitively all over the room. Then, while I was taking care of one of the picture files, one of the rings disappeared. I made a great show of looking for it and found it in the same place I'd hidden the other. She thought that was hilarious. We took refreshment breaks—coffee for me, juice for her—and also to change her soaking wet diaper.

Along in there, Dick Dennehy finally returned my call. Surprisingly, he readily agreed to what I thought was a real imposing request: to check with the departments who investigated the deaths of Alex Capitani and Betty Brody and the near-death of Linda Steckroth, to see if there were any parallels, any leads, anything we could work with. I also told him about the late Jenny Phelan and asked him to see what the cops had on that. Dick said, Fine, no problem, I'll get back to you, anything else? Weird. We agreed to meet Tuesday evening at Under New Management.

Meanwhile, the printer kept printing, disgorging smut at three- or four-minute intervals. Pictures of men and women, alone and together, in twos, threes, and more, grappling and grimacing, panting and penetrating, exerting and ejaculating—everything, in fact, but enjoying. All frozen in 300-dots-per-inch images in what passed, for them, for ecstasy. The pictures had the same dulling effect on me as before.

The difference was, this time I recognized some of the participants.

"Real security you've got in this place," Raeanne said easily as I let her into the apartment.

"I haven't added you to the authorized visitor list yet," I replied, shutting the door. "Good thing, too."

She eased to me and we hugged, barely touching. "Why is that?" she asked, bemused.

"Gave me a chance to quick-pick up this place before you got here."

She looked around the living room. "It looks . . . lived in," she said charitably.

"Bah," came Rachel's loud voice from out on the deck.

Raeanne's face lighted up. "Who's that?"

"Another woman," I confessed.

"Let me see."

I led her out onto the sun-flooded deck. Raeanne wore a simple white cotton jumpsuit, the front buttoned to the V neck and all four cuffs rolled halfway up. It looked comfortably loose on her long good build and offset her light baked-in tan. She seemed fairly relaxed, considering she'd never been at my place before, and had that quiet calm air about her, confident, content. "Well," she said, peering down at Rachel, "who's this?"

Rachel sat in her high chair, her plastic juice bottle in one fist, the white tray scattered with slices of cold cuts. She stared back at Raeanne without blinking her dark blue eyes, round face a tad baffled, a tad suspicious. *"Ma*-ma," she said, and flung the plastic bottle to the deck—her way of ordering a refill.

"This is the rookie," I told Raeanne, picking up the empty. "Rookie; Raeanne. We were just eating," I added. "Get you something?"

"Iced tea?"

"Coming right up." I went to the kitchen, recharged Rachel's bottle with juice, and grabbed an iced tea and a beer as well. In the living room I replaced Zanna's *Blues Angel* with Eric Clapton's *Unplugged*. Back on the deck, Raeanne had taken a chair in the corner, facing Rachel, the two of them bathed in the brilliant afternoon sun, adult woman and baby woman sizing each other up.

"She's beautiful," Raeanne commented, thanking me as I passed out drinks. "Her name's Rachel, though, right?"

"Yep," I said, sitting down next to the baby. "Rookie is a southern nickname for Rachel."

The baby muttered something and took a long noisy drink from her up-tipped bottle, watching Raeanne.

"You're kidding, right?" Raeanne asked.

"Yeah, I made that up," I admitted. "Didn't I, rook?"

She scooped up a piece of bologna and reached it toward me. I leaned over and let her put it in my mouth. "Oh, thank you, darlin'," I said, chewing. "Mm-mm, that's good."

"Ha," Rachel said, grinning and kicking her bare feet.

"So," I asked Raeanne, snapping open my beer, "how'd your looping go this morning?"

"Long and tedious," she answered. "And tense. The studio charges triple time on Sundays and the client was frantic, trying to rush us through. I imagine you've had a more relaxing time of it."

I drank. The first one of the day, cold, delicious, wonderful. "Not really," I said. "I got the little computer monster cranking out printouts back there." Rachel was holding out another sliver of meat. I let her feed it to me and thanked her. "E-mails and crotch shots," I added. "Ton of 'em."

"Find out anything?"

I drank. "Oh, yeah. I think so."

"The link among the victims?"

"B'lieve."

She tipped her head back, watching me. "You don't look pleased. Let alone triumphant."

I shrugged. "It's butt-ugly, is what it is."

"Can I see?"

Thing was, I wasn't positive about what I'd found. Pretty sure. But it was obviously an old shot, and not all that well focused to begin with, and at 300 dots per inch it was pretty damn fuzzy. It would help to get an independent opinion. Maybe more than one. "It ain't pretty," I told her.

"I can handle it."

"'Kay. Hang tight." I went back to the spare room, collected the printout, and brought it out to Raeanne. "Brace yourself," I said, handing it to her.

"Hum," Rachel said, holding out more bologna. I bent and let her feed me and on impulse gave her a hug. She drew back and shook her head and drank some juice from her bottle.

Inside, there was a knock on the door. As I stepped back in, I glanced at Raeanne. She was studying the printout, expression empty. I opened the door and Carole came in briskly. "Hi, we've got to run," she said. "Where's Rachel?"

"Outside." We went out onto the deck. Rachel chortled at the sight of her mother, as Raeanne stood. "Where's Buck?" I asked. "Did he have to rush off and defuse a bomb or something?"

"No, he's waiting in the car." Carole smiled at Raeanne, that pasted-on remote smile she usually reserved for opposing counsel. "Hi. I'm Carole."

"I'm Raeanne," she answered warmly. "I've just been enjoying Rachel. What a sweetheart."

Carole scooped the baby out of the chair. "Just changed her a bit ago," I told Carole, "and she ate some stuff."

"Thank you," Carole said to Raeanne. "I'm sorry to rush so, but we're late picking up my son. Nice meeting you."

"Same here," Raeanne said easily.

Rachel, bouncing in Carole's arms, had that put-upon cargo look as we went to the apartment door. "You be good for Mommy now, rook," I said.

"Thanks for keeping her," Carole told me, opening the door.

"It was great," I answered.

Carole looked at me, dark eyes skeptical. Softly she said, "She's a *kid*, Ben."

The comment, and its intensity, surprised me. "She's only five years younger than you. And hey, Ms. Lolita, you're five years younger than my good buddy Buck. So what's the difference?"

"I don't have time to explain," she said huffily. She turned to go and then turned back. "This 'paperwork'—does it have to do with the Chris Cloyd death?"

"Yup."

The baby struggled in Carole's arms, all fussy-face. "Still on that," Carole observed.

"He was killed," I said simply. "Dunno who or why, but there it is."

"Ah," she said. "Your next stop is the police, I take it?"

"Haven't decided."

Rachel howled and tugged at Carole's shoulder. Standing around in one place was never her style. "Take it to the police," her mother told me. "We have a deal, remember? No murderers. No violence. No Ben passing out in the hospital with a bullet fragment in his butt, no Ben crash-landing his ultralight—"

"Going to ease it along just a bit further," I told her.

Her facade of cheer fell away. "You're impossible," she said. "Say bye-bye to Daddy, Rachel."

"Bye-bye," she said, and then, being always ready to go, turned away from me.

"Bye-bye, babe," I said, and mother and daughter left.

I went back out onto the deck. Raeanne was standing at the rail, looking at the vista of lawns that ran between two of the Norwegian Wood buildings, down to the distant shore of Ford Lake. I stood beside her and felt her eyes on me. "It's pretty here," she said.

"So what'd you think?" I asked abruptly.

"She seems very nice," Raeanne answered.

"Not about Carole. That there."

She handed me the printout face down. "I see what you mean," she said. "And I think you're right. And I understand why you're upset."

"Not upset. Not really."

She was silent and then touched my hand briefly. "Let's not let it ruin the afternoon, okay?"

I grinned at her. "Aw, hell, no. What do you feel like doing?"

"Show me around?"

"You got it."

So we took a long walk. We went down the slope to the lakeshore, where my crew had been planting trees for a new picnic area. Strolled around the perimeter of the golf course to the clubhouse and pool, then along the row of widely spaced apartment buildings all the way to the far end of the property. Along the way we encountered several of the usual suspects—Mrs. Janusevicius, the Colonel, Debra Clark, a few others—some tenants, some friends, some both. There were smiles and waves and even a few introductions, and I could tell what they were thinking: Perkins's latest.

We ended up in the back forty, the big empty field south of the complex where the ownership was threatening to add several new units. An old tin-roofed cinderblock shed stood back there, no doubt left over from whatever farm had occupied this property way back when. I had appropriated it years before for personal maintenance and storage of my ultralight airplane and Harley Sportster motorcycle. If the development plans went through, I'd be losing it, and I had no idea what I'd do with my bike and airplane and tools. I didn't mention any of that to Raeanne, just wheeled the aircraft out for her dutiful and bemused admiration. Then I handed her a helmet and we boarded the big chopped Harley Sportster and took off.

We took a long late afternoon ride on the heavy bike, along Huron River Drive through the river parklands all the way to New Boston and back. On impulse I motored us over to the Star Flite Lanes on the Interstate 94 service drive, and we managed to squeeze three games into the last hour of open bowling. Though she claimed to be rusty, Raeanne did well, averaging 140 or so. I did my 200 but I wasn't really with it. I was thinking about the case. My thoughts had drifted back along a lineup of faces from the endless day of research with Barb, and back farther yet, to the spectacles and poor complexion of Gary Cockrum, the owner of the ContaXX network. I hadn't found any direct link between him and the victims, but I had all kinds of twitchy, sweaty doubts about him. There was Jenny Phelan's death, for one thing, and the general odor of malevolence that surrounded him. I thought I should take what I knew and double back on him— good and hard—and see what his thoughts were.

As the league bowlers poured boisterously into the lanes, we ate burgers and onion rings in the snack bar and then motored back to Norwegian Wood by way of downtown Belleville. I wheeled the bike into its corner of the shed and covered it, hung up the helmets, and slid the shed door closed and locked it. Raeanne, patting her hair, smiled at me, and we started walking across the field toward the buildings. "That was fun," she said.

"You like the bike, eh?" I asked, lighting a cigar.

"I've never been on one that big," she told me. "It's just incredible, the feeling of power."

"Wait till I take you up in the airplane," I told her.

She held out her hand and I took it. "Did I upset you last night?" she asked.

"No," I said, surprised. "Why?"

She didn't answer at first. We reached the steps up the slight slope between buildings two and three. "It's just that my days of recreational sex are over."

"You don't have to explain."

"But I don't want to wreck this," she said, all in a rush.

Her honesty touched me. "Hey," I said easily, "we like each other, right?"

"Well, of course," she drawled. "What I'm talking about is larger than that. We both have uncertainties about each other."

"Oh, we do?" I inquired. "Tell me what you're uncertain of about me, darlin'."

We reached the top of the steps and turned left on the sidewalk. The sun had fallen behind the trees by the lakeshore, leaving the fronts of the apartment buildings in deep warm shadow. When Raeanne answered, she sounded guarded. "I'm not sure what you're after, a friend or a fling."

"That's a fair question," I said easily. "I've been figuring we're friends already."

"We're getting there," she said with a smile. "Now tell me what you're uncertain of about me." I didn't answer. "It's because I'm an actor, right?"

"And so good it's scary," I admitted.

She laughed. "I understand."

Something stirred in the entryway of my building up ahead, and in the dimness I saw two people, a man and woman, Dennis Squire and Barb Paley. They had been sitting on the steps and they stood as we approached. They wore matching white denim shorts and bright blue, obviously new, T-shirts. Cute.

"Man," Dennis boomed, "we'd about given up on you, Ben."

"Makes us even," I said. "You said you'd get here before three. Hey, Barb."

"Hi, hon," she said, giving Raeanne quick eyes. "The guard told us you had a guest." All at once I knew what they'd thought: that Raeanne and I were inside, probably in bed, too busy to answer the door. "I'm Barb Paley," she said to Raeanne.

I made all the introductions. Barb and Raeanne were immediately friendly, but Dennis seemed hurried and elsewhere. I got out my keys. "Why don't we go in, open a few."

"Oh, Ben," Raeanne said, "I should really get going."

"You don't have to," I said. "We can hang out awhile."

"Early wake-up call," she said. "Do you mind?"

"Whatever you say." I tossed Barb the keys. "Be up there in a mo'," I told her.

I walked with Raeanne across the parking lot toward her white Pontiac Sunbird. "Glad you came out," I said clumsily. "Enjoyed it."

"Me too." We walked in silence. "My audition's Wednesday afternoon," she said. "Want to come along?"

"Sure," I said, surprised. "What time?"

"Pick me up at four-thirty?"

"You got it."

We reached her car. She stuck her key in the door, turned, and faced me. A stray streak of sun lighted up her face and she smiled, took both my hands, tiptoed up, and kissed me lightly on the lips. "Don't be uncertain about me," she said.

"I'm not."

"This is me, really me," she said, squeezing my hands. "All me and just me. For better or worse."

"I know," I answered. I kissed her, and this time we lingered with it a bit. "How're you doing in the uncertainty department?"

"I feel better." She let go, unlocked the car, dropped in limberly.

"Well," I said, grinning, "today you explored Perkins country. Machines and tools and wheels and wings. Not to mention bowling. What you got today was a full dose of the real me, kid. For better or for worse, like you say."

"And it was fun," she agreed, pulling the door shut. "But that isn't what makes me feel better about you."

"Well, what then?" I asked playfully.

She started the engine, gunned it twice, looked directly at me. "I saw the look on your face when they took your little girl away."

TWENTY-THREE

"Same deal," Dennis announced, sitting back in his chair. "Same deal exactly."

"Same deal what?" I asked.

He tapped the monitor of Linda Steckroth's computer, which sat next to Chris Cloyd's on the card table in my spare room. Its screen showed a series of interlocking multicolored boxes, with a small hourglass symbol that I'd come to learn meant "Hold your horses." Along the bottom edged a scroll bar, signifying the progress of the program Dennis was running.

"Somebody blew away a whole bunch of stuff the last time the system was used," he told us. "I'm running the undelete program. We'll see what's there." He looked at Barb, who sat on the edge of the spare bed. "How much time do we have?"

"Few minutes yet." She looked at me. "We're hitting a meeting at six and then going to my mom's."

"Appreciate your swinging by," I answered.

We waited and watched. Dennis had had his blond hair cut and it was crisp and smooth now, all business. He seemed nervous there as he waited, brimming over with restless energy. What we now had, I thought, was the old hard-charging go-go Dennis Squire, returned from the dead. Amazing what a week off the sauce, with regular meals and the patented Barb Paley exercise program, had done for him.

Barb seemed nervous too, but in a different way. Every time we made eye contact she beamed: bright, brilliant, and, I thought, fake. Trouble in lovebird land or what? I wondered. She lighted a cigarette and broke the silence. "So that was Raeanne," she said.

"Yep."

"Interesting," Barb observed.

"By which she means, 'a knockout,'" Dennis said.

"Hey," she warned, giving him a swat.

"Pretty much a kid, too, don't you think?" I commented.

Barb looked sardonic. "No way. Gotta be thirty, anyways."

Take that, Carole, I thought.

"Okay," Dennis said, squinting at the screen as it finally went still. "What did we uncover here? We uncovered—oh yeah, same deal, Ben," he said, pointing at a column. "Bunch of E-mails and some picture files. Ton of cross-linked and stray clusters too, who the Christ knows—"

"Never mind that," I said. "Tell me about the pictures."

"Want to look at them?" he asked briskly. "I can file them off and load them on the other—"

"Just the names."

"No problem." He skittered some keys. The screen went black and then listed a whole string of file names in white, each with the now-familiar suffix CHF. I skimmed the list. Bingo. "Okay," I said. "That's all. Thanks."

The two of them looked at me quickly. "What do you mean, that's all?" Barb asked, a little hot. "Aren't you going to tell us what's going on?"

"If you want to know, sure," I said. They faced me expectantly, Barb more intent than Dennis. "Cloyd and the other dead folks, they were all exchanging these amateur porno files. Steckroth had shots of herself. She was into lesbian stuff: girl-girl, dildos, butt plugs—"

"Thanks for sharing," Barb said dryly.

"Of course," I went on, "Cloyd was sending out shots of Roulette Brooks. You both saw those the other day." I turned to Barb. "Remember Alex Capitani, HardRodd10? The guy in Lathrup?"

"With the wife and daughter," she said, nodding. "Sure."

"He was sending out pictures of his daughter," I said.

Barb winced. "That sick, dirty bastard," she muttered.

"Okay, so they're all swapping smut," Dennis said. "What's the point, Ben?"

"The point is," I said, "they're linked by another picture they all received shortly before their deaths. I matched it up by cross-referencing E-mails and the picture files. I think Capitani got it first. He sent it to Cloyd and Steckroth and God knows who else. And they were all killed because of it. That's the way it looks, anyways."

"And," Dennis said thoughtfully, "whoever did it made it look like this asphyxiation thing—"

"And wiped off the computer files too," Barb said. "Or tried to."

"That's right," I answered.

"But," Barb said uncertainly, "why would someone kill a bunch of people because of a dirty picture?"

"Depends on who the picture's of," Dennis said, nodding at me. "Right?"

"And what the person's doing," I added.

Barb, looking unwilling, said faintly, "So let's see the picture already."

"Okay. Tell me what you see here, guys." Barb stood and looked over Dennis's shoulder as I laid a printout on the table by the keyboard, the same printout I'd shown Raeanne, the one called ZANNWICH.

The Fischer Library in Belleville was practically deserted the next morning. Looked like Mondays weren't exactly high-volume days in the library business. Which was fine with me, because it meant I had my pick of the microfilm machines.

I was spinning my way through a reel of the recent *Detroit Free Press* when Edna appeared at my elbow. "And what is it you're in need of today, Ben?" she asked, peering at the screen over her heavy glasses.

"Just some news pictures, mainly," I said, turning the reel.

Edna was a sawn-off bristle-haired bundle of energy, dressed as always in deep dark colors, down to the stockings on her stick legs. I'd been a regular customer of hers for years, and though I knew I'd changed, she sure as the world hadn't. She was a compulsive helper, cross and bossy, the kind who piled your arms high with books when you asked her what time it was. "Local or national news?" she asked.

"Well, state."

"Have you checked the video file?" she asked crisply.

"What the hell is that?"

She hesitated. "Number one," she said crossly, "no profanity in the library. Number two, I'm referring to our newscast videos."

"Come on, Edna, lead me along slow."

"We have tapes of all the TV newscasts, going back to the first of the year," she told me. "Didn't you see the poster in the lobby?"

"Really?" I answered. "All of them?"

"Every single one," she said. "We subscribe to the National Media Project for the network news. Their tapes come in once a week. We tape the locals ourselves. Getting to be quite an extensive resource for us."

"Hell of a thing, for a library," I commented.

"No profanity, Ben! Please!"

"Sorry, sorry."

"And it's no longer correct to call us a library," she added. "We're a media resource center."

"And," I said wearily, "I suppose you're not a librarian anymore."

"I," she said, "am an interpretive consultant."

"I see. Well, Ms. Interpretive Consultant, would you mind showing me where this video stuff is?"

"Step this way." I gathered up some of the prints I'd zapped off the microfilm and followed her brisk stick-legged pace among the empty tables toward the front desk area. "You can even make dubs if you want," she told me.

"Dubs?"

"Copies of the videos, or selected segments. Honestly, Ben," she said, glancing at me over her glasses, "you're really behind the times, aren't you? You'd better get with it."

"I'm gittin'," I answered, "as fast as I can."

She opened a door for me. "Why, I'd wager you don't even own a computer."

"Ha. Gotcha," I said. "In point of fact, I have two."

She hit the lights and shot me a look. "Oh, bullshit."

*   *   *

The maroon-uniformed bellhop led me up to an unmarked door and tapped on it politely. "Your Honor?"

After a moment the door opened and the judge looked out at us. "Ah, yes," he said, with a quick smile as he recognized me. "Come in."

"Thanks," I said to the bellhop, who scooted back down the empty hallway toward the elevator.

I closed the door behind me. The room was small and dark and luxurious, with plush carpets and heavily upholstered furniture and the faint reflections of light off glass and chrome. Though it was deep in the heart of the Radisson Plaza in Southfield, it wasn't a hotel room per se. It was reserved as a get-ready room for speakers at functions held at the hotel. All I knew, from having called the judge's Detroit office, was that he was speaking at the noon luncheon of a group called PAPA.

"Glad you could see me, sir," I said, setting my heavily packed brown paper bag down on the dark cocktail table. "This is kinda urgent."

"I'm sure," the judge said. He was a couple of inches shorter than me, a couple of decades older than me, lean and yet jowly with fine wispy gray hair. He had the big crooked-toothy grin of the hard-charging, deal-making, rubber-chicken-eating, back-slapping old Michigan pol— had all that still, despite the dozen years he'd been on the Michigan Supreme Court. His suit was dark and tailored to a T, and he held a squat-bowled briar pipe in one hand. "You couldn't save it till poker night?"

"You get pissed off when anyone talks business on poker night," I reminded him.

"That's true," he reflected. "So how can I help you, Ben? I've got—oh, fifteen minutes till I go on."

I began digging items out of the bag. "First of all, what the hell is PAPA?"

"Polish-American Priests Association." He grinned.

"Didn't you see all the elderly fellows in black suits downstairs?"

"Scary," I admitted. The judge seated himself on the sofa facing the big Panasonic TV as I spread papers out on the table.

After lighting his pipe, he listened thoughtfully, almost distractedly, for ten minutes, as the fragrant pipe smoke swam in gentle swirls around his head. More judge now than pol, and not shocked by any of it. After all, he'd started out on Detroit Recorder's Court and had seen it all. When I was done he said, "I have several questions. Of which the least important is, What do you want from me, aside from advice?"

"Wondering if you can get me into his organization," I answered, "so I can nose around up close."

"No, I can't," he said readily. "Two reasons." He adjusted himself on the sofa. "First, I don't know anyone who could arrange such a thing. I've stayed well clear of that crowd. They're out-staters, no friends to Detroit, no friends to my friends. Plus, there is something just the tiniest bit unpleasant about their methods." He gestured at the papers. "It would seem, from what you've found, that their methods are far uglier than even I ever dreamed."

"So you buy my idea?" I asked.

He snorted. "It's flimsy conjecture, of course, standing on a foundation of total supposition. But Paul is—um . . ." He tugged at his pipe, leaked smoke. "You know," he said thoughtfully, "in the heat of the struggle, you tend not to think. When you have people who are helping you, you tend to give them free rein and not question their methods too closely. Ultimately, only results matter. Loyalty is the coin of the realm, Ben, and the more intense it is, the greater the crimes it excuses."

"You're not suggesting the big guy knows."

"Probably not. What I'm saying is, he's more than capable of creating the type of atmosphere in which these kinds of methods can be used. An atmosphere of 'whatever it takes.'" He smoked, reflecting. "In such an atmosphere, it's not hard to understand how an operative, confronted with this—threat, would take the steps you're suggesting he took." He gestured at ZANNWICH. "Would you mind turning that over?"

"Sure." I did so. "What's the other reason, sir? You said two reasons."

"I know what I said," he said dryly. "The other reason is, Why haven't you taken this to the police?"

"'Cause it's my case. I'm working it—"

He held up a lean hand. "Ben, please. There is a critical difference between this and the other cases you've handled. And you know it."

"Reckon I don't, sir."

He sighed. "In most of your other cases—the ones I'm familiar with, anyway—you came in in the middle. The crime, or whatever, was ongoing, and you had to move fast to stop it, to protect people or whatever." He smoked. "With this one, the crime is over. The perpetrator tracked down the people who got the picture, and killed them, and tried to destroy the files to cover his tracks and to keep the picture from being distributed more widely. From what you've found, he got to them before they could send it to anyone else. There is no ongoing crime here for you to stop, Ben. All that's left is to catch the perpetrator and put him behind bars. That's a job for the police. Not for you."

I had not thought of it that way. "Doesn't seem right," I said. "For me to just . . . do the grunt work and walk away."

"I know it may violate your sense of detective

ethics," the judge admitted. "But you know, things are changing. Your life is different. Maybe it's time you moved on from this sort of thing. Certainly would be better for your health."

"My health is just fine, sir," I said, lighting a cigar.

He smiled, but not with humor. "Last winter, as I recall, you got shot. And damn near froze to death, while working a case."

"A case you dragged me into, sir."

He ignored that. "This past spring you crash-landed your ultralight. And you walked away. How many of your nine lives did that one cost you? Then," he said a little louder, to override my attempted interruption, "there was the shootout with the skinheads, skinheads with Uzis. Snowmobile chase across an icy lake. The guy with the strangling wire—"

"Two different guys."

"Beg pardon?"

"Two different times that happened, the strangling wire bit, sir. Just for your information."

"This isn't funny, Ben."

"No, it's not," I said, grinning. "It's all in a day's work."

He was clearly becoming annoyed. "I must also point out that your adversary here—if in fact your theory is correct—has committed at least three murders and gotten away with them. That makes—"

"So *far* he has."

He shrugged. "This may in fact be the most lethal professional you've ever faced. Ever think of that?"

"I'll keep it in mind. Anyway, you gotta run, sir. Can I show you some video first?"

"Very well." He glanced at his watch. "I've got a minute or two more. Wouldn't do to keep the good PAPAs waiting."

I slipped the video into the VCR, turned on the equipment, and used the remote to fast-forward a little. "I know you said you don't know most of these people," I said, watching the images contort in fast-forward frenzy, "but maybe you can give me some names."

"I'll try."

I slowed the tape to normal play. The sound was turned down, which was fine; who needed to hear the blather of the local newscasters? What was important were the images on the screen, of cheering crowds and banners and balloons, speakers on podiums, arm-in-arm waves, big toothy smiles.

"I know who the big shots are," I commented. "And her too, of course. I'm wondering about the other people up there with him. Must be his staff people. I need names to go with the faces."

"I understand," the judge said, squinting at the screen. "My God, they're so young."

"Everybody's young, sir."

"It's a young person's game," he grumbled. "I'm better off out of that and on the court, I suppose." The scene shifted, to a rally at Hart Plaza downtown. The camera panned over the people on the platform, by far the best such shot I'd been able to tape off the collection at the library. I reversed the tape and then played it again, on super slow this time, almost frame by frame. "I don't know, Ben," the judge said. "Nobody there I recognize."

"How 'bout that guy down yonder?" I asked. "Between the two of them." I hit STOP. "Him. Right there."

The image, full-face, color-grainy, shivered just slightly on the big TV screen. The judge looked at it and made a dismissive noise. "No. Sorry. Don't know him."

"You're sure?" I asked.

He threw me an irritated look. "If it makes you feel better, I'd have to say he resembles someone who . . . I don't know." He fussed. "I can't recollect the name. An actor, an old-time actor, that's who he looks like."

"Yes," I said. "My thought exactly."

CHAPTER

TWENTY-FOUR

rustration.

That's what I felt, as I headed west and then south, from the Radisson in Southfield toward home in Belleville.

And not just because of the awful traffic on the Reuther. That was in its usual dreadful state: four lanes of rapid, ruthless, rolling thunder, bumper-to-bumper demolition derby under gray hazy afternoon sky. Nope, I was frustrated because, against all odds and contrary to every damn expectation, I was on to something with this Cloyd case after all. Something big and lethal that reached high and wide, something that would upset one hell of a lot of applecarts if even a hint of it got out.

And I couldn't do a damn thing with it.

The cellular squealed. I grabbed it and turned down Buddy Guy. "Yeah, yeah," I said, "I'm on my way."

"Ben?" came Barb's voice.

"Oh, hi, darlin'."

"Busy?"

"Flyin'. What's up?"

"Can we talk?"

Oh, boy. "Sure. Where are you?"

"At home, but—"

"I'll meet you there."

"How 'bout the bar?" she asked. "I'll meet you at the bar, okay?"

I was just passing the Jeffries interchange. "'Kay, see you in a bit."

I hung up. What now? I wondered. More lovelorn laments, probably. I was sure I knew where Barb and Dennis were headed, but I'd had my say and now I'd provide shoulder service and keep my opinions to myself, tough as that was to manage. It would be good, also, to run the latest on the case past her. Get her opinion. See if she could think of something—anything.

As I neared Ann Arbor Trail, I could see smoke on the southern horizon. But my mind was on other things.

Such as: How was I going to catch the guy? I had no evidence. And I had no path to him. We had two strangulations: Capitani in Lathrup Village and Cloyd in Detroit. In Detroit, at least, the cops hadn't found squat for evidence. Then there was Betty Brody in St. Clair Shores, who'd been vaporized in a whole-house holocaust. That may or may not have been the work of our little perp, too. Nice clean professional job: no traces, no handles, no clues, no nothing.

The Michigan Avenue exit approached. The smoke looked thicker to the south. One of those new places along Haggerty, I figured. Chemical joint or something. Someone flicked a match into the wrong vat, and oopsy-daisy.

This much I knew. Capitani had received the picture first. I could prove he'd sent it to Chris Cloyd and Linda Steckroth. From there on out, though, all was supposition. The killer had gotten to Capitani first, done for him, and, by searching his computer files, found out who he had sent the picture to. Then he'd gone after Cloyd and whacked him, and made a determined try on Steckroth, and walked away clean. Betty Brody may have been a victim too. But I had no way of knowing.

Bottom line: Three people had gotten the picture—and of them, two were now dead and one might as well be.

Questions, questions. First of all, who sent the picture to Capitani? Without his computer, I had no way to find out. For all I knew, whoever had sent the picture to Capitani had gotten killed too. It could be that Capitani was just one branch of a sort of family tree of killings that spread out God knew how far and wide. But without access to Capitani's computer, I'd never be able to find out.

Another question: How did the killer get the names and addresses of the victims? That was easy: through Mr. Gary Cockrum. And now that the judge had bombed out on me, Cockrum was number one on the hit parade. I had to wheel back on his ass and stick all this in his face. Despite what had happened to Jenny Phelan, I didn't think Cockrum was *the* killer. I had my usual harebrained theory about that. But Cockrum had lent a witting or unwitting hand, and now I had to lean on him and see. Run some kind of huge con past him, maybe; get him to spill.

Ecorse Road approached. The smoke billowed across the expressway like roiling black bundles of cotton, thicker and thicker as I looked west past the ramp and the trees toward the Haggerty Road intersection. Haggerty and Ecorse, where stood Under New Management—

Which, I saw as I motored up the exit ramp, was invisible now, totally shrouded in rolling black smoke underpinned by hellish yellow-red flames. I rolled the corner without stopping, my heart at a standstill in my chest. Even the sight of the smoke and the flames, and the gaggle of gawkers gathered safely on the opposite corner, and the lemon-lime Van Buren Township pumpers and rescue squad—even that didn't make what was happening real to me. What made it real was the hot acrid stench of the blaze, and the sounds of it, an atonal, arrhythmic clattering punctuated by distant muffled flat explosions, as the fire gobbled greedily at the old wood-and-block building.

There was no getting near the place, even if I'd wanted to. The fire trucks had the lot blocked off. I wheeled a sharp U and parked half over the curb on the other side of Ecorse and popped out. I could feel the heat of the fire from where I was, thirty yards away. It was through the roof, dancing hotly and hungrily the entire width and breadth of the building. Firemen stood and watched, hoses ready, but they didn't give the blaze so much as a squirt. Too far gone. They'd see to it that it didn't spread, but that was all they could do.

"Ben!" I turned to see Jimmy Joe Putnam, gaunt and hawklike in his camouflage fatigues, hobbling along the weedy shoulder toward me, long dirty brown hair dancing around his head. He looked frantic. "Do you believe this, man?" he screeched. "Do you believe this?"

"Sickening," I said. "What the hell happened?"

He leaned on the rear fender of the Mustang, watching the fire with fearful eyes. "I dunno, man. Just started burning from the back and we all bailed out. There weren't but a half dozen of us—"

"Who was on?"

"Eddie. He got us all out. He's down yonder. Jesus Christ, Ben, look at the place go, just look at her go."

I didn't look. It would go whether I watched it or not. Instead I scanned the group of gawkers a few yards down from us. There was the massive, stoical Darryl Rockecharlie, of course, and Norris Johnston, impeccably dressed as always and staring shrewd and interested at the blaze, plus a handful of others: some irregular drop-ins I barely recognized, as well as a couple of women whom I took to be residents of nearby houses, down to watch something a tad more entertaining than *Oprah*.

Plus, at the end, staring dumbly at the inferno, Mr. Eddie Cabla.

I strode down to him. "What the hell, Ed?" I greeted quietly.

His bald head was glistening with sweat, but otherwise he stood there quite composed, almost inert, still wearing his white apron, sleeves rolled up, watching his business go up in smoke. "Wires crossed or something," he said.

Several muffled explosions issued invisibly from the building, and a shower of sparks arced over the top. The gawkers gave a soft unison *aaahhhh*. "Hope everybody got out," I said.

"They're all out," he answered, and looked at me. "I tried to stop it, you know. Spritzed it with the extinguisher. But it was inside the walls already; it caught me off guard, you know—"

"I know, Ed."

He was struggling for calm. "It just moved so fast!"

The sound of the fire receded momentarily, then increased to a louder din, as if the building were inhaling and exhaling in its dying agony. I heard a distant voice and turned to see Barb Paley, getting out of her gleaming gold Taurus, parked at the corner. She took an aimless step or two, gaped at the fire, at me, and back at the fire as I walked along the shoulder over to her. "Guess we won't be drinking here today, darlin'," I told her.

She looked stunned. "What happened? Did anybody get hurt?"

"Everyone's out," I answered, putting my arm around her as we watched the fire. "Eddie thinks it was electrical."

"Son of a bitch," she said, voice low and mournful. "It's burning down! Can't they save it?"

"Aw, sweetheart, it's way too late."

She looked stricken as she watched. "All those years, Ben. Look at 'em go. All those years."

The fire was raging higher now, yellowish red and pumping up smoke, almost hot enough to singe the nearby trees. I had the sudden mental image of a human figure, perhaps more than one, staggering out of the blaze, waving and flaming and collapsing in a smoldering heap on the gravel. I hoped to hell Eddie was right about no one else being in there. I wasn't about to rush in and see. My mother died in a fire like that, and all my life I've had the same unexpressed dread as the World War I pilots: dying in flames.

"C'mon," I told Barb. "Let's run down to my place. Nothing left for us here."

She disengaged herself from my arm. "Okay, see you there." She looked at the fire one more time, then got into the Taurus and started the engine.

As she wheeled out onto southbound Haggerty, I hoofed up the shoulder past Eddie and the crowd of gawkers. My thoughts were stuck in the groove of something Barb had said all those years—all those years—all those years. I didn't look at the fire until, with a mighty thunderous crash, the roof fell in, showering sparks skyward. I didn't realize that Ed Cabla had trailed along behind me until I heard his voice, just as I reached the Mustang. I turned. "What'd you say, Ed?"

He looked furtive, darkly triumphant. "I said, at least I don't have to worry about the fuckin' DNR digging up my driveway no more."

My apartment was dark and cool, having been closed up all day. I made a pitcher of iced tea and brought a big glass to Barb (double sugar, of course), as well as a Stroh's dark beer for myself. She sat on the sofa, dressed in dark brown slacks and a pale pullover top, looking drained. "Thanks, hon," she said absently, accepting the tea. "So that's her, huh?"

She was looking at the video I'd put on. The big fifty-inch Sony showed a typical political campaign rally, held somewhere in the state; could have been Erie or Ontonagon, it didn't matter. On center stage, surrounded by supporters, was the beefy, beaming Senator Paul Proposto. Beside him, holding hands with him, waving to the crowd, was the equally beefy, bottle-blond ex–blues singer, Ms. Zanna Canady. Big floppy red hat, dark sunglasses, explosively patterned outfit.

"That's her," I answered. I showed Barb the insert from the *Blues Angel* tape: "So's that," I added. I handed her a photocopy of a front-page *Detroit News* story: "And that." Finally, the infamous printout called ZANNWICH: "This too."

On the computer screen, the picture had been a

smudgy montage of pebbly pastel colors, mostly, as you might expect, various shades of flesh. On paper, produced by the laser printer, the picture was grainy black and white. It showed Zanna Canady, a little younger, a little thinner, and much more naked. She was on her hands and knees on a small bed—a cot of some kind. She had company. At the head of the bed stood a hairy-chested man whose penis was almost entirely engorged by Canady's mouth. At the foot of the bed another muscled, hairy-chested, dark-skinned male gripped Canady's large fleshy hips and half bent over her, piercing her from behind, more than halfway coupled with her. They were damp and straining, the three of them. Zanna's ringed fingers gripped the tousled sheets, and her medium-length hair was all a-scatter, and her eyes were fixed in a wild upward stare, frozen forever in what passed for passion, posed, pathetic, at 300 dots per inch.

"Doesn't show the guys' faces," Barb said softly. "Figures."

"Uh-huh," I said, shutting off the video.

"Sick shits who like this stuff need to pretend it's them doing her." She tossed the pictures onto the coffee table, blue eyes vague, freckled face pale. "So this is the reason those people—Cloyd and them—were killed," she said flatly. "Because they got the picture and if the picture got out it would destroy Proposto's campaign."

"That's the theory." I sat down on the recliner and drank a little beer. It didn't taste like much. The bar's gone, I thought. The juke, the stools, the Foosball, the booths.

Not to mention the years.

"Could this explain why she's not with the campaign anymore?" Barb wondered.

"Might." I picked up the remote and fast-forwarded the tape. Canady's exit from Proposto's campaign, after several turbulent, gossipy, high-publicity months, had been attributed by Proposto's publicity machine to "business commitments." But it could also mean she'd been taken out of the picture—forcefully.

"So if we're right," I said, "someone with Proposto's campaign either did the killings or jobbed 'em out. Motive—to stop the spread of the picture, protect the boss, and save the election."

"They'd kill for that?" Barb murmured. "Over a picture?"

"It's not about the picture, really," I answered, watching the screen. "It's about power. Hell, darlin'—in this country, people kill for Nike Airs. Lunch money."

"Or because someone dissed 'em," she added.

"Yup." I froze the tape on the same grainy color image I'd shown the judge. "Look at this. Look like anyone familiar?"

Barb leaned forward, squinting. "Yeah," she said slowly. "Sure. The actor. What's-his-name."

"You know who," I said encouragingly.

She snapped fingers, her lethargy lightening. "The one in the baseball movie."

"The what?"

"About the—you know, hon."

"I can think of—"

"The ballplayer who has a nervous breakdown. It was my dad's favorite flick, Ben. *Fear Strikes Out*," she said excitedly.

"The actor's name?" I asked patiently. She squinted. "Think about what Steckroth told us," I prompted.

"Steckroth?" Her breath caught. "Oh," she said. "Ohhh. Sure." She looked at me with a slow sly smile. "That's pretty wild."

"Something else," I agreed. "The problem is, doing something with it."

"You'll find a way, hon." She glanced at her watch. "Shit, I better boogie." She set her glass down and stood. "Walk me out?"

"Sure."

I'd been wondering when we'd get to it. It took her till we were down the stairs and out the front door and into the breezeless, humid evening air. She took my hand as we walked across the parking lot toward her car. "We're going to California," she said quietly.

In some remote way, that possibility had occurred to me. Still, I felt like I'd taken a good hard shot, like a broadsided car. I tried not to let it show. "To visit?"

"No. To stay." She spoke softly and quickly, sounding like she'd rehearsed it all in her head. "Dennis says it's hopeless, trying to start up a business here. All his contacts are out there. Besides, he has to get his divorce going."

"He don't need you to do any of that."

"I want to be with him."

"I understand."

"Do you?"

"If it's what you want, it's what I want." I was trying, anyhow. "Anyways, it kind of fits the pattern lately."

We waited for Boonie Snead to park his van, then walked around it to Barb's gold Taurus. "What do you mean?" she asked.

"Changes. I mean, look at it all. Norwegian Wood here, you won't recognize it a year from now. The bar's gone. The hardware store up and shut down; fifteen years I've been going there. And Carole, her and Longstreth—they're fixing to get married or move in together or something. Now you and Dennis and this."

She got her keys out. "It's a big adjustment," she noted. "For everybody."

I leaned against the front fender, folded my arms, and shrugged. "Every now and then, everything goes topsy-turvy. It's like the month my daddy died, and Kennedy was killed, and I went to work for the union."

"Yes," she said seriously. "I feel that way too." She moved close to me, reached up, and gave my jaw a light tap, smiling crookedly. "But at least for me there's you. Wherever I go, whatever happens, I know you'll always be here."

"Always, darlin'. Count on it."

She smiled, unlocked the car door, and opened it. "So what are you going to do about the case?"

I snorted. "Well, here's the opinion of the nickel seats. Judge wants me to hand it over to the cops. Carole too."

"What do you want?" she asked.

"What do you think?"

She studied me. "Well, then," she said lightly, "to coin a phrase, the judge and Carole can go pound sand crossways where the sun don't shine. You do what you want."

She kissed me lightly, and dropped into her car, and drove away.

TWENTY-FIVE

The guy was having a hell of a time.

I sat in the Mustang, parked along the fence on the west side of the long, low, flat-topped ContaXX building in Temperance. Tuesday morning was well under way, and the sun hung like a big red ball in the high eastern sky. Though it was past ten already, nobody was home at the ContaXX office yet. So I waited in the car, finished the dregs of a Donut Hole jumbo coffee, and entertained myself watching the guy who was trying to back a trailer into the loading bay at the rear.

He was driving a new teal Buick Roadmaster station wagon with WANDER INDIANA plates. The trailer was a chopped-off mottled bluish green job on big high tires, looking like one of those ammo trailers from World War I. Again and again the guy tried to reverse the trailer into the bay. He'd creep backward, and the trailer would edge crooked, and he'd throw the wheel to compensate, making the thing jackknife farther and farther, to the point where I was sure he'd rip his own bumper off. My hands felt fidgety, turning an imaginary wheel, trying to help him via telepathy.

After his sixth or seventh try, I couldn't stand it anymore. I got out and walked across the gravel-strewn macadam toward the car. The guy saw me and stopped and peered out at me. I called, "Good morning! What seems to be the trouble?"

"Can't back this thing in to save my soul," he called back. "That's the trouble!"

"Allow me."

"Oh, hey," he bubbled. "Thanks, mister. I 'preciate it."

I walked around to the driver's side as he got out. He was portly and balding and triple-chinned, with a fat grinning face and beaver teeth, wearing loud red shorts and an orange tank top that jutted out from the bulge of his gut. I got into the aromatic car—leather and one of those sweet fresheners—and shifted into reverse and backed the trailer into the bay, cleanly, on the first pass. As the man opened the door for me, I shut off the engine and got out and gave him the keys. "There you go, pal. It's all in the wrists."

"Thanks," he enthused, and looked up at the loading dock, shielding his eyes from the sun. "Now where'd that kid go? Tarnation."

There was no one on the dock. The big ribbed garage door was more than halfway down, and a sign above it said DIVERSIFIED PRODUCTS INC. On the lip of the dock sat a stack of cartons, a dozen or more. "That your stuff?" I asked.

"Guess so." The man grabbed one of the cartons and hoisted it down to the pavement behind the trailer and popped open the top flaps. "Yup," he said, "this is mine. Better get loaded. I have to get back to Indy today."

"Here," I offered, and he handed me the carton. I

leveraged it over the trailer tailgate and down into the empty bed. The carton flaps were still open, and I could see that the carton was packed tight with video-cassettes in glossy, colorful, and identical sleeves. This particular title was *Crack of Dawn*.

I turned and took another carton from the man and loaded it. This was stuck shut, but on the outside were stamped the words *Bed Spread*. There were several more of the same titles, and then another one: *Amazing Grace*. "You own a video store or something?" I asked.

"Distributor," he said shortly, handing me another carton. I loaded it. His moon face was shiny with sweat, and he was short of breath as we piled the boxes in. "Thanks, pal, I 'preciate it," he puffed when we were finished.

"Yeah, sure," I said shortly.

He squeezed himself into the front seat, started the motor, and wheeled away, tires crackling on the gravel-strewn macadam. I waited till he was gone, then walked around to the front of the building.

Distributor, huh?

Several more cars had arrived and were parked in a row along the front. After stopping by the Mustang, I went inside the building and walked down that same narrow hall I'd checked out earlier. The first door on the left, A Co. Inc. , was still closed, but the ContaXX door way down on the right was open now. As I headed toward it, the significance of the first name hit me. "A Co." : Accompany.

The late Jenny Phelan, according to the newspaper article, had worked for "a Temperance-based escort service" whose manager was Gary Cockrum.

Diversified Products, in the same building, sold dirty videos in bulk to out of town distributors.

And the ContaXX computer network was a hotbed of, among other less than savory activities, swapping of pornographic pictures.

Nice place there.

"You're out of your mind," Cockrum told me, leaning back in the chair behind his desk.

"Where else could the information come from?" I retorted. "It had to be you. Only you know the real identities of those people on the network, their names and addresses. Whoever you gave them to, that's the guy who killed them. I want to know who it was, Cockrum—and right this minute."

The office was cool and quiet except for the sound of the receptionist's word processor buzzing in the outer room. Gary Cockrum wore a wilted white short-sleeve dress shirt with the collar hanging open around his skinny neck. His bare arms were corpse-white, his fingers soft and unworked. Although he blinked a lot behind his dark glasses, I got the feeling he wasn't nervous or pressured at all. He was used to being grilled, by people with a lot more on him than I had.

Still, he had invited me in to talk instead of chasing me away. Obviously, he was as curious about what I was up to as I was about him.

Cockrum did his bobbing nod, his smile weak on his badly complexioned face. "This killing idea is nutty," he informed me. "Why would someone want to kill these people?"

"Never you mind," I said. "Who'd you give the names to?"

A silence stretched. Cockrum's pale fingers drummed the desktop. Then he said, "The feds."

"The who?" I asked, surprised.

"FBI," Cockrum said. "Guy came, had handles of ContaXX members—whole ton of them. Lot more than you. I gave him the names."

"Who was he?"

"I don't recall. Not sure he said, even."

"Was he out of Detroit, or—"

"Don't remember."

"Why'd he want the names?"

"Didn't say."

"Gary," I said after a moment, "you're not being helpful."

He smiled. "I'm doing the best I can."

Yeah, sure. "Would you know him if you saw him again?"

He considered. "Possibly."

I held up my videocassette and rattled it and grinned. "Care to have a look?"

He shrugged. "If you insist."

I tossed the tape onto his desk. He fielded it and rolled himself over to the caddy under the bookshelves that held a nineteen-inch RCA and some no-name VCR. He turned everything on, started the tape, and handed me the remote. Thoughtful.

I fast-forwarded through the rally shots for what seemed like the thousandth time and coasted the thing to a crawl when it came to the pan shot along the row of people up on the platform. When I came to the man at the end, I hit FREEZE. "Him?"

Cockrum looked at the set, head bobbing, fingers drumming on the desk. He had a gift, I saw, for fogging the air with all kinds of physical tics, to make it hard to read him. "I don't know," he said.

"Look at it," I said.

Instead he looked at me. "It could be," he said, entirely serious. "But it's hard to tell, Ben. He's such a plain-looking man. Anonymous. Could be anyone."

"You can do better, pal," I said, sounding feeble even to myself.

"No, I can't," he countered readily. He gestured at the set. "Was that a Proposto rally?"

Before I could answer, the door opened behind me. The receptionist said, "Interview, Gary."

Cockrum beamed. "Well, good! Please, come in!" He gestured at me to stay seated as a young woman walked in. At least at first glance she looked young. Up closer I could see she was well into her thirties: chunky, square-faced, heavily made up, blond curls cascading over her forehead, wearing a blue skirt and white blouse and sneakers.

"Have a seat," Cockrum said. Ignoring me, the woman sat on the other chair, looking expectant. "Worked escort before?" Cockrum asked.

"Yes," she answered. "In Dayton, when I—"

Cockrum held up a hand. It occurred to me that he had never asked for her name. "You want me to get you dates," he said.

"Well, sure," she said, smiling briefly.

"Give me a blow job, then," Cockrum said.

She didn't answer. I didn't say anything either. I was gaping at him, waiting for a punch line that never came. Cockrum looked his usual mildly bemused self, half smiling, head bobbing just slightly. "I'll give you twenty," he added.

The woman just looked at him. "Thirty."

"Twenty-five."

"Okay."

I found myself standing. "This is unbelievable," I said.

Both pairs of eyes watched me indifferently. Cockrum said, "If you want one too, stick around. Otherwise, could you excuse us, please?"

I felt myself teetering on the balls of my feet, every sinew straining—arms pumped—*lunge for his throat.* But I stayed cool, sort of. "That guy on the tape contacts you again," I said, "you call me right away."

Then I grabbed the tape and slam-banged my way out.

Back at Norwegian Wood, I channeled my anger into finishing up a carpet installation so that Randy, my crew chief, could knock off for the day. Though working on my hands and knees wasn't my idea of a great time—aside from in bed, that is—I found myself rather perversely enjoying the chore. As I stretched the carpet and pounded it into the tack strips with the rubber mallet—*whoppa, whoppa, whoppa*—I imagined myself pounding Cockrum's head into a shapeless pulp. And you can just imagine what I was thinking as I trimmed the excess carpet with the razor-sharp carpet knife. . . .

I finished just in time to meet Dick Dennehy, as arranged, at Under New Management.

Or what was left of it.

The state cop was leaning against the fender of his black state-owned Dodge Diplomat sedan, jacketless and smoking, as I wheeled the Mustang into the gravel lot and halted beside him. As I got out, he spun his cigarette butt in a cartwheel into the ashen wreckage of the saloon. "Of all the gin joints in all the towns in Michigan," he said, "you had to pick a burned-down one."

"Just happened yesterday," I said shortly. "Tried to reach you to meet somewhere else, but you were—ah, unavailable."

He caught something in my tone, and his sardonic

grin vanished, leaving him looking as remote as slate. "This is all right," he said. "Won't take long. You feeling okay?"

"Little tired," I said. I hiked up onto the fender of the Mustang, facing Dick, and lighted a cigar with the flick of a kitchen match on my thumbnail. "Had a carpet job today. That's always a bitch. Before that, I was down to see your friend and mine, Mr. Gary Cockrum."

"Ah," he said easily. "Do tell."

Though twenty-four hours had passed since the bar burned down, I could swear, as I sat there, that I could still feel residual heat from the ruins. And the stench was overpowering: sodden wood ash and acrid plastic, a confluence of smells sharp enough to bring tears to your eyes if you got too close. The roof had collapsed inside, and three of the walls also, leaving only the front wall, beside where Dick and I stood, still standing. Its wood facing had burned off, leaving only smoke-blackened cinder block and a hole where the door had been, gone now except for the large ornate hinges screwed into the steel frame and hanging bare in the air. I found myself studying those useless hinges, wondering how many times over the past dozen years I'd pushed my way through there, on my way to getting entertained, or stupid, or drunk, or laid, or sometimes all of the above.

Already it felt like way back when.

As I told Dick about my meeting with Cockrum, he lighted another cigarette and half watched me, arms folded across his white shirt. "Well," he said when I was done, "that's Cockrum for you. Cock*roach*, more like."

"I mean to tell you, that bit with the woman threw me, man."

"Wouldn't of, if you'd found out what I've found out," Dick said, voice light and lethal. "I been doing some more asking around about him. Would you believe he's got no convictions?"

"None?"

"Zero. He's slipperier'n a pig in Crisco."

"Mm."

"He's been worked for all kinds of wonderful stuff," Dick said. "Soliciting for prostitution. Contributing to the delinquency. Assault, extortion, distribution of obscene materials. Never seen the inside of a courtroom. Hell, he's hardly ever been in a squad car."

"Jesus."

"Attorney general's office thought they had him on a whole flock of labor law violations," Dick told me. "Put tons of hours into it, had everything checked off. Then the lawyers met with the judge, and Cockrum snaked out by signing a consent agreement. With a specific disclaimer of responsibility. Believe that? Little worm. Feds," he charged on, voice rising as he cut me off, "worked him on an income tax beef. Worked him for six years. Ended up with nothing. Had to write him a *apology* letter, do you believe that?"

A red Chevy El Camino slowed at the Ecorse Road entrance to the saloon lot, hesitated, then sped away.

"What about that dead woman last week, Jenny Phelan down there?" I asked.

"Sheriffs got nothing on that," Dick said disgustedly.

"I saw her with him."

"Was he doing anything special at the time? Like, say, beating her up?"

"Uh, no. Just talking."

"Did he threaten her?"

I thought. "No. Not exactly."

"See?" Dick said sourly. "Clever, slippery little ass-hole. Sheriffs know he did her. I know he did her. Everybody knows, and he knows everybody knows, but he goes his merry way, giving us the finger. Like this child-porn thing we dead-ended on, he stays just clear of us, just out of reach."

"Carole told me there's hardly any laws on computer porn and stuff," I commented.

Dick snorted. "That's right. Fucking politicians, them and the judges, they just make it easy for slime-bags like Cockrum to do business. I'll tellya, Ben, I got nothing personal with this guy, but he's got my back up, big time. These guys who do crimes and skate through, working the lawyers and the judges and the cops and the system—sticking it to us and walking away laughing, change jingling in their pocket—guys like him got to pay."

"Damn right," I answered.

"He's smart and he's slick," Dick commented. "When things get too hot for him, he finds a way to cool things off. Usually by ratting out someone else. Whatever happens, you can always count on Cockrum to take the easiest possible way out."

"Gotcha," I said, thinking.

"Well, somebody's got to put a stop to him. Gotta make him pay," Dick muttered. "Gotta make him go *away*. Got any ideas, offhand?"

"I don't know," I said, sounding more tired than I felt. "Did you check up on Capitani's death, and the Brody fire, and the assault on Steckroth?"

"Yes, yes, and yes," Dick answered. "And the word is: No evidence. No witnesses. No nothing."

I'd been afraid of that.

"But I'll keep working on it," Dick went on. "Whatever you need, I'm your man."

It took a long time for that to sink in. "Meaning what, Dick?"

His smile was tight and lethal. "You're calling the shots," he said evenly. "I'll work with ya. As long as it's headed toward putting Cockrum in the deep six, I'll do whatever you want, no questions asked."

"That's right neighborly of you," I told him, not quite believing my ears.

"Besides," he said intently, "I owe you from last spring. You did CPR on my career. I haven't forgotten," he said gruffly.

"Well, forget it anyhow," I answered, looking away.

"Can't."

"Okay, Dick. Okay."

As I pulled out of the lot onto Ecorse Road, a huge red Autocar tractor pulled up to the corner from the freeway. It was hauling a long flatbed trailer with a big yellow backhoe chained to it. I saw it turn awkwardly into the Under New Management parking lot and thought, offhand, This is good. They're clearing away the wreckage already, so they can rebuild the place.

Back in the apartment, I scooped up the mail by the door and carried it into the kitchen. Fetched myself a Stroh's dark and began sorting the mail into the wastebasket. All but one thing, a postcard. Simple, white, with the postage printed on it in red, white, and blue. On the back were a few simple words, written in clear, loopy blue cursive in which I could almost feel the warmth of their writer's voice:

Hey—

I really did have fun. Thanks again for the biking and burgers and bowling and all.

—R

P.S. See you Wednesday at 4:30.

Christ, that's right, I thought. Tomorrow was her audition. I called her house but there was no answer. Still out working somewhere, I supposed.

By now it was pushing seven. Still brilliantly bright outside; we were coming up on the summer solstice, when sundown wouldn't come till past nine out in the western fringe of the Eastern time zone. I ordered myself some pizza and ate out on the deck, reading the *Free Press* that I hadn't had time for in the morning. I had the old Zanna Canady tape going on the deck, and her husky mournful voice floated out at me as I ate and drank and read, keeping an eye on the red-ball sun making its evening descent toward Ford Lake.

God, Zanna, I thought, how did you end up like this, lady?

Talk about the right to sing the blues . . .

The tape was just ending when a knocking came at the door. I opened it and Dennis Squire stood there grinning, in jeans and sneakers and red Ban-Lon shirt. "Ah, pizza!" he boomed, sniffing. "Got any left?"

"Sorry," I answered, and let him in. "What's up, pal? Where's Barb?"

"Back at the house," he said easily. "It's just—you know we're headed out west, and I wanted to pick up those utility programs I left over here. Unless you need them."

"I wouldn't know what to do with them," I said. "Go help yourself." While he went back to the spare room, I ejected Zanna, inserted Jeff Healey, and dug through the mess of tape boxes and inserts till I found Zanna's. Dennis returned, disks in hand, just as I snapped the tape into its plastic box. "So when are y'all going?" I asked.

"Thursday morning," he answered briskly, "Detroit to Salt Lake City to San Jose." He stopped and faced me, ruddy face solemn, gray eyes serious behind his glasses. "Listen, Ben, I want to thank you, man."

"For what? Forget it."

"You came through when I hit bottom," Dennis said. "You put me back on my feet. Through you I met Barb. Through her I got sober. Through sobriety I've changed my life."

"I just happened to be around," I said uncomfortably. "Glad you're back on your wheels. But Dennis, look here. I . . ."

He paused, watching me. "What, Ben?"

"Nothing."

He smiled slightly. "I'll take good care of her."

"She can take care of herself," I said evenly.

"I know," he said, just as evenly. "What I'm saying is, I'm going to spend the rest of our lives trying to be as good to her as she's been to me. I promise you that."

"You'll never make it," I said.

He stiffened and his eyes narrowed. "Meaning what?"

"You can never be as good a person as she is. Me neither."

"Got that right." He stuck out his hand and we shook. "I'll see you again before we go," he said.

"Sure. 'Night, Dennis."

"So long, Ben."

He left. I trailed over to the couch and sat down as Jeff Healey's band roared into "Change in the

Weather." So they were really going. Barb Paley and the man of her dreams, headed for California to live. I felt sour and sullen about it, and worried sick, too. But I was minding my own business, being supportive and understanding, being a good boy.

But if I was being so good, how come I felt so bad?

Sitting there, I still had Zanna's tape in my hand. I looked at the faded color insert. *Blues Angel,* Zanna Canady. The picture showed her standing in a single spotlight, head bowed, acoustic guitar dangling by an embroidered strap slung from her shoulder. I tried to square her fleshy, serious, lived-in face with the image of her servicing those two faceless men, and I could not do it.

I turned the tape over. Scanned the song titles and credits and the logo of the long-vanished record company. All familiar to me, from those years I'd owned this tape before—Christ, went back to my brief fling on the east side, Jefferson-Chalmers, the big house along the Detroit River, and Charlotte, my very first all-consuming passion. Charlotte, disappeared into God knew where, like so many others. Like maybe Barb now, too.

In the lower left-hand corner of the sleeve were the words *For Zanna Fan Club and booking information, call Deirdre Wellcome.* There was a phone number in area code 212.

I looked at it for the longest time. I thought about how Zanna had vanished from the Proposto campaign—when was that?—a couple of weeks ago now, according to the clippings. Once more I wondered where she went, and why.

And I wondered if this twenty-year-old phone number was still any good. So I picked up the phone and mashed buttons.

Of course it was no good. It didn't even ring. A computer voice cut in and informed me that the area code had changed to 718.

So I mashed once more, half expecting another computer voice.

But got ringing, this time.

CHAPTER

TWENTY-SIX

All day Wednesday I waited for the callback. Not sure it would come. Not sure what I'd do if it did—or if it didn't.

Meanwhile I worked. I put in an honest-to-God full day—pretty close, anyways—at Norwegian Wood. In my repeated absences, my boys had gotten a little flabby about things. Lost their zest for precision work and for staying on schedule. I counseled them and worked with them and, in my own quiet way, got them back on track again.

Of course my heart wasn't in it. I was distracted as hell, plagued by thoughts of the case, of the trail of dead people, of dead Jenny Phelan, of the curly-blond woman visitor I saw in the ContaXX office selling fellatio, and of Cockrum himself: bobbing and nodding and jingling the change in his pocket, giving the finger to the law. Had to make him pay, as Dick Dennehy said.

And I thought of the anonymous man in the video-tape, lurking in the shadows behind the beefy, ebullient Senator Paul Proposto. Skulking there behind the

Man, doing his dirty work. Had to make him pay too.

But first I had to catch him.

And before that I had to find out who he was. . . .

I was on my way to Raeanne's house, a little after four in the afternoon, when the cellular phone whistled. I shouldered it and answered as I played dodgem with a couple of semis on Michigan Avenue. "Yo, Ben here."

"What's this about some trouble I'm in?" came a heavy, lazy female voice, southern-slow-syrupy and suspicious.

"Who's this?" I asked, not daring to believe it.

"This is Zanna," she answered, almost toneless.

"Wow," I couldn't help saying. "It's you, huh? Oh, man. Zanna Canady. How are you?"

"What's this all about?" she drawled, with little warmth.

I slid the car to a stop at Merriman Road. "You got my message?"

"That was my sister you talked to," Canady said. "You spooked the bejesus out of her."

"I'm such a huge fan of yours," I said, trying to keep my tone relatively calm and businesslike. "I mean, seriously. Goes all the way back to *Blues Angel.*"

"That's nice to hear," she said wearily.

"All your stuff. Just never made it over the top, I guess, a damn shame, in my opinion. Could have been another Janis Joplin," I added, acutely conscious that I was gushing. Me, gushing!

"I *was* another Janis Joplin," Canady said dryly. "I was Janis before there was Janis. She used to come to my club. Borried my look, knocked down a bunch of my riffs, too. But she didn't pick up that Southern

Comfort bit from me. I wouldn't drink that sicky-sweet slop at gunpoint."

"Good for you."

"I've always been a Wild Turkey gal." She cleared her throat. "And Janis and I were different one other way. Career-wise, I made one fatal move."

"What was that?"

"I lived. Listen, mister"—she veered abruptly—"does this have something to do with the Senate campaign? You're in Michigan, right?"

"Metro Detroit."

"What's this about some sort of trouble?"

A car honked behind me. I realized the light had changed, and gunned the car ahead, shifting up as I talked. "It *is* about the campaign," I answered, "in a roundabout sort of way." Shit, I thought, how do I *do* this? "Bad trouble. Bad ugly trouble."

"Who are you?" she asked.

"Private detective, working a case."

"Is Yinger mixed up in this?"

"Who's Yinger?"

Long pause. "Never mind."

Oh, shit, losing her. "Can we talk?" I pressed.

"No."

Damn, *damn.* "Come on, Zanna," I said bravely, "you know there's something going on, I can tell."

"Oh, I know," she drawled. "At least I know a little. But if you want to talk to me, you'll have to come here. To New York."

"Why New York?" Raeanne asked as I swung the car onto the northbound Southfield Freeway entrance ramp.

"Because that's where she is," I answered.

"I gathered that," she answered. "I mean, why won't she just let you—"

"My hands."

"Your what?"

"She wants to look at my hands," I explained.

"Your hands."

"Depending on what she sees in my hands," I said, "she may or may not talk."

Raeanne considered, then took my right hand off the gearshift knob and turned it palm up. I was watching the road, roaring north, threading my way among knots of cars and trucks, as her cool fingers lightly traced the deep grooves of my palm. Then she carefully put my hand back on the shifter knob.

"She'll talk," Raeanne said confidently.

But for the rest of the drive, we didn't. Raeanne was off in her own world, no doubt getting mentally prepared for the audition. I'd heard her singing some kind of curlicue musical exercise as I pulled into her driveway. Now she was quiet and, from all appearances, relaxed sitting next to me in the bucket seat. If looks counted, I thought, the part was hers, hands down. Her short black hair made a smooth cap around her oval pretty face. She wore a little makeup, a little lip gloss, a little something around the eyes. She also wore a long sleeveless black wrap dress with a V neck, an outfit that showed off the good lines of her neck and shoulders and was just snug enough to show off the rest of her long lithe body without being obvious about it.

"Nervous?" I asked as we turned east on 8 Mile Road.

"No," she said casually.

The audition hall was on the third floor of an anonymous building near 8 Mile and Woodward. We emerged from the elevator into a dim, darkly tiled hallway lined with shuttered windows on one side and a row of long tables on the other. There were women in the hallway, lots of women, young ones—much like Raeanne in appearance and demeanor, almost eerily so. I hung back and watched, arms folded, as Raeanne waited in the line that shuffled along ever so slowly toward the last table, where sat two chopped-off gray-haired battle-axes wielding forms and pens and detachment. Beyond it was a set of wood double doors. At intervals, the auditioners went through those doors, but I never saw any of them come out.

The auditioners were quiet, each off in some remote place, looking everywhere but at each other. I was disheartened at the sight of all that competition; I'd had no idea there were this many attractive, talented, and hungry young women in the world, let alone metro Detroit.

Too bad, I thought, they all had to waste their time going up against Raeanne. . . .

As she reached the head table, one of the battle-axes looked at me. "Wait downstairs," she ordered.

"Can't I go in?" I said.

"Downstairs," she repeated.

"Go ahead, Ben," Raeanne said remotely. "It's all right."

"But—"

"I'll be down in a bit," she said, patting my arm.

I grinned crookedly. "'Kay. Good luck."

"No," she countered. "Break a leg."

"That too."

I walked along the row of hopefuls to the elevator and jiggled down to the ground floor. There was a security desk in the small lobby, with the requisite big beefy blazered security guard seated behind it, but this one was reading the paper and didn't even notice me as I walked by him and up a hall that ran deep into the building on the other side.

I found the stair door, but it was locked. Past it, beyond the bathrooms, was an elevator with a sign that said EMPLOYEES ONLY. Well, I thought, I'm an employee, so I hit the button, boarded the elevator, and rode up to the third floor.

I emerged into another dim hallway, this one windowless and deserted. A door across the way, to my left, said NO ADMITTANCE. Taking the hint, I tried the knob. Locked. However, the door was old and its hardware was older; there was considerable play in the latch and lots of room between the door and the side jamb, so I flicked open the little knife on my key ring and, with some quick wiggle-jiggle, moved the latch far enough to open the door. Didn't break anything, not even a sweat. Professional.

I found myself at the rear of a small sloping auditorium with rows of old-fashioned curve-backed wood chairs divided into two sections by a single aisle. The stage at the other end was brightly lighted and thrust into the seating area a few feet, and it was empty except for a boom box and a couple of large speakers spaced far apart. A man stood by the double doors on the far side, and a woman sat at a card table next to him, presiding over papers and cards and stuff. As my eyes adjusted to the dimness, I saw that there were two other people in the auditorium. They were seated at the aisle, about halfway up: a man and a woman.

I stayed where I was. I heard murmuring from the others; the acoustics were pretty good in there. I wondered how long I'd wait for Raeanne's turn. The double doors opened and a woman came in, a woman dressed in black: Raeanne herself.

The sight of her jolted me. Christ, I thought, those others ahead of her must have whisked through in no time. Raeanne climbed the steps briskly to the stage. Around her neck dangled a sheet of white cardboard, the size of a trunk lid, with the number 33 printed on it. She smiled out at the empty auditorium, bent to put her tape in the boom box, then stood again, waiting. There was no introduction, no parley of any kind, just the sounds of the orchestral intro of the love theme from *Jubilee* emerging from the speakers, sounding far away in the long sloping room.

Under the bright stage lights, Raeanne swayed in time to the music and right on cue began to sing, her voice rich, right in time, captivating; I thought, Keep it up, darlin', keep it up—

"Thank you!" came a loud, impassive baritone voice from the pair of watchers in the seats.

She'd gotten six words into the song, maybe seven.

The music kept playing from the speakers. Dumbstruck, I watched as Raeanne very promptly and without expression bent to the boom box and stopped the tape. Before I knew it, I was on my way down the aisle toward the judges. "What the hell!" I heard myself bellow.

The two faces turned toward me. Man and woman, both in glasses, unkempt hair, tired eyes. "Jesus Christ," the woman muttered.

"You could let her finish the damn song!" I stormed as I reached them. "How the hell can you decide in three seconds, you—"

"Miss?" the woman called up to the stage. "Could you—"

"Ben!" came Raeanne's voice.

"—sons of bitches!" I fumed, waving my arms. "I *know* great singing when I hear it, and this woman here, she's *special*, she's *priceless*, and she's worked her *ass* off!"

The man was rolling his eyes. "Get the hell out before I call security," he said dismissively.

Raeanne was beside me now. "Let's go, Ben," she said quietly. "Please."

She was pale and composed. The sign was gone and the tape was in her hand. Stopped short, I thought I could hear the echo of my ranting from the distant corners of the auditorium, and I felt foolish and embarrassed—not for me, but for Raeanne.

"Okay," I told her.

"Thank you," she said graciously to the others, and led me out a door to the right of the stage. We walked down six short flights of concrete steps to the ground floor, and out onto the Woodward Avenue sidewalk, without saying anything. I couldn't get a fix on her at all. Angry? Understanding? Indifferent?

The Mustang was backed into a slot behind the building, facing the parking lot of one of those new retro diners, all chrome and neon and Dion music blaring from speakers mounted on the outside wall to get customers into the mood as they entered. I jingled my keys as we reached the car and said, "Sorry, kid."

She looked at me as I unlocked her door, and sighed, and said, "I can't help wondering what kind of comment they're writing beside my name up there."

"I know. I was out of line." I opened the door and she got in. "I just couldn't let them do that to you."

She looked at me. "You couldn't change it, Ben, any more than I could. All you could do was make things worse."

"Yup. I screwed up."

"Yup," she said. "You sure did."

I closed her door, went around, and got in my side.

She stopped me as I put the key into the ignition. "Just wait now," she said quietly. "Wait. We need to talk about this."

I sat back and rolled my window down. Raeanne did likewise. I didn't know what to expect. For all I knew, she was about to kick my ass but good. So I was surprised when she spoke in a calm, quiet voice, half smiling as she looked at me. "I understand why you did what you did," she said. "It's the flaw most men have, only with you it's worse. When something doesn't go your way, you always have to *do* something about it."

"Oh, not always," I answered.

"Yes." She nodded. "Always. It's central to you, Ben. You feel there must be something you can do, some way to change things or fix things or whatever. And when you can't change things to be the way you want them, no matter how hard you try, you get angry. That's why you're such an angry person."

"Hey, I'm not angry, most of the time."

"Oh, for heaven's sake," she said easily, "of course you are. And I understand why. From what you told me, your father was an angry, abusive man. Your mother was caring enough, but manipulative. I suspect she was no real source of warmth for you. You went to work on the assembly line, another harsh, inhumane, regimented place. Union work, ditto."

I felt fidgety, having my whole life, my act, trotted out like that. Where I came from, you didn't waste time staring into your own navel thinking those things. I'd been exposed to a little of it with Barb, with her AA and stuff, but she was almost completely self-absorbed. This was different. This was me in the crosshairs, and it made me uneasy.

Raeanne shifted her legs under the long black dress and stared pensively at her slim hands. "And your detective work, even that's related to this," she said. "It gave you an arena in which to assert yourself, to exercise control and influence over people and events. You've been successful. But there are always limits. The trouble is, you've never accepted those limits."

"Neither have you," I pointed out. "Look how you keep flinging yourself into these tryouts and stuff, running into these goddamned brick walls."

She looked quickly at me. "But of course," she said patiently. "I'm not saying you should ever give up. You have to keep trying." She reached out and touched my arm lightly. "Don't ever change what you do. Just try to change how you think about the outcome, how you react to rejection. Get off your own back, Ben. Let things not work once in a while."

"I've tried," I answered. "It ain't easy."

"No, it's not," she said. "And I'm only . . ." She let go and looked away, out the passenger window. "It's not that I'm not upset about their rejecting me up there. Tonight I'll cry. Just like I did when I tried out for *The Music Man,* when I was twelve. And when the band I was in replaced me with another guitarist. And when my husband moved out. And when my novel was rejected and rejected and rejected."

"And when you realized your mom wasn't coming back?" I asked quietly.

"Mm." She looked at me. "When was the last time you cried, Ben?"

"Me? Ha." I stuck a fresh cigar in my teeth. "I'm a detective. We're too tough to cry."

"Ha-ha, oh my, yes," she said, smiling. "So, when?"

I flamed the cigar and puffed. "When my Uncle Dan died."

"When was that?"

It took me a minute to figure. "Four years ago."

"Long time."

"Yesterday, darlin'."

"What?"

"To me," I told her, "it seems like just yesterday he passed on."

"Oh."

It was pushing suppertime now. The retro fifties diner in front of us was filling up with people, business commuters grabbing a quick one on the way home. The spaces around the Mustang steadily emptied as workers in the buildings around us left for the day.

"There was a woman I knew," I said presently. "Met her on a case last winter. Ardyce Brown. And we got pretty close. She was—um, she ended up needing a place to stay and she was fixing to move in with me, but instead she disappeared. Just plain vanished. No word, no nothin'."

"That's pretty rotten," Raeanne said quietly.

I shrugged. "Well, like you say, I couldn't let it go. I've been stewing, no doubt about it. But you know what happened?"

"What?"

"Pretty funny." I tapped ash into the ashtray. "She called me, I don't know, back in May, five months after she dropped out of sight. Just to say hi. Told me she'd been all confused, something like, I don't know . . . didn't know what to do for sure. Instead of coming to my place, she called up a reporter we met on the case. Went and saw her. Ended up moving in with her. She's living there now, in Boston-Edison."

Raeanne made the slightest whistling sound. "What did you do?"

"Well, I said I was glad to hear she was all right. And I wished her well." I looked at Raeanne. "I accepted it okay."

She was watching me curiously. "You haven't told anyone else about this, have you."

I tapped more ash. "Who'd give a shit, stupid little romance went bad, happens all the time."

"But it's important to tell someone about things like that," she said, looking closely at me. "It's okay to tell. Anything you want. As long as it's the truth."

"Never been much good at that," I muttered.

"Because you were punished for it, I suppose," she said softly. "I won't punish you, Ben. Not ever."

I smiled at her. "And I'll try not to trip and fall into my big fat mouth on you any more. Ready to go?"

"Whatever you say."

I fired up the Mustang, put it in gear, then abruptly shut off the engine again and faced her. "How about coming along with me tomorrow?"

"Where?" she asked readily, face lighting up. "New York?"

"Yes, ma'am."

"To work on your case."

"Among other things."

"To spend the night?"

"Be the most practical."

"Together? In a hotel?"

"I'm broke," I confessed, "but I'm sure we can find an appliance box in a park somewhere."

She considered. "Oh, I'd prefer a hotel."

"I'll see what my travel agent can rustle up."

"In that case, yes."

I grinned at her.

She smiled back, reached her hands behind my head, drew me to her, and kissed me. "Yes," she whispered.

TWENTY-SEVEN

"Ladies and gentlemen," came the female voice over the loudspeakers, "as we continue the boarding process for flight eight-seven-one, nonstop service to Salt Lake City and San Jose, we're now boarding passengers holding seat assignments for all rows. Passengers holding boarding passes for flight eight-seven-one may now board at this time through gate nine."

"Better get going," Dennis said briskly.

"Already?" Barb fretted. "Oh, well," she said, giving me a sunny smile.

The concourse and gate area at Detroit Metro's north terminal were jammed with people, the usual democratic mix ranging from borderline street people up to mega-rich socialites. Most of the passengers looked like business people: sleek, graying, purposeful, well dressed, skimming the headlines of *The Wall Street Journal* or talking urgently on a pay phone with a wary eye on the gate clock.

Dennis Squire fit the profile—sober business suit, briefcase, the works—but the rest of us didn't. Barb was dressier than usual but too casual for business, wearing blue slacks and an ivory blouse and medium heels. Her round freckled face was determinedly cheery under its halo of bright red curly hair. Raeanne wore pale blue pleated jeans and a blue-and-white striped top and white walking Nikes. I was somewhere in between: black denims and gray open-collar sport shirt. Traveling clothes, right down to the black sneakers.

"When's your flight?" Barb asked me.

"Not for an hour," I answered. Dennis, boarding passes in hand, was drifting into the departure area. Raeanne busied herself with the front page of the *Free Press*. I went up to Barb and took both her hands in mine. "You all right, kid?"

"Nervous," she admitted. "Little scared."

"Of flying?"

"Of everything."

"It'll be all right."

"I know." Her smile was fixed and forced. "I'll probably come back around Labor Day to put the house on the market."

"Anything I can do, holler."

"Well, there is one thing, hon."

"Name it."

"Come to my wedding?"

"Have to," I answered. "If I don't show up, who'll put gravel in your hubcaps and catch your garter and stuff?"

She laughed, squeezed my hands, and lowered her voice. "I do love him, Ben."

That was the one thing I did not doubt. But, keeping a promise I'd made to myself, I stayed bright and upbeat. "That's good, sweetheart. Now listen to me." I stepped closer to her and we held each other's arms. "You be good out there, hear? You take good care of yourself. You need anything, you call. I'll always be here."

She flushed, and her eyes filled, but she hung on with a big smile. "I know," she managed. "I can't tell you how much that means to me. That and everything else you've done for me."

"Detroit kids," I answered.

"Fellow survivors," she said.

"And best pals always."

"Always," she echoed.

We embraced, and hugged hard, and held on.

"Come on, babe, it's time," came Dennis's voice.

"Oh," she murmured.

I gave her one last squeeze. "It's all right," I whispered, and let her go. She stepped back and wiped a tear trail and turned to Dennis, who handed her a boarding pass. "Safe trip, y'all," I said.

Raeanne joined me, and we four did the quick handshake routine, then split into pairs and began our trips to opposite coasts.

I'd never been to New York City before. The closest I'd ever been was LaGuardia Airport. That time I was alone, chasing a trunkful of cash that had been separated from a client of mine sometime before. I ended up in Poughkeepsie, New York, of all places, only to turn around and go back home.

This time I was with Raeanne, which was a lot more pleasant. It was also fortunate, because, I learned as we talked on the way over, she'd been to New York quite a few times and knew her way around. So for once I didn't have to make things up as I went along.

We landed at LaGuardia a little after eleven and took a massive, crowded Carey bus into midtown Manhattan. We moved along briskly while still out in Queens, but after emerging from the tunnel into Manhattan the congestion slowed the bus to an inch-along crawl. Hell, sidewalk pedestrians were easily outdistancing us. Finally we reached Grand Central Station, disembarked, and retrieved our overnight bags from the luggage compartment.

"Where's the hotel, now?" Raeanne asked as people churned around us on the Park Avenue sidewalk.

I checked my ticket jacket, on which I'd scribbled the information the travel agent had given me. "Eastwood Arms," I read. "Thirty-ninth between Second and Third."

"This way," she answered, and marched off with me in tow.

We walked down 42nd to Third and then south. The sheer magnitude of the city was astounding—fabulous and terrifying all at once. Down on the city floor, at the broad expansive bases of the tightly packed sooty buildings that shot all the way to the sky in dizzying ranks of anonymous windows, I felt antlike and almost helpless, borne along by the swiftly moving crowds that flowed ahead of me, a sea of bobbing heads, as far as I could see. Cars, buses, and fleets of yellow taxis shunted herky-jerky with gaseous, clamorous, and, as far as I could tell, useless aggression between—and often through—the traffic lights that blinked to their own beat in every block. Commerce thrived in the shops and stores and even on the sidewalk, where vendors sold food and drinks and magazines and leather goods and probably flesh too, if you knew what to look for. I could tell Raeanne was enjoying herself already as we walked along, pulse elevated by the insistent adrenalized aggressive activity all around us. I felt I had to ratchet myself up a notch to do business here, which was no problem. I felt wary and on guard. I also felt suddenly uncertain about being here, about seeing Zanna Canady, about the whole deal. Jesus Christ, I thought, whatever made me think I could come out here and do this?

Just a touch of stage fright, I told myself. You're off your turf, but you'll do all right.

The Eastwood Arms was an anonymous-looking thirty-story brick job occupying half a block on a street that ran one-way east. Beyond its large green entrance canopy, the lobby was tiny to the point of being closet-like, but cozily carpeted in maroon and gold and glinting with walnut and bronze. A couple was just finishing business at the check-in desk. I gave Raeanne my Visa card with the worn-flat numerals. "Mind checking us in?" I asked. "I'm gonna call our friend real quick."

"Okay," she answered, and went to the desk.

I dropped my overnight bag by a pay phone next to the restaurant entrance and dialed a number off my tattered little spiral pad. Presently it was answered by a single-syllable grunt. "Ms. Canady, please," I requested.

"She ain't here," said the toneless voice. Sounded youthful and male, but it was hard to tell.

"This is Ben Perkins," I said, "just in from Detroit. Will she be back today?"

"I don't know."

"She's expecting me," I said. "Tell her I'm in town and I'll be over in a while. Okay?"

"Whatever," the voice said, and hung up.

Raeanne had finished, and handed me a key as I led her to the elevators; 23C, the green plastic fob said. I hit the floor button and we started the ride up, overnight bags slung over our shoulders. She seemed composed, almost tranquil. Which was more than I could say for myself; all I could think about was spending the night with her. I must admit I was a bit hyped. Don't screw it up, boy, I told myself. Don't screw it up.

We emerged from the elevator. "Do you want to go

to Zanna's right away?" Raeanne asked as we walked up the hall.

"Better," I answered, checking room numbers. "She seemed interested enough yesterday, but who knows. . . . Here we go."

I slipped the key into the knob of room 23C and it opened easily. Raeanne, however, had not stopped. She moved past me and down the hall and to the door of 23B, dropped her bag, and unlocked the door with a key of her own. "Okay," she said offhandedly, "I'll meet you out here in a minute." And went into her room, alone.

Two long walks, one swaying hot jam-packed subway ride, and ninety minutes later, we walked up to the revolving brass front door of the Nordstrom Manor at 99th Street and Fifth Avenue. A middle-aged doorman stood there in a maroon uniform, bouncing slightly on the soles of his glossy black patent leather shoes. "What can I do you for?" he asked briskly.

"Ms. Canady, please," I said. "She's expecting us."

So what? his hawklike face said. "Name?"

"Perkins."

He turned slightly away from us, held open his jacket, and murmured into a microphone strapped to his shoulder, similar to the ones I'd seen beat cops wear. I didn't hear the answer, but he grunted something else, eased out of the way, and said, "See the man inside."

"Thanks." He ignored us. We thumped through the revolving door and into a small foyer, floored and walled in mottled green marble with veins of gold running through it. The front desk was made of the same material, and behind it stood another man in maroon, gray-haired but, like the sidewalk man, tough looking. "Perkins?"

"Yep."

He stepped around, wielding a handheld metal detector. "Raise your arms." I did so and he probed me all over with the wand, then did the same to Raeanne with the exact same amount of thoroughness. The thing growled a couple of times but not enough to give him pause. Then he unzipped the black leather portfolio I'd brought along, glanced incuriously at the videotape and the manila envelope, and closed it back up again. "Elevator down the hall," he said. "Fortieth floor."

"Thanks."

We went down the hall. At the other end I could see another security guy lounging on a chair near a back door. The elevator was waiting, and as we rode up I said, "Seems like a lot of security for an apartment house. That typical of New York?"

"Does seem a bit extreme," Raeanne answered. "What I'm wondering, is the security to keep bad people out—"

"—or to keep tenants in?" I finished for her.

The elevator stopped and we emerged into a hallway that dead-ended at a door ten feet up. There was no number, no markings, nothing but a little peephole. I knocked briskly. "Hello?" I called.

From inside a muffled female voice said, "Show me your hands."

I looked at Raeanne, who smiled. Held my left palm over the peephole. "Not so close!" came the voice. I pulled back. "Other one," the voice commanded. I showed it too. Long pause, then the door opened and Zanna Canady looked out at us.

She was shorter than I expected, a lot shorter, probably five three tops; a shapeless moundlike woman with weary wary watery blue eyes and a puffy, full-lipped face and very even, very white teeth. She still had that ample mop of incredibly blond hair, middle-parted and splashing down over her shoulders in brittle streaky waves. Like many heavy people, she favored loose shapeless clothes: a large white short-sleeve shirt that billowed down the front of her loose-fitting, comfortable-looking blue jeans. She'd never been pretty, really, except when she was singing. Otherwise she'd always been more the road-weary folkie type. Now, well into her fifties, she looked, to coin a term, played out.

"So you really come all the way out here," she said. Her voice was low and hoarse and very southern, but was drawling and melodic rather than brittle and twangy like the north Georgia sounds of my parents. "Who's this?"

"Raeanne," she answered, extending her slim hand, which Zanna enveloped in her broader one. "Very nice to meet you."

"You're purty," the older woman said flatly. "You a detective too?"

"Singer," Raeanne answered, offhand.

"Poor child," Zanna replied. "Come on in, y'all."

We followed her inside. "Enjoying New York?" I asked, just to break the ice.

"Enjoy?" she echoed, leading us into a bright living room. "What's to enjoy? I'm in exile here."

"How come?" I asked.

"Ah'm just bad for the sinatah's bidness, I reckon," she said, exaggerating her accent with sour amusement as she crossed the living room. "Whatcha folks drankin?"

Raeanne requested soda, I declined with thanks, and the two of us glanced at each other and around the room as Zanna fussed with glasses and fluid at a bar next to the fireplace. The room was not large, but was definitely sumptuous, with a huge, brown U-shaped sectional sofa, numerous chrome and glass tables, an easy chair or two, a colossal wide-screen TV, and honest-to-God tapestries depicting still lifes hanging on the walls. The far wall was all glass with filmy white curtains pulled back; in the center was a double door-wall leading out onto a balcony. I could see the sunny skyline of New York City beyond a large open space over what I took to be Central Park.

"Nice joint," I commented as Zanna brought Raeanne her drink.

"Huh," she answered, flopping into one of the corners of the U. On the coffee table at her feet was an array of beverage glasses, presided over by a squat bottle of brandy. "That's what he said."

"Who?" I asked, sitting at one end of the U. Raeanne took the other, across from me. I held the small portfolio in my lap, unopened, waiting for the right strategic moment.

"Sinatah Paul, when he marooned me here," Zanna answered, plentiful face crabby. "He said, 'Zanna, darling, it's a gorgeous place right off Fifth Avenue; it's owned by one of my contributors.' You know the outfit," she added. "The one that does great thangs. Such as napalm."

Raeanne, playing right into it, asked, "But why did the senator send you here?"

"The numbers," the blues singer answered. With an effort she reached the square dark brandy bottle from the table and, upending it, gulped down a swig. "The tracking numbers."

"Polls," I guessed.

She nodded and let out an alcohol-flavored sigh. "What Paul said was, at first I didn't hurt, campaigning with him. At first I got him lots of press. But then the curve started down. Said if it kep' up, he'd be in trouble by primary time. Do you believe that?"

I considered. "Do you?"

She looked at me, and in her eyes I could see considerable street sense. I could also see, beneath the streetwise bluster, that she was worried, plenty worried, and scared too. "I don't know," she said finally. "It's fishy."

"Why let him treat you this way?" Raeanne asked evenly.

"Because I love him," Zanna answered, with absolutely no warmth, then upended herself another swig and coughed. "Look at me, kids. I got no career left. Nobody wants to see a fat old blues singer. I need a straight gig, and for me Paul is it. Plus," she added, "I love him. Now," she said to me, with sudden sharpness, "what's this trouble that dragged you all the way here?"

Raeanne looked away. I wasn't about to fill Zanna in, not quite yet. I wanted to ease her toward the theory I had developed, and get her to talk without prejudicing her one way or the other. So far, it all fit, and the picture I was getting made me very uneasy. If what I suspected was true, there was a lot more to Zanna's exile than some worrisome polls. If what I suspected was true, Zanna Canady was in great big trouble.

"Why do you think the numbers story is fishy, Zanna?" I asked.

"They're watching me," she answered.

"Who?"

"People. I'm being followed wherever I go. And," she went on in a torrent, "Paul ain't come to see me. He said he would but no, not a word, nothing. He doesn't call, either. I call him, but they screen me out. Something bad is going on, something real bad. So tell me, Mr. Perkins," she said, with just the slightest shade of pleading. "Tell me everything you know."

Like hell, I thought. "All right." I unzipped the portfolio and opened the manila envelope. Raeanne, who sensed what was coming, was watching me tensely but said nothing. I slipped the printout of ZANNWICH out of the envelope and reached it, image side down, across to Zanna. She turned it over and froze. The hand holding the picture began to tremble. Her plentiful mouth went to a tight angry line and she turned the picture back over and asked, after a long inhalation, "Where'd you git this?"

"It was transmitted over a computer network," I replied.

She looked sharply at me. "Computer?"

"Yes, ma'am. Don't know how it got there, but—"

"Computer," she said murmured. "Well, I'll be damn'."

Neither of us answered. After a moment Zanna looked from me to Raeanne and back. It was hard to read her expression, but suddenly I was glad she was holding nothing sharp or blunt. "Would y'all excuse me just a minute?" she asked politely.

"Sure, we got all kinds of time," I answered.

With an effort she got up and walked heavily around the sofa and over to a door that led off the room next to the fireplace. She didn't knock, just opened it and went through and closed the door behind her.

Raeanne and I exchanged looks, and she made a silent whistle. "Where's this headed?" she asked softly.

"That's half the fun of this work," I said. "Most of the time you just can't tell."

From the next room I heard Zanna's voice. It got louder, shouting, unintelligible syllables interspersed with *asshole* and *goddamn bastard* and *son of a bitch*—

Followed by a loud hard thump, a crash of glass, and a shout.

CHAPTER

TWENTY-EIGHT

Ten seconds later I was through the door, to find Zanna Canady down on the floor, straddling the torso of a young, skinny, and completely unresisting long-haired teenager. She swayed atop him, cursing and gasping and slapping the kid's acned face, back and forth with both hands. The blues singer's fleshy face was enraged, her blond hair tossing in the air as she swung her meaty fists, the blows on the kid's face crisp and wet: *biff-baff, biff-baff.* "Zanna, for chrissake," I said as I reached her, catching an arm in mid-swing. "That's it. That's enough."

Raeanne had come in too. The kid beneath Zanna, making wild-eyed damp pleading sounds, wore jeans and a Tasmanian Devil T-shirt. Zanna tore her arm out of my grip and lurched heavily off the kid, nearly kneeing him in the groin as she did so. "Little cocksucker," she shouted down at him, lumbering to her feet, and then kicked him hard in the side.

I grabbed her by the shoulders and swung her around and away from him. "That's enough!" I said, nudging her back. "Who the hell is he, anyway?"

"My worthless goddamn son, that's who." Zanna was breathing hard from the exertion, flecks of spit showing whitely on her lips. "Fucking little sneak. He found those pictures couple years ago. I made him tear them up. I made you tear them up!" she shouted over at the kid.

The bedroom was small, plushly furnished in very feminine pastel colors and fabrics. The kid was up on his rump, feeling his face experimentally, eyes emptily indifferent now. "You're a whore, Zanna," he said idly, "and everyone knows it."

"See?" Zanna said, looking wildly at Raeanne and me. "He hates me! He hates me! His own mother he hates."

"Let's go chat," I suggested, and eased Zanna toward the door. Raeanne, looking grim, came alongside and led her out and closed the door. I turned to the kid, who was still sitting on the carpeted floor, feeling his hatchet face with long white fingers. "What's your name, son?" I asked.

"Billy. Billy Wirkus," he answered.

"You were on ContaXX?" I asked.

He nodded.

"Sending out pictures of your mom?"

He nodded again, readily, almost proudly.

"Why?"

He rolled his skinny shoulders. "I dunno. Piss her off. Get her in trouble with those political assholes, maybe. That whole deal sucks, man," he said defiantly. "I want to go back to L.A."

"Who else knew you were sending out those pictures?"

"Nobody."

"Nobody?" I pressed.

He said nothing, just folded his thin white feet up

toward him and began picking absently at his toes.

"Billy," I said, "your mom could be in big serious trouble here."

"Good."

"People have gotten killed because of those pictures, Billy."

He quit his picking, and his eyes flicked at me, doubtful and defiant. "Who got killed?"

"People you sent the pictures to." He stared off into space. Down on the carpet in that girlish room, face reddening from the blows of his mother, Billy looked lost. In a flash I glimpsed his life, dragged from town to town by his feckless show-biz mom. I said softly, "Here's your chance to do in those political assholes and protect your mother at the same time."

"I don't care about her."

"Oh, cut it out. Of course you do." He did not answer. "Tell me who else knew, Billy."

Back in the living room, the women were sitting in their previous positions: Zanna in the comfortable curve of the U-shaped sofa, staring numbly into space, and Raeanne down at one end, looking tense. "He's all right," I said.

Zanna, I saw as I opened my portfolio, had been crying, but now she was brittle and remote. "So how much, Perkins?"

"How much for what?" I asked, taking out the videocassette.

"She thinks we're here to blackmail her," Raeanne told me.

I held up the video. "Not hardly. Does the VCR work?"

Zanna sniffed and blinked. "Sure. Why?" She focused

on the tape. "I never made no videos. Least not that I know of."

I didn't want to hear about Zanna's porno career. I went to the TV cabinet, turned on the VCR, inserted the cassette, and picked up the remote. "This isn't of you," I said, watching the screen as I fast-forwarded. "Want you to ID somebody for me," I said, slowing the images to a fast trot. "Here we go . . . him."

The big screen flickered, pausing on that same anonymous male face I'd shown the judge and Cockrum. The more I looked at it, the more bland and featureless it seemed. But I was close now, closer than I'd ever expected to get, and though my heart froze in my chest as I waited for the name, I knew what it would be—

"Yinger," Zanna said, eyes sharp, tone poisonous.

"Oh?"

"Who's he?" Raeanne asked.

"Del Yinger," Zanna repeated. "Paul's security consultant and designated asshole."

I pressed STOP and REWIND and sat back down on the sofa. Got you, you son of a bitch. "Tell me about him."

"He's a weasel," she said. "He was some kind of intelligence guy once, you know? That was the rumor. Been with Paul since the 'seventy-six campaign, started out as his pilot. Now he's the campaign cop. Keeps everybody in line. Snoop. Eavesdropper. Strong-arm. Scary little shit. All the girls on the campaign staff, they were scared shitless of him." Zanna reached clumsily for the brandy bottle. "He hated me. I think, if it was up to him, he'd of bounced me and Billy out of that campaign in two shakes. Hell"—she laughed shakily—"if it was up to him he'd of wrapped both of us in chains and dropped us into Lake Erie. But Paul made him be nice to us."

"At least until the picture," I answered.

She coughed on her swallow of brandy, got it down, and asked hoarsely, "The picture? What's he have to do with it?"

"Well," I answered, "I don't know for sure. But here's what I think. He found out about Billy and the picture of you. Maybe he snooped in Billy's computer or something. Anyway, he confiscated the computer—"

"He did what?" she asked sharply.

"He took it. Billy told me just now."

"Billy told me it was in for repair," Zanna said. "His own *mother* he lies to."

"Deal is this, I think," I went on. "Yinger found the picture. He realized if it got out—if even *word* of it got into the press—Proposto's campaign was dead. So Yinger went on Billy's computer to find all the people he sent it to. He got the real names of the users from the ContaXX network owner. Then he tracked them down and killed them. Made the deaths look accidental. And wiped their computer disks clean."

For a long time no one said anything. I was in dire need of a cigar, but I held my peace. Raeanne was looking at me without expression, and I wondered what she was thinking. Probably, Good God, what kind of man am I getting involved with?

"Man, oh, man," Zanna said, deathly pale.

"You really think Yinger would kill people just to protect the senator?" Raeanne asked.

"Del would," Zanna said coldly. "He'd do anything."

"It's not the senator he's protecting," I answered. "It's the power he represents. They're playing the ultimate in political hardball."

Zanna looked pensive. "You know what else this means," she said. "I got a big bullseye on my back. Billy too."

"Could be," I said.

Raeanne was nodding. "Yinger wanted you out of the way. He couldn't convince Proposto to dump you completely. But he did talk the senator into getting you away from the campaign."

"Stuck me in here," Zanna said. "Stationed people to keep an eye on me." She looked at me intently. "Reckon we should make ourselves scarce. Can you help us?"

"Why, sure." I went to retrieve the cassette. "And then you're going to help me."

"To fix that asshole?" she asked grimly. "Anything. Anything you need."

It took a while to put the caper together, a while longer for Zanna and her son to pack a small bag each, and the wait went into extra innings while we gave the two of them a head start on their trip down forty flights of stairs. I didn't have much doubt we could get them clear. Zanna knew the building, and from what she said the watch on her was a casual one. Yinger was counting on her feelings for Proposto to keep her on the reservation. Already I was thinking beyond that, to the next move, wondering what it would be. I had no evidence or anything. What I had, as the judge pointed out, was flimsy conjecture standing on a foundation of total supposition. But it all fit together, and I believed in it, and feeling the way I did, I knew I had to do something with it. Question was, what?

"Dunno," I answered Raeanne as we rode the small elevator car toward the ground floor. "I'll think on it and see."

She stood beside me, her relaxed, easygoing air giving way to a look of steely-eyed focus. Getting into character, I figured. "Ready?" she asked as the elevator eased to a stop.

"Sure," I said.

The doors opened. Raeanne started out, hurling words over her shoulder at me. "You sorry sick sack of shit," she said loudly, turning toward the lobby. "You just stay away from me."

The words stung, that's how good she was. "Aw, come on, Rae," I said, trailing along. "It's all in fun."

The desk guy was peering down at us. I hoped the guard at the other door was paying attention too, but I didn't turn to see. "Fun?" Raeanne shot back, her mouth a jagged ugly line. "It's the sickest of the sick, Dale. I'm going home."

"No, you're not." I grabbed her arm and stopped her. "We're going back up there. You're not going to embarrass me—"

She jerked her arm out of my grip. "I don't need to embarrass you!" she shouted. "You do a great job of that by yourself!"

The guard stepped around from behind his desk. "You folks have to move along," he said.

"Go screw," I advised him. "We're going back up. Come on, Rae," I said, trying to crowd her back toward the elevator. The guard from the other end was headed our way. Ah, good.

Raeanne ducked under my arm and made a break for the front door. I caught her arm and stopped her. She hissed and swung at me, missing me by a mile; I let her go and her momentum flung her into the arms of the desk guy. The other guard had reached us. "Okay, let's go," he boomed, giving me a big hard push toward the front door.

"You leave my husband alone!" Raeanne shouted, jumping in the way.

Now the guard from out on the front sidewalk had come in to join the party. I pounced on Raeanne and dragged her, kicking and swinging, toward the elevator. "We're going back upstairs," I said grimly, "and that's that."

"No way, buddy," one of the guards boomed. "You're outa here right now. You too, lady."

They split us, and not gently, and held us by the arms: two for me, one for the panting, red-faced Raeanne. "You know what this sick shit wanted me to do?" she asked them. "Make love with him and his boyfriend up there. How about that?"

"Aw, honey," I whined.

The three pairs of hardened New York eyes were not impressed. "The two of yez get lost," the desk man rumbled, "or we're calling the cops."

"Don't make me leave with him," Raeanne begged.

"Tough luck, lady." With well-oiled moves they hustled us to the revolving door, through it, and out onto the sidewalk. Raeanne bolted west toward Fifth Avenue while I exchanged fist-jabbing epithets with two of the guards. Then I stomped up the sidewalk toward the greenery of Central Park, crossed Fifth Avenue at the light, and found Raeanne, as scheduled, sitting on a park bench, waiting for me.

"Hi," she greeted, smiling. "Come here often?"

"My first time," I answered, sitting down beside her. "You?"

"Oh, I've been here lots of times," she answered. She took my hand in hers and we watched the Fifth Avenue traffic roar by: fleets of cabs, lane-straddling trucks, pedestrians on the sidewalk skating, bustling, ambling, floating. "Did Zanna and Billy get out?" she asked.

"I didn't notice either. I assume so. The ruckus we made, you could have snuck the Third Army out of there. You were good, kid."

"Trained professional."

"Obviously. I do have one complaint, though."

She shot me a look. "What?"

"You rewrote the damn script."

"I did?"

"It was supposed to be your *sister* and you I wanted to make love to," I said. "Not my *boyfriend* and you."

"Sudden inspiration," she answered, and squeezed my hand.

"Made me look like some kind of sicko," I grumped.

"This is New York," she explained. "Takes a lot to get people's attention."

"Well, you got theirs," I told her. "Those goons bought your act a hundred percent."

"Yes," she said happily. "It's very encouraging. If I can make it here, I can make it anywhere. What now, Mr. Detective?"

"Whatever you want."

"Whatever I want?" she asked slyly.

"Whatever."

She considered. "What I want," she said, "is a couple of hours in the Metropolitan Museum. After that, I'm yours to do with as you please."

"Okay," I said, and we stood. "When does your sister get in?"

She smacked my shoulder, laughing. I gave her a sidearm hug and we started down Fifth Avenue, hand in hand. "What do you want to do after this?" she asked.

"Can't think of a single thing," I confessed.

"Sure you can," she answered.

"Well . . ." I looked at her happy, expectant face. "This is going to sound hokey, darlin'. But I've never been in this burg before. I'd like to do the real cliché tourist things."

"Statue of Liberty? Empire State Building?"

"You got it."

"Absolutely." We walked a while longer. I didn't know where the Metropolitan Museum was, and I didn't care. I didn't know what I was going to do on the case next, and I didn't care about that either. What I cared about at that moment was being with Raeanne in the greatest city in the world, with the rest of the afternoon and all night to burn. It was a magical moment, dropped on me out of nowhere. Life was like that sometimes—except that usually, I did not recognize moments like that for what they were until they were long gone.

Raeanne was smiling. "While you were talking to Zanna's son, I asked her what she saw in your hand. Know what she said?"

"What?"

"She looked at me and said, 'Some gals have all the luck.'"

So we made a brief visit to the Metropolitan Museum of Art, where, at Raeanne's request, we lingered over the James McNeill Whistler stuff: *Pantomime in Platinum, Reggae in Rouge,* you get the idea. We subwayed south to the Empire State Building, went to the top, oohed and ahhed; then down to Battery Park, where we took the big ferry out to the Statue of Liberty. It was all touristy as hell, crowded, and hot on that beautiful late June Thursday, and everything cost money. But it was a great time and, like all great times, over way too soon.

Later, having grabbed dinner at a deli near Grand Central Station, we rode the elevator up to the twenty-third floor of the Eastwood Arms. Raeanne had gone quiet, and I had too. I mean, the next act was obvious, but I was hinky as hell. Lost confidence in my moves. Wasn't sure I was decoding the signals right.

We got off the elevator and I walked her to her door. "Maybe I should come in," I suggested. "Check under your bed and in the shower stall for prowlers and such."

"I checked already," she told me, unlocking. "It's all safe."

"Okay."

"Okay." She leaned up and kissed me briskly. "Lovely day," she said softly. "See you for breakfast?"

"Breakfast," I echoed.

"Good night." She went inside and closed the door.

Well, okay.

My room was a nice double, furnished plain and drab but clean and comfortable, with a big window looking west toward the remaining glow of the sun that had finished setting behind the phalanx of skyscrapers. There was also a desk, bureau, TV, closet, a dorm-sized fridge, and a closed door that obviously connected to the next room.

Hm.

I turned on the TV and kicked off my shoes. Opened the fridge and found it stocked with pop and beer, chargeable, according to a notice inside, at a rate of five bucks a can. I bought myself a Budweiser, cracked it, flopped down on the bed, and tried to watch the news. All I could think about was Raeanne next door. I wondered what she was doing. The grim news from around the world bounced off me in Peter Jennings's even, civilized tones, and I sipped beer and lighted a cigar and thought about Raeanne over there, and I wondered what she was thinking.

Finally I thought, This is nuts.

I got off the bed and went to the connecting door. Just as I reached it, my phone rang. I picked it up. "Yes?"

"Can I buy you a drink?" came Raeanne's warm voice.

Suddenly I could not seem to take a full breath. "This is incredible," I said. "I was just this instant coming over to ask you the same thing."

"What stopped you?"

"Phone rang. Some woman."

"Well," she said, "hang up on her and get your butt over here."

TWENTY-NINE

The room was monochrome, a dozen shades of gray and black, fuzzy. Outside and away and far below, I could hear and feel the mighty city rumbling at a steady, insistent, night-shift idle. We'd turned the air conditioner off, so the room was warm, but just pleasantly so. I lay under the bedsheet, head propped on two big pillows, wide awake in the darkness. It was 4:00 A.M.; I'd dozed, but only in fits and starts, and I knew there'd be no more sleep for me. Not that night.

Raeanne lay beside me in the double bed, on her side, facing away, shrouded almost completely by the sheet, visible as a curve of shoulder and another of hip and a smudge of dark hair from which came the soft sweet sound of her regular breathing. As I lay there and looked at her, it occurred to me that lovemaking was much much more than physical coupling and did not end with climax. Lovemaking, I realized, began well before that, with talking and touching and walking together, and laughing and fencing and wondering. And it continued long after the moist, fiercely gentle physical engagement, into this aftermath of quiet togetherness, one person awake watching the other sleep in a state of perfect sharing trust.

Had I been ten years younger, I'd have wakened her then. Probably by easing my naked body slowly, gently against hers, and slipping my arms around her, and kissing her neck, hands gently exploring her breasts, her belly, her thighs. But I did not want to tamper with the moment. I did not want to interrupt her sleep until I had to, around six, so we could catch our early plane home. And I needed that moment to think about the thing that had woken me up to begin with: the case.

Those dead people. Cloyd and Capitani, strangled and left for dead as sicko-sexual suicides. Linda Steckroth, forever trapped in a lump of useless flesh, dead in all but name. And maybe others besides, people who'd received that lethal picture, tracked down and done in, just to head off any possible problems for a damn politician. I didn't know much about Del Yinger, but if what I suspected was right, he'd committed a string of nearly perfectly executed, flawless murders.

Question was: What to do now? And that's what kept me awake.

The conventional route—cops—was out. Without evidence, there was nothing for the cops to work with. Proposto was powerful. Even without knowing what Yinger had done—and I had no doubt his deniability was airtight—he'd protect his people, and the minute his name came into the equation, the threshold for involvement by any police agency would go way, way, way up.

Did that mean I had to let Yinger walk?

If so, I'd be agreeing that it was okay for politicians and their aides to break the law in order to protect their own interests. I'd be agreeing that the rich, the powerful, the connected, the important were above the law, exempt from the rules, entitled to grind up anyone who got in their way. Of course, in the real world, all this was true. I could tell myself it was not my duty. I could tell myself I had no business putting myself at risk anymore. I could tell myself I had no financial interest, even; I was fulfilling an agreement with a public radio station, for chrissake. I could tell myself I'd made a deal with Carole. I could tell myself all kinds of things, and I did, in those long dark moments. But no matter how much I mentally wriggled and danced, I could not rationalize it away. If I went on with my life without doing something, I'd be signing off on the sons of bitches. And that I could not do.

What I had to do—somehow—was make Yinger pay for what he did and fix it so he could never do anything like it again.

The only way to do that was to set him up and then take him down.

Simple . . .

The ringing phone damn near made me jump out of my skin. Carefully reaching over Raeanne, I grabbed it, checking the time: only 6:00 A.M. Jesus. "Hello," I murmured into the receiver, turning my back on Raeanne.

"Well, howdy-do!" came a rich, cheerful woman's voice. "Hope I'm not disturbing y'all."

"Hi, Zanna," I said softly, relief overcoming annoyance. "Where are you?"

"I'm back on home turf. Espiritu Santu, Looz-iana. Gonna hole up here until you take Yinger out."

"Till I whuh?"

"Take him down," she answered casually.

"What makes you think I'm gonna do that?"

"'Cause I've known lots of old boys like you. You don't talk, you just do. Reckon you've been layin' there half the night, figuring out the ways and means. Am I right?"

"Close," I admitted.

"Or was it just layin' you were doin'?" she asked slyly.

"Keep it clean, now."

"Clean, hell," she said robustly. "I saw the way that little gal looked at you. You both got it bad."

"Glad you approve," I said dryly.

"It's cute," she reflected. "Makes even a hard-bowled ol' blues singer like me think there's hope for romance. So, whatcha gonna do about old Del?"

"Dunno yet."

"But you know I'll he'p, any way I can. Long as I don't have to stir from here."

"Don't want you doin' no stirring. Want you to sit tight. One thing I did wonder, though. Do you know anybody in Proposto's campaign? Somebody on the inside, somebody you could get to help me on the sly?"

"There's Katie Lynn," Zanna said readily. "She schedules transportation and the advance team. Her and me got to be right chummy."

Raeanne was stirring. I felt her arm slip around me, and as I turned she kissed my cheek. We smiled at each other and I kissed her back. "Good enough to help me if you asked her to?"

"You betcha. She's a good old gal. Besides, she hates Yinger's guts."

"Can you call her, ask her to help me out if I get in touch?"

"You got it. What else?"

"Nothing. Except, keep your head down." Raeanne slipped out of the bed and I watched her naked back, good hips, long lithe legs as she trotted lightly into the bathroom. "Give me your number, so I can get back to you."

Zanna did so. I scribbled it on the little spiral pad

that I fetched out of my pants pocket. From inside the bathroom came the thundering of the shower. Absently I asked Zanna, "Sure you'll be safe there?"

"Hell, I grew up here."

"Wouldn't it be the first place Yinger would look, if he decided to come after you?"

"I grew up here," she repeated obstinately. "This here village is just miles and miles of trails in the bayous. Half the folks in these parts is kinfolk of mine. He come anywheres near here, we'll know how to fix him." She paused. "Not that he'd dare." Another pause, and then, very softly: "Hope he don't."

"Scares you that bad, huh?"

"That bad. And if you've got any brains, you'll stay purely skeered of him too. 'Bye, Ben."

"'Bye, Zanna."

I lay back on the bed. In the bathroom, the shower thundered on. I really had to get my own rear in gear, over to my room to change and—ha—pack. But my thoughts had wandered in another direction, away from Yinger and onto Mr. Gary Cockrum. I wondered if there was a role for him in the upcoming drama.

Yinger, let's face it, was no dummy. He may already have known, or sensed, that someone was banging around on his trail. When I set the trap—assuming I came up with a decent one—he might be too suspicious of it to act.

But what if I double-dipped him? Waved one deal in his face and then came back at him from a whole other direction, sort of like General Jackson at Chancellorsville?

Might end up being a little rough on Mr. Gary Cockrum, but I didn't think anyone was going to feel much sympathy for a guy who, as Dick Dennehy had put it, spent his life "sticking it to the system and walking away laughing."

About then, Raeanne came out of the bathroom. She had a large white hotel towel wrapped around her from armpits to thighs, and her short black hair was damp, and she was giving me that look of wry appraisal as she came to the bed. "So how are we?" she asked, sitting on the edge.

I leaned up and we kissed. "I'm good," I said. "How about you?"

She took my hand and looked at it. "Good," she said seriously. "I'm just worried you think I've been toying with you."

"Hey," I said easily, "if that was toying, just think of me as your boy-toy."

"Seriously."

"I understand."

"It's just that it's scary," she said. "This is really powerful stuff for me."

"Me too."

"Is it?"

"It is."

She enclosed my hand in both of hers. "Bit by bit we open up," she said softly.

"There's a lot more you should know."

"You too."

"I want to tell you. I guess."

"It's okay to tell," she answered readily. "When it's time."

"Yup."

"I keep waiting for the other shoe to drop, and it doesn't."

"Oh, when you find out my bondage fetish, you'll cut and run."

She smiled. "What makes you think that would bother me?"

I reached for her and we kissed again. "Don't worry

about stuff," I murmured. "Like you keep saying, we got time."

Her lips had gone cool. She disengaged from me. "We should probably get going," she said, and went back to the bathroom.

To save time, we took a cab back out to LaGuardia and reached the gate right at flight time. Which meant, quite naturally, that the flight was then delayed an hour. We wandered the concourses, bought magazines, ate doughnuts and drank coffee, and waited. I felt a bit bummed, going home this quick. We'd just gotten started, and now we had to go back to our lives. I realized it wasn't just the trip, it was being with Raeanne. I hadn't had enough, and the giddily scary thing was, I wasn't sure there was such a thing as enough. I retreated from the thought and, as a test, tried to imagine never seeing her again. The pain of that thought was so fierce I could almost physically feel it.

Not going to happen, I thought. Not going to lose like that, twice in one year.

As we boarded the plane, I asked, "Working at all today?"

"Nothing that I know of," she said. "Why?"

I found our seats, opposite aisles halfway down the big crowded 757. "Tonight's Rachel night, at my place," I said. "Want to come?"

She was tucking her carry-on under the seat ahead of her. "Better not," she said, offhand. "Not yet. I don't want to intrude."

"Carole brought her guy to the last one."

Raeanne glanced at me. "It's really serious with them, then?"

"Reckon so."

The flight attendant went into his safety-for-all spiel. I reached across for Raeanne's hand and we gripped tightly. She asked idly, "Your singer friend's got herself a good hideout?"

I realized she meant Zanna, that she hadn't used the name because it was famous and distinctive, and you never knew who might be listening. Smart. "Sounds like it. Said she'd help me on this bit, if I get any big inspirations."

"Have you?"

"Ah. Buncha thoughts bang-clanging around."

"Any way I can help?"

I glanced at her. "You want a piece of this?"

"I want to help," she said matter-of-factly. "If you've got a role for an out-of-work actor, I'm your woman."

The aircraft suddenly thumped away from the gate. The tarmac, the luggage trains, and other aircraft moved by the small portholes of the plane as we edged along the taxiway. I looked at Raeanne and there was part of me that said no, no, keep her clear. But I needed her. And she was willing.

"You want a role," I prompted.

"Yes."

I considered. "How about bait?"

The door eased back, an eye peered through the crack, and then Herb Steckroth opened the door. "So here you are," he enthused, wheezing. "Hoped you'd get here in time for lunch, but too late. Ha."

"Flight was delayed," I answered, entering the foyer. "Had to make some stops. This is my friend Raeanne. Herb Steckroth, Linda's dad."

"Lovely home," Raeanne said as they shook hands.

"Thanks, thanks," he wheezed. Beneath the veneer

of cheer there was urgency as he faced me. "So, did you find out something? I've been dying to hear. Ha."

"Can we see Linda real quick, sir?"

"She might be asleep now," he fussed. "I just changed her. But okay, come on." As he led us up the curved carpeted stairs, he noticed the envelope in my hand. "What's that?"

"Possible evidence."

"I see, I see," he said importantly. "Ha."

As before, Steckroth wore nondescript pants and a faded patterned short-sleeved shirt and heelless carpet slippers. The house still smelled of new, and from the absence of sounds elsewhere and his offhand way of letting us in, I discerned that his wife was out. He led us upstairs and into the bedroom, a sweetly smelling riot in pinks and yellows. Once again, Linda Steckroth lay under a single sheet on the ornate canopy bed, thin body twisted toward fetal. She was facing away from us and almost motionless except for that periodic and unnerving tremor which shook her entire body, as if she'd been touched on the spine with a cattle prod.

Steckroth went to the bed, bouncy and cheery. "So you are awake!" he said happily to his daughter. "Our friends are back, dear. Well, one of them. Ben and his friend Raeanne."

Linda's huge dark eyes were locked open, staring at the sheet. A shudder went over her and she intoned, "Perkins."

I'd warned Raeanne, but I saw that she looked pasty. I could see why. For one thing, Raeanne was a naturally empathetic person. Besides, that husk lying there was about her age. Once, Linda Steckroth had, no doubt, been as vibrant and youthful as Raeanne. Once, she'd had similar sorts of hopes. Once, she'd had blind, unthinking faith in the future—that at least there'd be one. Linda Steckroth was living, breathing evidence that the future was just one more thing not a single one of us could take to the bank.

"Hi, Linda," Raeanne said, and touched the woman's sheeted shoulder. "How are you?"

Linda shuddered at Raeanne's touch, and she looked at me bleakly.

"So," Steckroth said to me, "what now, Ben?"

"Well, sir," I said, "I'm going to try something here, if you don't mind. Might turn up nothing. Might upset Linda a little. Just want to warn you."

His bulbous, amiable face was thoughtful. "What are you going to do?"

"Show her a picture." I opened the envelope and took out an eight-by-ten black-and-white glossy. "This is a still from a videotape. All I'm going to do, sir, is show it to Linda. Okay?"

"Go ahead."

I sat on the edge of the bed. Linda was on her side, facing away from me, skull-like head with its thin limp brown hair propped up on a big plump pillow. "Linda," I said kindly, "I want to show you something, sweetheart. Okay?"

Her only response was a quick, powerful shudder.

I reached the glossy out and held it in her line of vision, about a foot away from her wide staring eyes. It was a still of the man from the videotape, identified by Zanna Canady as Del Yinger.

At first, Linda did not react. Then I saw that her eyes were blinking more frequently. From somewhere inside her she unlimbered a moan that climbed in pitch and tone, and she shook with a mighty spasm, her thin fingers contorted. "Perkins!" she cried, then moaned. "Perkins!" I withdrew the picture and stood, but she stared where it had been, as if the image was etched on her eyes, and moaned again, louder this time, and now her feet were thrashing under the sheet.

"Perkins!"

THIRTY

"Oh, God," Raeanne said softly.

Giving me a quick look, Steckroth leaned over and gathered Linda's quaking shoulders into his arms. "It's all right, honey," he said soothingly as she continued to flail. "It's all right, all right, all right," he cooed, gently caressing her forehead. As Raeanne and I watched, Linda gradually settled down, and the piercing scent of fresh warm urine filled the air. Steckroth did not react, just held Linda, murmuring in low tones, eyes as mournful as a puppy.

"Jesus Christ, I'm sorry, sir," I said.

"So am I," the father answered. "But if it means what I think it means, it was more than worth it. Ha." He glanced at us. "Would you mind going out in the hall for a minute, so I can—?"

"Sure," I said, and we left.

Out in the hall, Raeanne leaned against the wall, gnawing a knuckle. Quietly I said, "Yup. Tough stuff in there."

"Confirms it though, right?" she asked.

"Far as I'm concerned. Never fly officially, of course."

"So we're go?"

"You still in?"

"I'm in," she said, quietly fervent, and in her eyes I saw something new. I'd seen her assertive, even resolute, but I'd never caught a hint of anger before.

"Then yes," I answered, and nodded toward Linda's door. "If he'll play along."

Presently, Steckroth padded out and closed the door quietly behind him. "Talk downstairs?" he asked, forcing a smile.

"Lead the way, sir."

We went down the curved staircase and into what my mother would have called the parlor, an impeccable, virtually dustless room jammed too full of rounded upholstered furniture in warm pastels, plus dark curved-leg coffee and end tables. It was the kind of room you wanted to look at but not use. I had the sense that the furniture had been bought for a bigger place.

Steckroth half sat on a love seat, and Raeanne and I sat on the sofa facing him. "Let me see the picture," the father said.

I slipped it out and handed it to him. He held it up and then out almost at arm's length. "Oh, sure," he said, realization dawning. "Ha. Anthony Perkins."

"Strong resemblance," I agreed.

His kindly face went cold as he looked at the picture one more time, then handed it to me. "Why did he do it?" he asked quietly.

I explained briefly. Through all of it—the ContaXX stuff, the porno pictures, the deaths—Steckroth's only reaction was to listen closely. When I was through, he nodded once. "What now? The police?"

"We could," I said slowly. "But I'll guarantee you right now, we don't have enough for the cops to move on."

The father's eyes flickered. "For me it is."

"Us, too," Raeanne said.

He looked at each of us. "Well, then," he said, "what do *we* do?"

"Katie Lynn's all set," came Zanna's voice over the phone, if anything even more syrupy-southern than before. Being back home did that to her, I guessed. "What about at your end?"

Rachel, sitting on my lap, reached out for the receiver. I ducked away from her as the excited voice of Will Somers came from the living room, against the backdrop of video game noises. "Nothing much yet," I answered. "Still putting things together. I should be ready by tomorrow. Now how do I reach this Katie Lynn person when I need her?"

"Now," Rachel demanded, grabbing at the receiver.

"You just hush," I told her, trying to catch Zanna's answer in the receiver. Rachel lunged for the phone again and I wheeled her down to the floor. She took a step on her bare feet, then wobbled and whumped down hard on her diapered butt and gave me a turn-to-shit scowl. "Serves you right," I told her, "trying to mess up Daddy's business."

"Mongo!" she declared, making a grin that showed several teeth.

Zanna had gone quiet. Now she asked, "Who're you woofin' with there, Ben?"

"My daughter," I answered, as Rachel scooted toward the living room on all fours. "Just takin' on, as usual."

"Does she look like her mama? I hope?"

"Sufficiently."

Carole appeared at the living room entrance and mouthed, "Pizza's here." I indicated the twenty on the table and she snatched it in one hand and scooped up Rachel and went back into the living room.

"Like I was saying," Zanna said, "there's a central campaign number with a computerized forwarding system, voice mail, the works. You know all this technology shit."

"No, I don't," I answered, "but go on."

"The system forwards calls to the campaign team, wherever they are in the state," she explained. "Don't ask me how. Got a pencil?"

"Shoot," I said, turning to the last page in my pad. She gave me the number. "That goes to Katie Lynn direct," Zanna added. "She'll keep you posted on what's happening."

"She know to keep her mouth shut?"

"She hates Del's guts. Skeered to death of him too. She'll keep quiet."

"Okay, Zanna. I guess we're in good shape for now."

"You keep me posted too," she ordered.

"Yes, ma'am."

In the living room, Carole had arranged open boxes of steaming pizza on the coffee table along with paper plates and napkins. Buck Longstreth was helping himself, and Will was playing his Big 10 Football video game, Michigan versus Illinois. I brought Rachel's high chair and her dinner—a jar of strained beef and vegetables, yum—in from the kitchen, inserted the wriggling, objecting Rachel into the chair, and snapped a bib around her neck. Will won his game with a last-second field goal. The TV boomed the Michigan fight song and Will sang along:

> "*Hail* to the victors valiant,
> *Hail* to our concrete hero,
> *Hail, hail* to Michigan—"

"Concrete hero?" Longstreth asked, between bites.

"Conquering," Carole corrected. "It's 'conquering heroes,' Will."

"I like my way better," Will replied, shutting off the TV.

"Me too," I told him.

"Have some pizza, son," Longstreth said, handing him a plate.

"Thanks, Buck ol' buddy," Will answered, rolling his eyes at me.

I began to feed Rachel her dinner, spoon by spoon. She sat quietly, putting away each bite as I gave it to her, her big dark blue eyes watching my every move. For a time, everyone was silent, focused on eating. Even so, the silence was awkward, thanks to Longstreth's presence. I found myself wishing Raeanne had come. She would have evened things out a little. Longstreth was tolerable, and obviously he and Carole were tight, but why did she have to drag him everywhere she went?

Carole finished her pizza and came over to me. "I'll take over," she said. "You eat."

I got myself some pizza and sat on the couch next to Will. Carole began feeding Rachel, with considerably less success than I had had. I ate and watched and grinned as Rachel bobbed and weaved, evading the spoon, refusing to swallow right away, stuff like that. Carole, annoyed, plugged on doggedly. Presently she said to me, "So what did you decide about the case?"

"The case?" I echoed politely.

"The Chris Cloyd death," she said, glancing at me.

"Trying to wrap it up," I said.

"What did the police say when you talked to them?"

"Haven't."

Rachel's mouth was closed, holding a mouthful of

food as she looked at her mother. "Swallow, dear," Carole said. Rachel did nothing. Carole gave me that narrow, prosecutorial look and made an exasperated sound. "I don't believe you," she said brittlely. I didn't answer. "You just have to go looking for trouble, don't you." I said nothing. Carole glared at me. "May I remind you that we made a deal?" When I didn't answer, she turned her attention to Rachel, who still had not swallowed. "Sweetheart, will you *please* swallow and—"

"Puh-*thuh*," Rachel answered, releasing the mouthful of food down her chin in a brown gush.

"Oh, God," Carole groaned, grabbing the bib to catch the mess. I got a towel from the kitchen and helped Carole mop up. The kid was grinning merrily, kicking her bare feet. Carole snapped the high-chair tray out and picked Rachel up. "I guess that means you're done," she said darkly, and set Rachel on her feet by the coffee table.

Longstreth leaned forward and held out his hands toward Rachel. "Come on, rookie." He beckoned, smiling.

I folded the high chair and set it around the corner in the kitchen. "Her name's Rachel, pal," I said. "When she walks for the first time, it'll be for me," I added. "Right, rookie?"

Longstreth just smiled. "Come on." He beckoned again.

She let go of the coffee table and started for him, but fell on her rear after the second step. Carole and Longstreth commiserated, but I said nothing; just ambled over to the sliding glass door, notched it, and lighted a cigar. "Hey, Carole," I said.

"Yes?"

"Long as we're asking pointed questions," I said, "why don't you tell me what's going on with you and Buck here?"

She smiled. "You mean, aside from we're good friends?"

"There's something going on," I said. "So spill."

Longstreth glanced at her. "Maybe you'd better tell him."

"Not yet," Carole said, and she and Longstreth exchanged smiles.

I had tried to reach Cockrum three times since returning from New York that morning. Not in, on the phone, up the hall. It was beginning to look like I'd have to go see him, but lo and behold, he called me back on Friday night about an hour after Carole and crew left.

"Frankly," he said in his nasal, whiny voice, "I'm getting a little tired of you bothering me, Perkins."

"I'm pretty sick of you too," I retorted, kicking my shoes off as I stretched out on the easy chair. "But for the moment we're stuck with each other. Just listen up and—"

"We really don't have anything to discuss."

"Who said anything about discussing?" I asked sharply. "What I want you to do is shut up and listen for a minute."

He did not answer.

"The guy on the tape," I told him, "is Del Yinger. Maybe you knew that, maybe you didn't. But you know him."

Cockrum was silent.

"He's security chief for the Proposto campaign," I went on. "Maybe you knew that too, but I doubt it."

Still Cockrum said nothing.

"He came to you for the names and addresses that went with some ContaXX handles," I told him. "And you gave them to him. That I'm sure of. And he then tracked those people down and killed them. Murdered them, Gary. You didn't know that, though. I'm pretty positive of that."

"How do you know?" Cockrum asked. "What makes you so sure I'm not working with him?"

"Because he'd have killed you too, when he was done," I answered. "I don't think he's the kind leaves witnesses around."

Again, silence from Cockrum's end.

"The new deal is this," I continued. "I've got the cops in the act now, and we're fixing to take Yinger down. We're going to do it fast and hard and permanent. If we all play our cards right, nobody else'll get hurt. If you play along, I guarantee you'll walk. But you have to play along."

"How can you guarantee anything?" he asked. His haughtiness and detachment had slipped. Now he sounded nervous. Coming along nicely.

"That cop who was with me when we visited?" I said. "State police inspector. Senior man. Tons of clout. Well, Gary, I own his ass. He's mine. I've got his pecker in my pocket. If I tell him Gary's my friend, your troubles are over."

Silence. Then Cockrum asked, "What do you want me to do?"

"Sometime in the next few days Yinger'll be contacting you," I said. "He'll ask you for the name and location of a ContaXX member. When he does that, you're going to call me and tell me about it. Right away." I paused, but Cockrum did not react. "And you're not going to breathe a word of this to Yinger," I added, "or I'll personally see to it that you get scooped up and hammered behind this. I'll make that my personal mission. I don't care how slippery you are, I'll get to you and fix you."

"I see," he said presently.

"So work with me," I said.

"All right."

I hung up. Naughty boy, I thought. Naughty *naughty* boy.

The mobile home was really little more than a small rectangular tin trailer set up on blocks, crammed in tight amid two hundred others in Imagine Acres in Livonia. It was a one-bedroom job with a living room at the front, a tiny one-person kitchen in the center, a bathroom across from that, and a bedroom at the back. Everything was various shades of faded brown, Formica and veneer and vinyl, and extremely neat and clean except for the dust that had accumulated over the past month or so.

Though it was early—very early on Saturday morning—the mobile home was uncomfortably hot. I guessed that was because it had been closed up tight in the summer heat. I had a couple of the sliding windows open, but there was no breeze to speak of, and the closeness inside was made worse by the presence of the two large men who sat side by side on the narrow shallow sofa, watching me work.

Darryl Rockecharlie was a massive man in his midforties. He was ex just about everything: boxer, cop, cabdriver, ship's cook, truck farmer, husband, you name it, with an enlarged beefy face and buzz-cut brown hair and eyes like small black bullets spaced widely in his face. He wore hiking boots and navy twill pants and an old chambray shirt with the sleeves whacked off, and he sat erect and inert, watching uninterestedly, maybe listening, waiting for instructions. He was a heavy lifter in more ways than one, good day labor, good old Darryl.

Next to him sat—make that lounged—Dick Dennehy. The big state cop had shucked his gray jacket and loosened the knot of his everyday tie, and he smoked a Lucky Strike with fine appetite, but he still looked ill at ease. Too early for him, I supposed. Too hot and humid in the trailer. Or maybe he was hungover. Or maybe he didn't like what I'd just finished telling them.

"Let me see if I understand this," Dick said presently. I positioned the CPU of Linda Steckroth's computer on the built-in dinette table. "Okay," I answered, plugging the AC cord into the back.

"You're going to make this Yinger guy think that Linda Steckroth is all recovered and living here again."

"Right." I set the monitor on the CPU and, checking the little tags I'd put on the computer when I took it apart at home, reconnected it to the CPU. I thought fleetingly of Dennis, then, and less fleetingly of Barb. I'd heard nothing from her since the airport Thursday. The two days she'd been gone felt more like a month. I wondered how she was doing out there.

"You're figuring Yinger'll come after her again."

"He'll come after her," I said, retrieving the computer keyboard from the box on the floor, "because he's gonna discover she's back on the ContaXX network passing that picture around."

"You think he's monitoring it, huh?"

"I would," I answered, plugging the keyboard in. "Wouldn't you?"

Dick exhaled smoke. "Okay. He finds out she's on the network—"

"As BiJudy," I put in. "Same handle as before."

"Swapping the picture," Dick continued thoughtfully. "What then?"

"He calls Cockrum to verify," I said, "and to get her address. He's not going to believe it's the same woman.

But when Cockrum gives him the address here, he'll know it's the same. That he has to do the job on her all over again—but more thoroughly this time."

"He comes here to take her out," Dick said, "and we catch him in the act, and I bust him. Is that about the size of it?"

"That's exactly it." Saying a quick prayer, I mashed the ON switch on the CPU. The computer began to hum.

Darryl just sat there, not reacting to anything. Dick was nerved up and bugged as hell. "Seems lame to me," he said finally.

After verifying that the computer was booting up okay, I faced the men. "Look, Dick. We've got to nail this Yinger guy. You know it and I know it."

"I know it," he said, "but—"

"There's no evidence to link him to those other killings. Or to the attempt on Steckroth," I rolled on. "You said so yourself. So if we can't get him for an old deal, why, we just set up a new one and get him on that."

In the long silence, Dick smoked and smoldered. I hoped to hell he was buying it, but I couldn't be sure. He asked, "What if Yinger isn't the perp, Sherlock?"

"He is, though," I answered. "If he isn't, he won't fall for any of this, and we'll have done it for nothing. But he's the one, Dick."

The state cop brooded. "Damn risky. Especially for the pigeon."

I shrugged. "We're all in this together. Besides, we've got the element of surprise, and we know his MO, and we outnumber his ass."

"Yeah," Dick agreed reluctantly.

"Darryl'll be out at the gate," I explained again. "When he spots Yinger or anybody who looks like him, he'll whistle us up on the radio. You'll be keeping watch outside here. I'll be hiding out in the bathroom, waiting for the right moment. When he does his deal, I'll jump him and either take him down or drive him out, right into your arms. You won't let him get away."

"No, I won't," Dick said sourly. "But tell me this, Mr. Genius. What if you don't take him down or drive him out? What if he gets past you? Huh?"

Just then the sliding door to the bedroom whonked open. Looking that way, we saw Raeanne come out of the bedroom and walk toward us slowly.

At least, the woman had been Raeanne, once.

"He gets past Ben," she said, eyes hard and gray as dirty ice, "*I'll* kick his fucking ass."

THIRTY-ONE

We all stared. Even Darryl's blocklike face showed a trace of awareness.

It was Raeanne, all right, and then again it wasn't. She had shortened her hair still further, and now it was merely a dark curly cap her head—gaminelike, I guess you'd say. Her outfit was, for her, quite outlandish: a black-, red-, and gold-striped shirt with little fleurs-de-lis all over it, its tails tied up under her breasts, leaving bare her smooth brown belly. Over that was an open black leather snap-up vest, and below she wore dark jeans held up by a wide black belt riddled with chrome studs. She wore no makeup and no jewelry. She didn't look butch, but she didn't look entirely feminine, either; she looked different, apart.

Besides that, her demeanor, her aura, had changed completely. From a quiet, easygoing, open, and friendly sort she'd become a tense, distant, suspicious person, calloused, resentful. She used all of herself to do it. A little in the eyes—narrow and wary; a little in the mouth—pressed in a straight lipless frown; a little in the posture—angular and somehow braced, as if ready to flee or attack.

She leaned against the small refrigerator, watching us. Dick, who had never met Raeanne before and thus had no basis for comparison, seemed unaffected. "So this is her, huh?"

"Raeanne," I said, not quite believing this was the woman I'd made love with in New York.

"Linda," Raeanne corrected. "You got my computer working there?"

I glanced at the screen. "Ready to go."

"Good," she said, and strode over. "Let me at it."

I got up from the dinette and Raeanne, insolently brushing her way past me, slid into the seat in front of the machine. "Soon as the phone line comes alive, we can start," I told her.

She nodded, and put her hands on the keyboard, and typed something. I noticed her fingernails, formerly well tended, were gnawed practically down to the bare skin. Yow.

"So," Dick said, standing, "when's the kickoff?"

"Probably tomorrow afternoon," I answered. "We'll go on the network later today, start chatting and swapping pix. I figure it'll take at least a day to start attracting attention. Then we better set up and hunker down."

"Okay," Dick said breezily. "I'll be back. 'Bye, Raeanne—I mean Linda."

She ignored us. Dick picked up his jacket, and he and Darryl lumbered out of the trailer. I brought up the rear, closing the tinny door behind me. The morning was uncomfortably warm and humid and somehow airless, the sky gray and featureless as slate. Around us, all was silent among the densely packed trailers of Imagine Acres. Saturday morning, I thought. Sleeping off Friday night.

I stopped the others by the prow of Linda's mobile home. "You're going to be over there, at the end of the trailer, in her parking space," I told Dick. "Darryl, you'll be at the visitor parking area in the front, by the mailboxes." They glanced around and nodded. Traffic hummed from Plymouth Road, a few yards away. "Y'all come on back after supper tomorrow night," I went on. "Bring heat, and stuff to drink and eat, and your wide-mouthed jar. Could be a long one."

Darryl nodded and waved and lumbered up the gravel lane toward his old mint-green mint-condition Caddy, parked in the visitor area. Dick lighted a cigarette. "Talkative type, huh?"

"Motormouth," I agreed. "But he'll get the job done."

"He'd better," Dick said quietly. "We all better."

"We will," I answered.

"Or that lady friend of yours will get bad hurt." Hands on hips, he looked past me and asked, "She the one you sent the flowers to?"

"Flower. Singular."

"And now you put her at risk."

"She volunteered," I shot back. "And it's under control. We're on the job, the three of us. We'll keep her safe."

"Hope so," he answered.

"I guarantee it," I told him. "Yinger'll never get anywhere near her."

Herb Steckroth had given us the keys to Linda's trailer. He'd let us take her car, a somewhat cranky and rust-holed Mercury Capri. He'd arranged for the phone to be reconnected and the utilities turned on. He let Raeanne look through Linda's wardrobe, such as it was, and showed her some recent pictures, so that Raeanne could get the look right. Raeanne was a few years younger than Linda, and taller, and less robustly built, but the idea was not to impersonate Linda anyway. Not really. Raeanne just had to be Linda at a distance, and in the trailer.

And on the computer.

The phone lines came alive at lunchtime. Raeanne and I sat side by side at the narrow dinette as she logged on to ContaXX using Linda's handle, BiJudy, and the password Steckroth had given us. The chat areas were busy. Each "room," which was really a subject or category, was crowded, the dialogue scrolling down the computer screen at a fast pace. Raeanne was in the room Women4Women when the computer beeped and a box popped up on the screen.

HOT FLASH!
from: Shadwbabe
Hi, Judy—
LTNS!

"Hey, I know that one," I said. "Shadwbabe. Lives over in—"

"What the hell does LTNS mean?" Raeanne asked.

I realized then that, until today, I had never heard Raeanne use profanity. I said, "I don't know."

She moved the cursor to a little box on the screen that said RESPOND, clicked the mouse key, and typed, NOT BAD, BABE, HOW U?

"Pretty good," I said. "You're getting the hang of this."

"Intuitively obvious," Raeanne answered.

HOT FLASH!
from: Shadwbabe
Wanna go private and
chat awhile?

"Uh, maybe we should move on to the pictures area," I commented. "Got to start advertising Judy's presence over there."

"I'll get to it, all right? I'm going to mess around with this thing, get comfortable with it." She glanced at me without warmth. "If you've got something to do, maybe you should go do it. I'll be all right here."

"You sure?"

She was typing, staring at the screen, and did not answer.

I slid out of the dinette and stood. "Guess I'll run down to the apartments, get caught up on the job a little before we hole up here. I'll be back for dinner, okay?"

The computer beeped. Raeanne, reading something on the screen, smiled. She typed for a moment, gave me a quick meaningless wave, and typed some more.

I went to the door. "By the way, I just figured out what LTNS means."

"What's that?" she asked incuriously.

"Long time no see." I left.

Considering I'd been away from the job two days, the mess at Norwegian Wood wasn't too bad. I did the end-of-week paperwork, signed off on purchase orders, glanced over the backlog, and made out the work schedule for the next two weeks. I also wrote a note for Randy, my senior maintenance kid, telling him to hold the fort for a few days. Fortunately, I was up to full staff. They wouldn't miss me, at least not right away.

Then, consulting my little pad, I called the Proposto campaign number that Zanna had given me. Quickly it answered. "Travel."

"Katie? Ben. What's up?"

The woman sounded very young, rushed, guarded. "Still in Alpena," she answered. "We're busing to Mackinac tomorrow, then Traverse City, then to the west coast, where we'll work our way down to Grand Rapids. Three rallies a day along the way."

"Our little buddy still on the job?"

"Very much so."

"I hear that. Hey, does he have a direct number?"

"He has a cell phone. Want the number?"

"Please."

She rattled it off. I wrote it down. "How's our friend?" she asked.

"Fine, last time I heard."

"Tell her I said hi."

"Will do. Holler if, you know."

"You bet. 'Bye, Ben."

I hung up the phone. Got up and paced across the chilly windowless maintenance office to the cold coffee percolator, paced back to my messy desk again. Lighted a cigar, blew out the match, sat on the edge of the desk, and thought.

Now or never.

I could, of course, give up on the plan and play it straight—make that straight*er*. Maybe it would work. But what if it didn't? Dick sure was skeptical. He understood what the stakes were. So did I. Acutely.

My way was not pleasant. My way, if it worked, would end up quite lethal. But it sure would solve all the problems. It would neaten things up right nice, as my mother would have said. As for guilt, how much would there be, really, considering the provocation?

What it came down to is, either I wanted the sons of bitches finished and off the street or I didn't. It was that simple.

So I made the call.

"Huh," Zanna answered.

"Hey," I said, knocking ash off my cigar. "How are ya?"

"I'm good, Ben," she answered, brightening. "Don't tell me it's over already."

"Not quite. Need a favor, Zanna."

"Anything. What is it?"

"Need you to make a phone call for me, by and by."

"To who," she asked, "and for what?"

"Just hold your horses and I'll tell you."

Ten minutes later we finished and said our good-byes. I hung up the phone and leaned back in the chair. So here we go, I thought. Here we go—

The phone rang. I grabbed it, thinking: a tenant with a problem, a vendor who hasn't been paid, one of my guys wanting time off, Marge in an uproar, maybe even Mr. Horner, my theoretical boss, wanting to rip me a new one. "Perkins, Maintenance," I said briskly.

"Ben?" came the male voice. It sounded familiar, and then again it didn't. "'Bout time I reached you, I tried you a hundred times. Where you been?"

"All over the place, Bill," I said, wondering. It was Bill Scozzafava, my bartender buddy from Under New Management, but he sounded odd. "What's cookin'? You boys started the reconstruction yet? I'll tellya, I can't wait for—"

"It's Eddie," Bill said, subdued. "He killed himself couple nights ago, Ben."

The words kind of bounced off me without registering. "What?"

Bill said nothing.

I found myself on my feet, pacing the area behind my desk, stretching the phone cord. "What happened?" I asked.

"I'd been trying to get hold of him," Bill said.

"The arson people had been questioning me, and—"

"Arson people?"

"Yeah," Bill said, mildly surprised. "Hadn't you heard?"

"I haven't been around much."

"They're sure the place was torched. I think they liked Eddie for it. And now that he's—"

"So he did what? Killed himself?"

"I went over to his house first thing Wed—Tuesday or Wednesday, I don't know which." He fussed, sounding tired. "He never answered his phone, and I knew he never went anywhere. Found him on the back porch glider, shot himself through the head."

At least it was a clear-cut suicide without ropes and straps and dirty pictures, I found myself thinking, the way you think of off-the-wall stuff when you don't want to face something that's just happened. "Christ," I murmured. "How come, you figure? On account of the bar?" Already I had a better idea, but I couldn't bring myself to voice it.

"The cops think he *done* the bar," Bill said. "Maybe he thought they were on to him for it."

"Yeah, maybe. Just doesn't make sense though, none of it." I remembered his fretting about the DNR, and that strange comment he made as the bar was burning down, about how they'd be off his back now. Too much pressure, maybe. Too much shit coming down on him all at once. Everybody had a limit. I thought about Eddie and all those years I'd known him. A strange guy in many ways, feisty, always a bitter little bitcher, like so many struggling small-business people. And I thought about the driveway again, and wondered what could be down there aside from dirt and clay and rocks. "So, they having services?"

"I don't know. They're trying to find kinfolk," Bill

said. "He's got nobody around here that I know of."

"Me neither. He never mentioned anybody." We shared a silence. "Well, let me know if they do something," I told him. "I'll be on the road but I'll call in."

"Maybe you could do some nosing around," Bill suggested, "and figure out why?"

"We'll see," I answered. "Once I finish up some business."

By Sunday, Raeanne had gotten herself well wired into the ContaXX network. As BiJudy, she took part in chats, exchanged E-mail, and began to swap pictures. She worked intently at the computer, quitting only occasionally for meals and rest and refreshment breaks. I sat beside her much of the time, reading over her shoulder, keeping track of the handles of people she contacted, trying somehow to divine which of these jokers, if any, was Del Yinger. It was impossible. The anonymity of the ContaXX network was virtually impenetrable.

Dick Dennehy and Darryl Rockecharlie showed up as scheduled on Sunday and took up their positions. Most of the time they sat in their cars and kept watch, especially at night. They traded positions every couple of hours and gave each other breaks. During the day, a less vulnerable time, they took turns crashing in a room they rented at the Holiday Inn up the road. Once each day, Raeanne went out shopping at Wonderland Mall, while I trailed her at a distance and the fellows took a break. Otherwise it was good old grind-it-out surveillance, sitting and watching and waiting.

They communicated with me, as needed, with short-range walkie-talkies. There wasn't much to communicate, though. Imagine Acres was big, and there was lots of traffic in and out at nearly every hour of the day and night. The men quickly got to know the residents and the regular visitors, which meant it would be that much easier to spot someone like Yinger snooping around, if and when he ever came.

I went to a night-owl schedule myself, catnapping during the day, staying up all night. Twice a day I checked in with Katie Lynn in the Proposto campaign as it worked its way west across the top of the state. I'd had both my apartment phones and car phone forwarded to the trailer's voice phone, so that I'd catch Cockrum and/or Katie Lynn when (or if) they called. At first, I jumped every time the phone rang. But it was always someone else: Carole, or Marge, or Bill Scozzafava, or one of my maintenance kids with some huge horrendous problem.

As for Raeanne, she stayed very much in character as the brittle, resentful Linda Steckroth. We spoke in short impersonal stretches; the rest of the time we were silent as she rattle-tap-tapped at the computer or watched TV, ate, or rested. It was the strangest damn thing. How many couples at the start of a love affair put it on hold because one of them has to pose as a lesbian? Not many, I'll betcha. Maybe, I thought, I should submit this to *America's Funniest People* or something. . . .

Not that what we were doing was funny. I hadn't lost sight, even for a second, of how dangerous it could get. I hadn't forgotten how Yinger got into the David Whitney Building and out again, leaving Chris Cloyd dead but nary a clue or a shred of evidence. I hadn't forgotten about Alex Capitani or Linda Steckroth, either. I hadn't forgotten what Zanna Canady said about Yinger's past . . . some kind of intelligence guy, she'd said. Big time at this stuff.

Well, now that the hunter had become, without

realizing it, the huntee, we'd see how good he really was.

By Wednesday, Raeanne had developed quite an acquaintanceship among the smut swappers in the ContaXX network. There seemed to be considerable interest in the ZANNWCH picture in particular. We didn't send it to anyone; I wanted her to tantalize with the thing. She described it to people, told them it showed Zanna Canady, crowed about it quite convincingly. As the hours went by, she started getting inquiring E-mails and hot flashes from people she hadn't chatted with before, asking about ZANNWCH. Word was getting around.

Still no calls from Cockrum down in Temperance or Katie Lynn up north.

By Wednesday evening, my second missed poker night, our watchdogs were getting grumpy. Darryl overslept on his afternoon nap, provoking a profane tirade from Dick on the walkie-talkie. Dick left his post to take a quick walk, causing Darryl to utter a sentence. Neither of them asked me how long we were going to push this yet, but I knew we couldn't go on much longer. Five days was pretty much my limit, six or seven tops. I hated waiting, anyway. That kind of waiting was the worst. And Raeanne was ice-cold standoffish, a whole different person. Unnerving.

Darryl and Dick thought they had it bad, sitting out in their cars, but for me it was no picnic either. I spent each night in the tiny bathroom of the mobile home with the sliding door shut, just waiting and listening as Raeanne slept in the bedroom. I didn't dare relax. Hopefully, Cockrum would call to tell me Yinger had contacted him. That would be the first warning. Then, hopefully, Dick and Darryl would spot Yinger coming in and alert me in advance. That would be the second warning. But I had to be ready, just in case my makeshift warning system failed for some damn reason.

So Wednesday night, when the noises came, I was ready.

THIRTY-TWO

I was sitting on the commode with both seats down. It was cramped and uncomfortable, but that was the whole point. If I sat on the floor, I might have dozed; this way, if I began to nod off, I'd slump off the thing and hit the wall or floor, and that would wake me up. Hopefully.

It was 3:15 A.M. I was using one of my time-tested time-passing techniques—mentally rebuilding the carburetor of my first brand-new car—when the sounds came from the back of the mobile home. I straightened and squinted and listened as a soft thump came, then a rustling, and then, as I reached for my .45 automatic, just the slightest vibration in the floor.

I braced myself, waiting. Then I heard the sliding door to the bedroom clonk open, and the bathroom door slid open too, and Raeanne stood there blinking, wearing a long white nightshirt. "I woke up," she said.

"Okay." I put the .45 back on the floor by the walkie-talkie and got clumsily to my feet in the narrow space. Damn right foot had gone numb on me again. "I'll get out of your way." I made to go out, to let her have the bathroom, but she blocked my way with a light hand on my chest, looked up into my eyes, and smiled. "I woke up," she repeated.

All at once I had this incredible flood of feeling for her, warmth and wanting that had been pent up for days. I took her in my arms and we kissed hard, clinging together, the whole length of us, standing by the bathroom sink. She broke the kiss and hugged me fiercely, her breath warm on my neck as she whispered. "I'm sorry," she said. "I know I'm overdoing everything."

"It's okay," I answered.

She was tugging my shirttail out of my slacks. "Sometimes, when I'm afraid, it's easier if I'm someone else," she whispered.

My hands couldn't help it, they moved with slow motions down her back to her rear end, feeling her firm skin beneath the shirt. She'd gone to work on my belt buckle and we moved clumsily in the tight space, heating up. "Don't be scared," I said. "He won't get near you."

"That's not what scares me," she whispered back, and kissed me again even harder.

I tugged her nightshirt up around her waist. She had nothing on underneath. As my slacks slid down, I lifted her onto the small vanity, her shoulders against the mirror. She spread her knees and braced, and I cleared the way and eased forward and in—and the phone rang.

We froze, just linked. The phone rang again.

"Oh," Raeanne said ruefully.

"Damn," I whispered. I kissed her quickly and we smiled and separated and I went out into the living area of the mobile home, awkwardly pulling up my pants as I went.

"Yeah," I answered the phone.

"Perkins?"

It was Cockrum's reedy voice, faint and distant. My heartbeat quickened again. "Yeah, Gary."

"He called." Cockrum spoke fast. "You were right, he called. He wants an address."

"Of who? What's the handle?"

"BiJudy."

Bingo. I glanced at Raeanne, who had come into the room also, and winked. "What did you tell him, Gary?"

"I stalled him. Told him we're taking the system down for maintenance. Said he could have it tomorrow."

"Good man. He bought it, I take it?"

"I think so."

"Beautiful," I said automatically, and felt a nudge in the old conscience, which I quickly quelled. Stick to the plan, man. I heard a thump and turned to see that the sliding door to the bedroom had closed, with Raeanne on the other side of it. Waiting for me. Yes.

"So what now?" Cockrum asked nervously.

Good question. "When he contacts you again, give him this address." I rattled it off and made him repeat it. "After that you're out of it, home free." Nudge of conscience again.

"And your state cop buddy'll take the heat off me," Cockrum said. "That was the deal."

"Don't worry about a thing, Gary," I said. "Pretty soon it'll be all over."

I hung up and took a deep breath. Dirty business, but, I reminded myself, there was no other way, and we were too far along to change course now. I went to the bathroom and flicked on my walkie-talkie. "We're in play, gentlemen," I announced. Darryl and Dick acknowledged briefly.

Then I went back out into the living room of the mobile home and sat down at the little dinette by Linda Steckroth's silent computer. There was no sound from the bedroom—Raeanne was waiting for me—but first, one more piece of business. I picked up the phone and dialed a number I knew by heart now. It rang and rang, and rang some more, and then Zanna answered sleepily. "Whafuck?"

"Pull the trigger," I said.

"Whuh?"

"Tomorrow morning, first thing."

"Oh," she said lazily, with some comprehension. "Okay. You sure?"

Well, sort of. "Absolutely," I answered. "Get back to me, hear?"

"Okay," she said, and hung up.

I stood up. My pulse was in overdrive, but by and by it calmed down. Here, I thought, is where the rubber meets the road. Nothing to do now, though, but wait.

I made the rounds of the tiny mobile home yet one more time, checking locks, and wound up at the sliding door to Raeanne's bedroom. No sounds from inside. I slid it open and peered in and froze.

The double bed filled most of the room. A small lamp, mounted on the wall over the bed, focused a spot down on the tousled white sheets. Raeanne lay on her side, facing away from me, knees drawn up under her nightshirt, hands folded together in an attitude of prayer. Her head was pressed into the pillow, and there was a darkness around it, a murky area that for one awful instant looked like a lake of blackish blood soaking the sheet—

But I heard her breathing evenly, and she stirred in her sleep, stretching out one long leg, and I saw that the murky area was just a shadow, a trick of the light and the pillow and the sheet.

That's when I knew for sure that my plan was the right one.

I slid the door shut and resumed my place in the bathroom, to keep watch.

"Perkins!"

I felt something nudge my side, and not gently. I cranked open one eye, closed it, mumbled, and shifted.

"Goddamn it, Perkins, wake up."

Eyes opened again, vision blurry. It sharpened, and then Raeanne, very near, scowling, gave me another sharp nudge. "What?" I fogged.

"Phone."

I blinked and she was gone. Turned over and looked at the ceiling. I was in the double bed, dressed except for my shoes. The clock on the built-in vanity said 11:15. Christ. Three hours I'd slept, maybe.

"Are you coming or not?" Raeanne called.

Shit. "On my way." I eased up, and then stood experimentally and stretched. I felt fragrant and scratchy with new beard, eye-achey, and in dire need of caffeine. The trailer was humid and seemed to have no air to breathe; Raeanne had cracked a couple of windows and turned on a fan, but all that did was shunt the sludgy air around the close confines of the mobile home. Outside the sun was beating down through a misty gauzy sky, raising temperatures and no doubt shortening tempers in Imagine Acres. Another hot sticky one in progress.

I plodded out into the living quarters. My feet were both numb and my balance wasn't working well. I'd forgotten what a bitch the midnight shift was. Well, with any luck I'd be back on human-being hours soon.

Raeanne sat longways on the dinette bench, leaning against the wall, reading the *Free Press*. She wore black suede short-shorts and a matching halter top, had gooed her hair into glistening dark spikes, and had dark circles under her eyes that I presently identified as makeup. On the table in front of her the computer hummed, screen showing the ContaXX signoff, and the phone receiver lay next to it, waiting.

"Morning, sweetheart," I said.

Her gray eyes flickered at me and she turned the page.

I picked up the phone. "Yeah, talk to me."

"Well, honey, I did it," said Zanna, from far away.

"Oh, that's great, darlin'."

"I don't know why I did it, but I did it," she said doubtfully. "Mind filling me in on just what you're up to?"

"Better off not knowing."

"Just hope it works, whatever it is," she said.

"Me too," I answered, thinking. "Tell me exactly what you told him."

"I can do better than that," she said. "I taped it."

"Oh, yeah?"

"Stuck one of those suction-thangies to the phone. Came out pretty well. Want to hear it?"

"Fire away."

"Just a minute, lemme figure this out," she muttered.

I heard the phone clonk and some even more distant sounds. Raeanne was studying the paper intently, paying no attention to me. I braced the receiver between shoulder and ear and shook myself a cigar out of the pack on the tiny counter. I was getting low on matches, though, just two or three left. Still bracing the phone, I turned on one of the gas burners and lighted the cigar from the flame and exhaled a nice long one as Zanna's voice returned.

"Okay, here we go," she said. "Hope it comes through clear enough."

"Ready," I answered.

I heard fluttering, little mechanical chirping sounds, then a steady low-grade hiss, and suddenly there was Zanna's voice, one generation removed. "—day for a long time, Del Yinger. A *long* time."

The next voice was male, even more distant, but very clear and precise. "Zanna," he said evenly, "where are you? Why did you leave New York? The boss is worried about you."

"Oh," she came back mockingly, "are we afraid the little gal done went off the reservation? Might go say naughty no-nos to the press? Well, that's the least of your worries, little daddy."

"What do you want, Zanna?"

"Oh," she answered airily, "after all we've meant to each other, Mr. Del, sir, I felt it was only fitting I'd be the one to tell you: It's all over."

"What are you talking about?"

"Them people you kilt. The cops know *all* about it, and they're about to take your skinny ass down."

"Tell you what," Yinger said tightly. "When you're sober, and ready to talk sense, call me back. Meantime—"

"That man in the building," she overrode, "the ad agency man? And the girl in the house trailer? And, uh . . . that other guy, the one sending around dirty pictures of his daughter?" Silence. "Oh," she cooed, "have I got your attention now?"

"We should get together," he said, "and talk about this."

"Ha!" she said richly. "Oh, no. I'm staying way outa sight on this one. My detective friend's handling it. He's the one put it all together, you know. Old Ben's gonna fix you, boy. He backtracked you, and he's putting it all together. Remember that computer network man, the one who gave you the addresses? Ben got him to sing. Tonight him and Ben are meeting with the cops to do a deal. You done been ratted out, boy. They gonna carve you up like a Thanksgiving pig, Mr. Del. Stretch you out on a sterling silver serving plate with a big ol' Paula Red apple in your mouth."

"You're crazy," he said, mildly disdainful.

"What I am, bubba, is thuh-rilled. See you on visiting day. Not."

More noise, then a snap, and the hiss quit as the connection broke. Clicking and a thump, and then Zanna was back. "How was that?"

"Great," I answered. "When was this?"

"'Bout half hour ago."

Ten-thirty or thereabouts. "You really dressed it up," I observed.

"Had to make it convincing. Besides," she said with a grim laugh, "it was fun. I've wanted to trash his ass for a long time."

"You did fine. Now we'll see."

"What do you think he'll do?" she asked.

"We'll see," I repeated. "Thanks, Zanna."

I hung up the phone and smoked in silence. Raeanne was watching me. "What did she want?"

"We got action," I answered absently. "Anybody else call this morning?"

"No."

Better whistle her up then, I thought. But first things first. I went to the bathroom, washed up with a few quick splashes, retrieved the walkie-talkie, and stuck the .45 automatic into the waistband of my slacks as I went back out into the living area. My feet had woken up, and most of the rest of me too. Now all I needed was some coffee, to feel a little alive. I poured myself a mug from the pot Raeanne had made, grabbed the phone again, flipped pages on my little pad, and punched out the campaign number. Katie Lynn answered right away. "Travel."

"What's up, Katie?"

"Wait a minute." I heard her mutter something, and when she came back her rushed voice was softer. "He's in Elberta with the advance team."

"Alberta? You mean—"

"Elberta. It's by Lake Michigan, near Sleeping Bear. We'll be there later today, after Petoskey."

"Okay, thanks."

I sat down and sipped some hot joe as Raeanne turned pages of her paper. Now the waiting would become, if anything, even tougher. I'd done all I could do, and now we'd see. I felt helpless. What if, after all this grief, my theory was wrong? Or, even if I was right, what if he didn't go for the bait? Well, I guessed, we'd just fold up the tent and go home and hope for better luck next time.

While the son of a bitch walked free.

"I need to go shopping later," Raeanne said absently as the computer hummed on the dinette table between us.

"Sure," I answered. "What's happening on the network?"

"Nothing," she said tersely. "You know, it gets pretty damn boring after a while."

"Really?"

She got up and refilled her mug. "Bunch of losers on there, with nothing better to do than write dirty stuff back and forth," she said. "They're like naughty little kids. Far as I'm concerned, they should grow up and get a life."

"I hear that."

She leaned against the stove, her long slim legs crossed. "I'll be glad to be off there."

"We'll all be—" The ringing of the phone interrupted me. I grabbed it. "Talk to me."

"He's not there," came Katie Lynn's soft rushed voice.

"What? Where is he then?"

"I don't know," she came back. "He was supposed to be in Elberta with the team, but he never got there."

"You're sure."

"Positive. It's happened before. He's that way; he vanishes for hours at a time. I thought you should know."

"Thanks. Call me if you hear anything."

"Right."

I hung up. This is it, this is *it*, I thought.

CHAPTER

THIRTY-THREE

Raeanne was watching me, expression sardonic and suspicious. I gave her a grin. "We're about out of this, darlin'."

"Cool," she answered, and sipped some coffee.

I pressed the SEND button of the walkie-talkie and said, "Who's on?"

"Me," came Dick's crackly answer.

"Where's Dare?"

"Up napping. We gotta talk, old buddy," Dick said.

"I know. Come on in and we'll do it."

"Come on in?" he retorted. "That'll blow our—"

"Just come on in," I said, and shut the walkie-talkie off.

I found my shoes and put them on. Located cigars and keys and wallet and extra ammo and loaded up. Raeanne watched all this without comment. I went to her and put my hands on her shoulders, but she made no move for me, did not respond at all, quite a different woman from the one who had clung to me in the bathroom the night before.

"Going home tonight," I told her, sounding more confident than I felt.

"Good. Be glad to get out of this shithole."

The door pounded. I peered out, unlocked it, and opened it up. Dick Dennehy came in, wired and blustery. He was coat- and tieless with dark circles under his wary eyes, and his short gray-blond hair was matted from many hours on the job. "What the hell?" he growled, peering back out the window. "This could blow our cover, you know. What if our perp's watching?"

"Good morning," I said easily. "And he's not. Trust me."

Dick snorted.

"Deal is," I went on, "I got to take off for a while. I want you to stay here with Raeanne and get Darryl back on the gate."

Dick looked incredulous. "Jesus H. Christ," he cut in. "What the fuck are you up to?"

"Just some business, nothing special."

He stepped toward me, all menace. "You're not going anywhere."

"Correction," I shot back. "I'm gonna do what I want."

"Boys, boys, boys," Raeanne called in a sharp, snotty voice. We looked at her. "Inspector," she told Dick, "I'm sure Ben knows what he's doing. If he wants to go, let him go. We'll be okay here till he gets back."

"Doesn't make sense," Dick grumbled.

"Doesn't have to," she answered. "I trust him."

Dick let out a long, frustrated breath. "Okay, all right. Hope you know what you're doing, old buddy."

"Guard her with your life," I told him, and left.

The way I figured it, Yinger would make the trip by car. The only other option was to fly, and that would leave a trail. And besides, it would take just about as long. On my way south, I called my friendly travel agent from the car phone, and she did some fast research. The nearest airport of any consequence to Elberta was Traverse City, fifty winding two-lane miles away, and from there he'd have to catch a series of puddle-jumpers to either Detroit Metro or Toledo Express airports. And then he'd still have to drive a good forty minutes to get to Temperance. He couldn't possibly get to Cockrum's place before midafternoon.

Nope. Driving was the most sensible thing. That put him five hours, easy, from Temperance. Figure three in the afternoon he'd get there. By then, I'd be more than ready.

I took the easy way down, Interstate 275 to 75 and then west to Temperance. On the way I ate lunch, picked up a *Belleville Enterprise* newspaper, smoked a couple of cigars, listened to Buddy Guy. I reached Temperance about twelve-thirty and rolled by Cockrum's converted strip mall on Hench Road about twenty to. It was lunch hour, and the parking lot was almost deserted, making the place look almost as desolate as the quarry next door and the abandoned drive-in theater across the road. The only sign of life was a navy Dodge utility van backing up to one of the truck bays in back. No doubt, I thought, another video store flunky picking up a shipment of dirty flicks.

I could not expect Yinger for at least a couple of hours. Plenty of time to get situated. I rolled by the place a couple of times on Hench Road, scoping it out. I couldn't exactly plunk down in the parking lot and wait. A tad too obvious. Yinger didn't know me or the Mustang, but Cockrum did, and I didn't want him knowing I was near. So I needed a place to hide out.

The quarry was no good. Whole place was fenced off with high chain link, and what had been the drive-way was blocked off with huge concrete tiles sitting in an irregular line like giant gray chunks of Tootsie Roll. East of the mall was a swath of forest, which had its possibilities—forests usually have trails, and I'd probably find a decent vantage point if I looked long enough.

But the best bet seemed to be the abandoned drive-in across the road.

It was fenced in too. The old rusty chain link was topped with barbed wire and thickly entwined with lush leafy grapevines. The entryway was still there, and what had been the gate was bent and twisted and crushed over to the side, leaving just enough room to get the Mustang through. Looked like somebody had mangled it open with a car or something, a long time before. I could just imagine why.

I eased the Mustang through the opening. The old wood ticket booth sat forlornly to the right, its glass long since busted out. Dead ahead was the gigantic white movie screen, its back to me; beyond it was the drive-in parking area, a gentle rise of ancient cracked blacktop with grassy weeds poking through it, dotted at military intervals by the yellow steel posts that once held the sound speakers.

I didn't care about that. I followed the fence about thirty feet west, turned the Mustang around so it was facing the other way, and shut it off. The weeds grew waist high here but had been matted down from time to time by earlier visitors. As I got out of the Mustang and went to the fence, I found the area was heavily littered with all kinds of stuff: old empty beer cans, flattened faded cigarette packs, potato chip bags, used condoms, a woman's sneaker, white once. Real party place, nice and private. Perfect.

At the fence, I used my pocketknife to hack at the grapevine, stripping away long oily strands until I had chopped a fairly decent hole. I got back in the Mustang and found I now had a useful view of Cockrum's building, the parking lot, and the driveway. Lovely.

Assuming, of course, Yinger showed up. If he did— *if* he did—what a hell of a thing it would be. After all, I'd never ever laid eyes on the guy, except on TV. I'd tracked him from afar, and now I was reeling him in, and then I'd put him down, all without having ever exchanged so much as a word with him.

If he was coming. To make sure, I decided to call Katie Lynn again. I dug for my little spiral pad and came up empty. Nothing in my pocket but matches and ammo clips. Must have left the pad back at the mobile home. Shit.

Oh, well. I knew Yinger would show. He had to. Cockrum was the sole link between Yinger and the victims. Cockrum, according to Zanna Canady, was meeting with the state cops and me this very night to rat Yinger out. Cockrum had to go, and Yinger was just the man for the job. So I knew he'd be here, and I knew what would happen then.

Didn't want to think about it, though.

So I assumed the position in the driver's seat. For extra comfort, I took the ammo clips out of my pocket and laid them on the floor of the back seat. Then I leaned back, lighted a cigar, snapped open the front page of the Belleville paper. The boxed story at the top, under the masthead, pounced on me like a cat off a tree limb.

STATE CREW UNEARTHS CORPSE

The Wayne County medical examiner is trying to identify the remains of a woman unearthed in Van Buren Township by an excavation crew, but so far has had no luck.

The corpse was discovered Wednesday morning

buried in an abandoned parking lot at Haggerty and Ecorse roads. The excavation crew that made the find was under contract to the state Department of Natural Resources.

A department spokesperson confirmed the discovery, adding only that the remains were found about twelve feet down and had been there, according to Van Buren Township detectives called to the scene, for a decade or more.

The body was transported to the Wayne County Morgue, where pathologists will try to determine its identity as well as the cause of death. Detectives would not rule out the possibility of foul play.

The parking lot is on the site of the former Lighthouse Bar and Grill, which was totally destroyed in a fire earlier this week. The investigation of that incident continues.

I stared numbly at the paper, flooded with so many thoughts that none of them stayed put: Eddie, the fuel tanks, 1968, tree huggers, Eddie, the fire, Eddie, shot himself dead.

And Lighthouse Bar and Grill. So that was Under New Management's real name.

I wondered who the woman was. I wondered what Eddie had done to her. I wondered at the naiveté of all of us stool fools, traipsing in and out of the saloon for all those years, not knowing a corpse lay buried below where we parked our cars. I realized, as I slowed down and thought about things logically, that none of us ever really knew much about old Eddie. Not even Bill, his longtime bartender. We knew he lived alone, we knew he kept to himself, but that was about all we knew.

Until now.

I kept coming back to the woman. Wife? Daughter?

Girlfriend? What happened? Foul play? Obviously. Eddie? Must have. All those years, thought he got away with it—and then came the notice from the Department of Natural Resources.

No wonder he was so upset.

I threw aside the paper and peered across Hench Road, inventorying the scene. Nothing substantive had changed. Keeping my eyes on the view, I went back to my old friend: waiting. I didn't think about Eddie and the corpse anymore. I didn't think about what would happen when—and if—Yinger arrived. I didn't occupy my mind with exciting things like carburetor rebuilds this time, either.

What I thought about was women.

But how can you just sit here and let Cockrum get—

I thought about Rachel, my little rookie, developing into her own person with terrifying quickness. Tomorrow was Rachel night again, and my main task now was to stay alive until then. Don't worry, kid, I thought, Daddy'll do his best not to get himself shot.

Sure, he's got it coming. Remember Jenny Phelan, found beaten to death? You know that was him.

I thought about Carole, tall lovely Carole, abrasive, self-confident Carole, forever my ex. I thought about our years together and apart, things said and done, unsaid and undone, a long, passionate, and traumatic trail that ended here, with her and Longstreth. I wasn't jealous. I wasn't even sad. Just a little wistful. If I'd listened a little more, thought a little more, cared a little more—would things have worked out differently?

He's a wart on the ass of society, destructive and poisonous and seemingly untouchable. He's got to be stopped. But isn't this the same thing as pointing a gun and—

I thought about Barb, out in California, with a new love, new life, new locale. Living proof that a person can work through the worst kinds of troubles and come out the other side and be happy in the end. Living proof also that when it came to being wrong about something, I took a back seat to no one.

How about that little job interview of his? An animal like that deserves what happens to him. Hell, you've done worse, a hell of a lot worse.

I even thought about my mother, dead these twenty years, crushed by a falling beam while rescuing elderly people from a burning house. She'd died convinced I was bound for prison, and I wondered what she'd think of how I had turned out.

It's murder, Benjy, murder, son. An evil thing.

I thought about Raeanne—

"Freeze, asshole."

I froze. The male voice was a low whisper, outside the car and behind me. Christ! I thought. Got the drop on me! Slowly I put my hands on the steering wheel. "Your call," I said, staring ahead out the windshield.

"Very good," came the voice, in a normal tone this time, chuckling.

Christ! I thought again. I turned and stared. "How the hell did you find me?"

Dick Dennehy holstered his Colt Python under his gray jacket and walked around the rear of the car to the passenger door, crunching weeds as he went. "The usual brilliant inductive and deductive reasoning," he said, as he got in. He left the door ajar and one trousered leg hanging out, his black street shoe buried in weeds. "Any action?" he asked, jerking a thumb in the direction of Cockrum's building.

"Quiet so far. Early yet, though." It was just past one. "Seriously, Dick, what the hell are you doing here?"

"Wanna be where the action is," he said airily, getting out a Lucky Strike.

"Wanted you to guard Raeanne."

"Raeanne's just fine," he answered, flaming his cigarette, "and you know it."

"I do?"

"You wouldn't have left her if you thought there was even a chance Yinger was on his way there. True?"

"True. But—"

He faced me. "Let me explain my reasoning, and you tell me how close I am. Fair enough?"

"Go ahead."

"First of all, you left something behind when you took off." He went inside his jacket and tossed me my tattered little spiral pad. "Took the liberty of making some phone calls. Called your blues singer friend, called the woman in the Proposto campaign. Put it all together and figured this was where you had to be."

"So it wasn't deductive reasoning," I said, grinning. "You got Zanna and Katie to rat me out."

Dick exhaled smoke and *tsk-tsk*ed. "Shoulda filled us in, buddy. Sometimes you carry this tight-lipped act way too far."

"I didn't want you involved in this," I told him. "Or Raeanne, either."

"Involved in what?" he asked evenly. "Yinger killing Cockrum?"

He really *had* figured it out. "Yeah, that. Fewer people involved, the better."

"You just want all the fun for yourself, old buddy. Damn selfish, if you ask me."

"You call this fun?"

"I call it brilliant," he answered, quite serious. "This is the way to go. Absolutely."

I didn't answer.

"Cockrum's an insect," Dick said. "A slippery slime-ball, needs wasting bad. Then take this Yinger guy. If your theory is right—and I think it is—he's responsible for at least two murders. What do we got for evidence? Jack shit. So what you do is, you give Yinger a good reason to waste Cockrum, and you catch Yinger in the act. The result? Cockrum's off the street for good; Yinger's under the hammer for murder. Two for the price of one."

Still I said nothing.

"Like I said," Dick commented. "Brilliant."

"Also wrong," I said quietly.

THIRTY-FOUR

"What?" Dick asked sharply.

"It's a wrong thing, man. I can't go through with it," I said.

"You're shittin' me."

"It's wrong, Dick. We're setting Cockrum up like a pigeon, and it's—"

"He deserves—"

"Maybe," I overrode, "but there is such a thing as due process."

"What due process did Yinger give those victims?" Dick asked furiously. "What due process did Cockrum give Jenny Phelan?"

"None and none," I answered. "Doesn't mean we should go the same route. There's got to be a better way."

He was getting hotter. "If that's how you feel, why'd you set it up like this?"

"Didn't think it through. Now I have."

Dick glared at me. "Never figured you'd go soft on me."

"Everything changes," I said. If I sounded a little jaunty, it's because that's how I felt. Relieved, too. It's amazing, how easily you can fall into doing a bad thing and press on with it, with blinders on your eyes and a gag on your conscience. That's what I'd done for several days, but now I saw how wrong I was, and moreover I knew how to fix it. And I felt good about it, as if an elephant's foot had been lifted off my heart. "But don't worry, Dick, we'll still get Yinger. I have a plan." The state cop smoked and fumed and stared out the passenger window toward Cockrum's building. "Remember," I reminded him, "you said I'm calling the shots. You in or out?"

"In," he said grumpily.

"Good man." I picked up the cellular, consulted my pad, and punched. After a moment Cockrum himself answered, which surprised me a little. "Heard anything from our little buddy?" I asked.

"No," came his reedy voice.

"Well," I said, "as it happens, I'm across the street with a friend of mine, and we've got a proposition for you. Mind if we stop by?"

"All right," he said tonelessly.

"See you in a minute." I hung up the phone, reached under the driver's seat, and extracted the .45 automatic. With a quick metallic snap I worked the action to put a round under the hammer, then stuck the weapon in the waistband of my jeans, under my shirt, against my spine. "Ready?"

"What's with the artillery?" Dick asked sourly. "I thought you wanted to go over there and talk the bad guys into giving up."

"I've maybe gone soft," I said sarcastically, "but I ain't gone stupid. Or stupider. Wanna do this?"

"Lead the way," Dick answered.

We exited the Mustang and high-stepped through the tall weeds toward the gap in the gate. A lone car breezed by on Hench Road, and then we walked across, the tarry blacktop soft under our shoes. It was the height of the summer day, a preview of July, the sun a blazing disk fixed in the deep blue sky, the air a still, solid, humid presence. Dick, obviously baking in his gray suit, loosened his nothing tie as we entered the parking lot. "Looks pretty deserted," he commented.

It did, too. There hadn't been much action since I arrived. Several cars had pulled in; none had left. The usual scattering of vehicles sat in the lot, waiting patiently in the hot sun. The blue van was still backed into one of the loading bays around back. The windowless brick building was silent as Dick and I walked toward it. "How do you think we'll get the drop on him?" Dick asked.

"Dunno," I answered. "We'll figure that out once Cockrum signs on. We got time. Yinger can't possibly get here for a while yet."

As we reached the heavy gray steel door, I saw that Dick had pulled his Colt Python and held it against his pants leg in his right hand. I thought that was a tad melodramatic, but I said nothing. I opened the door and stepped into the hallway. Dick followed.

The place looked just the way I remembered it; a long hall ran straight as a poker to the other end. Doors dotted each wall at intervals. The drop ceiling was cheap white acoustic tiles interspersed with indirect lights, and the floor was industrial-grade carpet glued to concrete, like a day's growth of blue beard. All the doors were closed: A Co., Welcome Productions, Diversified Products. All silent, a little ominous.

Dick asked, "What do you—" A sound came from behind us, the rattle of a door latch, faint. The faintness was the tip-off, and Dick sensed it too, and as we pivoted he was raising his weapon even as I was digging for mine. A shot boomed. Dick cursed, crouched, and

cut loose with his Python as I jerked my Colt free an
dumped a couple of wild shots, falling to the har
carpeted floor. Our fusillade peppered the cheap dry
wall down there and blew out a couple of ceiling tile:
leaving a scattered pattern of rough holes and fillin
the air with drywall dust. But there were no bodies, n
cries, no nothing—just abrupt silence in the smok
hallway.

"Fuck," Dick muttered, and slid suddenly along th
wall to the floor. His face was as gray as his suit, and hi
right knee had become a shapeless red mass, the le
folded at a bizarre angle under him. "Kneecapped me,
Dick moaned.

Weapon ready, I scooted over to him. "He went fo
you first," I said, heart pounding. "I'm truly insulted.
Cockrum? I was wondering. *Cockrum's* the shooter
What could he possibly hope to gain?

"Not funny," Dick said faintly, head lolling agains
the wall. "I'm gonna pass out on you, buddy."

"Hang on." I rose, leveling my weapon warily, an
darted back a few feet to a door on the left side. It wa
unmarked and unlocked. I pushed the door open an
saw that it was a long unfinished room, the unpainte
drywall showing its stark white mud seams, the bar
concrete floor scattered with scraps of BX conduit an
toe strip. Dick was so sickly pale his lips looked blue
but somehow he had found the strength to fight hi
way to an almost-standing position on his good foot.
took him under the arms and eased him along into th
room, where I lowered him to the floor with his bac]
against the wall. He'd left a trail of blood, and the kne
was bubbling red now through the cloth of his pants
and he was gasping, in borderline shock and obviousl
fighting to stay conscious.

"Just a scratch," he whispered.

"Sure." I stripped off his tie and dropped it in his lap. "You know what to do with that." I went back to the door and peered, quickly and furtively, up and down the hall. Nothing. I could hear sounds in the building, across the hall, low sounds like quick steps on carpet, a room or two away. What the hell's he doing? I wondered. Why hasn't he come after us?

When I returned to Dick, he had fashioned a tourniquet of sorts with his necktie around his thigh. He was slumped raggedy-doll against the wall, eyes shut. The pressure as I tightened the tourniquet revived him, and he looked at me blearily as I clapped his big Python into his hand. I didn't have to explain what I was about to do. He understood. "Keep your head down," I advised him. "Aim low. Shoot to kill."

"You too," he answered.

I clapped his shoulder and went back to the door, .45 at the ready. Still nothing in the hallway in either direction. No more sounds, either. I decided to work him from the far end. Back brushing the wall, I darted down the hall toward the ContaXX door, feeling incredibly vulnerable; anyone from either end could have plinked me easily, but fortunately no one did. Weapon ready, I kicked the ContaXX door open and swiveled in, ready to shoot.

Nothing.

The small waiting room was empty. The reception desk and its big phone console were spick-and-span, as if the receptionist had left for the day. I wondered then about her, about the other employees in the building. I'd seen no one leave. Where the hell were they?

The door to Cockrum's office was ajar. As I tiptoed toward it, I saw bright streams of coarse powder, an electric orange color, running along the carpet next to the walls. Some kind of carpet cleaner, or—

Motion behind Cockrum's door, and as I flung myself backward shots boomed, the slugs ripping through the cheap hollow door and slamming with terrifying force through the walls and off the steel desk. I was on the floor, panicky, rolling against the desk legs and trying to hide and waiting for it to stop, or to get hit, or to die, or something. But the firing just stopped. In the fresh silence I realized I was not even hit.

It was as if the shooter wanted to keep me busy while he did something else.

Slowly I rose. I was hurting now; after you've slammed yourself on cloth-covered concrete a few times, you start to feel it. The receptionist's desk had been knocked catty-wampus and was bashed in but good, and the hollow door to Cockrum's office was even more hollow, having had great chunks blown off it. Silence from back there. I stepped over, .45 ready, and gave a quick peek in. Nobody. Noise from another room, though: from the computer area, it sounded like.

Warily I slipped into Cockrum's office. All was as it had been the other times I'd seen it, mostly. Its owner was absent, a stray bullet had totaled the TV, the computer screen was dark, and those lines of bright orange powder streaked the carpet along the walls, almost as if someone had been drawing base paths or something.

Quickly I went to the opposite door, leading into the computer area. I edged it open and saw nothing. Noise again, still from farther back. The shooter was moving away, keeping his distance.

I went into the computer room. Nobody there, nothing awry except for that orange powder. The noise from farther away was more pronounced now. Getting careless? Getting bolder? *Getting away?*

The next door was locked. I snorted, stepped back, poised, and kicked the knob clean off. Stooping, I worked the spindle to move the latch and opened the door, ever so slowly.

The next room was a long dim warehouse with a high dark ceiling and unpainted cinderblock walls. In the distance I could see daylight, obscured by stacks of boxes and rows of gray steel utility shelves. All the lights were off, but daylight filtered in, no doubt from the truck bay doors that I'd seen earlier. I froze, uncertain, fearing a trap; the shooter could have been lying in wait in any of those rows. But then I heard sounds from the daylight end: footsteps again, rustling, a thud, and then, the most definitive sound of all, the slam of a vehicle door.

I took off running, hunched down, .45 automatic ready. As I burst out of the rows of shelves into an open area, I saw the navy Dodge utility van down low in one of the loading bays, backed up to the concrete dock. The driver's door was shutting, and I saw a face in the window as the engine fired up.

Not Gary Cockrum.

Del Yinger. Yes, indeed. Slender and dark-haired and dour, handsome in an anonymous sort of way, not quite Tony Perkins but close. Of course it was thoroughly impossible for him to be here. If he'd started in Elberta, he could not possibly reach Temperance for another hour or more—but there he was. He had, in fact, arrived about the same time I did.

He didn't stop to explain how he'd worked this miracle. He didn't even take any shots at me. All he did was slam the van into gear and floor the gas. The rear wheels screamed smokily as the vehicle lunged away from the loading dock. That put me in a real fix. My Mustang was all the way across the road; by the time I corralled it, he'd be on Interstate 75. I wasn't about to just let him take off, not without trying the obvious, ridiculous though it was.

I ran to the end of the loading dock and dropped into a one-kneed shooting stance, left hand bracing my right wrist as I—ha—aimed the .45. The van was screeching almost on two wheels in an arc to go around the building, bound for Hench Road. I trained my weapon as steadily as I could and fired five times, as fast as I could pull the trigger. The clumsy old gun bucked like a jackhammer, shell casings flew, and then the weapon locked open, empty.

I'd hit the van at least once, on the back end, but otherwise the shots did squat. The vehicle started to straighten its swerve toward Hench Road but suddenly, as I dug frantically in my pocket for another clip, the vehicle's front end dropped and the van started to slide and a line of bullet holes punched along the right front fender, *thunk thunk thunk*, as shots rang out from somewhere around the corner.

My hand was empty. No spare clips; left them in the Mustang. Damn. Without thinking, I jumped off the loading dock and ran in the direction of the van. It had hopped the curb and slid cornerwise on its wheels up the grassy berm, tires tearing the turf. I thought it might go right over the berm, through the chain-link fence, and down into the quarry on the other side. It hit the fence, all right, rear first, having spun almost 180 degrees by then, and punched through it with a metallic ripping-shredding sound, but that was all. The van came to rest at the top of the rise, half through the fence, right side up, engine smoking silently, right front tire flat.

By then I had trotted around the corner to the front of the building. The steel front door was half open and Dick Dennehy lay on the concrete, half in and half out, raised on one elbow, Python aimed in the direction of the van, about fifty yards away. He called something—could have been my name—but I didn't stop, not for Dick, not to think. I just tore on like a guided missile and charged the van, veering left a bit and crouching, to present the narrowest possible target from the side door.

More shots as I ran, from the building: Dick Dennehy giving covering fire. His bullets peppered the dark blue van, blowing out the windows and windshield and poking black holes through the steel skin. The run seemed endless. But in just seconds, as the shooting stopped, I slammed against the grille of the van, then turned and crouched and slithered around the fender toward the open sliding door, closing in on the bastard at last.

THIRTY-FIVE

Yinger was inside on his hands and knees, just behind the twin seats, covered in busted glass, crawling toward the empty rear of the van, reaching for a pistol that lay on the hard steel floor of the cargo area. I hurled my useless .45 at him like a Frisbee; it clattered somewhere behind him as he came up with his gun, but I had grabbed the van roof above the open door with both hands and swung in feet first, driving my shoes at him like a battering ram and slamming his gun hand hard. The gun fired, the bullet screamed past me, and Yinger stumbled and fell the other way onto the floor, his gun bouncing away as I swung my feet down and jumped into the van after him.

I thought I had him cornered, but man, was he fast. He drove his shoulder into me, knocking my wind out and throwing us both on the glass-strewn van floor against the front seats. He went for my throat but I kneed him and butted him, swiveled and spun him jiggly, and then, having created punching room, bashed at his face with a quick right jab. That rocked him, and I knocked him off me, but before I could take advantage he had my right arm in a twisting excruciating hold, and with that he propelled me against the wall of the van with an impact that made me see spots.

I was bigger and stronger than Yinger. But he was wiry, and powerful, and knew lots of moves. I was on my hands and knees, head swirling with shooting stars, and Yinger jumped on me from behind and gave me the old half nelson strangulation grip that would break my neck unless I suffocated first.

I could only barely breathe. I rose, lifting him, and pivoted on all fours, trying to spin him off me like water off a dog, but it was no good. I stumbled sideways, vision going red, and thrust myself backward between the two front seats, as if to knock him off by driving him into the bulbous engine enclosure that spanned the space below the dashboard. Of course that had no effect, but I didn't really expect it to. I had something else in mind.

Yinger, grunting, squeezed my neck tighter and tighter. I made a not entirely phony show of struggling, as I wormed the practically numb fingers of my hand into my pants pocket. Suddenly Yinger shifted and got a better grip, but by then I was as ready as I was ever going to be.

Without looking, but with a prayer the damn thing wasn't sodden with sweat, I flicked the kitchen match against my thumbnail, down near where I figured Yinger's elbow was.

"Hey!" he screamed, and in that blessed instant of release I caught a good breath, lunged him over to the left, and, with my right hand, slapped the shift lever of the van up one notch.

And the van lurched, and bumped, and started to roll backward.

Yinger came at me, but I popped him in the face again. That hurt him but didn't finish him. Outside the window, the fence went by as I came up to a crouch. Yinger parried my feint and I popped him again with a straight jab, bang on the nose, and he fell onto the passenger seat. The van bumped on its suspension and gained speed on the incline. Yinger grabbed at me as I scrambled by, but missed. We were really rolling now; time to leave. I stumbled uphill to the sliding door as the van took a hard bounce, and without thought or plan I flung myself through the opening and flew free. The sky, the building, the ground—I got my hands out just in time and caught myself with joint-wrenching impact on the edge of the stone cliff as the van sailed on past me.

For a moment I just dangled there on the gravelly stone lip, feet free and incredibly heavy, scrabbling at the edge with my ripped-up hands, breathing so hard it hurt, my arms screaming *enough already!* Almost at once a hard metallic crash sounded below. Don't look down *don't look down.* I tried to pull myself up—another crash from down there—not enough strength oh my God—a final *whoosh* of water from downstairs as I summoned everything I had left and shimmy-kicked myself over the lip of the cliff and collapsed on the rocky ground.

A wave of spots and swirling red blurred my vision. I blinked, and rose onto my haunches, and bent and violently threw up. Closed my eyes till my head cleared, rocking blearily on my haunches. All was silent now. I slid myself to the edge of the cliff and looked down into the quarry.

The smooth granite wall ran down about forty feet and ended in a wide pond of green water. Evidently the van had hit an outcropping on the other side, come back this way and hit another, and then went into the drink.

Amazingly, it was still there. The blue van floated on its side, slowly turning in the cool green water. The sliding door was halfway open, and caught in its opening was

Del Yinger, his face a blob of white agony way, way down there. As I watched, the van began to nose down, the motion making Yinger's head bob, and then, with a sudden nose-first plunge, the van was gone, the green water closing with finality over where it had been.

A sudden surge of bubbles, and it was over.

Slowly, I got to my feet. Everywhere, all over me, I was ripped and torn and bashed, as if I'd endured a ten-round tag-team stomping by Joe Frazier and Mike Tyson. All I could think about was ending this. Get Dick to the hospital and me back home, and then forget all this, forget it, it's *done*. I hoofed heavily up the berm toward the ripped chain-link fence, stopped to shake some broken glass out of my pants, and staggered on to the top.

But once there, I froze.

Cockrum's building was burning. Great sheets of yellow flame shot out the open truck bay doors, and blue-gray smoke floated in a haze along the flat roof. A half dozen people milled and gawked in the parking lot where a pair of cars parked nose to nose. I picked up speed to an easy aching amble, and as I neared the group I saw Dick Dennehy, slouching against a front tire of one of the cars, bad leg out at a funny angle. The people around him—evidently passersby from the road who'd swung in to rubberneck—were chattering and milling about and gaping at the building, hoping, I guess, to see someone fry.

They shut up when they saw me. Just shut up and stared and kind of edged back. I guess I was quite a sight. Dick's pasty face didn't change expression. I glowered down at him. "I thought you'da bled to death by now," I said.

"Had to see who won," he answered.

Someone came running up to us, shouting something about nine-one-one. "You mean, you had doubts?" I asked Dick.

The state cop ignored that. "Yinger say anything?"

"He said, 'Hey.'" I turned and looked at the building, then looked back at Dick. "Incidentally, you shoot better when you're hemorrhaging. That was a great shot, getting his tire like that."

"Thanks," Dick answered. "Trouble was, I was aiming for Yinger. Where's your piece?"

"Went down with him."

"Good. You couldn't hit anything with it anyway."

More vehicles were pulling in. Sirens sounded from far away. I looked back at the building again and knew what I had to do. "Stick around," I told Dick. "We'll grab some supper after." And with that I started for the building.

"Where the hell are you going?" a man asked, grabbing my arm.

I shook him off and glared, and he backpedaled quickly, hands up in surrender. Almost at once the spectators went silent again, all eyes on me. "There's people inside," I said, my voice tinny and loud. "See all these cars? That guy, Yinger, he must have locked them up someplace in there. I got to get them out."

Immediately there was a clamor of protest. But Dick was watching me, and he just nodded once. I turned and began to trot toward the building, headed for the flames that were rising higher and hotter now.

The man, the busybody who'd grabbed me before, caught up with me. "You crazy son of a bitch!" he screamed. "Don't go in there!"

"Get back from me, boy," I answered, walking hard.

"Whaddya tryin' to be?" He sneered. "Some kinda hero?"

"No," I told him. "No. It's not what I am. It's what I do."

He fell back from me as I made for the flames.

*   *   *

By early evening, a cool front had rolled in. The sky went to a cloudless azure as the sun headed downward and the humidity dropped below fifty and a light breeze picked up. It would be great sleeping weather.

Telegraph Road was fender-to-fender frantic, the four southbound lanes dense with trucks and cars and the occasional motorcycle jockeying for position as we shunted in bursts between red lights. I had to force myself to recall that this was, in fact, Thursday. A late June Thursday, and these were commuters, headed home from work.

And so were we.

Raeanne sat in the passenger seat, one long tanned leg crossed over the other. She still wore the black suede short-shorts and matching halter top, as well as sandals; her short dark hair was still in gluey spikes, and she was still made up.

Still Linda, aka BiJudy.

"How many people?" she repeated sharply.

"Six," I answered. "Yinger penned 'em up in the computer room. I got there just in time. They'll be okay."

"How about Dick?"

"He'll live," I said. "He'll be out of action for a while though."

She unbuckled her seat belt, turned to lean into the back seat, and came back with a white T-shirt and a small cosmetic bag. "Think Cockrum will make it?"

"Well, the EMS people got a heartbeat before the meat wagon took off. Beyond that, I don't know." She said nothing. "Yinger'd strung him up by the neck with his belt," I added. "God knows how long he'd been without air. He may never come out of it."

"But you carried him out anyway," she observed, shrugging herself into the T-shirt.

I shrugged. "You can't try a corpse."

She opened her makeup kit and got some tissues and stuff out and began working on her face, wiping it clean. "Oh," she said after a moment. "I get it. Yinger planned to make it look like Cockrum torched his building and committed suicide."

"Yep," I said grimly. "He didn't just want Cockrum out of the picture, he wanted to destroy the network's computers. Put an end to that Zanna picture once and for all." I pounded the steering wheel once. "Ha!"

"What?" she asked, brushing the spikes out of her hair.

I negotiated the Mustang through the cloverleaf onto eastbound Michigan Avenue. "That stuff I saw on the floor," I said. "Orange powder. That was some kind of thermal accelerant. One of the people we tried to track down, one of Cloyd's pen pals—can't remember the name, a woman in St. Clair Shores—her house had been torched. Burned completely to the ground. I'll bet Yinger did her too."

She considered that. "We may never know how many he killed," she said quietly.

"Nope," I agreed. "You never know everything."

She put her things away, turned sideways on the seat, and faced me, one leg tucked under her. "But what I want to know is, how did Yinger get to Temperance so fast?" She looked bemused now, more like herself. Coming back. "Did you ever figure that out?"

"He flew himself," I answered. "He was a pilot. Remember Zanna telling us that? Shoulda remembered." I paused, remembering. "He got there just as I did." Reeled him in, I thought faintly. That I did, all right. Did almost too good a job of it.

We were in her neighborhood now, the elegant old Ford homes glowing in the late sun. She touched my arm briefly and then let go. "Dick was really furious at you for taking off," she said. "I told him I'd be safe. I told him you'd never let any harm come to me."

"Should never have dragged you into the mess to begin with," I replied. "From now on, these things come up, I call Rent-a-Decoy."

She laughed as I pulled into her driveway and parked behind the white Sunbird. I shut the engine off and faced her. "So," I said, "are you going to let yourself be you with me again?"

"What kind of question is that?" she asked, smiling.

"Don't make me repeat it. Please."

And then she reached for me and we hugged tightly, leaning together over the console. For a long moment I heard nothing from her, not even breathing, and then she let go with a wet gasping cry. I held her tighter as she whispered against my neck. "I was so scared, I was so scared."

"Sweetheart," I said gently, "you knew I'd protect you."

She shook her head. "No no no, I was scared for you, scared you'd be—"

"Aw, don't be takin' on now."

"He killed all those others. And I was afraid you'd—"

"He had the drop on 'em," I said. "But I was ready for him."

"And I doubted you," she murmured. "I doubted me. I gave myself once, gave all my heart, and—"

"I never gave myself to anyone," I said. "Before."

Slowly she loosened her grip and sniffed and pulled back to look at me. Her oval face had lost its sardonic cast and looked almost gaunt at that moment, big tear trails running down her cheeks.

"Don't you be cryin' now," I said softly. "It's all right."

She reached out and brushed my cheek with her thumb. "You either, tough guy."

I straightened and looked away, drew a shaky breath, and plunged. "There's stuff you should know."

"Yes."

"I've done bad things," I said. "I've hurt folks. I haven't always been good to people, not even my own."

"It's all right."

I looked at her. "I've killed people."

"I know," she said gently. She drew near and kissed me hard. I kissed back, one of those from-the-soles-of-your-feet kisses that's like to never end. I held her and she held me, and we were like that for a long time.

But not long enough, in my opinion.

Finally we parted, and she touched my face, looking serious. "Let's go inside," she said. "I'll draw you a bath and wince over all your cuts and bruises, and while you're soaking I'll do a steak and we'll eat out on the patio."

"Sounds great. And then," I added, "I think, uh. . . I think we've got things to talk about."

"Really?" she asked, cocking her head. "What kinds of things, Ben?"

"Just things and stuff."

"Can you give me a sample? I'll be glad to give you one."

"Okay." I looked straight into her eyes. "Look here, kid. I—"

"Raeanne! Hey! *Raeanne!*"

We turned to look as a man in a blue sport coat, open-necked shirt, and slacks came briskly up the walk from a car parked at the curb.

"Oh, Lord," she murmured, "it's Derek."

"Who?" I asked, thinking, Ex-husband.

THIRTY-SIX

Raeanne was getting out, and I followed suit. Derek Whoever had dark curly hair and reddish half-dollar sunglasses and an arm-waving way of expressing himself, kind of like Jerry Seinfeld on speed. "Christ, babe, I've been trying to reach you for weeks!" He stopped and squinted at her, and glanced at me, and looked troubled. "What's going on?"

"This is my friend Ben," she said as I ambled around the rear of the Mustang. "I just got done with a job, Derek. That's why I look like this."

"Cool," he said exuberantly. "So what about the spot? Willya do it?"

"Derek, I told you," she said patiently. "I don't want to do the dumb blonde anymore. I'm super-super busy right now."

He smiled. "We'll double the money."

"As I said," she went on smoothly, giving me a wink, "I'm between shows at the moment. Where do I sign?"

* * *

The next night was Rachel night, back at my plac
this time. The cool spell had held, so I'd shut off th
AC and opened the deck door to let the breeze flow
through my living room. Eric Clapton sang softly from
the speakers; Rachel babbled happily at the coffe
table as she scattered plastic blocks hither and yon
Will sat silently in the recliner, engrossed in an X-Me
comic book; and the rest of us hunched over the car
table, playing some heavy-duty four-handed hearts.

And talking.

"Well," Carole said finally, "did you call the clien
and tell her how it all came out?"

"I called her," I answered, studying my hand
"Didn't exactly—uh, give her the whole scoop, not b
half. Told her her husband's death was an acciden
Which in a sense it was."

"Didn't that violate some detective ethic or another?"
Carole asked.

"It was a kind thing," Raeanne said lightly. "Nc
unethical."

"I suppose," Carole said darkly.

We passed cards, across this time. Buck Longstreth
seated to my right, made a slight hissing sound throug
his teeth as he inspected his new hand. Carole ha
given me the queen of spades. I gave her a look with
out changing expression. She twinkled and stuck ou
her tongue.

"Da da da," Rachel said.

"I'm here, darlin'," I answered.

Carole was looking at me intently. "Short year, hul
Ben?"

"Yes, ma'am."

"My," she commented. "How time flies."

"He did what he had to do," Raeanne said, and le
with the two of clubs.

"That's always the excuse," Carole grumbled, playing the four.

"Still," Longstreth said, playing the king, "you're lucky you got out alive, Ben."

"Pure skill," I said jauntily, spinning the queen of spades to the center.

The women laughed. Longstreth, too cool to be upset, simply said "Ah-ha" in that haughty tone of his as he scooped the cards in, including the lethal queen of spades.

Presently, he played a diamond. Raeanne and I followed suit. Carole was studying her cards. I said, "Now listen up. I done told you the whole story this time, Carole. Told you everything, for once. So now I want you to come clean with me."

"What about?" she asked, taking the hand with the king of diamonds.

"What's up with you and Bucky boy here?"

"Why, nothing," she replied, playing a club.

"Nothing at all," Longstreth said airily, as he tossed the five of hearts in.

I didn't play. "I know there's something going on," I told them. "Y'all been whispering and grinning for weeks now. If y'all are planning on getting married, you might as well tell me."

Carole's eyebrows shot up. "Married?"

"What a notion!" Longstreth said, laughing richly.

"I'm not ever going to marry again," Carole said. "I don't see why any woman should get married." She glanced at Raeanne. "Take the hint."

"I hear you," Raeanne answered, smiling.

Rachel swiped at her blocks and sent them flying toward the window wall. I watched her drop to all fours and quick-crawl to retrieve them. Then I looked narrow-eyed at Carole. "C'mon. Something's going on. I'm a trained professional, I can sense these things."

"You're right." She looked at Longstreth, who shrugged. She laid her cards face down. "It's not confirmed yet, which is why I've kept quiet. But I'm about to be appointed district judge in the Thirty-third District up in Plymouth."

When that sunk in, I grinned. "Hey. That's great."

"Congratulations," Raeanne said.

"It's not official yet," Carole cautioned, obviously pleased with herself. "But it's ninety-nine percent certain."

"Be quite a drive for you," I noted.

Carole inspected her cards. "Good old practical Ben," she mused, and looked at me, dark eyes serious. "Fact is, I'm selling the house and moving to Plymouth. Hopefully before school starts."

"Oh," was all I could manage. So the venerable Cape Cod in Berkley, where I'd spent so many hours and put in so much work, was becoming history. A little sad, that. "Be closer to here, anyway," I said.

"A lot closer," Raeanne agreed.

"That's a plus," Carole said. "I'll have a built-in babysitter nearby."

"Any time," I answered cheerfully.

We played out the trick, and another one, in silence. After the next deal, Carole left her cards face down. "Now," she said, in her courtroom-inquisitor tone, "why don't you two tell us what's going on with *you?*"

"Who, us?" I asked airily.

Carole just nodded, waiting. Raeanne and I looked at each other. "Go ahead, Ben," she said, smiling. "She's your ex."

"And my *best* ex," I affirmed. The phone rang. "Oops," I said, getting up. "A pause in the action, gang."

"Go ahead," Carole grumped. "Keep us in suspense."

I picked up the phone and leaned in the entrance-way to the kitchen, watching the threesome at the card table and, beyond them, Rachel, who was looking out the screen door onto the deck. "Perkins Card Sharps, Ben speaking," I answered.

As the caller introduced himself, I knew, I just knew, what had happened, and my heart sank. I was surprised, but not terribly. In a selfish way, I was even relieved. Whatever else was going on, at least she'd come home. "What's up?" I asked the deputy.

He told me, in that brisk crisp cop tone, wasting no words. What he told me wasn't pretty, not at all. I groped my little spiral pad out of my pocket, but there were no blank pages left, so I tossed it aside.

"Is she okay?" I asked.

He answered at some length, and my eyes went to Rachel again. She had returned to the coffee table and was holding on to it with both hands, blue eyes cheery as she grinned her two teeth at me.

I smiled back and answered the caller. "Yep, she's mine. Paley, Barbara Elaine." I sighed. "Where'd she come in from?"

He answered. Rachel let go of the coffee table and stood on her own. Put one bare foot forward, then another. Headed for me.

"Do you have to lock her up?" I asked the caller, "or can I just come get her?"

Rachel took a third, fourth, fifth step toward me, arms out for balance. "Hey," Raeanne said to the others, "look at this." Longstreth and Carole went silent and watched as Rachel made for me.

"I know, I know," I said into the phone, stooping, reaching out my hand to my daughter. "Gettin' to be a habit."

I grinned at Rachel and she toddled to me and

grabbed my hand in both of hers. The others applaude
and I picked the little girl up and hugged her.

"Fifteen minutes," I said into the phone, and hun
up.

"How about that!" Carole marveled. "All on he
own! That was—what, six or seven steps!"

"Fabulous," Longstreth agreed.

"Who called, Ben?" Raeanne asked.

Rachel was struggling in my arms a little, and
shifted her. "Gotta go run an errand, gang. Can you si
tight for a half hour?"

"Sure," Carole answered. "Will? Come over and pla
Ben's hand."

"Be all right?" I asked Raeanne.

"Of course."

"Okay." I put my face to Rachel's. "Whaddya say
rookie? Let's go help somebody."